'Holy Mother of ~~God~~, the second Argentine screamed. 'We're going to crash.'

His companion switched off the throttle and hurled himself on the wheel, swinging it desperately to port. The launch spun dizzily, its deck tilting beneath their feet. Water lashed their faces, and a series of shudders ran through the vessel's tortured frame as it hurtled sideways through the tossing waves. The rocks loomed up, jagged and menacing, hovering above them like crouching giants.

Crrrraaaacck. The force of the impact was almost unbelievable. The two Argentines were hurled bodily to the deck, rolling over in a tangled flurry of arms and legs. Stunned, they lay motionless for several moments while the stricken vessel bobbed impotently on a maelstrom of foam. In the starlight, they dimly discerned the shadowy outline of a Gemini boarding craft picking its way towards them. Bruised and defeated, they dragged themselves to the gunwhale and raised their arms in a gesture of surrender.

Also by Bob Langley in Sphere Books:

The Churchill Diamonds
Death Stalk
Conquistadores
Autumn Tiger
East of Everest
Warlords
Traverse of the Gods

Bob Langley

AVENGE THE BELGRANO

SPHERE BOOKS LTD

A SPHERE BOOK

First published in Great Britain by Michael Joseph Ltd 1988
Published by Sphere Books Limited 1989

Copyright © Bob Langley, 1988

Printed and bound in Great Britain by
Richard Clay Ltd, Bungay, Suffolk

Sphere Books Ltd
A Division of
Macdonald & Co. (Publishers) Ltd
66/73 Shoe Lane, London EC4P 4AB
A member of Maxwell Pergamon Publishing Corporation plc

PROLOGUE

The submarine moved silently through the dark waters of the South Atlantic, its metallic hull blending with the grey currents surrounding it. The tripod projections of its twin snort masts and periscope looked aesthetically incongruous against the sleek lines of its oval conning tower, and it made no sound as it sped through a world of total stillness at a speed of eleven knots.

Inside the control room, the air seemed surprisingly chill. The bitter cold of the Antarctic ocean seeped insidiously through the bulkheads' insulation. Clad in jumpers and padded over-jackets, the crew watched in silence as their captain studied the complex array of instrument readings, his eyes crinkling in the subdued lighting.

For more than twenty-five hours, they had been tracking three Argentine warships, the *Piedra Buena*, the *Hipolito Bouchard*, and the eleven thousand-ton *General Belgrano*. The date was 2 May 1982. Britain and Argentina were locked in conflict over the ownership of the Falkland Islands, and barely an hour before, in a direct signal from Northwood, England, the submarine had received the order to attack. None of the crew had ever fired a shot in anger, and their eyes were taut as they went through the preparatory procedures with an air of mingled excitement, anticipation and dread.

The captain's gaze flickered over the dials and gauges in front of him. Youthful and clean-cut, it was his first voyage in command.

'Course starboard thirty,' he ordered. 'Enemy speed eleven knots. Bring tubes to the ready.'

'Bow caps open,' answered the WEO. 'Fire control set.'

'Stand by numbers one, two and three.'

Tense and expectant, the men waited for the order which would send the torpedoes on their deadly way.

Four thousand yards away, in the *Belgrano*'s junior ratings' quarters, Corporal Signalman Alex Masters, blissfully unaware of the killer submarine stalking his vessel, was preparing to go on watch. Tall, bony, tousle-haired, Alex Masters was not part of the *Belgrano*'s regular crew, most of whom were trained cadets from the Buenos Aires naval college, but one of three hundred conscripts who had been mobilised during the prelude to the Falklands invasion. Though he was Argentine to the core, Alex's ancestry was British; he had been educated at the exclusive St George's College in Buenos Aires and now formed part of the city's substantial Anglo-Argentine community. An athletic young man with pleasant features and a frank, engaging manner, his anglophile heritage had made him the butt of numerous jokes, but affable by nature, he had accepted the raillery with characteristic good humour. His one hope had been the report on the morning news bulletin that a peace settlement was imminent. American diplomats were acting as emissaries, the newsreader had said, and a major announcement was expected within hours. This news had cheered Alex Masters immensely. He was relieved and gratified that there would be no war.

In the submarine's control room, the 'tubes-ready' lights glowed eerily.

'Enemy speed eleven knots. Angle-off spacing set.'

'Stand by,' the captain said. 'Check firing bearing.'

The men waited, muscles tense, nerves stretched to breaking point. Only the captain looked cool, unruffled, imperturbable. The tension mounted as he paused, judging his moment. Then . . .

'Fire,' he shouted.

*

Alex was half-way up the companionway when the first torpedo struck. There was no explosion, only a dull muffled thud. The ship shook and seemed to lurch forward with an upward grating motion as if they had suddenly run aground. He paused, frowning, his hand gripping the metal rail. The air filled with an acrid burning odour and the lights blinked into darkness. He remained where he was, puzzled by the strange eventuality, not understanding it fully, his brain racing, assessing the possibilities while he waited for the electrical system to correct itself. He counted the moments: one, two, three, four . . .

Then the second torpedo hit. This time the cause of the impact was terrifyingly apparent. A blast of white-hot air swept along the companionway and Alex saw a flash of orange-tipped flame as the warhead detonated in a thunderous brain-stunning roar, ripping through the metal decks above. Choking black smoke filled the narrow corridor.

Coughing, he clambered back down the companionway ladder, trying hard to hold on to his senses. He could see flames rippling and billowing, and something like terror swelled inside him. He swallowed it down, fighting for balance on the rapidly listing deck. A cluster of figures burst through one of the cabin doors. Coated from head to foot with slippery black fuel oil, they looked grotesque as they scrambled past him, heading for the open air.

A great jet of oil shot along the corridor, taking him completely by surprise. There was no escape from it, nowhere to run. He was caught helplessly in the first breathless rush, the oil drenching him, knocking him from his feet as his head went under and he found himself choking for air. The slippery torrent swept him along the companionway, its force washing against his torso and limbs. A momentary panic struck him. What if it reached the flames and ignited? The entire deck would become a maelstrom of fire. Desperately, he seized a metal rail, holding on grimly, his arms aching in their sockets. His muscles strained and twisted as he struggled to keep himself in place, the current sucking at his lower body. He felt his grip steadily slackening. In the dark, he dimly glimpsed a narrow escape hatch slightly to his left. It led, he knew, to the deck above, but it was slender and constricted, just wide enough to encompass a man's shoulders, and already the oil was swirling inside it in a slippery black vortex.

He coughed hard, choking and spluttering as he struggled to keep his head above the surface, his fingers growing numb with each passing second. He loosened one hand and reached across the companionway, grabbing the rim of the escape hatch. His skin crawling, he held his breath and ducked under, dragging himself into the suffocating funnel. The oil poured into his nostrils and he had consciously to refrain from spewing out in disgust as, with stomach tensed and legs shaking, he began to wriggle his way up the flooded shaft. The walls seemed to close in, holding him fast. He felt dizzy and nauseous from the liquid's touch, and his insides cringed as he battled upward, hysteria threatening to engulf him at every second. He had never been so enclosed before. The darkness was overwhelming, smothering him like a shroud. There was no light, no hope, no substance, only the interminable skin-coating cavity-oozing liquid, shutting off the world beyond. Panic coiled like a filament in his brain. He felt tremors of revulsion running through his body, but somehow, desperate and half-senseless, he reached the hatch top and wallowed out of the slimy oil, gasping frantically for air.

Black and dripping, Alex struggled to fix his bearings as the deck listed dangerously. He still had another level to go before he reached the open. Stumbling along the companionway, he found Hugo Bechar, a young Patagonian of Italian descent lying where the initial blast had thrown him.

The entire left side of Hugo's body had been charred beyond recognition and he was shaking like a man possessed. Somehow, Alex managed to swallow back the bile, and gritting his teeth, he slipped one arm around Hugo's stricken shoulders, manoeuvring him towards the companionway ladder.

A flashlight shone into his face. '*Qué va*. Anyone still alive down there?' a voice demanded.

'I have an injured man here,' Alex croaked. 'Help me, please.'

Boots clattered on the ladder as someone dropped a rope from the deck above. Looping it under Hugo's armpits, they dragged him, shrieking and protesting, into the misty South Atlantic day.

Alex knelt at Hugo's side, comforting him as best he could. Hugo's one remaining eye bulged from its ravaged socket, and his spine arched as he lay on the deck, twitching spasmodically.

An officer came running toward them. 'How bad is he?' he asked.

His face sickened as he stared down at Hugo's mutilated form. '*Mierda*,' he breathed. 'Is that a human being?'

'Where are the medics?' Alex cried.

Gently, the officer squeezed Alex's shoulder. '*Compánero*, this man is dying. No one could survive in such a state. Get him into the life rafts quickly.'

Around the vessel, Alex could see blackened figures scrambling for the water. Everyone had been coated with oil and churning columns of black smoke belched across the tilting superstructure, turning the upper deck into a nightmare vision of hell. On the dancing wave-crests, the rafts, bulbous and canopied, bobbed just beyond the cruiser's reach.

Hugo shrieked as the icy water touched his gaping flesh. Closing his ears to his friend's torment, Alex held him tightly and kicked towards the dancing life rafts. He could see men framed above the inflated rims, their torsos swathed in heavy lifejackets. Spray leapt into his face, stinging his eyes. He felt the swell take him, lifting him bodily like the spine of some incredible beast, balancing him for a moment on its rippling crest before plunging him into the valley beneath.

A raft loomed up and willing hands took Hugo from his grasp. Someone hauled at his windcheater and he felt his muscles lighten as, sodden and dripping, he was dragged over the glistening rim. He collapsed gratefully on the rubberised deck, and wriggling forward on his belly, began to vomit over the side.

It was more than thirty hours before the tugboat *Gurruchaga* finally picked them up. Chilled to the bone, lashed by the angry seas, they spent the night singing and praying to maintain their spirits. For Alex Masters, the physical suffering was minimal compared to the torment in his head. Riven with exhaustion, he could not rid his mind of the fact that the attack had come without warning of any kind. He felt betrayed, humiliated, his fury transmuting into a crisis of identity that was difficult to define. He was conscious of only two overwhelming emotions: an irrational fear of confined spaces, and a burning hatred for the country of his ancestors.

CHAPTER ONE

At 9.15 on the morning of Monday, 20 November, Mike MacNally, fair-haired, thickset, twenty-four years old, set out with his fishing-rod from the tiny Scottish hotel he ran with his sister Julie, unaware that he was about to plunge the British government into its gravest military crisis since the Falklands War.

It was a chill wintry day, the sky dark and menacing, as he cycled towards Barracula Sound, a narrow strip of water tracing the coastline above Arisaig. To the north, he could see the wild slopes of the Drium Nam Leagh and the rocky chasm of Salach D'Aim where fresh snow dusted the stony ramparts of the Charrach Dam. He was whistling happily as he rode, for despite the coldness of the morning, the prospect of the day's fishing filled him with a feeling of pleasant anticipation.

On the slopes overlooking Barracula Sound, he propped his bicycle at the roadside, and dropping through the heavy curtain of spruce, was half-way down the bank when he heard a shout ringing discordantly above the treetops, harsh, startling, authoritative.

'*Freeze.*'

Taken by surprise, Mike halted, blinking as he stared back at the woodland from which he had come. The firs formed a blanket, shutting off the upper slopes above and trickling down the gullies in thin straggling lines. A man moved out of the shadows, easing into the pallid daylight – a soldier. Mike's eyes noted the heavy arctic anorak, the webbing-belt and respirator, the dark green commando beret. A Sterling

7

sub-machine-gun rested casually across the man's left arm. Mike spotted other figures filtering out of the woodland, circling in opposite directions to cut him off at either end.

Mike was a cheerful young man with a natural easy-going manner, but the cold determined attitude of the approaching troops filled him with a sudden irrational alarm. Though he had done nothing wrong, he felt his muscles tightening spasmodically. For a moment he stood perfectly still, then without thinking, he dropped his fishing-rod and plunged blindly into the undergrowth. Voices echoed in his ears, but he shut his mind to their clamour, concentrating on the simple task of flight and escape. He scarcely knew why he was running – his sudden burst had been little more than a spur-of-the-moment impulse, but having started, he seemed unable to stop.

Branches tore at his cheeks and throat as he leapt and sprinted down the steepening hillside. Then suddenly he was over, cartwheeling forward in a desperate flurry of arms and legs, the bracken catching him full in the face. Someone came crashing through the undergrowth behind him, and a hand grabbed his jacket, hauling him to his feet. Without hesitating, Mike swung backwards with his elbow, grunting with satisfaction as he felt it sink into his assailant's stomach. A boot kicked his ankle and he went down hard, his shoulder striking a rock. His pursuers, panting, grouped around him in a heavy cordon, their machine-guns menacingly aimed at his chest. He counted eight altogether – not soldiers, he realised now, but Royal Marines, identically dressed, identically armed.

Their leader, a heavy-shouldered sergeant with a thin moustache, came striding towards him as, gasping, Mike clambered to his feet. The sergeant's eyes had a piercing shrewdness which contrasted strangely with the woodenness of his features.

'What are you doing here?' he snapped.

'Nothing,' Mike answered, his chest heaving.

'You must be doing something.'

'I'm going fishing.'

'Fishing, is it?' The sergeant's eyes looked mocking. 'Without a fishing-rod?'

'I dropped my rod in the trees up there.' Mike jerked his head at the slopes above.

'Why did you run?' the sergeant demanded.

'Your men came at me wi' machine-guns. What, in God's name, did ye expect me to do?'

'What's your name?'

'MacNally,' Mike growled.

'Address?'

'The Barracula Hotel.'

'You're lying. The Barracula Hotel's been closed since October. It's out-of-season, didn't you know?'

'I'm no' a guest,' Mike told him wearily. 'It's my home. I own the place.'

It had been three years since he had bought the Barracula with life insurance money after his father died. With his sister Julie doing the catering and Mike himself handling the general maintenance, the hotel offered an idyllic existence during the out-of-season months when he was able to fish to his heart's content.

The sergeant motioned with his machine-gun at a nearby tree. 'Place your palms against the trunk,' he ordered.

Mike stared at him in bafflement. 'Look, can ye no' tell me what this is all about?'

'Shut up, fart face,' a soldier snapped. 'Do as you're told, or you'll get a bullet through your kneecaps.'

Mike flushed, but he turned without a word and laid his hands against the tree trunk.

The body search was rough and thorough. The sergeant scrutinised his driver's licence and his membership card to the Barracula Social Club. He examined an envelope from

9

the Inspector of Taxes in Edinburgh, then with casual impudence, took out the document inside and calmly read it. When he had finished, he tossed the papers contemptuously on the ground. Mike felt his anger rising.

'Turn around,' the sergeant commanded.

His face had an almost featureless symmetry, as if the bone structure had been consciously honed into a precise and characterless mould.

'I'm going to ask you again,' he said quietly. 'I'd advise you to be frank and communicative. What are you doing here?'

'I've told ye what I'm doing.'

'Don't you realise you're trespassing?'

'What the hell are you talking about? That's Barracula Sound down there. I've been fishing those waters for years.'

'You must've seen the signs at the entrance gate.'

'I did'na come via the gate. I left my bike on the top road and cut down through the trees.'

The sergeant pursed his lips, and Mike sensed a softening in him. It was nothing immediately apparent, just an easing of tension in the cold grey eyes, but the sergeant looked marginally less sure of himself.

'If I follow the road, it means doubling back on my tracks,' Mike explained darkly. 'I can save a two-mile pedal by detouring through the woods.'

'Ah.' The sergeant's features visibly relaxed, and when he spoke again his voice had lost some of its harshness. 'The Sound has been placed out of bounds,' he said. 'No civilian personnel are allowed in the area from today.'

Mike looked surprised. 'On whose authority?'

'Ministry of Defence. You should've seen the announcement in your local newspaper.'

'Can they do that?' Mike muttered. 'Just take it over?'

The sergeant smiled thinly. 'The Defence Ministry can do as it damn well likes, didn't you know?'

He hesitated, running one finger along his thin moustache as if trying to reassure himself it was still there, then bending down, he picked up the documents and thrust them into Mike's jacket pocket. Mike guessed he was beginning to regret his earlier belligerence.

'Look, squire,' the sergeant said reasonably. 'I'm sorry if we gave you a fright just now, but there are warning posters all along the Bay entrance, and when we spotted you sneaking through the trees, we took you for an intruder. The Ministry'll have high-wire fences and security watchtowers around this area in a few weeks' time – it's been designated a military training ground. For the moment though, I'd be obliged if you'd spread the word among your friends. It might save any more embarrassing incidents like this one.'

He smiled, sticking out his hand. 'No hard feelings, I hope.'

Mike took the proffered hand, shaking it in a desultory fashion. He was not to be won over so easily. He had detected a faint Liverpudlian lilt in the sergeant's voice and realised the soldiers were English. He wasn't the one who did not belong here.

'This Sound belongs to the people of Scotland,' he said in a surly tone. 'Not the bloody Westminster government.'

The sergeant looked surprised. He chuckled and shrugged. 'Don't tell me, squire. Write to your local MP. I'd say you've left it a wee bit late though. The builders are moving in at the end of January. They're converting the Sound into a total exclusion zone.'

Mike was filled with an anger he could scarcely contain. Without a word, he turned and, still shaken, began to pick his way up the hillside. His chest ached and there was a nauseous sensation in the pit of his stomach. He'd been scared back there, no getting away from the fact. He couldn't forget the way he'd trembled, or the cold queasy sensation in his belly when the sergeant had dressed him down. But even worse was the realisation that Barracula Sound was being requisitioned by the English government. Mike hated the English. It was something inherent within him, a burning resentment that found its root in his earliest beginnings. For a brief period, during his younger days in Glasgow, he had been part of the Scottish National Liberation Army, a raggle-taggle collection of eccentrics, patriots and extremists who modelled themselves on Ireland's Provisional IRA, but managed little more spectacular than the sabotaging of power lines in the border counties. Nevertheless, the sentiments which had moulded Mike's youth still stuck doggedly in his memory.

When he reached his bicycle, he stood for a moment, breathing deeply, glaring across at the distant mountains. Something was happening here, something important. Something they didn't want him to see.

On an impulse, he unstrapped his saddlebag and rummaged inside until he found what he was looking for, a battered old 35mm camera, its casing scratched from constant wear and tear. He thrust it into his jacket pocket, and gently massaged his temples with his fingertips. His anger was gone now, transmuted into a cold motivating force, channelled, controlled, directed.

Clambering over the wire fence, he started back the way he had come. He moved cautiously, pausing every few feet to listen hard. If the marines caught him a second time, there would be no question of talking himself out of it. He had to proceed with the greatest possible care.

The ground began to steepen and Mike spotted a craggy outcrop protruding above the treetops like a schooner's prow. Silently, he wriggled his way along its crest. The grassy rim commanded an almost unobstructed view of the Sound itself, a slender crescent of glistening water, flanked by the tumbling screes of Barracula Island on one side, and the Scottish mainland on the other.

Breathing hard, he raised himself on his elbows, peering across the shimmering surface below. His eyes widened, and an exclamation of surprise burst from his lips. His heart was thumping as, with trembling fingers, he fumbled inside his jacket for the camera.

Mike spotted the little group of sailors entering the village pub. They were laughing uproariously at some remark or other, their faces shiny and pink in the pale light of the afternoon. Senses tingling, he pressed his foot on the brake, bringing the battered van to a halt. Beside him in the passenger seat, his sister Julie glanced at him with surprise. Julie MacNally was a pretty girl, twenty-two years old, slim-hipped and high-breasted. She was the opposite to Mike in every imaginable way: where he was fair, she was dark; where he was thickset, she was slender and supple, and where he was ruddy-complexioned, she was pale-cheeked and delicately featured, with a smattering of freckles across her forehead and nose. In some ways he felt protective towards her, yet in others he could not rid himself of the suspicion that it was Julie who controlled things, Julie with her quiet thoughtful perspicacity who shaped and guided their lives together.

He worried endlessly about her welfare. Though she looked happy enough – she loved the mountains, the grandeur, the solitude – the hotel seemed a poor place for a girl as pretty as his sister.

'What are you stopping for?' she asked, her face creased in puzzlement.

Mike tried to sound casual. 'Let's pop into Taggart's an' get ourselves a drink.'

She glanced at her watch. 'At this time?'

'Why not?'

'You go, Mike. It's too early in the afternoon for me.'

13

He took her arm, his fingers gripping the flesh. 'Please Julie, I want ye to come,' he insisted.

She looked surprised. 'What on earth for?'

'Dinna ask. I just want ye to, that's all.'

Julie frowned, but she said nothing as he parked the van, and together they walked to the pub. The bar was crowded as they entered; it was market day, and farmers from all over the county had converged on the village to buy and sell their livestock. Mike recognised Willie Dury, Charlie MacGregor, Stuart Hamilton. He felt his pulses racing as he glimpsed the little party of sailors grouped in a corner, talking animatedly. As he watched, a man rose to his feet and pushed his way to the bar, clutching an empty glass. Mike saw him glance appreciatively in Julie's direction.

'Smile at him,' Mike whispered into her ear.

She blinked in astonishment. 'What?'

'Smile,' he ordered fiercely.

'I'll do no such thing, Mike MacNally,' she snapped, glaring up at him indignantly.

Mike's eyes looked pleading. 'Please Julie, I wid'na ask if it wis'na important. Do it for me just this once, will ye?'

Startled by the fervour in his tone, Julie glanced uncertainly at the young sailor, and with a conscious effort, forced her lips into a thin smile. The sailor seemed taken aback at the unexpected response. Flushing, he raised his empty glass in a formal salute.

Mike elbowed his way forward and threw his arm around the man's shoulders, slapping him amiably on the back. 'It's no' often we get a chance to welcome our boys in blue,' he said with an ingratiating grin. 'What're ye drinking, Jimmie?'

Mike stood in the makeshift darkroom he had fashioned under the stairs, and watched the photographs take on definition in the developing tray. He let them lie for a few minutes, then examined them critically in the dim glow of the lightbulb.

His pulses throbbed with excitement as he switched off the lamp, closed the cupboard door and hurried up to the tiny office. Swivelling a sheet of paper into the ancient typewriter, he began to hammer breathlessly at the keys.

For Billy Hannah, short, wiry, sparse-haired, coarse-featured, the morning of 28 November began like any other. He left Glasgow's Salvation Army Men's Hostel which had been his home for the past twenty-one days and made his way to Charlie Andrews' pub from which, at 11.00 p.m. the previous evening, he had been summarily ejected while trying to carve his initials into the cheek of a drunken rival with a broken beer bottle.

A small-time hoodlum, Billy had, in his early days, forged quite a reputation for himself as a strong-arm collector for the area's tally men, but alcohol and years of dissolute living had taken their toll of Billy's spare physique. During his sober moments, which were few and far between, he reflected bitterly on his deteriorating status and vowed that one day he would regain his former notoriety. But it seemed a forlorn hope, for Billy's good intentions seldom lasted longer than the first drink.

Charlie's bar was empty when Billy entered. It was too early for the lunchtime crowd, too late for the nightshift drinkers. Charlie himself was wiping down the counter with a damp cloth. Billy's head throbbed, and there was a sour sensation in the pit of his stomach as he approached the bar.

'Hey, Charlie,' he said in an anxious voice. 'Gie's a wee Scotch, will ye, and put it on the slate. I seem to've run mesel' a bit short this mornin'.'

Charlie glared at him as he wiped his fingers on the cloth and tossed it into the washbasin at the back of the counter.

'Get out, Billy,' he said mildly. 'Ye're no' wanted here any more.'

'Aw, Charlie,' Billy's voice became plaintive, wheedling, 'I'm sorry about last night, man. I did'na start it, Charlie. The bastard provoked me. He was trying to make a name for hissel'.'

'A name?' Charlie's eyebrows lifted in contempt. 'Christ, Billy, ye think he was tryin' to make a name by beating you? Still fancy yerself as a hard man, do ye? Silly sod. Can ye no' face the truth, man? Ye went ower the hill years ago.'

Billy's face hardened at the insult, but he needed a drink badly and was careful to keep his voice apologetic.

'All right, all right,' he said with a sigh. 'I was out of order and I admit it. Ye've been a good friend to me, Charlie Andrews, an' I should'na hae started trouble in yer place. I wis'na acting the way a friend should. I'll never do it again, ye have my word on that, Charlie.'

Charlie stared at him as Billy's voice grew pleading, desperate. 'A wee Scotch, Charlie, for God's sake.'

Charlie sighed. Taking a glass from the shelf, he filled it from the automatic dispenser at the back of the bar. 'This is yer last, Billy,' he said bluntly, 'until ye settle yer account. I'm no' running the place on charity.'

'Thanks, Charlie, ye're a prince, tha's what ye are, a real prince.'

Billy picked up the glass with trembling fingers and Charlie studied him in silence, disgust mingling with the pity on his face. He had seen Billy in his early years. He'd been a hard boy then. The 'Clydebank Hammer', they had called him. A wizened little runt, but tough for all that. Quick with a knife, quick with a razor. Not one to fall foul of. Now ... Charlie grimaced ... now, Billy was a paltry shadow of the man he had been.

'Another thing,' Charlie murmured. 'This is'na a post office. I dinna want the GPO delivering mail here just be-

16

cause ye've no fixed address any more. It gie's the place a bad name.'

He dropped an envelope on the counter and Billy stared at it, frowning. The writing had been crossed out and someone had scrawled across the top: *Try Charlie Andrews' pub.*

Billy was puzzled. He rarely received letters these days. Even his creditors had lost track of him.

Picking it up, he made his way to a table in the corner and settled down in front of the window. He took a swift gulp of the whisky to calm his nerves, then ripping open the envelope, tipped out its contents, grunting as half a dozen photographs scattered across the tabletop. Taking out the letter, he held it up to the light and began to read painfully, moulding his lips with each individual syllable. When he had finished, his eyes were blazing with excitement.

He stumbled to his feet, nearly knocking the whisky over in his haste. His cheeks were flushed, and a tiny pulse had begun to throb high on his left temple.

'Hey, Charlie,' he yelled, his voice screeching in the morning stillness. 'Gie's a loan of yer telephone, man. Billy Hannah's about to make his long-awaited comeback.'

They sat in a little council house on the outskirts of town, six men with sober nondescript faces, their ages ranging from twenty to thirty-five. Their eyes were dark, reflective, calculating, as they studied the wiry frame of Billy Hannah slouched in the frayed leather armchair in front of them. The curtains had been drawn to shut out the sun. Despite the chill of the November day, the heat from the gasfire was almost overpowering.

Billy squirmed uneasily in his seat. He could feel the contempt of the men surrounding him and wished Charlie Andrews had staked him to another Scotch to soothe his jangled nerves. These men, staid, ordinary, working-class, made up the ruling council of the Scottish National Liberation Army. Together, they controlled the operations and policies of a movement which had dedicated itself to the establishment of a Scottish parliament in Edinburgh. They passionately wanted sedition, withdrawal from the English constitution and a return to the interests and concerns of their own homeland. Individually, they were not intimidating, but encountered as a group they carried an air of elusive menace and Billy felt uneasy in their company. Spurned by the local racketeers, he had tried to regain past glories by joining the Army's ranks, but though he was tolerated, and to some extent even patronised, he knew he was regarded by the council as an embarrassing handicap, erratic and unreliable.

Their leader, a raw-boned young man with a hooked nose and sallow cheeks, spread the photographs dubiously across the tabletop. 'These pictures prove nothing,' he said. 'They might have been taken anywhere. They're too distant to be identifiable.'

'I told ye,' Billy protested nervously. 'It's no' just the pictures. My man chatted to a sailor in one o' the local pubs.'

The leader grunted, shuffling the photographs together. 'Who is he, this man of yours?' he demanded.

'His name's Mike MacNally. He used to live over Rutherglen way. His old man died and left him some money, and he and his sister bought a little hotel near Sheilington three summers ago. I had'na heard from him since, until today.'

'Was he a member of your unit?'

'Aye,' Billy nodded.

'Reliable?'

'Solid as a rock. A wee bit hot-tempered from time to time, but nothing I could'na handle.'

Billy paused to let the implication of his leadership register, but the man's cold features made him hurry on. 'He's no' a tearaway,' he added. 'He's no' in this for personal motives.'

'What, then?'

'Why, the cause, of course. Scotland a nation again.'

The leader grunted, accepting the explanation totally. It was the one thing they all had in common, a sanguine belief in autonomous government. Slogans had become meaningless in themselves, but a slogan offered a conglutinant of sorts, welding them into a cohesive force.

'It's true about Barracula Sound?' the leader asked.

'Aye, they're turning it into a training area right enough.'

'How do the local residents feel?'

'They hav'na much say in the matter. Ye ken how the English system works.'

'No protests, rallies, that sort of thing?'

Billy shrugged. 'The men wi' the big cigars kept it under wraps. Och, they went through the legal procedures all right, but they made bloody sure nobody heard until it was too bloody late.'

The leader glanced down at the letter on his lap. 'And this . . . suggestion. D'ye think it's feasible?'

Billy moistened his lips with his tongue. 'If Mike Mac-Nally says it's feasible, then I reckon I'd put my life on it.'

The man considered this for a moment, before turning to the council. 'What's the general feeling?' he enquired.

There was a moment of silence as the committee reflected on the idea, then a chalk-faced man with a sprinkling of grey hair said: 'It's ambitious. More ambitious than anything we've ever attempted before.'

'Too ambitious, would ye say?'

The man shrugged. 'If we pulled it off, the rewards could be incalculable. For a start, it would catapult us into the same media status as the Provisional IRA.'

'Aye, that's right,' another man stated. 'The John Bull press would'na be able to ignore us any longer.'

'But we haven't the muscle for an enterprise like this,' the leader protested mildly.

'We could get the muscle,' a man suggested. 'We could approach the Provos. Willie Gifford has a contact in Londonderry.'

'The Provos are no good,' the chalk-faced man snapped. 'They'd take all the credit. What we want is someone who'd be happy to carry out the operation and let us claim responsibility.'

'Och, what ye're asking is a bloody miracle,' the first speaker grunted.

The chalk-faced man smiled thinly. In the filtered light from the curtained window, his cheeks were a strangely greenish hue.

'I think I ken where we can find one,' he said.

Entre Rios, Argentina
17 December

The *jineatada* was already in full swing when the convoy of limousines swung off the *pampa* road and slid gracefully to a halt on the cindered car-park, dust rising from wheels in a thick dark cloud. A festival official scurried forward as a tall man in his early sixties emerged from the leading saloon and stepped elegantly into the sunlight. He was dressed in a suit of pale cream which looked expensive and beautifully tailored. His hair was white and flowing, and his face was slender and suntanned with strong Hispanic features. Señor Roberto Runcana was the sixth richest man in Argentina, once the tenth richest country in the world. His *estancia*, or cattle ranch, covered 40,000 hectares of the neighbouring province. In addition, he mined lead and uranium in the foothills of the Andes, grew wheat, sugar, cotton and tobacco in the Gran Chaco region south of the Pilcomayo River, and controlled forty per cent of the oil wells in western Patagonia. A millionaire many times over, Señor Runcana's standing, in a country where inflation soared like a raging disease, had been elevated to the level of minor royalty, and a smattering of applause greeted him from the throngs of leathery-faced *campesinos* and their gaily-clad womenfolk.

He acknowledged the compliment with a casual wave and glanced at the cordoned-off arena where, to roars of approval from the watching crowd, a peon in tightfitting *bombachos* was careering across the ring on a wild *criollo* pony which was vainly trying to hurl him from its back. Runcana followed the man approvingly with his eyes. As one of Argentina's leading *domadors*, he had a shrewd appreciation of good horsemanship. The pony, having failed to dislodge its unwanted passenger, was now arching its spine in a violent corkscrewing motion which caused the rider to hang on like grim death.

Señor Runcana snapped his fingers, waiting in silence as a member of his entourage placed a cheroot between his lips and lit it with conscious deference, then smoking amiably, he began to stroll through the lines of brightly-painted stalls, accompanied at a discreet distance by his impassive henchmen. He moved wth a fluid grace and an economy of effort which befitted a man who controlled nearly an eighth of his nation's wealth and as he passed, the *campesinos* touched their flat-brimmed sombreros in the manner of serfs recognising the power of a feudal overlord.

In a clearing near the centre of the field, carcasses of beef were being roasted over open fires; splayed on upright spits, their ribcages had been spread outwards to allow white-coated chefs to slice off the meat and distribute it generously among the passers-by. Gaucho cowhands exchanged *maté* bowls with solemn formality, while señoritas drifted among the crowds, flirting outrageously with their eyes.

A soldier approached Runcana and executed a crisp salute. 'Colonel Jaurez presents his compliments, señor,' he declared, 'and asks if you would be good enough to join him for a few moments in the members' tent.'

Señor Runcana frowned. He had been looking forward to watching the horse-breaking, but in Argentina, as in any country in South America, the military, even for a man of Señor Runcana's eminence, were not easy to ignore.

Runcana took the cheroot from his mouth. 'I shall be delighted to meet with the colonel,' he declared.

'If you will kindly follow me, señor,' the soldier said.

The members' tent was a large marquee which had been sumptuously decorated with tapestries so that its interior resembled a maharajah's palace. It was reserved for local landowners and visitors of distinction, but when Runcana arrived, he found it almost deserted, for most of the occupants had drifted outside to watch the excitement at the horse-ring.

He spotted Colonel Jaurez, however, cradling a glass of iced gin in one palm. Jaurez was a plump but stately man, who had been a stalwart supporter of the military junta during the years preceding the Malvinas conflict, and was one of the few army officers Señor Runcana still trusted. With him was a tall red-cheeked individual whom Runcana recognised as Gustavo MacAngus, an Anglo-Argentine of Scottish descent who owned most of the cattle land in the surrounding area. MacAngus's grandfather had been forced from his Highland home by avaricious English landlords in the middle of the last century and had travelled to Argentina to help build the country's railroads. Reared to revere all things Scottish, MacAngus hated the English with an unbridled passion. During the Malvinas conflict, he had been a stalwart supporter of General Galtieri, and was, Runcana knew, as passionately Argentine as it was possible to be, despite his roots.

Runcana liked MacAngus. They had met on numerous social occasions, both on the *pampa* and in the capital, and Runcana approved of the Scotsman's blunt manner and forthright approach. His smile was genuine as they shook hands, poured fresh drinks and made the obligatory speeches. The ritual was intrinsically Argentine, and as a member of the armed forces, it was Colonel Jaurez who started it off.

'May the sun shine on the jewel of our country,' he declared solemnly.

The others nodded their approval, and Gustavo MacAngus followed.

'To our great capital, Buenos Aires. May it be eternal as the sun, and its name be sacred always.'

Señor Runcana rounded off the ceremony with habitual panache.

'To Argentina, Queen of the Americas, land of scented grasses caressed by southern winds. We adore you.'

The three men stood at attention as they drank. Then, the formalities concluded, they settled themselves in the foldable armchairs. Señor Runcana nodded to his entourage to remain at the door.

'You are looking well, Roberto,' the colonel smiled, studying him approvingly. 'There must be something in this *pampa* air. You remain as youthful and vigorous as a stud horse.'

'I will let you in on a secret, *compadre*,' Señor Runcana told him. 'It is not the air which keeps me young. I make it a point personally to break in all the female members of my household staff. Women, like horses, have to be gentled, and there is nothing like freshness and variety for rejuvenating a man's appetite.'

MacAngus and the colonel laughed politely, and outside, the crowd roared as a fresh rider entered the ring.

Colonel Jaurez crossed his legs, dusting an imaginary speck from his thigh. 'Señor MacAngus has some news which, I believe, may be of interest to us all,' he said softly.

Runcana made no comment. Experience had taught him to move delicately in Argentina; survival often depended on

23

the ability to read a man's eyes, decipher the complexities inside his mind.

'I have a cousin living in Scotland,' MacAngus said. 'A distant relative on my father's side. He is a member of an organisation called the Scottish National Liberation Army. Perhaps you have heard of it?'

Runcana shook his head.

'It runs rather on the lines of Ireland's Provisional IRA though it is less effectively organised and far more stringently financed. It is dedicated to freeing Scotland from English domination.'

Señor Runcana said nothing. He drew hard on his cheroot, letting the smoke drift lazily from his nostrils.

'Yesterday morning, I received a letter from my cousin,' Señor MacAngus continued. 'It contained an interesting piece of information, and an equally interesting proposal.'

MacAngus took the letter from his jacket pocket and handed it to Runcana. Frowning, Runcana unfolded the paper and began to study it closely. As he read, his face grew very still. In May, 1982, Runcana's only son Régis had been serving as a young subaltern on the battleship, the *General Belgrano*. Torpedoed during the Malvinas conflict, Régis had been one of the 368 Argentines killed. He had been a good boy, Régis – handsome, charming, intelligent. He had chosen the navy as a career because he had recognised the military as the key to power; only in South America could a young naval lieutenant aspire one day to become president. When the Admiralty's cable had arrived, Señor Runcana had felt as if his entire life had fallen apart. Despite the sophistication of his upbringing, Runcana was a simple man in many ways, his character honed by the inherent Argentine notion of *machismo*. He had never forgiven the blow to Argentine pride, the affront to Argentine honour. Most of all, he had never forgiven the death of his son. He believed in the old ways, blood for blood, insult for insult, *muerte* for *muerte*. Now, he sensed his hatred hardening, strengthening.

He rose to his feet, staring at the tent wall. Dropping his half-smoked cheroot on the ground, he crushed it beneath his heel. 'Who else knows about this?' he whispered.

'No one,' Colonel Jaurez said. 'We were hoping you would agree to finance the venture, Roberto.'

'It's dangerous,' Runcana breathed.

The colonel nodded. 'Yes, Roberto, yes it *is* dangerous. It is also too tempting to miss.'

Runcana hesitated. In a strange way, his face seemed to lose its compactness as if, caught between fury and indecision, the muscles had grown limp and flaccid. He rubbed his cheekbone with his thumb. 'You really believe it can be done?'

'I am convinced of it, *amigo*. With proper planning, it should be a simple procedure.'

'Can you get army support?'

Colonel Jaurez pulled a face. 'I have a few friends in high places, but I doubt if they'd be prepared to risk their reputations and careers, to say nothing of their necks. You know how sensitive this government is. However, documents can be doctored, signatures forged. With a little subterfuge, we can get, not only the equipment we require, but perhaps even the use of military training facilities also.'

Señor Runcana closed his eyes. The image of his son flitted stubbornly through his consciousness. He looked young, handsome and reckless, his eyes filled with ambition and hope. It was not, Runcana reasoned, a simple question of revenge. He could never condone that. He was a civilised man who saw in the loss of his only son a situation which had to be faced and dealt with. Vengeance, in its purest and most vindictive form at least, was foreign to his nature. But there was something else at stake, something which went beyond the realms of personal rancour —

the honour of his country. It was simple, immutable, inescapable.

'You must give me time,' he whispered. 'I need to think it over.'

'Time, Roberto, is the one thing we cannot afford. By this time next month, the opportunity will be lost.'

'But we'll need the right men,' Runcana insisted. 'Members of the armed forces are no good. If things go wrong, we don't want the British government imagining this is an official operation.'

The colonel nodded. 'That's understood.'

'They must be civilians with military backgrounds. Loyal, dependable, and patriotic. They must be malleable — that means a weakness, some kind of personality defect we can utilise and manipulate.'

'Agreed,' the colonel grunted.

'Above all, they must believe in the justness of our cause.'

Colonel Jaurez ran his fingers down the front of his tunic, as if trying to reassure himself of his rank. In the pale light of the afternoon, his face looked confident and composed. Reaching down, he gently patted his briefcase.

'Roberto, we have already found them,' he said.

CHAPTER TWO

Leopold Collis straightened his tie and eyed himself approvingly in the washroom mirror. His face was scrubbed, his fingernails trimmed, and the tip of a spotless white handkerchief peeked demurely from his jacket pocket. He looked, if not exactly handsome, at least haughty and autocratic – qualities which certain ladies found attractive, he knew, for his arrogance made them feel they were stepping above themselves.

Looking appealing was vital to Collis's survival, for he made his living among the bars and dance halls which thronged the old Buenos Aires waterfront district of La Boca. Once the most notorious haven on the South American coastline, La Boca's shady past had fallen victim to the shifting influences of police harassment and governmental concern, until today it was little more than a showpiece for the tourists, a colourful reminder of Buenos Aires in its prime. But it was among La Boca's narrow streets and ramshackle buildings that a new culture had been born, the music which reflected the emotional heartbeat of Argentina itself – the tango. From dingy bars and whorehouses, the dance had spread across the globe, taking Europe and America by storm. Now, decades later, spurned and forgotten by the rest of the world, it still reigned supreme in Argentina, and in no place was it performed more passionately, more devotedly, than the squalid halls in which it had found its birth, the cantinas of La Boca.

Collis was a dancer. He moved with a dancer's grace. His muscles were supple and fluid, displaying a lyricism of motion only a dancer could understand. He made his living teaching the tango to ladies who paid handsomely for the thrill of being whirled around the floor in the arms of a man whose body understood every nuance of movement and feeling. Sometimes, if they paid enough, he rewarded them with favours which went beyond his dancing talents.

It was not an agreeable way of making a living, Collis had to admit, but in Argentina, the tango was more than just a dance – it was a declaration, an expression of will, a ritual of national integrity. When Collis performed, the lady in his arms, whatever her age, became young, desirable, alluring, and in the convolutions of his body, he sensed the traditions of centuries unfolding. All of which was decidedly strange, for Collis's ancestors did not come from the derelict shacks of the La Boca waterfront, but from the leafy lanes of Kent. His grandfather had been a civil engineer employed in opening up the Argentine hinterland, and with his own construction company, had helped build many of the highways linking Buenos Aires with the surrounding provinces. Indeed, his own life might have been both comfortable and affluent, Collis reflected, if only he'd handled things more delicately. After being expelled from school, cashiered from the officer training corps, and imprisoned for fraud during an inglorious episode involving forged football tickets, his long-suffering family had at last disowned him, and Collis had been obliged to make his way by whatever means he could find. Happily, his balletic grace, his profound self-esteem and his inherent charm for the opposite sex had provided the perfect solution.

A slim young man with sharply-pointed features and an air of perpetual disdain, he took one last look at himself in the washroom mirror, then running his fingers through his wavy hair, made his way along the echoing corridor to the ballroom beyond.

The dance hall had unquestionably seen better days. Its floorboards were scratched and worn from the passage of a million feet, and the huge glass ball which had once reflected a myriad fairy lights from the ceiling arch, now hung motionless and neglected, its studded mirrors peeling shabbily from their metal casing. The music came from a small combo in the corner – old men mostly, dressed in out-of-date tuxedoes, their faces pasty masks of indifference as they belted out the tango strains with neither sensitivity nor feeling.

Only two couples were on the floor. They looked incongruous as they spun and gyrated, the women plump and elderly, their chubby arms glittering with extravagant displays of jewellery, the men young, trim, athletic, guiding their unlikely partners through the intricacies of the dance with expressions of fierce concentration. At a cluster of tables flanking the dance floor's outer rim sat a group of similarly-dressed young men, unattached, awaiting the arrival of potential customers. Collis moved across to join them, lighting a cigarette with the unhurried gracefulness that seemed to characterise everything he did.

'Quiet night,' he observed to no one in particular as he settled into a chair.

One of the men nodded in agreement. 'It's always quiet on Thursdays.'

'I heard there've been storms down Dolores way,' another young man remarked.

They all knew what he meant. Despite Buenos Aires' reputation as a modern industrial city, a simple thunderstorm could bring it to a standstill, cutting off telephone lines, shutting down roads and railroad links, snarling up traffic in the business centres. Out in *el campo*, the countryside, heavy rain could turn the unpaved roads into ribbons of ankle-deep mud.

Collis grunted as he smoked his cigarette in silence. He'd

been counting on a busy week. He had run himself short at the races on Saturday, and the concierge of his little residential hotel was beginning to get anxious about the unpaid rent.

For nearly an hour, he sat moodily watching the couples on the dance-floor, ruminating on the depressing subject of his dwindling finances when suddenly, a little before ten, the door opened and a woman entered. She was hardly beautiful, Collis told himself; in fact, there was a certain severity to her features, but she carried an air of such arresting allure it was impossible to look at her without feeling strangely aroused. She was, he estimated, about forty years old, slim-waisted, full-breasted, with thick black hair which hung in a tangle almost to her shoulders. Dressed in a simple gown which hugged the expressive contours of her body, her skin had the delicate hue of rare ivory.

A young man approached her and bowed stiffly. Collis heard the woman's voice above the screeching of the dance combo.

'I have been told to ask for Señor Leopold Collis,' she said.

The young man looked disappointed, but with a gallant air, turned and waved in Collis's direction. Collis felt his muscles tighten as the woman moved towards him. Hurriedly, he dragged himself to his feet and bowed.

'Señor Collis?' she asked.

'At your service, señora.'

'They say no one in La Boca can dance the tango as you do.'

Collis kept his face expressionless. 'Does the señora require instruction?'

Opening her purse, the woman took out a handful of banknotes and tucked them into his jacket pocket. 'I wish simply to dance,' she whispered.

Collis felt his pulses racing. He held out one arm and as the woman stepped forward, pressing her body against his, a ripple of electricity passed through his limbs. He was surprised at his reaction. Normally, such encounters left him cold. He took a deep breath and paused for a moment, judging the beat, then nostrils flaring, launched across the floor.

The woman moved like a cloud, her supple form responding freely. Though she spoke not a word, Collis could feel her communicating with each shift of her breast, each brush of her thigh, each intimate touch, pressure, gesture. In his mind, the dance hall faded, and they went through their ritual in magical seclusion, improvising wildly. He let his body take him, swinging into the twists and turns with an abandonment he hadn't experienced in years, the woman reciprocating, matching his performance in total harmony.

Only when they paused at last to rest, their limbs aching with the effort, did she finally speak.

'I'm glad I wasn't disappointed,' she said as they sat at one of the tables.

'You dance like an angel. Are you a professional?'

'The tango is not for professionals,' she smiled. 'It's something you feel. In here.' She pressed her fist against her breast.

He smiled, watching her take a silver cigarette case from her handbag. She did everything slowly, he noticed, and with a fluid sensual air that was utterly beguiling. He shook his head as she offered him a cigarette.

'Are you married?' he asked.

'Does it show?'

'I can always tell. It's something you get to recognise in my job.'

'What *is* your job exactly?' she asked.

'Dance instructor,' he told her.

She glanced around the seedy ballroom. 'And this is where you make your living? I'm sure you could do a great deal better.'

She leaned forward to accept his profferred light. 'Your ancestry is British, is it not?'

He blinked in surprise. 'I'm an Argentine. I was born an Argentine. I shall always be Argentine.'

She studied him thoughtfully, exhaling smoke from the corner of her mouth. 'Tell me,' she said in a quiet voice, 'what would you be prepared to do to save your country's honour?'

Collis frowned. 'My country's honour?' he echoed. 'Why, anything necessary, I suppose.'

'Even if it were risky?'

'I like risks. It's the only time I feel alive, except for when I dance, that is.'

The woman considered for a moment, then nodded in satisfaction. Opening her purse, she took out another handful of banknotes and pushed them into his jacket pocket.

'What are you doing?' he protested. 'You've paid me already.'

'The last fee was for the tango,' she told him. 'This is for something else. I have a room in a nearby hotel. I would like you to accompany me there.'

Collis sat back, the breath catching in his throat. He was not an artless man. He knew he was attractive to women, knew too the erotic rhythms of the tango often incited his partners to levels of fierce physical awareness, but rarely did he find himself responding with such urgent enthusiasm. Strange, unaccustomed emotions stirred inside him as he nodded gently, and rising to his feet, pulled back her chair.

The hotel stood close to the waterfront, where the skeletal wrecks of ancient ships lay rusting along the empty quayside. It was small and sparsely-furnished, with a massive ceiling fan which clicked monotonously in the ornate entrance hall.

The concierge gave the woman her key and Collis followed her up the rickety staircase, his eyes fixed longingly on her trim behind. Inside the room, he kissed her before she had a

32

chance to switch on the light. She reacted just as he'd hoped she would, her mouth warm, moist, searching, her body locked against his in a fevered embrace. His hand groped upward, clutching her breast. Suddenly, she pushed him away. Gasping, he peered at her in the twilight.

'What's wrong?'

'You mustn't,' she whispered.

'Mustn't what?'

'Make love to me. It's not why I brought you here.'

Collis frowned in puzzlement as she walked to the window and drew back the shutters. The streetlamps cast slivers of orange light across the double bed, and he could see the outline of her body through the flimsy dance-gown.

'I am sorry if I have given you the wrong impression, Señor Collis. It was not romantic fancy which caused me to approach you tonight. I had something far more serious in mind.'

Collis's muscles tightened as anger and disappointment flooded through him. His dreams of amatory bliss had been nothing but an illusion.

'God damn you,' he choked. 'You think I'm some kind of machine you can switch on and off like a bloody computer?'

'Forgive me, Señor Collis,' she said honestly. 'I did not mean you to become so aroused. You must calm yourself. You will need all your faculties during the next few hours.'

'To hell with my faculties,' Collis snapped. 'There's only one faculty I bloody well care about.'

Crossing the room in two strides, he grabbed savagely at the front of her dress. There was a harsh ripping sound as it came away in his hand. Collis stared at her naked breasts, the nipples rising sharply in the cool evening air.

'Stop,' she cried in a hoarse voice.

But Collis was beyond stopping. Picking her up in his arms, he threw her on the bed, tearing at her clothing as she pounded his head and shoulders with her fists. He was on the point of entry when something cold and metallic pressed against the nape of his neck, and a soft masculine voice said gently: 'Señor Collis, please pull up your pants. We have great deal to talk about, and it will be such a terrible waste if I have to spread your brains across the bedroom wall.'

From Argentine military files:

NAME: Leopold Collis.
RANK: Lieutenant.
BORN: Buenos Aires, October 1959.
DESCRIPTION: 5'11" height, slim build, sandy hair, blue eyes, no distinguishing features.
SERVICE: Santa Rosa, Rio Gallegos, Malvinas Campaign.
SPECIAL QUALIFICATIONS: Demolition and explosives expert.
QUOTE FROM PSYCHIATRIC OFFICER: 'Subject is shrewd and intelligent, with a strong self-survival instinct. Cashiered from Bariloche Military Academy for dishonourable conduct. Liable to be unpredictable at times, but ingenious in his own field.'

Luke and Harley spotted the tracks as they guided their *criollo* ponies along the bank of the Venado River. They had been riding all morning, following a criss-cross pattern over the acres of scrubland which surrounded their father's *estancia*, searching for a small group of maverick strays which a passing *campesino* claimed to have glimpsed in the region of the dried-up riverbed. The brothers were not unduly worried, but there had been warnings of rustlers lately, and the military had been called out three times to investigate deficiencies in the neighbouring herds.

Luke wheeled in his wiry mare, whistling to catch his brother's attention. Harley came galloping towards him, his horse's hooves raising dust clouds on the sundrenched *pampa* air.

'What's up?' he asked, hauling hard on the reins.

'Take a look at this.' Luke nodded at the trail skirting the riverbank. 'Three ponies. Strangers.'

'How can you tell?'

'See the metalwork? Those hooves weren't shod by local craftsmen.'

'Rustlers?' Harley breathed.

'Could be.'

'We'd better warn the old man.'

Luke glanced at him sharply. 'What in the hell for? We can handle it.'

'Three against two?'

'You're not scared, are you, Harley?'

Harley looked exasperated. He knew his brother of old. Luke never paused to consider pitfalls or consequences. He was the supreme optimist, ready to plunge into everything without thought or compromise. 'For Christ's sake, Luke, supposing they're armed?'

Luke grinned as he reached back and gently patted his *facón* handle. The *facón*, a fourteen-inch skinning knife, was thrust into the sash at his waist. Like most of the other *campesinos*, Luke regarded the *facón* as his staunchest friend, using it for all the basic necessities of living. Now, as he stared at the tracks by his horse's feet, he said softly: 'We're armed ourselves, aren't we?'

Harley looked doubtful. '*Facóns* against guns? Not much of a contest.'

'Harley, don't be such a defeatist. If we go back to the *estancia*, the trail could run cold.'

Harley shook his head, grinning wryly. 'You know your problem, Luke? You think whatever happens, luck'll somehow carry you through.'

'Why not?' Luke demanded. 'It always has until now.'

35

Harley laughed in defeat. 'Okay,' he agreed. 'When you get that glint in your eye, I know there's no point trying to change your mind.'

Nudging their ponies with their heels the brothers set off in cautious pursuit, their eyes scouring the trail ahead. Dressed in *bombachos* and flat-brimmed sombreros, they looked like typical gaucho ranch-hands, but in reality Luke and Harley were Anglo-Argentine and had been educated at one of the most expensive English public schools in Buenos Aires. They mixed freely with the *campesinos* of the surrounding countryside, conversing in their guttural provincial dialect, but they were each ambivalent in language, culture and temperament.

Harley was the handsome one; medium-sized, square-jawed, he had his pick of the local señoritas, a fact his brother never allowed him to forget. Luke was small and wiry with dark tangled hair and a fierce gaucho moustache. He was, as he was fond of telling himself, infuriatingly ordinary. Though he was popular and universally liked, he had lived his entire life in the shadow of his brother. He was not ugly by any means, but he had no illusions about his physical allure and knew that by no stretch of the imagination could he be termed good-looking. His adventures with the opposite sex seemed doomed to failure before they even began, while his brother continued his amatory forays with the vigour and vitality of a prime stud, a fact which afforded Luke much indignation and envy.

Nevertheless, he was an indefatigable young man, incurably sanguine, friendly, impetuous and filled with an inborn conviction that whatever happened, the future would take care of itself.

The sun hung low, casting a shimmering brightness across the empty *pampa* as the two brothers left the river, following the tracks through prickly scrub and parched open grassland. They spotted the gravel scar of the provincial highway, and perched at its side, the ugly outline of Santana's *boliche*, a combination of grocery store, wine bar and frontier saloon.

Someone called them from the stable door, and Luke recognised Beatriz, Santana's youngest daughter, a dark-eyed vivacious girl with glossy black hair and a strong beautiful body. He reined in his mount.

'*Hola*,' he said, smiling thinly.

Beatriz was dressed in faded dungarees and a thick flannel shirt. 'What are you doing here, Luke Culpepper? You're a long way from home.'

'Looking for strays,' he grinned shyly.

Though he was talkative by nature, for some infuriating reason he always felt tongue-tied in the presence of the opposite sex.

'Strays, is it? You'll not find any strays around these parts. Except the ones who drink in my father's *boliche*.'

Harley chuckled as he reined in at Luke's side. Luke could sense the easiness in him. Harley felt at home with women, knew how to act, how to talk. A ladies' man, he had the looks and the style.

'What are you up to, Beatriz?' Harley demanded.

'Grooming,' she grinned. 'Somebody's got to do it.'

'Need any help?'

She peered at him coquettishly. 'I thought you were after cattle?'

'Not me,' Harley chuckled, sliding from his saddle. 'That's Luke's department. He's our cattle expert.'

'And what kind of expert are you?' she asked innocently as he sauntered towards her, taking the brush from her hand.

'Step inside and let me show you,' he said.

Luke shook his head envyingly as he watched Harley slip one arm around the girl's narrow waist, and guide her back into the stable. He heard her laughter rising shrilly on the hot afternoon air. That was Harley all over. He could charm the hide off a donkey.

'What about your *criollo*?' he heard the girl's voice saying.

'Luke'll take care of it. He's good with horses.'

She giggled again, her voice bright with merriment. 'He should be. He looks like a horse himself.'

A flicker of pain crossed Luke's face. The remark hadn't been meant to hurt. People laughed at Luke because Luke laughed at himself, but every once in a while, he hated his physical shortcomings.

He took the sombrero from his head, wiping one arm across his cheek, then suddenly his spine stiffened and his eyes narrowed. In front of the *boliche*, he could see three horses tethered to the hitching rail. Instinctively, he knew they were the three he and his brother had followed from the riverbank. For a moment, he contemplated rousing Harley from the stable, then decided against it. Harley had other things on his mind at the moment. Luke guided the two mounts to the open porch, and slipped lightly from his sheepskin saddle. Senses tingling, he stepped over the narrow verandah and pushed through the bead curtain which hung across the open door.

The proprietor, Luis Santana, a plump bristle-cheeked man with an oily skin, was wiping glasses behind the chest-high counter. Despite the brightness of the afternoon, the hurricane lamps had been prematurely lit, and they filled the room with a heavy roaring sound. At a table in the corner sat three men in traditional *pampa* clothing. Their faces glistened with sweat and they were watching him closely as if they had been awaiting his arrival. A tremor of surprise passed through Luke's body as he recognised the leader of the trio. In April 1982, the man had been Luke's sergeant in the *Buzo Tactico*, Argentina's underwater commando unit. His name was Mario Rodriguez, and he was chuckling deep in his throat as he waved at Luke benignly.

'*Hola, compadre,*' he said with a welcoming smile. 'I see you've changed little since the old days. Nearly two hours we have been sitting here, but as usual, you are late again.'

From Argentine military files:

NAME: Luke Culpepper.
RANK: Corporal.
BORN: San Nicola, February 1961.
DESCRIPTION: 5'5" height, slim build, black hair, brown eyes, no distinguishing features.
SERVICE: Necochea, Punta Alta, Comodoro Rivadavia, Malvinas Campaign.
SPECIAL QUALIFICATIONS: Diving and sabotage expert.
QUOTE FROM PSYCHIATRIC OFFICER: 'Subject is cordial and gregarious, a good mixer with strong social compatibility. Impetuous at times, but reliable at his job and popular with his men.'

Alex Masters heard the sound above the roaring of the wind. He paused in his tracks, feet straddling the narrow chimney he was climbing, and peered upward, struggling to assess the meaning of the eerie clamour above. He was at the foot of a narrow crack eight hundred feet up the Cerro Natales in Patagonia; on all sides, the jagged snowcapped peaks of the surrounding Andes rippled away in craggy confusion. Northward, he could see the gleaming buttress of Mount Alegre, and the craggy pinnacles of Torre Milonga and Aiguille Ciavinca etched against the sky. Dark storm clouds hung over the sharktooth ridge of Manantiales, but here on the Cerro Natales the sun was high and strong, biting through the thick flannel shirt he wore. Below, his fellow climbers, Ricardo and Simón, stood belayed to the rock, waiting for him to reach a convenient stance and bring them up on the rope.

The noise grew louder, developing into a muffled roaring sound like a train thundering through a distant tunnel, then a handful of dust granules came clattering down the rocky wall, and with a chill of horror Alex realised what was happening. The sun was melting the ice on the mountain's summit, loosening chunks of jagged moraine which were now dropping in a deadly salvo straight down the front of the fractured cliff. Trapped in their narrow chimney, he and his two companions were directly in the bombardment's path.

Alex frantically strove to think. He was perched in a perilous position, his feet splayed out against the rock. There was no time to get a peg in. The nearest belay was Simón's thirty feet below.

Choking deep in his throat, Alex tore the haversack from his shoulders and jammed it above his head.

'Rockfall,' he bellowed to the others below. 'Hang on.'

A few light pebbles came dancing down the cliff face, filling the air with a melodic tinkling sound, then in a breathless rush, the full power of the mountain's artillery cascaded around them. There were rocks everywhere, bouncing and careering crazily earthward. Alex felt the haversack almost torn from his grasp, but he gritted his teeth and hung on grimly, the roar deafening his ears, disorientating, demoralising, a great thunderous roar that took away even the capacity to think. His skin crawling, he crouched against the craggy surface, the rocks swarming about him, the air infested with missiles. Something caught him a glancing blow on the shoulder, and a debilitating numbness spread through the muscles of his upper body. He wrapped an arm around the haversack, thrusting the other defensively above his head, ignoring the thundering salvo as if, by some conscious effort of will, he could actually cease to exist. But the deafening clamour in his eardrums set the hair on his neck prickling, and dizzy and nauseous, he moved his lips in a silent howl of protest and fear.

Then, as swiftly as it had started, the bombardment ended. There was no transitional interlude. The tumult simply faded away, and raising his head, Alex blinked in the last peppering of feathery dust grains. He glanced down through the billowing haze and saw Simón, bruised and battered, giving him the thumbs-up signal with a painful grin on his face. Alex squinted, struggling to see, and an icy band settled round his chest as he glimpsed Ricardo's motionless frame dangling helplessly from the rope.

Cupping his hands to his mouth, Alex bellowed down the mountain face: 'Ricardo's hurt. Can you reach him?'

Simón glanced down, and after gingerly exploring the footholds around his narrow ledge, looked back at Alex and shook his head. Alex grimaced. He felt around with his fingertips until he found a convenient crack, then taking a piton from the rack at his waist, he hammered it firmly in, clipped on a nylon sling and looped the rope to it, testing it firmly before beginning his precarious descent. Trailing the rope S-wise between his legs, he leaned out from the mountain face and abseiled expertly downwards, leaping out from the rock in great fifteen and twenty-foot jumps.

As he approached Ricardo's inert body, Alex slowed his momentum. Ricardo was swaying like a pendulum, his head thrown back, blood from his face trickling down the steep curve of his throat into the collar of his flannel shirt.

Drawing alongside, Alex hung for a moment, his feet propped against the wall, trying not to think of the void below. He hammered in a fresh piton and clipped the rope to it, breathing deeply as he leaned back. Reaching up, he pressed his fingertips gently against Ricardo's carotid artery. An almost indetectible pulsing sensation ran along his wrist and forearm. Still alive, thank God, though how badly injured it was impossible to say.

Alex glanced at the scree eight hundred feet below. They would have to lower him in stages, using the slings in a makeshift pulley-system. It would be a precarious descent, frighteningly exposed every inch of the way.

Pulling Ricardo against the cliff, he belayed him to a narrow ledge, easing the pressure on Ricardo's kidneys, then carefully, patiently, he fashioned a seat-harness out of the nylon slings and manoeuvred Ricardo into it. He pegged the spare rope to the mountain wall and secured its free end to the harness handles, then he threaded it through a series of nylon pulleys, tying a sliding friction knot to serve as a brake. When he was satisfied the system was secure, he signalled to Simón, and working in unison, they began to ease Ricardo earthwards. Alex gritted his teeth, sweat trickling down his face as gently, tentatively, his muscles took the strain. His eyes watched the sling-pulleys, hoping to God they would hold, hoping he could maintain his balance as bit by bit, they lowered their unconscious cargo.

It was a slow tortuous process. Every fifty feet, the operation had to be brought to a halt while Alex abseiled down and hammered in fresh pitons so they could begin the harrowing ritual all over again. Over buttresses, grooves and overhangs, Alex and Simón, working together, took it in turns to free the rope of snags and rocky projections, their movements growing more erratic and clumsy as they approached the foot of the massive cliff. By the time they reached the first straggling screeslopes, their palms were bloody where the nylon line had scraped the skin raw, and their faces hung slack with tension and fatigue.

They collapsed against the rockface, panting hard. Their camp still lay five miles down the valley where the river ran into the open lake.

'You go on ahead,' Alex whispered. 'Radio Comodoro for help. I'll stay with Ricardo.'

'*Vaya*, when night falls, he will freeze to death,' Simón observed grimly.

'I'll keep him warm. Just get back as soon as you can.'

Simón nodded breathlessly, and struggling to his feet, began to shuffle down the screeslope, his scrawny body grotesque in its padded duvet jacket.

Rolling over, Alex examined Ricardo in earnest. The wound was ugly, but not as bad as he'd first imagined. Though there had been a lot of blood, the cut looked shallow and superficial. Ricardo's eyes were closed, his breathing heavy and regular, and there was a faintly yellowish hue in the hollows beneath his cheekbones. Brain damage? Alex wondered. It wouldn't have surprised him. Nothing had gone right with their expedition from the beginning.

He flopped back against the rockface, sighing wearily. In a strange way, he felt almost envious of Ricardo. Oblivion might be a welcome state if a man could find some use for it, he thought. He'd like that, a chance to forget, to wipe clean the memory slate, scour the inner recesses of his brain. There were too many things to haunt him there.

Something had changed in Alex after his ordeal on the *General Belgrano*, something he couldn't explain, even to himself. It was a kind of numbness, an emotional apathy, as if he had been anaesthetised inside his psyche. Was it possible, he wondered, could a man lose his feelings in the same way he could lose his life? Could his body die inside, not swiftly, as a soldier might die in battle, but slowly, insidiously, section by section, as if from some terrible disease? He'd never minded death, not really; some men feared it, he knew, and there had been times, he had to admit, when the thought of extinction had filled him with mortal dread, but not any longer. It was living he minded now. Going through the motions with his insides taken out. He had lost the capacity to feel, that was the size of it. Even the basic things – affection, desire, anger, sorrow – had become brittle and unmeaning. He was a cripple, not in the corporeal sense, the solid tangible material sense, but in the imponderable complexities of the spirit. Sometimes he felt he wasn't a man any more, merely a vessel in which the fear and anguish of war had somehow simmered and distilled, leaving him empty, ravaged and burned out. How blissful it would have been back there to have let the rocks take him. Everything would have settled into place. No soured fragments of a left-over life to live. Only death, soothing and final. Death would have absolved him completely.

His mind wandered as the minutes sped by. Dimly, on the edge of his consciousness, he heard a distant roaring sound and for one wild moment imagined his prayers had been answered – imagined the rockfall, by some supernatural process, had somehow started up again – then his brain identified the sound. A helicopter. He blinked. Even if Simón had run all the way, he couldn't have radioed for assistance in such a short time.

Narrowing his eyes, Alex saw the helicopter soaring in over the open pastureland. It circled once, then hovered motionless as the pilot settled, the downdraught from his rotor blades beating the grass like a giant threshing machine. Uniformed troops burst from the chopper's interior, scrambling up the screeslope towards him. Their windproof smocks looked incongruous against the splendour of the mountains.

A young officer drew to a halt and saluted smartly. 'Señor Masters?'

Alex nodded. The officer's chin was almost obscured by his helmet strap, his face shrunken beneath the metal rim.

'We have been sent to collect you, señor. It is a matter of the gravest urgency.'

'Sent? Sent by whom?'

'That will be explained later. If you will kindly board the helicopter.'

'I have an injured man here,' Alex said.

'*Sí*, I understand, señor. We picked up your companion. My men will take care of the casualty.'

The officer nodded to two of his soldiers, and lifting Ricardo

44

between them, they carried his body to the helicopter, loading him tenderly on board. Alex followed, clambering into the darkened cabin which smelled faintly of diesel fumes and sweat. He spotted Simón strapped against the bulwark, his dark face almost indiscernible in the heavy shadows.

'What, in God's name, is going on?' Alex asked, squeezing into the bucket-seat opposite, but the roar of the rotor blades obliterated his voice. He shrugged helplessly, settling back as a soldier clipped a safety harness around his waist. The helicopter rose into the air, hovered for a moment above the ragged screeslope, then sped off eastward, the darkening landscape flashing by in a dizzy blur.

Alex could see soldiers administering to Ricardo from a medical kit in the cabin corner, then exhaustion filled him, seeping through his limbs like a progressive malady. It was too difficult to speculate, too difficult to think. The present and the future were out of his hands. Everything would be explained in time, but for the moment, there was nothing to do but accept gracefully, and relax. Closing his eyes, he laid his head against the shuddering bulwark and drifted into sleep.

From Argentine military files:

NAME: Alexander Masters.
RANK: Corporal Signalman.
BORN: Buenos Aires, September 1962.
DESCRIPTION: 6'1" height, slim build, brown hair, grey eyes, no distinguishing features.
SERVICE: Necochea Naval Base, *General Belgrano*.
SPECIAL QUALIFICATIONS: communications expert. Also, trained mountaineer.
QUOTE FROM PSYCHIATRIC OFFICER: 'Subject is suffering emotional distress following *Belgrano* sinking. Signs of severe psychological disturbance. Recommend he be released from the service with full rights and benefits forthwith.'

CHAPTER THREE

Alex heard the engines change and dragged himself from his reverie. For one wild moment, he imagined he was still inside the helicopter, then his memory sharpened into focus. At Comodoro Rivadavia, Ricardo and Simón had been transferred to the local hospital while he himself had continued north in a tiny biplane through the early hours of the December morning. Only once had they put down to refuel, at a military airfield on the outskirts of Buenos Aires, but the pilot had taken off almost immediately, banking high over the mouth of the River Plate. Now, in the pale light of the afternoon, Alex realised they were coming in to land.

Below lay the open *pampa*, studded with lakes and clumps of bristling scrubland. He glimpsed a whitewashed *estancia* fringed by broad lawns and surrounded by a vast prairie sea. A narrow airstrip lay baking in the sun.

The pilot circled and made his approach, descending in a series of graceful arcs, touching down expertly and taxi-ing to a halt on the grassy runway. He indicated that Alex should disembark and, without a word, Alex unstrapped his seatbelt and clambered stiffly to the ground. A jeep stood parked at the apron rim; its driver, a young man in army uniform, saluted casually as Alex approached.

'Señor Masters?'

Alex nodded.

'Please get in. I will drive you to the house, señor.'

Alex watched in silence as the soldier started up the engine. They drove over the bumpy ground, heading towards the line of trees where the *estancia*'s estates began.

'Why have I been brought here?' Alex demanded at last.

The soldier looked puzzled. 'You do not know, señor?'

'Nobody's told me a damn thing since I was picked up last night. I've been fed, pampered and humoured, but I still haven't the faintest idea of what this is all about.'

'Then I cannot help you, señor,' the soldier told him. 'I was ordered to pick you up at the airstrip, nothing more.'

'Ordered by whom?'

'Why, by Colonel Jaurez naturally.'

Alex frowned as they pulled off the open *pampa* on to a narrow drive. He had never heard of a Colonel Jaurez, but in Argentina being abducted by the military was a dangerous novelty, and he resolved to keep his wits about him until its meaning became clear.

The trees fell back and he caught his first clear glimpse of the house itself. It was built in the style of a Roman temple, with mock pillars, stone arches and elegant terraces bristling with blue thunbergia. Cypress trees framed a turquoise swimming-pool, and gardeners tended the adjacent lawns, their movements slow and laboured in the breathless humidity.

The driver drew to a halt, and Alex saw a liveried butler waiting on the entrance steps.

'Señor Masters, will you please come this way?'

If anything, the building's interior was even more opulent than the luxurious estates bordering its surrounds. Louis XIV furniture decorated the marbled entrance hall, and the walls of the corridors were panelled with sheets of polished oak.

The butler led Alex into a sumptuously-appointed sitting-room commanding a splendid view of the pastures beyond. There were four other occupants, Alex saw, young men like himself, curiously watching his arrival.

'Señor Runcana will be with you directly, señor,' the butler said. 'Perhaps you would care for a drink while you are waiting?'

47

Alex shook his head, and the man withdrew, closing the door behind him. Alex waited until he had gone, then turned to examine his companions with fresh interest.

'Where did they find you?' one of them asked. He was tall and sandy-haired, with the musculature of a professional athlete.

'Patagonia,' Alex said.

'They grabbed me in La Boca. I'm Collis. This is Luke Culpepper. His father runs a spread up by the Venado River.'

Alex nodded at a small gypsy-looking man whose features were accentuated by a fierce moustache.

Collis indicated the two remaining members of the group. 'This is Carrillo and Masetti, both from Buenos Aires.'

Carrillo was medium-sized and nondescript, but Masetti was a giant of a man, a weight-lifter from the look of him, six feet three or four in height, with an olive skin, thick curly hair and a mean-looking face.

Alex shook hands warily. Before the *Belgrano*, he had been an easy mixer, but now strangers made him surly and defensive. 'Any idea what this is all about?'

'Search me, *compadre*,' Collis said. 'Haven't been doing anything naughty, have you? Political subversion, stuff like that?'

Alex shook his head.

'Somebody's coming,' Carrillo hissed urgently.

They fell silent as the door opened and three men entered the room. Two were in their early sixties; the third, dark-skinned and uniformed, looked about forty-one or forty-two. Colonel Jaurez, Alex guessed.

The leader of the trio was a striking man with flowing white hair and an imperious, autocratic manner. He was sunburned and good-looking, with a thin mouth and an aquiline nose. He smiled at them briefly, but his cold eyes did not soften with his features.

'Good afternoon, gentlemen,' he said. 'I apologise for keeping you waiting. My name is Roberto Runcana. This is Colonel Jaurez and my good friend Señor Gustavo MacAngus.'

He indicated a circle of chairs around the window bay. 'Please be seated. From this point on, I intend to conduct our conversation entirely in English. I shall be grateful if you will do the same. I know that each of you speaks that language fluently and, for reasons which will quickly become apparent, I want you to forget for a time that your Spanish tongue even exists. You must talk like Englishmen, think like Englishmen, act like Englishmen.'

Wonderingly, Alex and his companions took their seats while the colonel and Señor MacAngus settled themselves in the armchairs opposite. Only their leader, Roberto Runcana, remained standing. He was dressed in a suit of pale cream and a dark silk shirt which emphasised the bronze hue of his features. Opening a drawer, he took out five small bell-pushes, the type used on suburban front doors. He gave one to each individual group member and they stared up at him in bafflement.

'I am going to ask you a question,' he declared. 'How you reply to that question will determine how far we are likely to proceed with this matter. You have in your hands a button. If I were to tell you that by pressing that button, you could help to vindicate the honour of our country, but at the same time place yourself in grave personal danger, how would you react?'

The five men hesitated. Alex heard someone go by in the corridor outside, feet clattering on the polished wood floor.

He cleared his throat. 'It's not enough,' he said. 'You can't expect us to make such a decision without at least some idea of what it's all about.'

Señor Runcana considered for a moment. 'Very well,

49

supposing I said that by pressing that button, you could avenge the sinking of the *General Belgrano*?'

Alex took a deep breath, momentarily shaken. He stared at Señor Runcana in silence, then without a word, his thumb stabbed the bell-push.

Luke followed suit, grinning crookedly as if he found the gesture too theatrical for words. Carrillo and Masetti did the same.

Only Collis remained motionless, his face dark and pensive. Moistening his lips, he calmly and deliberately pressed the button with his fingertip.

The white-haired man nodded in approval. 'Good,' he said. 'If you'd refused, we would have had quite a problem finding replacements in the time available. You five have been chosen deliberately and for a variety of reasons. First, with the exception of Carrillo and Masetti, you are Anglo-Argentine and speak English as fluently as your native tongue. You understand the subtleties, the idiosyncrasies of British culture and society. Second, you are all unmarried. You have no dependants and no emotional strings. Third, you are all specialists in your individual fields. You, Culpepper, are an ex-member of the diving commando unit, the *Buzo Tactico*. You, Collis, are an experienced explosives expert, adept at infiltration and demolition techniques. Carrillo is a seasoned boatbuilder with an intricate knowledge of nautical structures, Masetti a champion swimmer, and you, Masters, are not only a versatile mountaineer, but as an ex-member of *Belgrano*'s crew, have a personal reason for desiring revenge.'

Runcana hesitated, and for a fraction of a moment, his voice seemed to falter. 'As it happens, I myself also have a personal reason.'

Keeping his face expressionless, he collected the bell-pushes and tossed them into the cabinet drawer. Alex watched wonderingly as Runcana leaned against the window-sill, ribbons of light tracing the hollows of his cheekbones. Intense emotion fascinated Alex. A man without feelings, he'd discovered, became a kind of spiritual voyeur, attracted to the very sensations he was incapable of experiencing.

'On 2 May, 1982,' Runcana said, 'without warning, and at a loss of 368 lives, the *General Belgrano* was torpedoed by the British nuclear submarine, HMS *Conqueror*.'

He hesitated, his voice subtly changing key. A strand of hair hung across his eyes, and his face looked hard, blunt, inscrutable. 'Gentlemen, we are going to commemorate that event by setting straight the balance. We are going to sink the *Conqueror*.'

Alex felt a small tremor of shock. It was as if, in some strange way, he had stepped outside himself and was standing now, watching the bizarre little scene with the placid detachment of a casual outsider. Somewhere nearby, the drone of a power saw echoed in the hot summer air.

He shifted on his chair. 'Is this a military mission?' he asked.

'Military, yes. Official, no – despite the colonel's presence here. It will be financed by me, and by certain associates in Buenos Aires. If it succeeds, you will each receive the sum of one hundred thousand dollars, paid into the bank of your choice anywhere in the world.'

'In pesos or austral notes?' Collis demanded.

'In American currency.'

'And if it doesn't succeed?'

'In that event, you will receive nothing. I do not believe in rewarding failure.'

Alex was silent for a moment. The thought of retaliation, of actually striking back in some elusive indeterminate way had never occurred to him.

'I know what you're thinking,' Señor Runcana went on. 'It seems a rash idea, sending a sabotage team into the very heart of Britain. But consider for a moment that during

World War Two, the British warship *Royal Oak* was sunk in the middle of Scapa Flow under the noses of the entire defence fleet, and that was at the height of hostilities. Here we have a vessel operating within its own boundaries, under minimal security cover, in peacetime conditions. We'll have a strong element of surprise on our side.'

Alex frowned. 'It'll take a lot more than surprise to get us within striking distance of a nuclear submarine, particularly one as celebrated as the *Conqueror*.'

'You're quite wrong. At the moment, the *Conqueror* is carrying out secret torpedo trials on a remote stretch of water in the Scottish Highlands. The region is soon to become a military training area, but no attempt has been made so far to cordon it off. Apart from a small party of marines policing the surrounding hillslopes, the vessel is virtually unprotected.'

'How do you know this?'

Runcana glanced at Gustavo MacAngus. MacAngus leaned forward in his chair, locking his fingers in the manner of a presiding pastor. 'I have a cousin in the Scottish National Liberation Army,' he told them. 'That's a subversive organisation dedicated to Scottish independence. They're anxious to sabotage the submarine for publicity reasons, but lack the necessary firepower. What they're suggesting is a co-venture, financed by Argentina, conducted by Argentine commandos, but with the SNLA claiming responsibility.'

'And how would this attack be carried out?' Collis demanded.

Colonel Jaurez answered. His English was slurred and uneven, but he spoke with the fluency of an experienced lecturer. 'There are two methods by which it might be achieved,' he explained. 'The first is the *Missile d'Assieger*, a French-built missile launcher with a warhead of shaped explosive charge designed to burn through armoured plating. It carries a computer-controlled wire-guided system which can be operated effectively by three men at a time. The problem is, we can't guarantee how successful it will prove on a target like a nuclear submarine. If, for example, we have to use several missiles, not only will we run a serious risk of the *Conqueror* heading for the open sea, but we'll betray our position to the British marines patrolling the surrounding hillslopes. The second option is by using French-built *Fouillis* limpet mines, museum pieces really, but still the most effective weapons around for sabotage attacks of this nature. Placed at strategic points around the *Conqueror*'s hull, they should be powerful enough to blow a series of four-foot holes through the outer casing.'

'*Mi coronel?*' Luke Culpepper grunted. 'How will the limpet mines be fixed in position?'

'They will have to be put there manually, of course. It will require a diving operation, similar to the ones you conducted with the *Buzo Tactico*.'

'But a submarine like the *Conqueror* will be capable of remaining submerged for extremely long periods of time.'

'You are quite correct, Señor Culpepper. The *Conqueror* is one of five SSNs, or nuclear-powered hunter/killer submarines in the British naval fleet, and she is indeed able to stay under water for weeks, if necessary. But at the moment, she's trying out the new Python, a torpedo which can be guided around obstructions by the submarine's computer system. Barracula Sound has been selected as the testing area because the bed is shallow, uneven, and littered with ancient wrecks. So the vessel is forced to operate either on the surface or at periscope depth – what the sailors call PD – making her conveniently vulnerable to sabotage attack.'

'How many men does *Conqueror* carry?' Alex asked.

'One hundred and three,' Runcana answered.

'What happens to them?'

'We are not barbarians, Señor Masters. As soon as the mines are in position, a telephone call will be made to the local police. The Royal Navy will have just enough time to evacuate the vessel before the explosions take place.'

He paused, glancing down at the floor, his white hair catching the refracted light. He looked, Alex thought, everyone's idea of a favourite uncle.

'What we are asking you to do is both politically sensitive and physically perilous. It is a personal statement, gentlemen, and we need patriots, not mercenaries. I must be certain in my own mind that money is not your primary objective. You will need to undergo an intensive training course before leaving Argentina. It will be strenuous and exhausting. When it is over, you will be placing yourselves at grave personal risk. We are making no attempt to minimise the dangers. It's true we have the co-operation of a British subversive group, but in operational terms, the hazards will be yours alone. I am being as honest as I can with you, gentlemen. I cannot blame you if you decide now to withdraw.'

Alex hesitated, then gently shook his head. Señor Runcana glanced at the others and they grunted in agreement.

Satisfied, Runcana rose to his feet, and opening the cocktail cabinet, took out a bottle of whisky.

'Sixty years old,' he announced with a smile. 'I'd been saving it for a special occasion. It's probably the last you'll get until your training is over, but I think that in the circumstances, gentlemen, we could all do with a drink.'

Julie MacNally found the letter lying in the passageway. It was addressed to her brother Mike, and scrawled across its front were the words 'Strictly Private and Confidential'. The postmark was Glasgow.

Julie was puzzled. Mike seldom received letters, unless they were bills or income tax demands. Customer enquiries generally came addressed to the hotel itself.

She hummed softly as she laid the letter on the breakfast table and scurried into the kitchen where the timer had begun to buzz, warning her Mike's egg was fully boiled. She took it out of the saucepan, switched off the gas, and shouted as loudly as she could: 'Mike, breakfast's ready.'

She could hear him moaning in his bedroom above. She knew the sound and understood its meaning. Hangover again. He had been at the pub until well after midnight, drinking with Dougal Dunelly.

She heard the stairs creak as Mike came tumbling down, buttoning up his shirt. His hair was tousled and his face looked pale and sickly. He stared at the egg on the breakfast table.

'Wha's that?' he muttered in a thick voice.

'What's it look like?' she said primly. 'Sit down and eat. You'll feel better.'

'I'd bring it up,' he mumbled.

'Do you good. Absorb some of that alcohol.'

'I'd be sick, I tell ye.'

She stared at him accusingly. 'Mike MacNally, how can you drink yourself silly with the hotel falling down around our ears? You've been promising to mend those central heating pipes for weeks now. And the door frames need replacing. And the outside sign is crooked. You really are the most exasperating man I have ever met.'

Mike grunted as he reached for the teapot. 'I ken what bothers you, Julie. Ye've always resented the fact that you inherited the virtues of this family while I ended up wi' the brains. Wi' you, life is always immediate, superficial. Wi' me, it's a matter o' the intellect. That's something ye'll never understand.'

'I understand it very well,' she cried indignantly, pressing her trim diaphragm against the tabletop. 'You are lazy, shiftless, irresponsible, idle and indolent.'

Mike peered anxiously at his reflection in the milk jug. 'D'ye think it's beginning to show?'

'Really, Mike, it'll be just like last year, a mad dash to get everything ready at the last minute. Businesses are like rose-gardens, they have to be looked after.'

'Well,' Mike stated firmly, 'this particular business is presently in hibernation. On the first day of April, when the tourist season begins, it will awaken refreshed and revitalised, but for the moment it'll no' be bothering its head about central heating pipes, or anything else for that matter.'

His eyes narrowed as they settled on the envelope on the tabletop.

'What's this?'

'Arrived this morning from Glasgow.'

'Why did ye no' call me, dammit?'

'It's only a letter, for Pete's sake.'

Eagerly, he tore open the flap and began to read. She watched a flush of excitement spread across his pallid cheeks.

'What's it say?' she demanded.

'Business,' he grinned, tucking the letter into his jacket pocket. His hangover seemed to have vanished completely.

'You mean customers?' Julie muttered.

'Aye. Friends of mine from down south.'

'But the hotel's closed, Mike. It's out-of-season.'

'Och, they'll no' be any trouble,' Mike insisted. 'We can put them in the Hamilton suite. They'll no' mind sharin'.'

'When are they coming?'

'Soon.'

'For how long?'

'A week maybe. They're mountaineers. They want tae climb some snow gullies.'

Julie watched in astonishment as he grabbed his coat from a hook on the wall. She had never seen such a transformation. 'Where on earth are you going?' she demanded.

'I have to make an important phone call.'

'Well, what's wrong with the telephone here?'

'This is personal. I dinna want anyone listening in on the party line.'

'Mike,' she called as he scuttled across the entrance hall, 'what about your breakfast?'

'Give it tae the dog,' he shouted, slamming the door behind him.

Gazing through the window, she watched him take his bicycle from the toolshed and pedal off furiously in the direction of the village. Shaking her head in puzzlement, she began to clear the table, carrying the dishes into the kitchen. If she lived to be a hundred, she decided, she would never understand that man.

CHAPTER FOUR

The truck swung in through the camp gates, drawing to a halt on the cindered forecourt. Crouched in the rear, the five Argentines looked expectantly at the duty sergeant.

He nodded. 'This is it, gentlemen. Welcome to your new home.'

They clambered into the night, stretching their cramped muscles with expressions of weary relief. In the darkness, they could see the high-wire periphery fence, and the long rows of barrack huts set in neat little blocks. A flag fluttered above the dusty parade ground, and beyond it glimmered the Parana River.

'This way,' the duty sergeant said.

He led them through the sleeping army camp, pausing at a small Quonset hut set slightly back from the others.

'Sleep well,' he advised, his teeth gleaming faintly in the darkness. 'It's probably the last chance you'll get. You'll find a daily routine order sheet pinned to the back of your barrack hut door. Chow's in the central mess at the opposite end of the parade ground. If you want the latrine, it's that dark Nissen building under those trees over there. *Vaya con Dios*.'

They watched him wander off to his own quarters, his feet crunching on the gravel drive. Wearily, they entered the Quonset hut. It was small, bare and primitive. Double-tiered bunks flanked one complete wall. On the other, individual lockers stood between the window frames. A crude wooden table occupied the centre of the floor, and filmy nets had been hung across the ventilation shafts to keep out mosquitoes.

58

Luke grabbed a towel and made his way briskly to the wash-house. Fireflies danced on the warm night air, and somewhere over west, a night-owl hooted mournfully. He felt good, he decided, glad the interminable truck journey was over at last. He'd had a lot to think about during their long drive south. Runcana's proposal had taken him completely by surprise, but he was a cheerful young man, full of buoyant enthusiasm. The thought of the dangers ahead didn't bother him in the slightest. He welcomed the excitement, the sense of challenge. It was like being back in the army again. He'd missed that, in a way. Life at his father's *estancia* seemed dull and uninspiring compared to his days in the *Buzo Tactico*.

He whistled happily as he soaked himself under the shower. He didn't care about the ethics of the affair. Luke's considerations seldom went that far. For him, there was only the fulfilment of the moment. His motives were simple. An escape, a blessed relief from boredom.

The barrack hut was dark by the time he returned. He could see the outlines of his companions huddled under their blankets. They were a strange bunch, and no mistake. Collis with his boyish charm; Alex Masters, truculent and withdrawn.

Luke tossed his towel over the wall rail and quietly undressed. There was only one bunk still vacant. It lay directly above Masetti, the giant. Even in the shadows, Luke could see the corded musculature of Masetti's powerful arms and shoulders. He was like a human battering ram, a brute of a man. Not one to fall foul of.

Carefully, Luke clambered into the upper bunk, pulling the blanket around him. He could faintly hear night sounds from across the river. Somewhere nearby, a generator throbbed with a low insistent rhythm which seemed to reverberate inside his skull.

'Hey, *amigo*,' Masetti crooned softly from below. 'Where have you been?'

Luke hesitated. Something in the man's tone alerted his senses. 'Taking a shower.'

Masetti chuckled dryly, his voice echoing in the barrack hut stillness. 'Taking a shower? Why, that's nice, that's nice, *amigo*. You'll be pink and clean, just like a little *princesa*.'

Luke's muscles tightened. There was no mistaking the taunting tone in Masetti's voice. He was goading Luke deliberately. Luke could tell by the silence from the other bunks that the men were awake and listening. Perspiration beaded his cheeks.

'Did you remember to wash between your toes, *princesa*?'

Luke didn't answer.

'What's wrong, *amigo*? Didn't you hear me? Maybe you don't like mixing with the rest of us scruffs?'

Luke stared fiercely at the rafters above. He's trying to rattle me, he thought. I mustn't respond. I mustn't retaliate. He's showing off his *machismo*, that's all.

'Is that true, *princesa*? Are you afraid we'll contaminate your pretty pink skin?'

Luke forgot his resolution as his cheeks flushed and his temper flared. 'You could do with a shower yourself, Masetti. You stink. You stink worse than a suppurating latrine.'

He heard Carrillo's sharp intake of breath as a heavy silence settled on the bunk below. Idiot, he thought, you've fallen right into Masetti's trap. He cringed.

When Masetti spoke again, his voice had lost its sing-song quality; it sounded harsh, threatening, brutal. 'I smell like a man, *amigo*. Have you forgotten what that smells like? Perhaps I should roll you in the dust a little bit, just to remind you.'

The bunk creaked as Masetti began to sit up. Jesus, he's coming up here, Luke thought wildly. Panic seized his body. Tossing back the blanket, he leapt to the ground, grunting as his foot collapsed under him, hurling him full length to the floor. He tried to rise, but a fist seized his ankle. Without hesitation, Luke twisted to one side and kicked backwards with his left heel. He felt Masetti wince in pain as his foot connected with something soft and fleshy, but before he could take advantage of the respite, his breath was driven from his lungs as a monstrous weight thudded on top of his body. He gasped for air, choking in the shadowy stillness, glimpsing the blunt outline of Masetti's head rearing dimly just above his own. He lashed out, his fist grazing Masetti's jawline, then his face exploded with pain as something pounded into his nose. Hard fingers clawed at his throat, shutting off his windpipe. He saw the hut reeling dizzily, the ceiling rippling in and out. He's killing me, he thought, the maniac is killing me. The pressure tightened, causing his cheeks to swell, his chest to creak dangerously as if ready to collapse of its own accord. Then a foot flashed past his face, and he saw Masetti's head disappear in a welter of blood and spittle.

The awesome weight lifted from Luke's body, and his chest rose and fell in grateful relief. Painfully, he rubbed his throat with his fingertips. In the corner, Masetti lay where he had fallen, sprawled against his wooden bunk, his eyes murderous with rage, glaring up at the man who had dared to interfere. Focusing his gaze with an effort, Luke saw Collis standing in the centre of the floor. Collis was wearing only his undershorts, and his body looked trim and athletic. His eyes were cool, his manner confident, but against Masetti's enormous bulk, he seemed, Luke thought, a dubious contender.

Masetti rose to his feet and stood swaying balefully, blood dripping from his lips to the coarse hair matting his naked chest. Collis made no attempt to speak and no attempt to back away.

Masetti eyed him in silence for a moment, then with a bull-like roar, he lowered his head and charged forward. Collis danced back, clipping Masetti with a sharp left hook to the side of the neck. Masetti thudded into the wall and teetered, shaking his head to clear it as he glared at Collis, speechless with fury. He spat on the ground, and a tooth rattled across the floor. Lowering his head, he charged again. This time, Collis went to meet him, catching Masetti with a running drop kick in the stomach. Masetti crashed headlong into the empty bunk, and it collapsed under his weight in a screech of splintered wood and tortured metal. As Masetti floundered among the wreckage, dragging himself painfully to his feet, Collis stepped forward, his hands moving like pistons. There was no finesse to Collis's attack, just a cold determined ruthlessness which bore Masetti back by its sheer savagery. Though Collis was no match for Masetti's muscular power, he was fit and supple, and against such athleticism, Masetti simply had no defence. He slumped against the wall as Collis went to work on his stomach. Only when Alex, clambering from his bunk, took Collis's arm and drew him gently aside, did Collis finally desist. Masetti slid to the floor, holding on to his mid-section. For a moment he stared at them in anguish and disbelief, then began, noisily, to be sick.

Gasping for breath, Collis helped Luke to his feet. 'Are you okay?' he asked.

'I'm fine. Except that I've got a pumpkin instead of a nose.'

'Come on outside,' Collis told him.

In the cool night air, Collis examined Luke's face critically. 'I don't think it's broken. Badly swollen though. You won't look as pretty as you used to.'

'That'll break the ladies' hearts,' Luke said dryly.

'Wait here.'

Collis returned in a minute or two with tiny wads of cotton wool. Gently, he pushed them into Luke's nostrils, padding the swollen flesh with delicate expertise. 'Just in case the bone's fractured. It'll stop it collapsing. You'll have to breathe through your mouth for a day or two. Think you can manage that?'

Luke nodded, and after a last cursory glance at his handiwork, Collis turned towards the hut door.

'Collis?' Luke said.

Collis paused, glancing round at him.

'Took a lot of guts tackling a monster like that,' Luke whispered, his voice almost indiscernible. 'Masetti would've killed me. Thanks.'

Collis shrugged and ignoring Masetti, who was still retching on the ground, clambered into bed, gathering the blankets around his chest. He was already snoring softly when Luke entered the hut and gently closed the door behind him.

Alex sat on the riverbank, listening intently as Colonel Jaurez outlined the workings of the *Fouillis* limpet mine. On the mine's underside, three small magnets protruded like the legs of a shallow tripod. The magnets could be extended or withdrawn inside the metal casing by turning a tiny handle. The detonating device was simple to operate and could be set effectively either under water or before the sortie began.

The colonel's voice droned monotonously on the humid air. He was dressed in combat fatigues, the five trainees in small nylon bathing trunks. They crouched in a circle, watching the colonel absorbedly – Masetti with his scarred face and bruised trunk, Luke with his swollen nose, Collis with his skinned knuckles. It had hardly been, Alex thought, a brilliant start to a successful team relationship. But he had to admire Collis for standing up to Masetti the way he had. A man that size made a formidable adversary. And it wasn't over yet, not by a long shot. Alex could see Masetti glowering murderously at Collis. He knew sooner or later they would clash again. The realisation depressed him, made him wonder what on earth he was doing here. After all, what did he hope to achieve with this mad little escapade? Revenge? Hardly. He didn't need the money either. It was something else he wanted. Reassurance. A purge for his emotional languor. Proof positive that he was still alive.

The colonel's voice rose and fell on the hot summer air as he went through the details with the impassivity of a well-oiled machine.

'The *Conqueror* has a maximum speed of 28 knots,' he said. 'She carries Harpoon anti-ship missiles plus Tigerfish and Mark-8 torpedoes. In addition, she's equipped with sophisticated sensor devices, thousands of sonar "ears" fitted to her hull, capable of picking up the sounds of a moving object and transmitting the details to a panel of video screens. However, since the only metal you'll be carrying will be the mines themselves and your oxygen cylinders, it's unlikely you'll be noticed among the rusting wrecks on the Barracula seabed.

'Your biggest problem will be the *Fouillis*, which was originally designed for use with midget submarines and is heavy and cumbersome to carry. Your weight-belts, which you'll wear to neutralise buoyancy, will have to be kept to a minimum. This is fine during the outward journey, because the mines will drag you down in the water, but coming back, the nitrogen bubbles in your neoprene wet suits will automatically lift you to the surface. This means that once the mines have been attached, you will have to make your retreat in full view of the submarine's deck.'

He paused to let the implication register. Across the river, a donkey-cart went by, driven by two peons in battered felt hats and ragged ponchos. The creaking of its wheels rose eerily on the afternoon stillness.

'The first thing we must do,' Colonel Jaurez declared, 'is familiarise ourselves with both carrying and operating the limpet mines. You will see, in the centre of the current, two metal posts placed thirty yards apart. One man will carry the *Fouillis* to the left-hand post and fix it in position. As soon as he has returned, the second will swim out, de-activate the magnets and transfer the mine to the right-hand post. We will continue moving the mine backwards and forwards until the carrying and placing have become virtually instinctive. Now, who will make the first sortie?'

He looked at Alex, and Alex nodded. The colonel picked up the mine, withdrew the magnets into the metal shell, and pushed it into Alex's hands. Alex's stomach tensed as he felt the weight of the thing. For a moment, he considered tucking it under his arm, then changing his mind, clutched the mine in front of him, poised himself on the riverbank, and executed a neat forward dive. The water closed over his head, cool and refreshing. He broke the surface and began to swim, rolling inelegantly as his feet lashed at the drifting current. The heavy *Fouillis* remorselessly dragged him under, like a monstrous albatross, hauling at his arms and wrists. Holding it in position involved a constant battle for air. He could see the opposite riverbank bobbing and dipping in his vision as he struggled to stay afloat, then his head went down and spluttering wildly, he fought his way to the surface again.

The river's movement distorted Alex's senses, washing over his face each time he swung his body into another stroke. He floundered gracelessly, no longer co-ordinated, the undertow sucking at his legs.

Somehow, panting, heaving, kicking, he reached the first metal post, and hugging the limpet mine against his chest, trod water as he brought the magnets into position. The *Fouillis* clamped into place with a dull metallic thudding sound. Gratefully, Alex turned and swam for shore.

Carrillo went next, cutting his way through the sleekly moving current with long confident strokes. He reached the mine, retrieved it from its emplaced position, and began the awkward journey to the second post. This time, his rhythm seemed completely broken. He wallowed and threshed in the water, dipping under for long moments at a time as the mine's insidious weight dragged him down. They could see his face, bug-eyed and desperate for air, fighting to regain the surface.

It took him nearly four minutes to swim the thirty yards, fix the *Fouillis* in position and make his thankful way back to the shoreline.

Collis followed. Collis fared better than his predecessors. His natural athleticism gave him a subtle advantage. Nevertheless, he found the transfer awkward and destabilising.

Only Masetti seemed completely at home. Masetti's prodigious strength overrode the limpet mine's weight, and retrieving the *Fouillis* from the point where Collis had placed it, he tucked it under his arm like an irksome toy and began to strike for the second post. He looked entirely at ease, sleek, sure, controlled.

Alex watched him silently, the afternoon sun making him drowsy. He saw the river rippling gently. He saw the metal posts rearing above the current. He saw Masetti, his bruised torso moving rhythmically, his blunt head glistening in the sun.

And then, without warning, a great mushroom of water shot into the air. Before Alex's astonished eyes, the river seemed to erupt upon itself, rising in a flash of brilliant flame, spewing out a grotesque welter of feathery spray, red-hot metal and shredded flesh. A thunderous explosion reverberated along the riverbank, and the waters boiled into a churning cauldron, lashing at the shoreline.

Alex felt a coldness settle on his limbs. He hunched forward, clenching his teeth as nausea started in his stomach like a tight little ball. Colonel Jaurez had risen to his feet in horror and was moving his lips in a silent impassioned fashion, his cheeks white, his eyes stunned with disbelief. A severed arm bobbed macabrely on the wave-crests.

For a long moment, nobody spoke. They sat transfixed by

the terrible inevitability of the scene before them. The river was settling now, and in the twisting waters, they could see Masetti's entrails dragging through the current like shredded seaweed.

'Now that's what I call going out with a bang,' Collis observed in a droll voice.

Alex turned on him, fury rising in his chest. 'What did you do to that limpet mine?' he hissed.

Collis looked surprised. 'Do, *amigo*?'

'It wouldn't go off of its own accord. You must've set the timer when you fixed it in position.'

'What the hell are you talking about?'

'You were the last one to touch that mine before Masetti reached it.'

'The mine was faulty, for Christ's sake. It dates back to the Second World War.'

'That's enough,' Colonel Jaurez said softly. He was struggling hard to maintain his dignity, but they could see his muscles trembling. 'Return to your barrack hut. We'll take the rest of the afternoon off. I'll organise a fatigue party to clean up the mess, and we'll get statements from each of you this evening.'

He tugged unhappily at his parka draw-cord. 'It's the worst thing that could have happened,' he whispered. 'We'll have one hell of a job keeping the operation under wraps now. There's bound to be an inquiry. Let's hope to God we can provide some satisfactory answers.'

Alex lay on his bunk, staring gloomily at the ceiling. Luke and Collis were sprawled at the table, playing cards in a morose desultory kind of way. Nobody spoke. Masetti's death had affected them all. He'd been a brute and they were better off without him if the truth were known, but the suddenness of the explosion had caused them all to reconsider. What was this madness upon which they had embarked? How stable was their equipment? If a man could lose his life in the opening stages of training, what would it be like in the field?

The questions stirred relentlessly in Alex's brain, but there was something else which bothered him more, and that was Collis. Only one man could have primed the *Fouillis*, he knew. Only one man could have set the timer. Was Collis capable of such barbarity, or had the mine been defective as he claimed? There was a coldness between Collis and himself now. Hostility had crept into their relationship, a bad beginning. They had no time for enmity or resentment. They would need each other in the days ahead.

The door opened as Carrillo came in. He was carrying a rucksack on his shoulder and his eyes looked sheepish as he hesitated on the threshold.

'I've just been to see Colonel Jaurez,' he said. 'I'm pulling out.'

'Already?' Luke sounded surprised.

'After what happened this afternoon, I ... I thought it over. I've decided it's not for me.'

'What did Jaurez say?'

'He's transferring me to Hidalgo military prison and placing me in solitary until the operation's over. He thinks you three have enough experience to carry it off between you. I just came over to say goodbye.'

Solemnly, he shook hands with each of them in turn. 'I wish you luck, *compadres*,' he said. 'I'm sorry I can't be with you.'

'We'll miss you, Carrillo,' Luke told him with a smile. 'It's getting to be like "Ten Green Bottles" here.'

The door closed as Carrillo left, and a heavy silence settled on the room. In the space of a single day, they had lost two-fifths of their commando team. The enterprise seemed jinxed from the beginning.

It was Luke, with his natural buoyancy, who tried to snap

them out of it. 'Well,' he said with a grin, rubbing his hands together, 'looks like it's down to the Three Musketeers.'

Alex stared at Collis stonily. The Three Musketeers? he thought. The idea didn't cheer him at all.

Nine days. The words drummed at their senses. There was no time to reflect on Masetti's death, no time to consider the implications of their enterprise. They could scarcely have withdrawn even if they'd wanted to, for their training took every ounce of physical, mental and emotional commitment they possessed. They worked and studied and practised until they were almost asleep on their feet. Every night found their bodies drained and exhausted. Most of the activity took place in the water, learning to operate almost by reflex, carrying out numerous sorties in the indoor training baths where a wooden replica of the *Conqueror*'s hull had been hastily assembled by military craftsmen.

Their diving instructor was an olive-skinned man who spoke English with a Spanish/American accent. Under Señor Runcana's instructions, even the training was conducted in the language of the country in which they would be operating.

On the morning of the second day, the instructor led them to a Nissen hut with a huge cylindrical water-tank in the centre of the floor. The tank was rounded at the top, with a sealed metal hatch and a porthole window allowing its interior to be viewed from outside.

'Aqualung diving is impractical for military purposes,' the instructor explained, 'because it gives off too many air bubbles. So we're going to concentrate on oxygen rebreathing, where carbon dioxide exhaled by the diver is chemically absorbed and replaced with fresh oxygen as he goes along. The problem is, oxygen poisoning can sometimes cause the diver to black out without warning, which means it's vital to your survival that you learn to recognise the telltale warning signals before an attack can occur.'

The instructor patted the metal tank affectionately. 'We call this the "sweatbath". It'll give you some idea of the sensations to watch out for. Inside, you will find a dial fitted to the tank wall. When you are ready, you will turn the dial in a clockwise direction one complete revolution. This will pressurise the cabin to a simulated depth of fifty feet. At some point during your submersion, you will experience a twitching sensation in the lips and other extremities. As soon as this happens, you must turn the knob back to its original position and make your exit through the ceiling hatch. Is that understood?'

They nodded in silence, and Luke went first. Dressed in nylon bathing shorts, he fitted his breathing set and eased himself into the pressure tank's aperture while the instructor battened down the lid. Through the glass, they watched Luke operate the wall-dial. Luke waved at them playfully and began doing acrobatics. He stood on his head, turned somersaults in the eddying water, and marched up and down the tank's vertical walls. Suddenly, he went very still. A series of convulsions ran through his narrow frame and he lunged forward, groping desperately for the dial. They waited until the pressure had returned to zero, then opened the hatch and dragged him to the Nissen hut floor.

'*Mierda*,' he coughed, spluttering wildly.

'How do you feel?' the instructor demanded.

'Like a rag that's just been wrung dry.'

'You were clowning around so much, you almost missed the warning symptoms. You're lucky you didn't make yourself sick.'

Collis took Luke's place. Unlike Luke, he made no attempt to entertain them, but sat motionless on the metal floor, his outline undulating through the reinforced glass. They waited in silence as the minutes passed, then suddenly Collis's body jerked into movement and they saw him dive forward, grappling with the pressure gauge. The instructor uncoupled the ceiling hatch and Collis emerged, choking and spluttering.

Next, it was Alex's turn. He tugged on his cylinder straps, slotting his face-mask into position. Lowering himself through the opening, he winced as the cool water touched his naked skin. A metallic clanging sound echoed above his head, and he glanced up to see the instructor slamming down the lid. A heavy weight seemed to settle in Alex's solar plexus. Moving almost in a dream, he reached out and turned the metal gauge carefully to the right. A gentle hissing sound filled his head as the chamber swiftly pressurised. Minutes passed. Numbly, he sat on the floor, staring back at the faces of his three spectators. He felt a twitching in his upper lip and swallowed hard. His mouth seemed out of control, the cheeks bulging like an inflated balloon. He could feel his lips writhing, his teeth clanging together. The chamber seemed to contract and lose substance. A band of pain fastened around his chest, and suddenly he was drifting helplessly, lost in the tortured labyrinths of his mind. In one wild hallucinatory moment, he imagined he was back on the *Belgrano*, struggling to crawl up the oil-filled escape hatch. Oxygen spilled from his throat, almost dislodging the rubber mouthpiece as he floated backwards, his body jerking and twitching in a series of helpless convulsions.

Watching through the porthole window, Luke gave a cry of alarm. 'He's passing out,' he yelled at the instructor.

The man scrambled to his feet, and running to a pipe which led from the tank's rear, twisted at the pressure release valve protruding from its coupling. His knuckles gleamed white as he focused his strength on the metal handle. 'Bloody thing's stuck,' he groaned.

Collis swore under his breath. Leaping forward, he began to tear at the pressure tank's fastenings.

'What are you doing?' the instructor yelled.

'Getting him out.'

'You bloody fool. Open that tank before it's de-pressurised and it'll rip your bloody arms off.'

Collis ignored him. He spun back the screws and the lid shot into the air with a resounding crack, hurling Collis to the floor. Without hesitating, he struggled to his feet and wriggled into the narrow aperture. He saw Alex's body caught in a macabre unwilling dance, bobbing against the metal ceiling. Ducking his head beneath the surface, Collis wrapped his arm around Alex's ribcage and dragged him to the circular opening. He grunted in approval as Luke hooked his wrists around Alex's shoulders, hauling him to the Nissen hut floor.

Collis followed, swinging lightly to the ground. Alex was retching and choking as the instructor tore at his breathing set. His cheeks looked ashen and there were flecks of vomit on his pale lips. Collis leaned against the metal tank, breathing hard in the warm dank air.

The instructor glared at him over his shoulder. 'Didn't you hear my warning?'

'I heard it.'

'Then why didn't you obey?'

'He might have died in there.'

'Rubbish,' the instructor scoffed, mopping Alex's face and throat. 'He got a little dizzy for a moment, that's all. But you disobeyed orders, and that's even worse than oxygen poisoning. A man who can't obey orders is a dangerous liability on any operation, remember that.'

Collis's face hardened. 'How many more of us d'you intend to kill before this lunatic venture gets off the ground?' he demanded.

The instructor glared at him, and for a long moment their eyes locked in silent duel. Then Collis relaxed, shrugging dismissively as outside on the parade ground, a bugle began to blow.

The incident had a stabilising effect on Collis's relationship with Alex. Since Masetti's death, something about Collis had worried Alex greatly; a brittle and inescapable aura of self-interest, but he had to confess he felt grateful for Collis's intervention in the pressure tank, and that night, as they strolled back together from the mess-hall in the cool softness of the summer evening, he said: 'I never got to thank you for pulling me out of that tub today.'

'Damn all to thank me for.'

'It's crazy, I know, but I lost my head completely in there. I thought I was back on the *General Belgrano*, suffocating in a shaft full of oil.'

'Does that happen often?'

'From time to time. This may sound strange, but sometimes I get the feeling I'm only fooling myself when I imagine I wasn't killed when the ship went down. A man who can't feel anymore isn't really a man at all.'

Collis nodded as if he understood. Through the periphery fence, they saw a steamer gliding by on the Parana River, its decks ablaze with light. The breeze stirred Collis's hair, brushing it backwards from his brow.

'Ever ask yourself what we're doing here?' he wondered.

'All the time.'

'It's a mad stunt, whichever way you look at it.'

'You're right. We have to be certifiable to be taking part.'

'Think we can really pull it off?'

Alex shrugged. 'To tell the truth, I don't care one way or the other. I've got my own reasons for doing this.' He hesitated. 'I'm trying to jolt my emotions into working order again, sort of like ... like souping up a worn-out car battery.'

Collis grunted. 'With me, it's different. I dance in La Boca, and I've made up my mind I'm never going back. That's why I need the money.'

Alex smiled. 'How simple life must be when money's all you've got to worry about.'

73

Collis drew hard on his cigarette, then crushed it beneath his foot. In the darkness, his profile had a filmstar quality, unconsciously arresting.

'No, it isn't simple,' he said softly. 'It isn't simple at all.'

On the morning of the fifth day, the three trainees were introduced to a new element — darkness.

'From now on,' Colonel Jaurez explained, 'all diving practice will be conducted in the gloom.'

It was an unsettling experience for Alex who had just come to terms with the sensation of being submerged in daylight. Then, there had still been the rippling paleness of the surface to give him a feeling of substance and hope. In the dark, it was impossible to tell where the water began and the air left off, but despite his misgivings, he learned to relax in the novelty of his new surroundings, discovering the wonders of phosphorescence, the myriad tiny lights which, even in inky blackness, could pinpoint the outline of a hand or the proximity of a friendly fellow diver.

When they were not engaged in underwater swimming, they studied the internal workings of the *Fouillis* limpet mine. In accordance with Colonel Jaurez's instructions, their hours were strictly regimented.

0430 hours:	Reveille. Quick dash to the latrine and a cold shave in the first thin light of day.
0500 hours:	Breakfast. Queuing with the troops at the mess-hall hotplate.
0600 hours:	Weapons instruction. 9mm Browning automatics, FN-MAG machine-guns, M3-A1 sub-machine-guns.
0800 hours:	Diving practice.
1200 hours:	Lunch.
1245 hours:	Demolition deployment. Dismantling, reassembling, charging, timing, detonating the *Fouillis* limpet mine.

1600 hours:	More diving practice.
1800 hours:	Dinner.
1930 hours:	Lecture period and familiarisation programme. Bellowing out the *Conqueror*'s features from Colonel Jaurez's illustrated wall chart: 'Bow caps and shutters, forward escape tower, snort induction mast, sonar transducer . . .'
2030 hours:	Calisthenics and cross–country run.
2130 hours:	Recreation.
2200 hours:	Lights–out.

On the evening of the ninth day, Colonel Jaurez held his final briefing in the lecture room. A diagram of the *Conqueror*'s anatomy had been suspended from the blackboard offering, in vivid detail, a graphic impression of the submarine's internal workings.

'It is critical that the mines are placed in exactly the right positions,' the colonel pointed out. 'Keep away from the nose cone and the area behind the conning tower. This is where the MTBs and the nuclear reactor are housed, and the hull has been specially reinforced at these points. The best locations are immediately below the frontal portion of the tower, under the Cool and Cold Rooms, the Senior Ratings' cabins and the fuel oil tanks. Detonations here will cause the maximum amount of damage and take the vessel directly to the bottom. Remember you'll be operating under water, but since you've memorised every inch of the hull, you should know your way along it blindfolded. There's a slight danger the *Conqueror* will be employing her active sonar gear, which means you'll face the hazard of being rendered unconscious by the sonic booms. We will provide you with protective headsets designed to muffle the effect. Keep them on as long as you are in the water, and you should be able to perform comfortably and safely.'

75

A hint of excitement shone in his small brown eyes. 'You will enter Britain through the customary channels, carrying British passports made out in your own names. We've decided to stick to genuine identities to avoid any psychological slip-ups. By the time the British authorities discover who they're looking for, you'll be out of the country anyway. The passports are forged, of course, and will hardly stand up to a sophisticated computer check, but as ordinary holidaymakers, there's no reason to suppose you'll be subjected to individual scrutiny. The limpet mines and diving equipment will be smuggled in two or three days after your arrival. That should give you just enough time to establish yourselves and become familiar with your surroundings.'

'How will we get there?' Collis asked.

'A contact from the Scottish National Liberation Army will pick you up at the airport. He'll handle transportation.' Jaurez paused. 'Remember, you'll be going to one of the most secluded corners of the British Isles, but Scotland is also an important NATO stronghold and a major buffer between the Soviet Union and the United States. There are numerous military bases there, including nuclear weapon emplacements. Do not imagine your isolation makes you immune to the attentions of the security forces.'

'What about getting out?' Luke enquired darkly.

'You'll be transported to Glasgow and held in a "safe" house until it is considered prudent to ferry you to the continent. We'll pick you up from there.'

'Who's in overall command?' Collis demanded.

'We've decided that Masters, with his mountaineering background, should assume supervisory responsibility. However, you are each specialists in your own field, and we feel it more desirable that you work as a team, rather than a military unit. Remember your training. Avoid mixing with the local populace any more than is necessary. And speak

76

English at all times, even among each other. That includes you, Collis.'

'*Qué lastima, no entiendo inglés,*' Collis muttered with an impudent grin.

The colonel's face hardened, but Collis, trimming his fingernails with a pocket knife, looked blissfully unperturbed. Thirty feet away, watching the proceedings from the doorway, Señor Runcana and Gustavo MacAngus glanced at each other dubiously.

'He's not taking this seriously enough,' Runcana whispered.

'His psychiatric file warned he was liable to be unpredictable. We could have trouble there.'

Runcana's features tightened as he stared across the lecture room to where Collis was balancing himself lazily on his chair's rear legs. Anxiety flickered in the older man's eyes.

'We'll just have to take a chance,' he grunted. 'It's too late to find a replacement now.'

CHAPTER FIVE

Belayed on the rocky ledge, Julie MacNally payed out the rope as her brother deftly scaled the precipitous cliff-face. Mike was a good climber, strong, dependable and agile as a monkey. She watched with approval as he edged from groove to chimney, from chimney to buttress, picking his way with a deceptive loose-limbed grace which made it look so easy. To the north, she could see the distant sweep of the Charrach Dam, its grey parapet partly obscured by a wisp of heavy cloud; beyond it, the jagged ridges of Drium Nam Leagh rose against the sky like the wings of a soaring bird.

Mike reached the summit, belaying himself securely before gathering in the slack and bellowing for her to follow. Julie took a deep breath, and reaching up, located a narrow fissure with her fingers. She gripped it fiercely, jabbing her boot against a sharp nobble of rock which offered a precarious toe-hold, then shifting with an expert sideways motion, she slithered skilfully upwards. She could feel the reassuring tautness of the rope rubbing hard against her chest, and jamming her fingers into fresh holds, she moved on up the steepening pitch, taking care not to hug the rock too closely and ignoring the great immensity of space below.

It was Mike who had started her rock climbing. The hills, she'd always liked – walking, rambling, hiking, but the towering crags had been an unknown world to her until Mike, with his infectious enthusiasm, had taken her on an exploratory scramble. Now she loved it, the strain and stretch of muscle and sinew, the nerve-tingling sense of exposure and the feeling of peace and splendid solitude climbing always gave her.

She was gasping hard when she reached the clifftop, and Mike grinned at her admiringly.

'You're getting better,' he admitted. 'Six months ago, ye'd never have managed that slab. See how your confidence is growing?'

'D'ye really think so?' she asked as he gathered up the rope.

'Aye, at this rate there'll be nobody in the Highlands to touch ye. No lassie, anyway.'

Julie was silent as they started back down the narrow ridge. Despite his cheeriness, something had happened to Mike in the last few days. Ebullient, he'd always been, but lately she'd sensed another element, a tenseness, a slow-burning excitement. He seemed to be waiting for something, but whenever she tried to broach the subject, he withdrew into his shell. His strangeness worried her deeply, and she said little as they clambered down the steeply-descending hill track.

It took them more than an hour to reach the path which led from the lower slopes to the back of the Barracula Hotel. Around them, russet-clad peaks rippled in every direction, and over west, the distant Atlantic shimmered in the winter sun. As they approached the rear of the building, Julie glimpsed a car parked on the hotel forecourt.

'Looks like we've got visitors,' she said, frowning.

Mike showed no sign of surprise. As they drew closer, she spotted two strangers sitting in the vehicle's front. Mike's breath caught in his throat and she glanced up quickly, frowning as she saw a flush of excitement spreading across his ruddy cheeks.

'D'ye ken those men, Mike?'

'Aye,' he nodded gruffly.

Taking the rope from his shoulder, he slung it over her arm. 'Drop it in the toolshed for me, will ye, Julie? I have to drive to Glasgow right away.'

'Glasgow?' she echoed disbelievingly.

'Aye, I've just remembered our guests are arriving this afternoon.'

'Mike?' she exclaimed as he strode briskly towards the waiting car.

'Dinna worry,' he called. 'I'll give ye a call from the city.'

Baffled, she watched him speak to the car's passengers, then turn and run swiftly to his battered grey van. The engines started and the two vehicles pulled slowly out of the forecourt. Julie stared after them as they vanished round the bend, but Mike did not look back.

Shaking her head in bewilderment, she shouldered the climbing rope and turned towards the hotel.

The 'No Smoking' sign flashed on as the pilot began his descent. Luke peered excitedly through the aircraft window, glad their journey was over at last. Sixteen hours it had taken to cross the South Atlantic, then a four-hour delay in Madrid while they waited for a connecting flight. Now, they were coming in to land. It was the first time in his life he had glimpsed the country of his forebears. The great sprawl of the city swung into view, cold and bleak in the January afternoon. Luke could see giant tower blocks and beetle-like lines of traffic filtering along narrow highways. It looked like a city anywhere, he thought, and following the stewardess's instructions, sat back in his chair, fastening his seatbelt.

He was whistling softly under his breath as the pilot touched down, filled with impatience for the challenge ahead. It had never occurred to Luke their venture might possibly fail. Inchoate anxieties had no place in his psyche. His optimism was total.

He felt the sharp bite of the Scottish cold as the passengers disembarked, and shivering, hurried briskly in to the comparative warmth of the baggage reclamation lounge. Alex and

Collis were already waiting, their dark jeans and ski jackets scarcely distinguishable among the jostling throng. There were no soldiers, no armed policemen in sight. Everything seemed normal, orderly, subdued.

Luke grinned at the customs man as they passed through the 'Nothing to Declare' gate and wandered across the arrivals lounge to the taxi rank outside. He had never before in his life been abroad, apart from a two-week visit to neighbouring Uruguay. Scotland was a new continent, a new hemisphere, beckoning and mysterious.

One minor incident marred their arrival, casting a faint air of unease over Luke's excitement and enthusiasm. Stepping through the self-opening doors, Collis collided with a lady pushing a metal trolley. The bag was torn from his shoulder, bursting open as it hit the ground. The lady apologised as Luke and Alex stooped to pick up Collis's belongings.

Alex frowned and rose to his feet, clutching a small oval-shaped object made from polished wood. It was Collis's *maté* bowl.

'What the hell is this?' Alex hissed, handing it back.

'I don't like British tea,' Collis told him mildly.

'You bloody fool, if the customs man had opened that bag, he'd have guessed immediately where we've come from.'

'How's that? It could be a tourist souvenir.'

'They don't sell *maté* bowls in Spain, you idiot. Get rid of it quick. You had no right to bring it along.'

'Okay, squire,' Collis promised, tucking the offending implement back inside his shoulder bag. 'Keep your hair on. I'll dump it at the first opportunity.'

Luke frowned as he listened to the exchange. Though they did their best to get along in a civilised fashion, it was clear to anyone with half an eye that Alex and Collis were ready to explode at any moment. The realisation depressed Luke.

They couldn't afford disputes or personality clashes. They had to work as a team.

A car pulled up at the taxi rank and a man clambered out, small and dissipated-looking. 'Any o' ye's named Masters, by any chance?'

'I'm Masters,' Alex told him stiffly.

The man came forward to shake his hand. 'Name's Billy Hannah. Sorry I'm late an' all, but I had a hell of a job getting through the lunchtime traffic. Pile in, the lot o' ye. There's some people want tae take a look at ye.'

Billy Hannah was silent as they headed into town. He sat in the front, his hands lightly stroking the steering wheel, his thin straggly hair curling in clumps above his dirty frayed collar. There was something ratlike about the man, Luke thought. A professional criminal, he was willing to bet. He had seen the type before.

He sat back, watching the city build up around them. It looked strangely disappointing, rather like the outskirts of Buenos Aires. A thin rain was falling, and the dour buildings seemed to huddle together for comfort and warmth. A few drunks meandered along the pavements, and a police squad car idled by, tyres hissing on the glistening asphalt.

Billy Hannah drove through a network of deserted side-streets until they saw the skeletal cranes of the Glasgow docks looming up ahead. He drew into a deserted factory yard, pulling to a halt and switching off the engine. A smell of diesel fuel and stale urine hung on the icy air.

'This is it, gents,' Billy said cheerfully. 'Everybody out.'

They followed him into an empty warehouse, their feet clattering eerily. A small cluster of men stood waiting in front of a line of parked cars. As they approached, a figure disengaged itself from the main group and came forward to meet them, tall, raw-boned, hook-nosed.

'Who's in command?' the man demanded.

'I am,' Alex said.

The man held out his hand. 'Ferguson. Chief of Staff, SNLA.'

His eyes scoured them keenly as if they were visitors from another planet. 'I'm glad to see ye. We were half afraid ye might pull out at the last minute. Come an' meet the rest of Brigade.'

Luke blinked as each individual member of the group was introduced in turn. There was an air of quaint formality about the proceedings. The Scotsmen seemed nondescript, faintly eccentric. It was hard to think of them as dangerous revolutionaries.

'Is there anything ye need?' the man named Ferguson asked.

'Not for the moment.'

'What about your equipment?'

'It's arriving later. We have to establish ourselves first.'

'Ye'll be on your own most of the time. That all right wi' ye?'

'It's the way we prefer it,' Alex told him.

'If ye need us, we'll be here. Just get on the blower.'

The Chief of Staff gave a sharp whistle, and a man climbed out of a battered grey van and came towards them, smiling amiably. He was thickset and tousle-haired, and there was a pleasing symmetry to his features.

'This is Mike MacNally. He'll be looking after ye for the next few days. Anything ye require, tell Mike.'

'Thanks,' Alex said.

'One other thing. Mike's got a wee sister. Her name's Julie. She knows nothing about this. Stick to your cover stories. Ye're a bunch of English climbers on holiday. She'll understand that. She's expecting ye.'

'Right.'

They shook hands again, conscious that they were being appraised, then with a final word of goodbye, they followed Mike MacNally to his van.

'Just toss your gear in the back, gents,' Mike ordered. 'Ye'll hae to squeeze in wi' it, I'm afraid. One of ye can sit in the passenger seat, but it'll be a bumpy ride for the rest. We're no' exactly the Ritz.'

Alex and Collis clambered into the rear, and Luke settled beside the driver as they started their long journey northward. Cruising through the darkening Glasgow suburbs, Luke peered eagerly through the window at the traffic drifting by. Beyond the city, grey hills loomed into the night. Now it looked different to Argentina, he thought.

The young Scotsman, Mike MacNally seemed pleasant and cheerful. He rambled on for a while in an amiable kind of way, curious about his new-found companions, and Luke chattered back, gratified to find someone else as loquacious as himself. Alex and Collis, wary of their surroundings, remained sombre and taciturn. After an hour or so, Mike gave up his efforts to draw them into conversation and switching on the van radio, filled the interior with heavy rock music as they drove steadily north through the darkening hills.

They stopped twice for petrol, and once for coffee at a hot-dog stall in a tiny village north of Tyndrum, but by the time they arrived at their destination, Luke's limbs felt stiff from the long hours of confinement.

He gasped as the mountain air stung his cheeks and throat. Framed against the night sky, he glimpsed the hotel which would be their home for the next few days. Its stone walls looked dour and austere.

'This way, gents,' Mike announced cheerfully, grabbing two of their suitcases and sauntering into the entrance hall.

To Luke's surprise, the hotel proved cosy and inviting, the flagged dining-room, low beams and roaring log fire warm and snug in the chilly evening.

Mike grinned at them happily. 'I hope ye dinna mind

sharing. It's no' worth our while heating the entire place in the middle of winter. To tell ye the truth, we canna afford it, so I've put ye in the family room on the floor above. It's the warmest spot in the house. Ye get the glow coming through the boards from the kitchen stove.'

He opened the door and shouted, 'Julie, are ye there, lass? We've got company.'

They heard a scuffling sound outside and a young girl came into the room, drying her hands on a kitchen towel. She was slim and pretty, with a smattering of freckles across her healthy cheeks. Beneath her floppy jumper, her figure looked full and firm.

'Ye must be half-starved,' the girl said welcomingly. 'I don't suppose it entered Mike's mind to get ye something to eat. I've hot broth on the stove, an' some steak-and-kidney pudding. Sit at the table and I'll bring it through. Gie's a hand, Mike.'

They clattered off together, the girl's trim haunches rolling tantalisingly beneath her tight blue jeans. The three Argentines followed her with their eyes.

Luke heard Collis chuckle, and glancing up, saw his companion's lips pucker into the shape of a silent wolf-whistle. Collis winked at them knowingly.

'Just so we understand each other, gentlemen,' he announced with a crooked grin. 'That one's mine.'

The wind bit into Alex's anorak, chilling him to the bone. To the east, he could see craggy mountains with snowcapped peaks rolling into the sky. Scotland was a strange country, he thought, not a bit the way he'd imagined; sometimes, though he'd been here only a bare few hours, he had the wild idea that the sun never shone, the birds never flew, the wind never dropped. Luke had said it was like the Malvinas, and he could believe that. There was a hint of desolation that chilled a man to the bone.

Below, the flat waters of Barracula Sound nestled in their cradle of spruce woods. He could see the island shutting off the sea beyond, and the ominous tips of submerged rocks poking, whale-like, out of the twitching currents.

They were still panting from the long haul in, dropping cautiously through the dried bracken and tree clumps to a rocky outcrop which commanded an excellent view of the Sound. Alex could see the water curving in a ragged half-moon shape, widening at the middle where the Sound was broadest, narrowing at each end as the island dipped towards the shoreline. He felt his stomach tighten as he glimpsed the submarine directly below – almost as if it had been awaiting their arrival, he thought. Motionless, feature-less, its dark hull and conning tower looked eerily familiar to Alex who had studied every facet of its outline for days on end. There was no sign of life on its narrow deck, and no sign either of the foot patrol assigned to police the surrounding shoreline.

'Give me the field glasses,' he ordered.

Collis, breathing heavily from the steep descent, fumbled in his haversack and passed across the binoculars. Alex raised them to his eyes, swivelling the lens into focus. Close to, the submarine looked strangely vulnerable. There were no markings that he could see, and in the pale grey of the winter morning, the vessel might have been a mirage, a reflection cast by the surrounding hills.

'Is she always in the same spot?'

Mike shook his head. 'Last time she was closer to the shoreline.'

'See anything of the crew?'

'They come into the village sometimes, tae drink at the local pub.'

'Anyone paid her a visit yet? Carrying out supplies, that sort of thing?'

'She was fully stocked before she got here. Nae civilians

are allowed anywhere near the Sound before the end o' the month. Ministry of Defence ruling.'

'What about diving?'

'She canna dive fully. The bed of the Sound is cluttered wi' old wrecks. The trials are being carried out at periscope depth, or on the surface.'

Alex lowered the field glasses, rubbing his chilled cheeks with his fingertips. It all looked too simple, he told himself moodily. Were the British really so stupid?

'When are ye planning tae do it?' Mike asked.

'Soon as the equipment arrives,' Alex said mildly.

'How soon's that?'

'Couple of days, maybe. No more than three.'

'What'll ye be using?'

'*Fouillis* limpet mines.'

Mike laughed shortly. 'Museum pieces.'

'You know the *Fouillis*?' Alex asked, glancing at him in surprise.

'Only by proxy. We used tae study military ordnance and demolition charts when I was wi' the SNLA. I could put a *Fouillis* together blindfolded, but I've never actually held one in my hands.'

Alex grunted, glancing at the surrounding hills. Mist cluttered their summits, blending the ragged contours into the swirling gloom of the winter sky.

Suddenly, Mike's eyes narrowed as he gazed across the incline below.

'Look,' he hissed, pointing at a line of ragged scrub. 'Ye can see the marine patrol.'

Alex raised the field glasses. His vision blurred, merged, solidified. He spotted a troop of men dressed in windproof anoraks, their faces blackened to help them blend into the surrounding woodland. They carried Sterling sub-machine-guns, and as Alex watched, they fanned out, vanishing stealthily into a straggling clump of spruce.

He handed the binoculars back to Collis. 'Let's get out of here,' he grunted. 'We don't want the bastards spotting us unnecessarily.'

Alex was quiet as they drove back to the hotel through the January chill. He felt the *Conqueror* should have produced some emotion in him – anger, hatred, resentment. After all, it had wrecked his life. But there'd been nothing. No fury, not even fear. He'd expected a Goliath waiting for its David. It had been a submarine, nothing more.

Maybe I'm too far gone already, he thought. Maybe you can't salvage the totally dead. It was easy for Luke and Collis; their motives were clear-cut and simple. With him, there was only the pitiful desire to trigger his body into life again, a half-baked idea of a new awakening.

He came out of his reverie as Mike swung the van into the hotel forecourt. There was a touch of frost on the glistening cobbles as they clambered from the rear, and Mike drove the vehicle into the adjoining garage. Alex spotted Julie coming out of the toolshed, clutching a wicker basket filled with heavy logs. Dressed in the familiar floppy jumper, her hair fluttered wildly in the wind. He moved towards her, taking the basket from her grasp.

'Think I can't handle it?' she smiled, peering up at him.

'I'm sure you can. But there's no sense straining yourself with four able-bodied men around.'

She chuckled as she led the way through the narrow entrance hall, Luke and Collis staring after them. Collis's face was dark and hostile, and Luke glanced up at him anxiously.

'Don't take it to heart, Leo. He's only helping her with the logs.'

'The girl is mine,' Collis breathed.

'Hey, remember what we came for. We haven't time for petty jealousies.'

'Is that what you think this is, jealousy?'

'What else?'

Something in Collis's face made Luke wince. Collis had it bad, he realised. Whether it was Julie MacNally's attractiveness, or his inherent rivalry with Alex was difficult to define. Either way it spelled disaster.

Luke liked Collis. He liked Alex too, if it came to that. It was rotten luck having them at loggerheads like this. They were both good men in their individual ways: Alex moody and withdrawn, solid as a rock if the need was there; Collis haughty and superior, able to turn on the charm at will. Luke couldn't forget how Collis had saved him from Masetti. Clearly Collis wasn't lacking in the guts department. He knew how to handle himself, a born fighter, supple and athletic. A ladies' man, too, Luke was willing to bet. He studied Collis enviously, suddenly intrigued. Ladies represented the one feature of life in which Luke's natural optimism faded. In matters relating to the opposite sex, he was, he realised, an utter novice.

'What's it like?' he asked suddenly and unaccountably. 'Going with a girl.'

Collis stared at him. 'What're you talking about?'

'I mean, what's it like? I've never done it.'

'You're kidding me.'

'Would I joke about a thing like that?'

'At your age?'

'I'm not exactly an oil-painting, Leo.'

'My God,' Collis breathed, shivering in the chill.

He was eyeing Luke with an expression of bafflement. He doesn't believe me, Luke thought. Well, who could blame him, for Christ's sake? Half the time, he didn't believe it himself.

'I never know what to say,' he admitted, surprised at his own candour. 'I've never told this to a solitary soul, but when I'm alone with a girl, I get tongue-tied.'

'I've never seen you at a loss for words before.'

'I'm telling you the truth, Leo. I just seem to shut up like a clam.'

Collis was silent for a moment as he considered his friend's problem. The unexpected confession had deflected his attention. His anger at Alex seemed momentarily forgotten. He thrust his hands into his anorak pockets, his hair flapping wildly in the wind. Then he smiled.

'As soon as this is over, I'll take you to Rio. We'll celebrate in style.'

'Girls?' Luke queried, eyeing him keenly.

'All you can handle.'

'You really mean it?'

Collis chuckled dryly. 'It's a promise,' he said.

In the kitchen, Alex emptied the basket of timber into the metal container. His cheeks were flushed, his hair tousled. Julie eyed him curiously. He was not like the other two, she thought. Not like Mike either. He was quiet and subdued. She liked him.

'Would you care for some tea?' she asked, filling the kettle and setting it on the stove to boil. Something about Alex drew her like a magnet. It was hardly his looks, she told herself. Not that he wasn't attractive; he had a pleasant face and nicely-placed features, a wee bit on the bony side perhaps, but agreeable, for all that. No, it wasn't his appearance, it was his manner, the hint of strangeness in his eyes. He was a haunted man, this friend of Mike's. She was careful to keep her expression neutral as she said: 'How d'you like it here? It's no' exactly the Dorchester.'

'It's better than I'm used to,' he admitted.

'Where are you from?'

'Newcastle.'

She smiled. 'Ye didn't get that suntan in Newcastle.'

'I . . . I've been in the Canaries,' he told her, colouring swiftly. 'On holiday.'

Odd reaction. What on earth had she said that was so upsetting? 'Och, it must be a braw job ye've got, holidaying in the middle of January.'

'Well . . .' He shrugged. 'I work for myself. It's part of the privilege.'

'Lucky you.'

Yes, no question about it, her comments were making him nervous. He was a strange one and no mistake. They all were. Ever since their arrival, she'd noticed oddities in their language and behaviour. Sometimes they used expressions which had gone out of fashion decades ago. It was nothing she could put her finger on, but something about their visitors didn't sit right. Mike claimed they were friends from the old days, yet there was no sense of intimacy between them. They never reminisced. They behaved like strangers.

Alex's eyes lit on Mike's battered guitar, tucked behind the kitchen cupboard.

'Who's the musician?' he asked, picking it up.

'Mike. He used to strum it when we had parties. He hasn't touched it for months though.'

'I used to play myself,' he said. 'Back in the old days.'

His fingers hovered over the strings, tuning the instrument expertly.

'Let me hear.'

'Oh . . .' He looked embarrassed. 'It's been too long.'

'Please.'

He hesitated. Then bending his head, he began to play. The music filled the room, full of strangeness, sadness, isolation. She stared at him enthralled, caught in the spell of the moment.

'Don't stop,' she pleaded when he had finished.

He shook his head, putting down the guitar. 'I'm out of practice. My fingers need to loosen up a bit.'

'That was beautiful,' she said. 'It sounded Spanish.'

'South American.'

'Have you lived in South America?'

'Never.'

The intensity in his voice surprised her. God knew, she wasn't probing. Reticence she understood, but not this impassable defensive barrier. She changed the subject. 'Think you'll find enough around here to keep you occupied?'

'Well,' he said hesitantly, running his fingers through his thick dark hair. 'We thought we'd try a few snow gullies on the west face of Ben Rualin.'

'Watch it up there. It's a dangerous mountain in winter. Don't let the weather catch you out.'

'We'll be careful.'

'Climbed in Scotland before?'

'Once or twice in the Cairngorms.'

'I'm not boring you, am I?'

He looked startled. 'Of course not.'

'I just thought ... well, ye look a wee bit ill-at-ease somehow. I know I prattle on a lot, Mike's always telling me that. It runs in the family. My mother was the same.'

'Where *is* your mother?' he asked.

'Och, she's been dead for years. I was only six when that happened. Pleurisy, the doctor said. Mike and I were brought up in Glasgow by our father. He was a lovely man.'

'Is he dead too?'

She nodded. 'Three years ago. We used the insurance money to buy this place. It's not much, I know, but we like it here. Mike sometimes worries that I'm missing out on things, boyfriends, dances, stuff like that. But I prefer the mountains to the city any day.'

'Aren't there any local lads around?'

'Oh aye, one or two. Jamie Blackmore sometimes takes me to the village hops, but it's nothing serious.'

'He's a lucky man, Jamie Blackmore.'

She smiled, acknowledging the compliment. 'I'm not one

for playing about much,' she admitted. 'With me, a relationship like that, it has to mean something. Does that sound silly and old-fashioned?'

'Not if you mean it.'

'Of course I mean it. If you care about someone, it has to be completely. I mean, enough to give your life if necessary.'

'Dying's easy,' he told her. 'It's living that's the hard bit.'

She frowned. The matter-of-fact way he'd spoken seemed to emphasise the strangeness of his words. 'Could you do it?' she asked. 'Die for somebody, if you really had to?'

'A man who's lived through his own death can die for anything,' he declared.

She hadn't been mistaken, there was something about this man that was impossible to ignore.

'Will you be going on the tops tomorrow?' she asked casually.

'I imagine so. Weather permitting.'

'Mind if I come along?'

He looked surprised. 'You?'

'I'm a good climber, ask Mike. I love snow-and-ice work, and I'd like to get away from the house for a while.'

She watched his features settle into an obstinate mask.

'Impossible,' he said, shaking his head.

'Why not?'

'A woman on the rope, it's bad luck. Collis wouldn't like it.'

The answer confused her. 'What about you?' she asked.

She could feel the barrier strengthening between them. He was shutting her out, coldly and deliberately.

'I wouldn't like it either,' he whispered.

A wave of disappointment swept through her. She felt angry and humiliated. He'd rejected her without reason. Biting her lip, she turned her back so he wouldn't glimpse the hurt in her features.

Mártin Segunda smoked a cigar as he lay in the bath, watching the woman appreciatively. She was beautiful, he decided, even better in the nude than she'd appeared gowned and bejewelled at the French Embassy ball. Her breasts were firm and full above the jutting cradle of her ribcage, her stomach flat, spreading into the delightful curve of her loins and thighs. Her hair, unpinned at last, hung around her shoulders in an unruly tangle. Her eyes were smiling as she watched him through the swirling steam.

'What're you looking at?'

'I was thinking how lovely you are,' he told her.

She pouted. 'Compliments drip so easily from your tongue.'

He grinned, chewing on the cigar tip. '*Usted me honra,*' he answered politely.

She tested the water with her toe and he grinned as she eased herself into the bathtub opposite him. Steam rose around her ample breasts, beading the nipples with tiny moisture droplets. She shook her hair, loosening the thick dark curls.

'You look so different without clothes on,' she smiled.

Segunda's body was hard and lean, the muscles glistening in the foamy water. A ragged scar ran from his navel to his lower breast. His hair was grey and tousled, and there was a gleam of humour in his merry eyes. He looked like a man to whom life was one long permanent joke.

'I was thinking the same thing about you,' he admitted.

'Did I intrigue you at the embassy?'

'Totally.'

'Did you dream about me?'

'Every night.'

'What did you dream?'

'I dreamt about this,' he smiled, his eyes crinkling at the corners.

She reached out, taking the cigar from his lips. 'I have heard of your reputation,' she breathed.

'Never listen to rumours.'

'They say you are insatiable.'

'Exaggerated.'

'They say you are . . . unique.'

He considered a moment. 'They might have a point, at that,' he admitted modestly.

Leaning forward, she kissed him on the mouth. His lips tasted of tobacco. Reaching beneath the water, her fingers located his manhood.

'*Duro*,' she breathed huskily.

His arms locked around her, pulling her hard against his chest. Her mouth opened beneath his and his hand found her breast in the steaming water, the soft flesh slippery against his fingers. She whimpered softly deep in her throat.

Segunda was on the point of positioning himself when a voice reached them from the floor below. 'Rosa?'

He frowned, drawing back. 'Who the hell is that?'

Her eyes widened. 'My husband.'

'Christ,' he groaned.

Water cascaded around her as she clambered from the bathtub, her splendid breasts shimmering in the steamy air.

'Get out,' she hissed. 'You've got to leave quickly.'

'Like this?' he protested.

'Please. You mustn't let him find you here.' Her face was frantic with concern. She tore open the window and he felt the cool draught of the night air. 'You can cross the roof and escape through the garden. He won't see you if you keep to the shrubbery at the side of the lawn.'

'Without clothes on?'

She grabbed a towel from the bath-rail and wrapped it around his waist.

'Please go,' she pleaded, pushing him desperately towards the window. 'You've no idea what he's like. He's quite capable of killing me.'

'But how am I to maintain my dignity?'

'No one need see you. There's a taxi rank at the end of the street. I'll parcel up your clothes and send them back in the morning.'

He was laughing as she bundled him on to the roof outside. The air chilled his glistening skin. He stared across the sloping tiles at the garden beyond. Through the trees, he could see the lights of the city casting an orange glow against the night sky.

Shivering, he danced back into the bathroom.

'What d'you want?' she cried hysterically.

'My cigar,' he grinned.

He picked it up, jamming it between his lips. There was a creak on the landing outside, and the bathroom door swung open. Through the swirling clouds of steam, they saw a man staring at them disbelievingly. Segunda heard the woman's sharp intake of breath.

To Segunda's surprise, she began to attack him, pummelling his face and shoulders with her fists.

'Leave me alone,' she cried. 'Take your hands off me, raping *bastardo*.'

Her fist caught his cigar, squashing it flat. Segunda blinked. Turning, he clawed his way back on to the roof, his bare feet sliding on the slippery tiles. He heard the man shouting behind him. Deftly, Segunda dropped into the darkness, grunting as he landed on the open lawn. From the window above, a shot echoed wildly through the stillness. *Dios mio*, he thought, the lunatic has a gun up there.

He tore through the shrubbery, chuckling wildly, the underbrush catching at his naked feet. A bramble bush ripped the towel away, and he had to go scampering back for it, private parts merrily jangling. He saw the wall rearing

96

out of the darkness and scrambled to the top. The street beyond looked silent and deserted, the office blocks empty, the storefronts shuttered for the night. A solitary car sped by, heading towards the open *campo*, its passengers blissfully unaware of Segunda's presence. Naked and glistening, his body wrapped in the flimsy bathtowel, he dropped to the pavement and collapsed against the wall, laughing helplessly. Doubling over, he held his stomach with both hands, his shoulders shaking with merriment. A lady, approaching, crossed discreetly to the opposite side of the street. Eyes streaming, Segunda tightened the towel at his waist, and began to stroll along the sidewalk, looking for the taxi rank. Automobiles hooted, going by. A streetcar drew to a halt at the traffic lights and the passengers stared out at him in astonishment through the misty windows. Solemn and dignified, Segunda saluted them gravely.

He saw a vehicle cruising towards him, and glimpsed a police signal lamp on its roof. The squad car drew to a halt, the eyes of the men inside widening at the sight of the incongruous figure wandering along the kerbside. A uniformed sergeant rolled down the window.

'Stop,' he commanded shrilly.

A flicker of surprise crossed the man's features. 'Why, it is Señor Segunda.'

Segunda bowed. 'Gentlemen?'

'Señor, we have been looking for you all evening,' the sergeant declared, opening the car door. 'You are required immediately at the presidential palace '

'*A su servicio, señores*. But first you must allow me to return home and make myself presentable.'

Unbuttoning his tunic, the sergeant handed it to Segunda.

'*Con su permiso, señor*. We have been ordered to deliver you as quickly as possible.'

Segunda sighed as he pulled on the tunic. There was no point protesting, he knew. It was typical of the police department to take the order literally. They always over-reacted. In matters involving state security, they insisted on doing everything by the letter. Sighing, he climbed into the squad car and settled back against the seat cushions as they drove through the darkened streets to the Plaza de Mayo. The broad lawns and plane trees looked murky in the lamplights' glow. He saw the pink walls of the presidential palace, and the stone balcony where generations of dictators had harangued cheering hysterical crowds.

The sergeant parked the car at the palace entrance and shepherded Segunda past the astonished guards at the security checkpoint. He led him along a series of marbled corridors to an elegant reception room where a young lieutenant sat writing at a mahogany desk. The lieutenant blinked disbelievingly when he saw Segunda standing there.

'Señor?' he breathed, swallowing hard as he stared at the apparition in front of him.

'I have been ordered to report here,' Segunda told him.

'You are . . .?'

'Mártin Segunda.'

'Oh yes, of course, Señor Segunda. Please go in. The general has been waiting for you all evening.'

General Emilio Guayabero, head of Argentina's security division, rose to his feet as Segunda entered the office. Guayabero was a small man, unimpressive in appearance, but he had gained a reputation among his colleagues for incisive intelligence and astute ingenuity. He had held his post throughout the turbulent years of *la guerra sucia*, the 'dirty war' against the terrorists, and continued to hold it now under the critical scrutiny of the new administration through both shrewdness and personal cunning. Guayabero had learned at a very early stage how to survive in the fluctuating tempos of a country where governments changed with the regularity of football teams. He was constrained in his attitude, ambiguous in his loyalties, and dedicated to the cause of self-survival.

For a moment he stared dumbfounded at Segunda's bizarre appearance, then waving him to a chair, opened his cocktail cabinet and poured them each a drink.

'Do you always dress in such an eccentric manner?' he asked. 'And where on earth have you been? We've been trying to locate you since six o'clock.'

Segunda grinned, crossing his legs as he relaxed comfortably in the armchair. 'I was busy,' he declared simply.

Guayabero grunted. He knew perfectly well how Segunda had been occupying his time. According to his psychiatric report, which Guayabero saw no reason to dispute, Segunda was imbued with an exorbitant sexual appetite. Handsome as a filmstar, Segunda took full advantage of his looks to indulge his implicit belief that life – particularly with respect to matters of the flesh – was meant to be enjoyed.

'One of these days,' the general warned, settling into his chair, 'you'll grow old and decrepit like the rest of us. It'll happen so fast, your body will disintegrate like a worn-out steam boiler.'

Segunda chuckled. 'I am not afraid of death, *compánero*. I should like to depart with dignity, that is all. Preferably at the age of ninety-four, shot by a jealous husband.'

'I see you are working at it already,' the general said dryly.

Though he liked Segunda, for some reason he never felt relaxed in the man's company. Segunda's air of merriment was, the general knew, only a façade. Segunda was a snake, deadly and unpredictable. During *la guerra sucia*, he had acted as a professional assassin for the military junta, eliminating anti-government suspects in the reign of terror that raged in Buenos Aires throughout the mid-seventies. Segunda's speciality had been his skill with the *facón*, the fourteen-inch *pampa* skinning-knife, which had earned him the nickname of 'The Gaucho'.

Guayabero shivered as he thought of Segunda's exploits

during the anti-terrorist campaign. Fifteen thousand people had disappeared from the streets of Buenos Aires alone and Segunda, he knew, had been responsible for a goodly proportion. It had taken all Guayabero's ingenuity to prevent Segunda being arrested after the junta's downfall. Now, though he was an invaluable asset to Guayabero's intelligence department, the general could never rid himself of a certain unease at the thought of his agent's macabre past.

Guayabero's face grew grave as he came to the subject in hand. Opening a silver cigar box, he offered one to Segunda, lighting another for himself.

'I have called you here because I find myself in a slight dilemma,' he confessed. 'There may be no cause for alarm, but after fifteen years in this business, I get a prickly feeling at the back of my nostrils when something isn't sitting right, and I've got it now. I'd like to find out why.'

Segunda said nothing. He slouched in silence, smoking his cigar. Even in repose, he carried a certain animal quality, the general thought, a physical presence it was difficult to ignore.

'Last Sunday, we had a fatality at Chalia army base on the Parana River. A man was killed, blown by up a *Fouillis* limpet mine.'

'*Fouillis?*'

'A French antique. Hardly the sort of weapon we'd expect to be employed on training exercises in this day and age. They should have been cleared out years ago.'

'Who authorised the exercise?' Segunda asked.

'Colonel Jaurez, an officer of impeccable reputation.'

Segunda knew Guayabero of old and had learned over the years to recognise the tell-tale nuances of expression and tone. 'You don't like him much, I take it?'

'Frankly, no. I find him arrogant and dull-witted.'

'Is he a rival?'

Guayabero shrugged. 'In a manner of speaking. He may

be junior in rank, but he has powerful friends in the government.'

Segunda chuckled deep in his throat. 'He sounds a troublesome fellow, this Colonel Jaurez.'

Guayabero drew hard on his cigar, settling back in his chair. His eyes were mild and reflective. 'Do you know how long I have served my country, *compánero*?'

Segunda shook his head.

'Thirty-one years. Thirty-two in April. I was seventeen years old when I left home for the Bariloche Military Academy. Presidents have come and gone, but Guayabero continues for ever. I'd like to keep it that way. I have thirteen years left before retirement, and I intend to see them out.'

'Why shouldn't you? You're irreplaceable.'

'Surviving takes a special kind of mind,' the general said. 'A special kind of ingenuity. An essential part of the process is the ability to recognise a threat before it grows too big to handle.'

Segunda tapped his glass with his fingernail. 'I'd hardly describe Colonel Jaurez as that,' he smiled.

'Colonel Jaurez is both younger and richer. He has powerful associates. Most important of all, he's inordinately ambitious.'

'You think he's after your job?'

'I think he could one day prove a distinct embarrassment to this department, and that's a possibility I'd like to avoid.'

Segunda chuckled. 'In other words, you want me to discredit the man?'

The general paused, taking the cigar from his mouth and studying its tip with more than usual intensity.

'I want you to investigate,' he declared. 'If Colonel Jaurez is acting honourably, he has nothing to fear. Without actual proof of misconduct, I am reluctant to proceed further, but the use of *Fouillis* limpet mines is a puzzling occurrence. Something smells about this incident, and smells badly.

Knowing your talent for detective work, I feel sure you'll be able to set my mind at rest regarding the good colonel's character and integrity. If, on the other hand, you discover something improper has been taking place . . .' – the general's eyes were bland – '. . . then of course, my duty will be clear.'

Segunda smiled, swirling his drink in the glass. Laughter lines creased the corners of his eyes as he hooked an arm over the chair-rest and studied Guayabero amusedly.

'I'll see what I can do,' he promised.

The party was in full swing by the time Segunda arrived. He heard music droning in the marbled rooms upstairs, and the muffled murmur of conversation. He paused in the hallway and took off his coat. The butler bowed, his voice carefully deferential. Dressed in an immaculately-cut tuxedo, Segunda looked suave and important.

'You have an invitation, señor?'

Segunda shook his head, smiling. He lit a cheroot, his movements deft and precise. The butler looked flustered. 'I am sorry, señor,' he stammered, 'but this is a diplomatic affair. No one is allowed to enter without written authorisation.'

'I have authorisation,' Segunda told him.

Reaching into his pocket, he showed the butler his ID card. The man's cheeks blanched as he recognised the name.

'Señor Segunda?' he breathed, taking half a step backwards. 'I am sure your presence will be acceptable, sir.'

Segunda grinned to himself as he ascended the massive stairway. It amused him to see the fear in people's faces when they realised his identity. In government files and in Western intelligence records alike, he was still listed under the nickname he had made notorious, 'The Gaucho'. Killing meant little to Segunda. He had killed since boyhood – predators on his father's *estancia*, injured animals, cattle scheduled for slaughter. He saw little difference in the destruction of human beings. Devoid of pity, he could massacre the innocent with neither feeling nor restraint. His irrepressible humour and his powerful sexual urges baffled his superiors, but as a programmed killer who could be called upon in any emergency, he continued to be irreplaceable to the secret police.

Segunda was amused by his commander's obsession with Colonel Jaurez. Guayabero could be an old woman sometimes. Nevertheless, he was cunning, devious, and had a nose for impropriety, and Segunda owed him a lot. He was a useful friend and a generous benefactor. It was very much to Segunda's advantage to keep Guayabero happy.

Segunda found General Vasquez standing by the punchbowl. Vasquez was a squat little man with crinkly black hair. He seemed surprised at Segunda's presence.

'Segunda,' he exclaimed. 'What on earth are you doing here?'

'I was looking for you,' Segunda told him.

The general's eyes narrowed as he glanced quickly across the seething throng of partygoers. The jewelled gowns and bright uniforms looked strangely unreal in the glare of the crystal chandeliers.

'What have I done that could possibly warrant the attention of the security department?'

Segunda filled himself a glass from the punchbowl, smiling pleasantly. There was nothing half-hearted about Segunda's humour. He exuded merriment and charm. It had proved a useful faculty in his years as an assassin, when his cheerful countenance had often helped to throw his enemies off-guard.

'Two days ago, you chaired a committee investigating a death at Chalia army base,' he said.

General Vasquez blinked in surprise. 'That's true,' he admitted.

'What were the findings of that investigation?'

Vasquez looked affronted. 'You know better than that. I can't disclose evidence before it's gone through the proper channels. It would be unethical.'

'General, just answer me one question. Was the cause of death deliberate or accidental?'

The general's eyes narrowed. 'What are you getting at? It was accidental, of course.'

'You're certain of that?'

'Why shouldn't I be?'

'Then can you explain why *Fouillis* limpet mines were being used on a routine training exercise?'

The general glanced unhappily across the sea of faces. 'This is highly unorthodox,' he protested.

'*Compánero*, I have no wish to embarrass you, but I need the information urgently.'

The general sighed. 'The victim was a reservist practising buoyancy techniques during a refresher course. The team was using the *Fouillis* because of its reputation for unwieldiness.'

'Is that customary?' Segunda asked.

'No, but it seemed a reasonable enough explanation. The committee did not question it.'

'Where did the limpet mines come from?'

'The military stores at Los Flores.'

'Do you know who authorised them?'

General Vasquez's cheeks flushed. He put down his glass. 'This has gone far enough,' he hissed in an exasperated voice. 'You have no right to question me in this manner. Until our findings have been published, they come under the heading of privileged information. Excuse me, señor.'

Segunda's eyes crinkled with amusement as Vasquez strode brusquely away. Irreverent by nature, he cared little for rank or authority. Many officers regarded him as insolent and insubordinate, but Segunda viewed their disapproval with an almost mocking disregard.

Making no attempt to mix with the chattering guests, he collected his coat and drove quickly across the darkened city. The army supply stores were, he knew, manned twenty-four hours a day, and though he was cursory by nature, Segunda was totally dedicated in matters relating to his job.

He showed his ID card to the sergeant on duty and was escorted immediately to the central administration hall. The night-clerk was a studious young corporal with heavy-rimmed spectacles. Segunda gave him the date of the Chalia army camp fatality and asked for details of the equipment being used. The clerk checked his record books.

'Eight *Fouillis* limpet mines were withdrawn on 30 December,' he declared. 'One was discovered to be defective, another was returned five days later, six are still being used on specialist training exercises.'

'Do you have the authorisation signature?' Segunda enquired.

'It's right here. Major Otello Bravo.'

'Which battalion?'

'Just a minute,' the night-clerk said. 'I'll feed it into the computer.'

Segunda watched his fingers rattle across the instrument keys. There was a moment's pause, then the screen flashed the word INVALID in sharp red letters.

The night-clerk frowned. 'That's odd,' he muttered.

He typed the details again. A second time, his input was rejected. 'I don't understand it,' the clerk said in embarrassment. 'The computer must be malfunctioning. There's no record of a Major Bravo at all.'

Segunda's eyes glittered with excitement. 'It's no malfunction, corporal,' he said. 'The answer's quite simple. The authorising signature was a forgery.'

The night-clerk blinked in astonishment as Segunda turned and strode briskly from the hall.

*

The MP stopped his jeep in the centre of the compound. He pointed across the barrack huts at a thickset man in a rubberised diving-suit who was demonstrating emergency hand-signals to a group of new recruits gathered at the edge of a swimming-pool.

'That's Sergeant Gomez,' the MP stated. 'Want me to give him a shout?'

Segunda shook his head. 'Don't bother. I'll talk to him myself.'

He climbed out of the jeep, nodding his thanks as the MP trundled back the way he had come. Segunda lit a cheroot, and breathed deeply in the morning sunlight. As he approached the swimming-pool, he heard the sergeant snap out a crisp command. The little group of divers plunged into the water in fountains of feathery spray.

'Sergeant Gomez?' Segunda asked.

The man glanced up, squinting against the glare of the sun. Segunda flashed his ID card, smiling inwardly as he watched the sergeant's features tense. Old habits died hard, and during *la guerra sucia*, he knew, a visit from the security forces meant torture, interrogation, death.

'I must speak with you,' Segunda said.

'*Qué va*, I have done nothing wrong,' the sergeant said sullenly.

'Hey, *amigo*, did I say you had?'

The sergeant stared at him in silence for a moment, then he shouted something at the soldiers in the pool, and clambering to his feet, began to stroll across the compound with Segunda at his side. He moved with a deceptive agility, despite his girth.

'What's this all about?' he mumbled.

'A few days ago, you conducted a special training course, reference number G3208.'

The sergeant nodded.

'Who ordered you to do that?'

'Nobody. We get our instructions from the daily roster. I didn't see the authorising certificate.'

'Is that usual?'

'Well, it's not *un*usual, let me put it that way.'

'What was your brief precisely?'

The sergeant ran his fingers through his long lank hair. 'They told me it was a refresher course. Diving, underwater navigation, that sort of thing.'

'Did it include the use of the *Fouillis* limpet mine?'

'That too.'

'For what purpose?'

'It wasn't explained. The men were being prepared for some kind of military operation, but the details were kept strictly classified. In fact, even the lessons had to be conducted in a different language. English.'

Segunda looked at him in surprise. 'English?' he echoed.

The sergeant nodded. 'Security, they said.'

'Who were these men? Any idea where they came from?'

The sergeant shook his head. 'The order arrived with an F–1 classification. That's the highest category in the handbook. In a situation like that, we use numbers, not names.'

'How many?'

'Five, to begin with. One died in the river accident, another quit – that left three.'

'What happened to the equipment after the course was over?'

'It was carted away in an unmarked truck.'

'Destination?'

Gomez shrugged. 'God knows. I recognised the *hombre* behind the wheel, though. We used to serve in the same regiment together. His name was Carhue.'

'Where's Carhue now?'

'Well, that's the odd thing. Carhue left the MT division years ago. I happen to know he's Colonel Jaurez's personal driver.'

Segunda was silent for a moment. Colonel Jaurez had a disturbing habit of popping up in the most unlikely places, he thought. And what in God's name was a colonel's chauffeur doing in an unmarked truck? Diving-suits and limpet mines hardly seemed the sort of equipment an officer and a gentleman should be playing with.

Segunda took the sergeant to the guardroom and spent an hour going over the details of the accident. He got the sergeant to scribble out a full report, and include, for good measure, detailed descriptions of his three charges. Then he thanked the man graciously, and drove back to Buenos Aires, pondering over the curious irregularities of his findings. Too many questions pointed to the one man he couldn't approach, the mysterious Colonel Jaurez.

When he reached his office several hours later, Segunda called for the colonel's personal file and sat studying the man's history, background and psychiatric reports. By all accounts, Jaurez had been an exemplary soldier, a graduate of the Bariloche Military Academy, and a veteran of the Malvinas Campaign. He had also been, Segunda was quick to notice, a staunch supporter of Galtieri's junta. There were several warm commendations signed by Galtieri himself, and it was clear Jaurez had been considered a loyal and dependable officer.

When he had finished the file, Segunda sat for a time, drumming his fingers on the desktop. One thing was apparent from the evidence in front of him. Jaurez was hardly a man who changed with the seasons. How would such an individual react, he wondered, to the overthrow of a regime in which he had placed not merely his faith, but his entire future?

On an impulse, Segunda called the central transportation department and asked if any recent dispatches had been arranged in the colonel's name.

'Oh yes, señor,' the clerk told him. 'Two days ago we

flew a consignment of military equipment to Bilbao in Spain.'

'What was the consignment exactly?'

'Oxygen re-breathing sets, diving-suits, M3–A1 sub-machine-guns and *Fouillis* limpet mines.'

Segunda took a deep breath. 'Wasn't that rather unusual? Guns, limpet mines? Did nobody question the legitimacy of this equipment?'

'No, señor, the end-use certificates were all in order.'

'And what did the certificates signify?'

'The equipment was for use in joint training exercises with the Spanish army.'

Segunda frowned as he hung up the telephone and sat staring at the office wall. He'd expected the missing mines to be destined for terrorist attacks on the Argentine mainland. Suddenly, the matter had entered a completely new phase.

Segunda picked up the phone and began to call General Guayabero's number. Then half-way through, he stopped. What could he tell the man? He had nothing concrete to go on beyond his own intuition, and that wasn't enough. He was deeply in the general's debt, Segunda knew. After the downfall of the military junta, Guayabero had saved him from a Buenos Aires prison. He was a patron to be cultivated, and it was well worth Segunda's while to help him indict the nebulous Colonel Jaurez. On the other hand, Jaurez was an important man with powerful and influential friends. He needed proof, facts, names.

Slamming his fingers on the receiver rest, Segunda re-dialled. There was a click on the end of the line, and a voice said: '*Si?*'

'Get me a seat on the next flight to Bilbao,' Segunda ordered crisply.

CHAPTER SIX

The wind was dry coming off the land. It carried a hint of peat and moorgrass, mingled with the unmistakable odour of cow-dung. Sitting in the motor launch cockpit, the two Argentines found the smells reassuring. They were not seafaring men, and the twelve-hour cruise through the heavy curtain of darkness had strained their concentration to the limit.

The sky was clear and full of stars. To the east, they could see the ragged line of the Cumbrian coast, its lights twinkling along the rocky foreshore, offering an illusion of sanctuary and warmth. The air was chill, and as the launch chugged steadily northwards, the Argentines' breath steamed from their lips and nostrils.

They were young men, late twenties or early thirties, with glassy expressions generated by tension and fear. They spoke little as they traced the line of the distant land, for the long hours of anxiety had caused their throats to dry and their voices to tighten.

Just north of Maryport, the first Argentine noticed a vessel approaching rapidly from starboard. He struggled to see through the enveloping darkness, eyeing the cluster of signal lights bobbing and dipping in the heavy swell.

'Look,' he hissed.

His companion tilted his head. 'Fishermen,' he suggested.

'It's coming too fast.'

Frowning, the second Argentine squinted into the gloom. The vessel was taking shape now, its grey hull rearing out of the night, and the two men felt a surge of dismay as they realised their worst fears had materialised. A searchbeam lanced across the open water, vividly illuminating their craft, and a voice, hollow and tannoyed, boomed above the wave-crests in solemn commanding tones: 'This is the Royal Naval Fisheries Protection vessel *Sagamore Prince*. There is no cause for alarm. Please switch off your engines and prepare for inspection party.'

The two Argentines stared at each other. They knew it was nothing more than a routine enquiry, but the cargo in their hold made it impossible for them to comply.

'What are we going to do?' the second man demanded.

'We'll have to run.'

'You're crazy. They'll blow us out of the water. We'll have to try and talk our way out of it.'

'Talk, hell. We can't let them search the boat. I say we run.'

'Oh Christ. Sweet God in heaven.'

The first Argentine pushed in the starboard clutch and swung the launch in a tight right-hand curve, the roar of its engines reverberating above the rolling swell.

The loudspeaker echoed again. 'This is the Royal Naval Fisheries Protection vessel *Sagamore Prince*. Repeat: this is the Royal Naval Fisheries Protection vessel *Sagamore Prince*. Switch off your engines and prepare for boarding party. Do not attempt to escape. This is an order.'

The engines thundered and the motor launch's bow rose in the darkness. The two Argentines felt the power of the screws biting at the water beneath. Pushing in the port clutch, the first man opened up the throttle and the launch leapt forward, surging across the waves like a seabird pre-paring for take-off. Spray lashed the salt-flecked windshield, and the slipstream scoured their throats and cheeks.

'You're going too fast,' the second Argentine wailed, watch-ing the speedometer rapidly climbing. 'You'll blow her out of the water.'

'Shut up,' his companion snapped, hanging on to the wheel.

They could feel the launch bucking now, pounding relentlessly against the waves. The night erupted with the piercing shriek of the minesweeper's siren, and glancing back, the Argentines spotted the vessel hurtling terrifyingly in their wake.

'They'll outrun us easily,' the second Argentine sobbed.

'Not if we reach the shoreline. We can hide among the rocks. A vessel that size will never take the shallow water.'

Chunk-chunk. Shots from the minesweeper's 20mm cannon made a chilling sound on the cold wintry air. Ahead, they saw water mushrooming just in front of their bows.

'They're shooting at us,' the second Argentine cried.

'Over our heads. They're trying to scare us, that's all.'

The launch was almost out of control now. Muscles slack with fright, the first Argentine battled to steady the wheel. They could feel the vessel lifting bodily into the air like some wild directionless trajectory. Through the droplets beading the windshield, the two Argentines spotted huge columns of fractured rock rising out of the boiling ocean, towering in their path like the ramparts of some incredible fortress.

'Holy Mother of God,' the second Argentine screamed. 'We're going to crash.'

His companion switched off the throttle and hurled himself on the wheel, swinging it desperately to port. The launch spun dizzily, its deck tilting beneath their feet. Water lashed their faces, and a series of shudders ran through the vessel's tortured frame as it hurtled sideways through the tossing waves. The rocks loomed up, jagged and menacing, hovering above them like crouching giants.

Crrrraaaacck. The force of the impact was almost unbelievable. The two Argentines were hurled bodily to the deck, rolling over in a tangled flurry of arms and legs.

Stunned, they lay motionless for several moments while the stricken vessel bobbed impotently on a maelstrom of foam. In the starlight, they dimly discerned the shadowy outline of a Gemini boarding craft picking its way towards them. Bruised and defeated, they dragged themselves to the gunwale and raised their arms in a gesture of surrender.

The sea shimmered brightly as Luke strolled along the craggy promontory. Ahead, high mountains rose into a faultless sky, their snowcapped peaks catching the refracted light. He did not like mountains, he decided; unlike Alex, who had spent his entire boyhood scrambling about the Andes foothills, mountains unsettled Luke, always had.

Luke's optimism had almost begun to desert him during the past few days. Everything seemed to be going wrong. The limpet mines had failed to arrive on schedule, and to cap it all, Collis and Alex were snapping at each other like a pair of sulky schoolboys. It was the girl who'd started it all, of course. Luke had watched Collis hanging about her like a stallion at stud, when any damn fool could see it was Alex she really wanted. She eyed Alex secretly when she thought he wasn't looking, watching his movements from under her dark flowing hair. But Alex had only one thing on his mind. The submarine. HMS *Conqueror*. Nothing else existed.

Every morning, they took to the hills like genuine climbers, going through their ridiculous charade with the singular absorption of actors on a stage, but as their tensions grew and their differences strengthened, Luke realised he couldn't keep Alex and Collis apart much longer. Sooner or later, they were going to explode.

As he turned away from the promontory, the wind stirring his hair, he glimpsed a farmhouse nestling among the folds of the pasture, and two men standing in a fenced enclosure at the building's rear. Remembering his orders to avoid the local populace, Luke started to detour. Then suddenly, he paused, the breath catching in his throat. Pacing around the enclosure was the most magnificent mare he had ever seen. She stood, he estimated, around sixteen hands, her eyes bold, her muscles rippling beneath her silky chestnut skin.

Impetuously, Luke changed direction, cutting down through the trees. The two men watched as he strolled towards them. They were both youngish, Luke saw. One was in his early twenties, the other about thirty-two or thirty-three, with craggy features and reddish blond hair.

Luke grinned. 'Good morning,' he said politely.

The men nodded in silence.

'I hope I'm not trespassing.'

'Tha's all right, Jimmy,' the older man declared. 'We dinna stand on ceremony in these parts. Ye'll be one of the Englishmen staying at the Barracula, no doubt.'

Luke nodded.

'Mountaineer, are ye?' the younger man enquired.

'That's right.'

'Och, ye've more nerve than sense,' the older man stated flatly. 'Ye wid'na catch me on yon fells for love nor money, and that's a fact.'

Luke hooked his elbows over the enclosure fence, staring at the mare still pacing restlessly.

'I was just admiring your horse,' he said.

The older man spat on the ground. 'Like her, do ye, Jimmy?'

'She's beautiful.'

'Aye, I thought that myself when I first clapped eyes on her. But she's a devil, that's what she is. I bought her from some Irish tinkers at Selkirk horse fair. They said her father was an Arab stallion who'd won races from Dublin to Kentucky. What they didn't tell me was that nobody'd managed to strap a saddle on her back, let alone ride her.'

'She's unbroken then?'

'Unbroken is right. Wild as a tiger. She's costing us a

fortune in winter hay. Nobody'll buy her, that's the trouble. A small community like this, the word gets around.'

Luke was silent for a moment, his eyes fixed on the animal in front. Rarely had he seen a creature so full of fire and vitality, even on the Argentine *pampa*.

'Mind if I take a closer look?' he asked.

'Daft, are ye? Yon mare'll tear yer bloody head off an' eat it for breakfast.'

Luke grinned. 'Let's see, shall we?'

Deftly, he slipped over the wooden rail, and moving step by step, began to ease towards the horse pacing the other side of the compound. Sensing his approach, the animal stopped, and throwing back its head, delivered a warning whinny, pawing menacingly at the ground.

Luke paused. For a long moment, he stood perfectly still, fixing the chestnut with an almost hypnotic stare. Then he began to move again. The two Scotsmen watched in wonder as, inch by inch, he edged towards the wary animal, crooning softly under his breath. The mare danced on her feet, turning as if to flee then, backing her haunches against the fence rail, she braced her legs defensively.

Luke stopped. He was now barely a yard in front of her nose. One lunge, he knew, and she could pound him into the dirt with her hooves. Bending forward, he tilted his face towards her, and with a short, deliberate, nudging motion, blew gently into each of her nostrils. The Scotsmen blinked in puzzlement, baffled by this strange behaviour. Luke went on blowing and crooning, then with infinite slowness, reached up and lightly stroked the chestnut's neck. A shiver ran through the mare's entire body, but she made no move to break away.

Stepping forward, Luke tenderly fondled her ears, a feeling of triumph flooding him as the two Scotsmen uttered exclamations of astonishment and disbelief.

'Why, man,' the older one declared, 'nobody's managed to do that since we brought her here.'

Luke spotted a bridle draped across the fence post. 'Mind if I ride her?' he asked.

The man blinked. 'Without a saddle?'

'I don't need a saddle. Just toss me that halter.'

Eyes glittering with excitement, the man turned to his younger companion. 'Open the gate,' he ordered hoarsely.

He hurled the bridle to Luke who slipped it deftly over the horse's skull, and holding on to the rein, inched his way along its quivering flank, still crooning in his soft hypnotic monotone. In one fluid motion, he vaulted neatly on to the animal's back. For a full second, the chestnut stood totally still, baffled by the strange and unfamiliar presence, then as Luke jabbed his heels lightly into her belly, she sprang across the compound in a mighty leap and tore through the open gateway. Luke heard the Scotsmen whooping as he steered her expertly along the adjoining foreshore. He rode western-style, the reins clasped in one hand, his weight balanced in the centre of the chestnut's spine. A surge of exultation swept through him as he felt the exhilarating power of the muscular body between his thighs. The world unfolded dizzily around him; he saw the cliffs blurring, the ocean breakers crashing white against the sand, then he was pounding through the shallows, spray from the horse's hooves showering his cheeks and throat. In his mind, the mountains had gone and he was back on the *pampa* in the first cool of the early morning. Nothing existed except himself and the horse. A wild ecstasy coursed through his veins and his lips drew back in a grimace of demented joy.

By the time he returned to the farmhouse, the mare's hide was steaming freely. The two Scotsmen watched in wonder as he slipped from her back and tugged free the bridle.

'I never saw anything like that in my life,' the older man exclaimed, slamming the gate. 'Nobody's been able to touch that mare since we brought her back from Selkirk. Where did ye say ye come frae, Jimmy?'

Luke hesitated. 'Winchester,' he grunted.

The Scotsman held out his hand. 'I'm Joe Robben. This is my brother Barry. After a gallop like that, ye could do wi' a wee bit refreshment. Coffee maybe, or something a little stronger?'

Luke was about to decline when he noticed a girl standing just inside the farmhouse doorway, her reddish brown hair contrasting sharply with her creamy skin. Her lips were full, her nostrils flared, and there was a roguish glint in her soft green eyes.

Luke felt a thickening sensation in his throat and he wiped his lips with the back of one hand. 'The mare could do with sponging and picking,' he muttered. 'There'd likely be shells along that beach.'

'Barry'll see to it,' Joe Robben told him. 'Come on up tae the house.'

The farm kitchen was muggy and pleasant, its flagged floor heated by a huge metal stove. There were heavy hooks on the walls which Joe explained had been used in centuries past to hang poultry and carcasses of meat.

'Our pa usually runs things,' he said with a grin, 'but he's away in Inverness on business. That's our sister Deborah over there.'

The girl was staring at Luke with an almost impudent curiosity. There was a hint of suppressed merriment in her eyes which caused his cheeks to flush hotly. She was no great beauty, he realised; her face was too plain, her nose too broad, but there was something inescapably alluring in the tilt of her head, the thrust of her pert young breasts. She carried herself like a queen, and Luke felt his instincts responding warmly.

'Sit yourself doon at the table,' Joe said. 'I'll put the kettle on.'

For the first time, Luke noticed the curious stiffness in

Joe's left thigh and with a small sense of shock realised Joe was wearing an artificial limb.

'What happened there?' he asked. 'Accident?'

Joe grinned. 'Shrapnel blast. I lost it in the Falklands War. I was on the *Sheffield* when the Exocet hit her.'

Luke stared at Joe strangely. In Argentina, he had met many men mutilated in the South Atlantic, but this was the first time he had encountered a casualty from the opposite side.

'I did'na even realise the bloody thing had gone,' Joe laughed. 'Ye could'na see for bloody smoke. I could'na understand why I kept falling down. Then three of ma pals dragged me up on deck. Those bloody Argies, they didn't even gie us a warning.'

'Like the *Belgrano*,' Luke whispered softly.

Joe glanced at him in surprise. 'Aye ... well, that was different, wasn't it? I mean, it was the Argies that started it all.'

'Maybe they don't see it that way.'

'Hey, man, whose side are ye on anyhow?'

Luke hesitated. 'Ours, of course,' he muttered. 'I just like to get it in perspective, that's all.' He glanced at the girl shyly.

'I watched ye wi' the mare,' she smiled. 'Where did ye learn to ride like that?'

'Nowhere special,' he told her, his cheeks crimsoning.

'How long're ye staying at the Barracula?'

'Just a few days. Then it's home to Winchester.'

'And what d'ye do in Winchester?' she demanded.

'Breed horses.'

'Och, that explains it. I wondered how ye could ride so well. Joe and Barry are braw horsemen right enough, but they canna hold a candle to you.'

It was the first time in his life Luke had met a girl he felt he could talk to. She wasn't like the ones on the *pampa*. There was no pretentiousness about her, no posturing or affectation. Even when she laughed at him, it was laughter without ridicule. He felt himself beginning to relax.

'Ever ridden in competition?' Joe asked, as they sat sipping coffee.

'Couple of times. Nothing professional.'

'It's just that Wednesday's Burns Night, ye ken.' He grinned. 'Och, that would'na mean much to an Englishman, but for us, it's one of the big days o' the year. The older men hold traditional suppers, haggis, neeps an' the like, and the younger ones celebrate wi' a dance at the village hall. But it's no' just the dance. Every Burns Day, we hold a horse race between ourselves an' the folk frae Dunaven. There's a lot of money riding on the winning village. For the past eight years Dunaven's won hands down, and tae tell the truth, I was hoping to change our luck when I bought the mare. Trouble was, nobody's been able to ride her, until now.'

Luke shifted uneasily in his chair. 'I couldn't,' he stated firmly. 'I'm not even a local.'

'Ye're living at the Barracula Hotel, aren't ye?'

'Only as a guest.'

'Makes no difference.'

'It's out of the question,' Luke said.

'Och man, it's no' yer right arm I'm asking for. It's just a race, that's all. It mebbe means nothing to you, but it's an awful lot to us.'

Reaching across the table, Deborah seized Luke's hand. He felt a tremor run along his forearm, and his cheeks flooded with colour.

'Ye'd be doing us a big favour,' she whispered. 'Truly.'

Luke seemed tongue-tied. Something about the girl threw him into total confusion. It wasn't simply a question of physical attraction, he reasoned. That, he could have understood. But this was more, a kind of instinctive and immediate compatability.

'Let me think about it,' he whispered.

She smiled, squeezing his wrist gently.

For almost two hours, Luke sat chatting to Deborah Robben. Never in his life had he talked so freely to a girl before. It was as if a dam had opened, allowing him to express feelings and sentiments he'd thought beyond definement. She listened attentively, sometimes putting in a word or two, sometimes expanding on a theory of her own, and always her eyes carried that disconcerting brightness, that glow of merriment he found so charming and beguiling.

It was early evening when he finally took his leave. Deborah walked him to the door. Outside, it was already dark and they could see stars shining through the distant trees. The wind carried a hint of the sea.

'Thanks for the coffee,' he muttered.

Her red hair shone like soft silk. 'We'll see ye at the dance after the race then?'

'It's possible.'

'Och, nobody could accuse ye of being over-eager,' she remonstrated.

'I didn't mean it that way,' he said hastily. 'It's just...' He hesitated.

She smiled, her teeth gleaming in the darkness. 'Well, here's something to help ye make up your mind.'

Stepping forward, she kissed him hard on the mouth. For a moment, he was taken completely by surprise, then the softness of her body sent his pulses racing, and with a low moan, he wrapped his arms around her, pulling her close.

'Deborah,' he whispered hoarsely.

But in one deft movement, she slipped from his fingers. 'It's up to you, Luke Culpepper,' she said. 'Are ye coming to the Burns Night dance, or is it only horses ye're interested in?'

She laughed gaily, her voice tinkling on the chill night air. Then the door closed and she was gone.

*

Luke slept badly that night. The memory of the girl hung doggedly in his mind. Her green eyes, her reddish hair, her roguish smile excited his senses, galvanised his emotions. He could still feel the soft insistent pressure of her lips as she'd kissed him. His brain imbued her with an almost indefectible level of perfection. There were no half-measures with Deborah Robben, he thought, nothing quiet or withdrawn, delicate or conservative. He liked her boldness, her direct approach to things. He was no prize, he knew that. No girl had ever considered him attractive before, and he found the experience unsettling.

Luke would not have been human if Deborah's advances had not wrought in him a new conflict of loyalties. He had come on a mission of destruction – was, even at that moment, awaiting the implements by which the mission could be carried out. But he was, by nature, an ebullient young man, incurably optimistic, full of enthusiasm for the allurement of the moment. In Luke's mind, the submarine was forgotten. Only one thing existed: his memory of the girl.

Next morning, when he strolled downstairs for breakfast, he found Alex and Collis sitting at the kitchen table. Their faces looked grim and cheerless, their eyes filled with an anger it was difficult to ignore. Luke's memories of the girl were momentarily forgotten as, frowning, he reached for the coffee pot.

'Where are Mike and Julie?' he asked.

'Gone shopping.'

A feeling of uneasiness rose inside Luke. 'Something wrong?'

Alex pushed across the morning paper. 'This just arrived,' he said.

Picking up the paper, Luke held it to the light, his eyes scanning the lines of newsprint. He read slowly, phrasing the syllables with his lips:

A major diplomatic row has broken out between Britain and Argentina following the disclosure that a boat carrying arms and military equipment, picked up in the Irish Sea early this morning, was manned by two officers of the Argentine army. The boat was arrested by the Royal Naval minesweeper *Sagamore Prince* after a high-speed chase in which several shots were fired and the Argentine vessel badly damaged. A Defence Ministry spokesman refused to comment on speculations that the arms were intended for the Provisional IRA, but a strongly-worded protest has been sent to the Argentine government. The launch is now under heavy guard at Brownfield Naval Base in Cumbria, and the two Argentines detained have been transferred to London where a representative from the Spanish Embassy is expected to call on them later today.

Luke whistled under his breath as he dropped the paper back on the tabletop. 'Think it was ours?'

'Of course it was ours. Who else's could it have been?'

'It's over then? The submarine?'

Alex shifted uncomfortably on his chair, his eyes filled with the weariness of defeat. 'We'll think of something,' he promised bravely.

Luke shrugged as he sipped at his coffee. 'Thinking doesn't come into it,' he said. 'Without mines and diving equipment we're finished. It's over, that's all.'

The village store was crowded as Julie and Mike sorted through their provisions list. Mike carried the basket to the pay counter where Mrs Murgatroyd, the store proprietor, was chatting to Constable Whitgreave, the local policeman. Julie liked Mrs Murgatroyd, but she could be exasperating at times the way she kept nosing into everyone's business.

Little took place in the village without Mrs Murgatroyd knowing about it, and that was as good as a full-scale broadcast on the BBC. For as long as Julie had known her, Mrs Murgatroyd had been an incorrigible gossip, unable to keep anything to herself for longer than a few minutes at a time.

'Aye,' she said, as she went through Julie's purchases, ringing them up on the cash register, 'I had a feeling ye'd be in. I heard ye'd some customers staying with ye. Unusual, is it no', to be opening in the middle of winter?'

'We wouldn't normally,' Julie admitted, 'but they're friends of Mike's.'

'Is tha' a fact? An' where would he be knowing them, I wonder? Glasgow mebbe?'

'Aye,' Mike said gruffly. 'Glasgow.'

'One of them's quite a rider, I hear,' Constable Whitgreave put in. 'A bonny lad wi' the horses.'

Mike blinked. 'What?'

'Why, man, have ye no' heard? He's representing the village in the Burns Race on Wednesday.'

'Where did ye get that?'

'It's all over town.'

Julie glimpsed the panic in Mike's eyes.

'Funny, they hav'na said a word tae me,' he muttered evasively.

'Some friends,' the policeman grunted. 'I'd have thought ye'd be the first they'd tell.'

Julie paid the bill and they made their way across the cobbled market-place, Mike clutching the grocery bag to his chest. As he loaded the purchases into the van, she said, 'Mike, what in God's name is going on?'

He looked at her blankly. 'Going on?' he echoed.

'Those three men – Alex, Luke and Collis – who are they?'

'I've already telt ye. Mates from the old days.'

123

'Strange, you never mentioned them before.'

'I dinna tell ye everyone I know, do I?'

'Mike, there's something odd about those men, I can feel it.'

'Odd, in what way?'

'It's nothing I can put my finger on, but every once in a while they say something silly. Or miss the point of something that shouldn't need to be explained. Mike, it's as if they've been shut away in a time capsule for the past twenty years. They look like us, they talk like us, but they belong to a different universe.'

Mike's eyes looked dark and troubled. Reaching out, he gently squeezed her arm. 'Julie,' he said in a soft voice, 'I knew it was a mistake bringing you out of the city. You've been spending too much time on your own.'

'Don't humour me, Mike, I'm not having a nervous breakdown. Those three men are not what they seem, and I'd like to know why.'

He sighed, running his fingers through his thick curly hair. 'All right, I didn't want to tell ye this, but ye've given me no choice. The tall one, Collis, is on the run from his wife. She's after him for alimony payments. Alex and Luke figure if he can keep his head down for a while, she'll lose track of the poor bastard.'

'You expect me to believe that?'

'Either ye trust me, Julie, or ye don't.'

She stared at him shrewdly, feeling a slackness inside her, a sense of uncertainty and unrest. 'Get in the van,' she said darkly.

Julie was silent as they drove back to the hotel. It was the first time in her life, she thought, her brother had knowingly and deliberately lied to her.

Alex, Luke, Collis and Mike strolled drearily through the drizzling rain, following the line of sea-cliffs meandering north to Brachaigg Bay. A swirl of gulls rose yelping above their heads, sweeping westward across the churning ocean. In a nearby meadow, cows huddled against the dry-stone wall, their steaming hides drenched and sombre.

Luke shivered as he thrust his hands deep into his trouser pockets.

'It's a crazy idea,' he mumbled.

'I know it's crazy,' Alex agreed, 'but it's the only one I can think of. We're running out of time. The *Conqueror*'ll be gone in a day or two, and we can't hit that sub without proper equipment.'

'Why don't we just call it off?'

'It's too late to call it off,' Alex insisted stubbornly. 'At least we know where the motor launch is being held.'

Luke blew moisture droplets from the tip of his nose. He was surprised at the intensity of Alex's reaction. Collis, he'd expect to be disgruntled, but not Alex.

The news of the motor launch's capture had cheered Luke immensely. He had lost his stomach for the venture, if the truth were known. There were too many problems, too many uncertainties. Alex and Collis fighting. The instability of their Scottish allies. Most of all, there was the girl, Deborah Robben. He'd thought he could go back to her, stop the stupid charade he was playing, face her like an equal instead of an enemy. But Alex clearly had other ideas.

Somewhere they heard a cock crowing, the sound shrill and discordant on the morning air. 'It'll never work,' Mike declared, his hair dripping with moisture.

'It will if we plan it right. It's the last thing in the world the bastards will expect.'

'For Christ's sake, we canna walk into a fully-armed naval base and lift the launch from under their bloody noses.'

'We don't need the launch. Only its cargo.'

'But what're we supposed to frighten them with?' Mike protested. 'Pop-guns?'

'Either we get that equipment back,' Alex said fiercely, 'or everything we've gone through has been for nothing.' He glanced at Collis. 'What about you?'

Collis shook his head. 'It's crazy, *compadre*. A raid like that would take weeks to prepare. We know nothing about the naval base lay-out or how its defences operate. We'd need proper resources, weapons, back-up.'

'We'll improvise,' Alex said.

'The idea's insane.'

'That's the biggest thing in our favour. We'll have surprise on our side.'

Collis chuckled. 'You really think we could pull it off?'

'I think we should at least drive down and take a look at the place. It's stupid jettisoning this operation until we're absolutely sure it's a no-go.'

'We'll end up being killed,' Mike cried.

'I didn't say it wouldn't be risky, but if we want to finish the job, we must get that equipment back. Let's vote on it. Those in favour, raise their right hands.'

Silently, Alex and Collis thrust up their arms. Mike hesitated, then joined them sullenly, his ruddy cheeks glistening in the driving rain. Luke felt a sense of dismay. He'd thought it finished – no mines, no submarine. He'd thought his hopes of amatory bliss were about to reach fulfilment. Now, in one heartstopping second, Alex had shattered everything. Infiltrating a top-security naval base seemed foolhardy to the point of madness, but Luke was a genial young man, easy-mannered and companionable, his decisions forged by the needs of the moment and the influences of his friends.

He saw Alex, Mike and Collis watching him, their eyes questioning and expectant, and with a wry grin, Luke slowly lifted his hand. 'There must be something in this Scottish air,' he said sourly. 'It's got me even crazier than you are.'

*

Charles Palmer, head of Section 4, DI6 (formerly MI6), the Foreign Office branch which dealt with international espionage, had barely finished breakfast when he heard the front door ring. He glanced at his watch, frowning. It was seven-thirty in the morning, a strange time to be receiving visitors.

He rose to his feet, wrapping his dressing gown around him, and striding into the hallway, switched on the TV security set fitted into the wall above the ornate umbrella stand. The screen flickered, blending into focus. A tall tweed-jacketed young man in his early thirties stood on the outer landing. Palmer recognised him as Major Anthony Kerrwood of the Directorate General of Intelligence, an amalgamation of the intelligence units of the three armed forces which operated from the main Ministry of Defence building in Whitehall. Palmer let himself relax. A lifelong bachelor, he knew he was often dangerously lax about his personal security, a fact which afforded his subordinates many anxious moments.

He switched off the TV set and opened the door. 'Kerrwood,' he said. 'What on earth are you doing up at this time of the morning?'

Kerrwood smiled wearily. His chin looked stubbled and there were heavy shadows under his eyes. 'I've been up all night,' he grunted. 'I'm sorry to trouble you at home, Charles, but something rather important has come up, and my section chief thought you might be interested.'

'Come on in. Care for some coffee?'

'No, thanks, I'm on my way home.'

Palmer led him into the sitting-room and gently closed the door. He looked at Kerrwood queryingly. 'Well?' he murmured.

Kerrwood ran his fingers down the front of his coat, straightening the lapels. He looked ill-at-ease and strangely defensive. 'The Argentine motor launch picked up in the

Irish Sea, I understand it's being handled by your department?'

'It was the Home Secretary's idea, not mine, Kerrwood. Take it up with him, if you feel we're poaching on your territory.'

'It's not that,' Kerrwood said quickly. 'We were just wondering if anything had transpired yet?'

'There's a bloody big row blowing up among the diplomatic boys. The Argentines are getting on their high horse again. They claim we've conjured up the entire thing to embarrass them at the United Nations.'

'Are they telling the truth?'

Palmer shrugged. 'Well, the two officers are sticking to their story. They say the weapons were for use in a joint training exercise with the Spanish army, and our sources in Madrid have certainly confirmed that. The equipment they were carrying included diving-suits and an underwater direction-finding device, hardly the sort of stuff the IRA would be interested in. On the other hand, there's still the question of what they were doing so wildly off-course. They claimed to be lost, and there could be an element of truth in that also. Neither man was an experienced sailor, and the charts they were carrying covered the whole of Western Europe, making it difficult to prove they were heading for any particular area.'

Kerrwood paused for a moment. Then he said softly, 'It may be nothing more than coincidence, Charles, but I think you ought to know the Gaucho has been spotted in northern Spain.'

No expression crossed Palmer's face, but his facial muscles seemed to contract as if they had gone into involuntary spasm. He took a deep breath.

'You're sure? There have been sightings before.'

'This time it's certain. It's Segunda all right. One of our men clocked him at Bilbao airport.'

Palmer's thin mouth tightened. He strolled to the window and stared down into the street below. The faint murmur of traffic reached them through the wintry sunlight.

'Segunda,' Palmer breathed. 'So he's back in Europe.'

'Of course, it may have nothing to do with the motor launch. Could be something completely un-operational.'

'Don't be absurd. The Argentines wouldn't risk the Gaucho on a milk run.'

'You can't know that, Charles.'

'I know Segunda.'

He was silent for a moment as the clanging of a fire engine rose on the chill morning air.

'I want him, Kerrwood,' Palmer breathed.

Kerrwood sighed. 'Segunda works for the Argentine security forces. The Spanish authorities would never agree to extradition. Besides, technically speaking, he's committed no crime on British soil. We have no power to detain him – officially, that is. You must leave personal feelings out of this.'

'Are you telling me I should let him go?'

'Not telling, Charles. Asking. If Segunda's involved with those captured arms, sooner or later he'll make a move. It's only a question of waiting, Charles. Elliott felt you should be informed.'

'Thank Elliott for me,' Palmer said.

Kerrwood hesitated. 'He also ordered me to contact Mosstrooper.'

'Mosstrooper?' Palmer echoed.

'No one knows as much about the Gaucho as Mosstrooper,' Kerrwood murmured.

'You're quite correct.'

'No one has more of a right to be kept in touch.'

'I agree.'

'Will you do it, Charles, or shall I?'

'Mosstrooper is my department,' Palmer said.

'I can leave it to you, then?'

'Yes,' Palmer promised stiffly. 'Yes, I shall call her right away.'

Kerrwood noticed his hand was trembling as he reached for the telephone.

CHAPTER SEVEN

Mike stopped the van on the opposite side of the square, facing the naval base entrance. Crouched in the rear, the three Argentines peered dubiously through the windshield at the stronghold they would have to penetrate. High walls topped with barbed wire framed both sides of the heavy metal gates. Cars cruised in and out, pausing while uniformed sentries checked the occupants' identities. Frost coating the fence wires had melted with the afternoon sun, and now the metal strands glinted sharply, catching the refracted light, emphasising the infrangibility of the sanctum they were guarding.

Mike drummed his fingers against the driving wheel. 'Och, it's nuts,' he declared. 'The place is sealed up tighter than Fort Knox. Even if we get in, we'll never make it out again.'

'All it takes is a little nerve,' Alex said softly.

He felt stiff from the long day's drive down the Scottish coastline. His muscles were aching and his head throbbed with tension and anxiety. He still couldn't fathom why on earth he was doing this. He had his chance to pull out now, proudly and with dignity, head held high and no blame attached. Any doubts he'd had about their dubious enterprise could be resolved by one simple wholly understandable act. Withdrawal. But something had happened to Alex since the limpet mines' confiscation, something he couldn't put a name to, a hardening of resolve, a sense of direction; it was as if, in some strange and indeterminate way, adversity had wrought in him a new stubbornness. Luke would be willing to quit, he sensed. Luke hadn't cared for the idea from the beginning. Like everything else in his life, it had been a challenge, an adventure, a giggle, a welcome respite from the monotony of life on his father's *estancia* — until they had come to Britain. In Britain, Luke seemed different. Something in the surroundings, something in the nature of the people had weakened his resolve. No, Luke would be happy to call it a day. Not Collis though. It would take a battering ram to stop Collis. And with himself, there was still that awful obstinacy.

'Ye said we'd look at it,' Mike growled sullenly. 'That's all, just look at it. Well, we've looked. Now let's bugger off back home.'

'There must be a way in,' Alex whispered.

'Aye, there's a way. We could hire a tank and bulldoze the wall down. Of course, they'll probably blow our heads off before we reach the dockside, but at least we'll have the satisfaction of knowing we made it through the front gate.'

'Scared, Mike?' Alex asked him gently.

Mike turned and glared at him. 'Aye, ye could say I'm a wee bit scared,' he snapped. 'Those sentries are armed, we don't know the camp's lay-out or the surrounding area, there's upwards of a thousand men in that base and we hav'nae a single weapon among the four of us.'

'We'll improvise,' Alex told him.

'With what, for Christ's sake? Use your head, man. It was a grand idea in the beginning, but the party's over. That's a top security stronghold over there. It's madness to think we can break in without any kind of plan at all.'

Alex glanced at the others. 'What's the time?'

Collis peered at his watch. 'Five-thirty.'

'Are the pubs open?'

'Just.'

Alex nodded. 'We'll park the van and hit the bars. If it's drinking time, there'll be sailors off duty and that's where we'll find them. We'll talk, we'll listen, we'll circulate.

There's got to be a way into that pickle jar. The only problem is finding it.'

The Spanish general was a courteous man who looked, Segunda thought, more like an elegant maître d' than a high-ranking military officer. At the camp gate, he showed his pass to the sentries on duty, and after parking the car in front of the guardroom, led Segunda through the rows of barrack huts flanking the central office building. Flags fluttered above the nearby parade ground, and troops in camouflaged combat jackets saluted smartly as the general strolled by.

'The equipment you speak of,' the general explained, 'was claimed by the Argentine contingent immediately upon its arrival. According to my information, it was loaded on to a launch chartered by the two Argentine officers for recreational purposes. They left on a fishing trip, telling us to expect them back the following evening.'

'A fishing trip, with *Fouillis* limpet mines?' Segunda murmured.

The general shrugged. 'They were our guests, Señor Segunda. We did not question what they chose to do with their own equipment. When the news came through that they'd been arrested in the Irish Sea, we were astounded.'

Segunda pursed his lips, thinking deeply. He could visualise the general's reaction. Disbelief. Embarrassment. A simple man who didn't like the machinations of politics and hated intrigue. He had probably been asked by the British to corroborate the prisoners' claims and disliked being drawn into it. Segunda almost felt sorry for him.

Segunda rubbed his forehead with his fingertip. He was still a little dazed from his long flight across the Atlantic, and the sudden transition from the Buenos Aires summer to the Bilbao winter left him shivering in his light seersucker business suit.

'Where were the Argentines billeted?' he enquired.

'In one of the vacant barrack huts. The camp is a little over-crowded at the moment, otherwise we would naturally have accommodated them in the officers' mess.'

Segunda smiled at him. 'I wonder, general, if you would be kind enough to show me their quarters?'

The general hesitated, glancing at him curiously. He was puzzled by Segunda's presence here, but being an inordinately polite man, and having checked his guest's authority with the Argentine consulate and the Spanish Ambassador in Buenos Aires, he had refrained from probing any more than was necessary.

He pursed his lips, then he nodded. 'I cannot see that it will do any harm.'

Leading the way to the barrack hut, he opened the door and waved Segunda inside. The interior was small and basic, with two army bunks arranged against opposite walls. There was a metal stove in the centre, a pair of primitive wardrobe lockers, a small table and a number of high-backed chairs.

Segunda tried each of the lockers in turn. They contained exactly what he expected to find, clothing, underwear, toilet accessories, personal letters. He sifted through the papers, his fingers moving deftly, expertly, while the general stood watching in silence, his face grave. He was, Segunda knew, unhappy at the intrusion, but inherently diplomatic, felt too constrained to say so.

Segunda sighed as he shut the locker doors. There was nothing in the officers' personal effects to offer the slightest indication of what he might be looking for. He thumbed quickly through a sheaf of papers spread across the wooden table. There were several Spanish magazines, a number of daily routine reports, and an empty blotting-pad. Segunda felt the hopelessness of defeat. Everything seemed normal. No clues, no evidence. Nothing out of place. Well, what did he expect? he wondered. The entire trip had been little more than an impulse, and he'd failed, that was the size of it. Had gone off half-cock. No results, no revelations.

Wearily, Segunda thanked the general and took a taxi back to town. He found a hotel and telephoned Guayabero in Buenos Aires. Guayabero's voice sounded strained when he came on the line.

'Where are you, for God's sake?' he demanded.

'Spain,' Segunda told him.

He heard Guayabero's sharp intake of breath and quickly explained the reasons for his visit. When he had finished, Guayabero said, 'Don't you realise all hell's breaking loose here?'

'I've seen the papers,' Segunda grunted, lighting a cheroot with one hand. 'Embarrassing, being picked up by the British navy, of all people.'

'"Embarrassing's" hardly the word. It's a diplomatic disaster. Pereyra's office is in an uproar. In fact, the entire Foreign Service is being turned upside down. The British think the government is running guns to the IRA.'

'Is that what you think, general?' Segunda enquired.

'Of course not. It's something far more complex. And Jaurez is in it up to his neck.' He paused. 'I want you to go to England,' he declared.

Segunda looked surprised. 'What good will that do?'

'You must interrogate those Argentine officers.'

Segunda almost laughed out loud. 'The British authorities would never let me near them.'

'Use your charm. A request from the Gaucho – they're bound to be intrigued.'

'Intrigued? They'll either toss me in gaol, or throw me out on my neck,' Segunda protested.

'I don't think so. Not if they believe you can help them get to the bottom of this. So far, the evidence against Jaurez is purely circumstantial. It's damning, I agree, but not nearly concise enough. If I have to show my hand, I want his downfall to be total. That's the second essential rule of survival. Always take care to finish the job.'

Segunda grinned, and reaching over, tapped his cheroot lightly into the bedroom ashtray. 'I'll fly to London this afternoon,' he agreed.

The man standing in the departure lounge was plainly-dressed and nondescript. He wore a light gaberdine raincoat and a pair of heavy-rimmed spectacles which did little to alleviate the deceptive blandness of his features. He watched Segunda move through the gate leading to passport control, then stepped into a telephone booth and dialled an international number. After letting the phone ring four times, he hung up the receiver and called again. This time, a voice answered almost immediately: 'Crawford and Lang, Package and Delivery Company.'

'Uncle Algernon will be coming to Tracy's party after all,' the man said simply, and stepping from the booth, strode briskly away.

The sky was brightening rapidly as Leading Seaman Albert Hopkins drove through the rugged Cumbrian countryside. He hummed softly under his breath and turned up the radio, drumming his fingers to the rhythmic beat of the heavy rock music. Through the lifting shadows, he could dimly see the rolling hummocks of the Lakeland foothills. Slivers of snow traced the narrow gullies, but the pasturelands below looked lush and green in the early morning.

Hopkins glanced at the illuminated clock on the dashboard in front of him. It was barely eight o'clock. He fumbled in his pocket and stuck a piece of chewing gum in his mouth, working his jaws methodically. He'd had breakfast in the mess-hall before leaving the naval base, but he was trying hard to give up smoking and the gum helped take his mind off things.

Something moved in the headlamps ahead, and he leaned forward, blinking excitely. A fox, he realised. Lean and red, it shot across the roadway, vanishing into the hedgerows on the opposite side. Hopkins grinned to himself. He liked to see wild creatures in the countryside. They made him think of freedom and independence, an existence uncluttered by petty restrictions and red tape. He envied Captain Matthews living so far from the naval base. The captain had rented a farmhouse cottage in Caldale and spent his off-duty hours, Hopkins knew, living a life of peaceful and rural tranquillity. Every morning, Hopkins picked up Captain Matthews in his limousine and every evening delivered him safely home again. The daily excursions had wrought in Hopkins a deep dissatisfaction with the daily grind and all the problems it engendered. A man needed a place to escape to. A sanctuary. A retreat.

He frowned suddenly as the highway dipped and he spotted in a hollow ahead, the body of a man sprawled motionless at the roadside. A bicycle lay on the grassy verge, its frame buckled, its wheels twisted in tangled disarray.

Muttering with alarm, Hopkins eased his foot on the brake and scrambling into the growing daylight, bent over the supine form in the gutter. Pressing his fingers against the body's carotid artery, he frowned as he felt the unmistakable rhythm of the pulse-beat, strong, steady and vital.

Suddenly, the chill muzzle of a heavy revolver thrust itself against the base of his skull and a voice hissed: 'One move, and you'll never live again.'

Leading Seaman Hopkins had no way of knowing that the handgun was merely a harmless replica purchased in a souvenir store the evening before. He was conscious only of a freezing sensation in his vitals and a panic which seemed to numb his entire skull.

On the ground in front of him, the body he had been examining burst suddenly into life; scrambling to its feet, it pulled out a second revolver and pressed it deftly against the centre of Hopkins' forehead.

'Stand up,' the man commanded.

Leading Seaman Hopkins was shaking as he rose to his feet. In his mind, the beauties of the winter morning had completely vanished. He had never in his life been faced with a situation which directly threatened his well-being, and he was filled with a terror he found difficult to control. He stood totally still, staring down at the gun barrel with a sickly fascination.

The man gestured towards the bushes. 'Walk,' he said.

Hopkins moved almost in a dream, his legs strangely unwieldy. He could think of no reason for this abduction, and no earthly explanation of why his kidnappers should choose, as their victim, a lowly insignificant seaman. He saw the scrub looming out of the semi-darkness, then the bushes fell back, and he glimpsed a fence-post rising up in front. Beyond it lay a battered stone barn.

Under his captors' instructions, Hopkins clambered weakly over the fence and made his way to the building's interior. It was dark, musty and smelled of manure. Straw littered the ground and Hopkins could see slivers of early morning daylight gleaming between the ragged stone bricks.

'Take off your uniform,' one of his kidnappers ordered.

Hopkins blinked. 'My . . . my uniform?' he echoed.

'Strip, you bastard. We haven't got all day.'

Whimpering deep in his throat, Hopkins began to peel off his tunic. When he was down to his underclothes, one of the men tossed him a padded sleeping-bag. 'Pull it on,' he ordered. 'We don't want you freezing to death.'

The command cheered Hopkins somewhat. Men who cared about his welfare could hardly have murder in mind, he reasoned.

He wriggled into the sleeping-bag, pulling the drawcords tightly around his throat and neck. One of the men slipped his revolver inside his jacket pocket, and taking a rope from around his waist, knelt down and began to tie Hopkins up. His fingers were deft and professional. When he had finished, Hopkins was helplessly cocooned, his arms and legs inexorably pinioned. He lay blinking in the semi-darkness while the two men gathered his discarded clothing and made their way into the lifting daylight. Two minutes later, he heard the roar of the limousine as it thundered along the road to the west.

Captain Raymond Matthews rose promptly at eight-fifteen, did his Royal Air Force eleven-minute exercises on the bedroom floor, shaved, showered and brushed his hair, then made his way downstairs clutching the morning paper. When he reached the kitchen, he stopped in surprise. Facing him on high stools sat his wife and two young children. His wife, Matthews noticed, was sobbing in a dry, wracking kind of way. Behind her, three men in stocking masks stood covering the family with heavy blunt-nosed revolvers.

Captain Matthews was not a cowardly man; he had demonstrated his bravery many times before – in combat in the South Atlantic, in the fear-ridden streets of Ulster, but the unexpectedness of the confrontation seemed to deprive him of his senses, and all he could do was stand and blink helplessly.

'You are Captain Raymond Matthews,' one of the masked men said. 'Supply officer at Brownfield Naval Base?'

Matthews nodded silently.

'We wish you no harm,' the man declared. 'We don't want to hurt anyone. We'll do it if we have to, but that's not what we've come for.'

'Who are you?' Captain Matthews whispered in a hoarse voice.

The man ignored the question. 'In just a moment, we are going to drive to the naval base,' he said. 'It will be your job to get us through the front gate. One of my friends will remain here with your wife and children. As long as you co-operate, they will not be harmed. If however, you do anything which draws attention to our presence, or if either I or my companion fail to return, at least one member of your family will be shot. Do you understand that?'

Captain Matthews swallowed hard as, for the first time, the terrible reality of the situation dawned on him. He felt his body tremble. 'I understand,' he croaked.

'Early yesterday morning, an Argentine motor launch was picked up by the minesweeper *Sagamore Prince*. You know about this?'

Matthews nodded.

'Where is the motor launch now?'

'Moored to the dock inside the naval base.'

'And its cargo?'

'Transferred to the magazine for safer protection. I understand it may be returned if the Argentines prove they'd genuinely drifted off-course.'

'We are going to collect that cargo,' the masked man told him simply. 'When the equipment is in our hands, your family will be released unharmed. Can I count on your co-operation, Captain Matthews?'

Matthews hesitated. Now that the first flush of astonishment had receded, a new sensation began to take its place. Anger. Silently, he glared at the masked intruders, weighing up the chances of resistance, calculating risks, odds, possibilities.

'Daddy?' his little girl said in a strangled voice.

Captain Matthews felt his senses melt. One look at his daughter's terrified eyes, and every shred of defiance flooded out of him. Sighing, he nodded resignedly.

'Good,' the masked man said. 'Now collect your coat and make your way to the entrance hall. You'll find your staff-car waiting at the doorstep.'

A strange driver sat behind the wheel. He was dressed in the uniform of a leading seaman, but Matthews didn't recognise his features.

'This is your new chauffeur,' the masked man told him. 'From now on, you will follow his instructions. I shall be directly behind your seat. Should you fail to get us through the entrance gates, or should the guards stop us for any reason whatsoever, I will shoot you through the chair-rest before turning the revolver on my companion and myself. Is that understood?'

His face stricken, Captain Matthews nodded silently. The masked man waved him into the passenger seat, and clambering into the rear, tucked himself surreptitiously on the floor. Matthews glanced back at the farmhouse, thinking in a dull and desperate way of his wife and children trapped in the kitchen with a homicidal maniac. Then the driver engaged gear, and with a gentle purr, the limousine pulled on to the open highway.

Segunda lay on the narrow bunk, staring fixedly at the ceiling. The cell was small and practically unfurnished. There was a bedside locker, a tiny sink, and a chamberpot in the corner. The only light came from the reinforced glass window, barely six inches square. Segunda had been in the cell for almost three hours. They had picked him up at the airport as he'd passed through Customs, and the efficiency with which the arrest had been carried out led him to believe his arrival had been expected. The security forces must have been watching him. He blamed himself for that. He'd been too eager, too impatient.

Prison cells were no novelty to Segunda. The brick-and-tile walls, the metal bars, the wired lightbulbs, he'd seen them many times before. But always from the other side, he told himself wryly, when visiting detainees in the interrogation centres of the *Olimpo*, the *Club Atlético*, the *Omega*, and the most notorious of them all, the *Escuela de Mecánica de la Armada*.

How he'd hated the dark unventilated chambers, the odour of vomit and excrement, the squalid 'operating theatres' with their metal beds and leather wrist-and-ankle straps where victims were brought to the brink of despair. Prisoners howled under torture, Segunda reflected darkly. There were rarely screams. The idea of screams was erroneous. There was only the howling until the dehumanising process was complete. Despite the brutal nature of his own profession, Segunda had despised the torturers, regarding such men as barbarous, sub-human and depraved. He had treated them with contempt and disdain. And yet, surprisingly, he had felt no compassion for their victims. Mercy was a weakness. He was beyond pity or remorse.

He was contemplating this when he heard feet scraping in the passageway outside. The lock clicked heavily and the door swung open. Segunda rose to his feet as a man entered, pale-cheeked, grey-haired, immaculately dressed in a dark blue suit and sober necktie. The man wrinkled his nose with distaste as he eyed the austerity of the surroundings.

'Hardly hospitable,' he muttered. 'Is this the best they could do for you?'

'I forgot to book,' Segunda said with a grin.

'I'm Palmer,' the man said, extending his hand.

Segunda nodded. 'Head of Section 4. I've heard of you.'

'I've heard of you too, Mr Segunda. In fact, we have quite a comprehensive file on your activities in headquarters. Mind if I sit down?'

'Be my guest. Sorry I can't offer you a drink. It's the maid's day off.'

Palmer settled himself on the edge of the narrow bed, balancing delicately as if surrounded by contamination. Segunda watched as he brushed a fleck of imaginary dust from his trouser crease. He studied Segunda in silence for a moment, his eyes bland, shrewd, intelligent.

'Coming here was ill-advised, to say the least,' Palmer murmured. 'You must have realised we'd have a tail on you, surely.'

'Why? I've done nothing wrong in Britain.'

'You were responsible for the death of one of my leading officers,' Palmer said dryly.

'For God's sake, that was years ago. And it was a mistake. I thought he was a member of the French DST.'

'We have long memories at DI6.'

'Do you seriously think your people at Westminster would let you put me on trial, Palmer?'

'Who said anything about a trial?' Palmer asked blithely.

Segunda smiled. '*Amigo*, I was part of *la guerra sucia*, remember. Do not threaten a veteran.'

Palmer inclined his head, acknowledging his prisoner's astuteness.

'Nevertheless, running guns to the IRA is a serious offence in this country. And you'd be surprised how far we'd go in defence of the realm.'

'Don't be a fool. You know damned well I had nothing to do with that.'

'My dear fellow, I know no such thing. Two of your countrymen are caught red-handed in the middle of the Irish Sea, and suddenly you, of all people, turn up on our doorstep. I'm too old a hand to believe in coincidence.'

'Didn't you read my report? I came here to help.'

Palmer nodded. 'Most interesting.'

'The smuggling of the limpet mines was a freelance operation,' Segunda insisted. 'It had nothing to do with my government.'

'The detainees are Argentine officers.'

'Pawns, both of them. The poor fools probably don't even realise they're being exploited. Think about it, Palmer. What would the Provos do with a cargo of limpet mines and diving-suits? Why not guns, bombs, explosives?'

Palmer nodded. 'That thought had occurred to me.'

'This is more than just a routine arms-smuggling incident. That's why you've got to let me talk to those men.'

'I can't do that,' Palmer said.

'Of course you can. You're head of Section 4.'

Palmer studied his fingers. His hands were long and slender, the nails carefully manicured. His eyes were bland, the pupils filled with a lazy unconcern which Segunda suspected was a deliberate front. They heard footsteps clattering in the corridor as a guard went by, whistling softly. Segunda recognised the tune. It was 'Help Me Make It Through The Night'.

'Mr Segunda, our Foreign Office is going berserk. Any involvement between Argentina and British terrorist organisations is bound to cause a flap at the highest level. There are telegrams of protest rattling backwards and forwards across the Atlantic. I have no intention of ending up with egg on my face.'

'You'll look a damn sight sillier, Palmer, if the situation escalates. My government is just as embarrassed by this as you are. You've got to let me help.'

'You must realise you've been on my personal Wanted list for years.'

'This goes beyond private vendettas, Palmer.'

Palmer sighed as he rose to his feet. There was no softening in his features. He looked like a man who preferred issues to be clear-cut and precisely-defined, who hated compromise at any level.

'Let me sleep on it,' he said. 'I'll give you my answer in the morning.'

Segunda groaned under his breath as Palmer stepped from the cell, slamming the door loudly behind him.

*

Alex's palms were sweaty as he drove towards the naval base. The seaman's uniform was ill-fitting, the tunic stretched tightly across his chest, constricting his lungs and shoulder muscles. Fear lodged like a leaden ball against his ribcage. He hated what he was doing. There seemed something despicable in terrorising the poor captain's family, but he could think of no other way. It was either this or pull out altogether, and for whatever crazy reason, he'd made up his mind that quitting was out of the question. Their scheme was a wild one, whichever way you looked at it. Success depended on its sheer unlikelihood. They'd had no time to plan properly. A few drinks in the local pubs, picking the sailors' brains, casual questions, delicately delivered, nothing too direct. Gradually a picture had begun to emerge, a fragmented compendium of base routine, timings, schedules. The stratagem was half his, half Collis's and nobody with an ounce of brainpower would consider it feasible, but Alex had learned from many years of mountaineering that sometimes the most improbable route would go if you tackled it boldly enough.

Throughout the journey, Captain Matthews had sat in total silence. A good man, thought Alex, worried about his family. Co-operating grudgingly, but ready to retaliate, he was willing to bet, if they let their defences slip. He wished he could have explained things, compromised, spelled it out to stop the captain worrying – but he had to keep up the pretence. It was the only way he knew to get the job done.

He slowed down as the streets of the little Cumbrian town gathered around him. There was an air of fragile normality in the early morning bustle. When he saw the naval base entrance approaching, he took a deep breath and said in a quiet voice, 'It could get tricky at the gate. I'm carrying someone else's ID card. When I show it to the sentry, I want you to divert the man's attention, understand?'

Captain Matthews nodded. His face looked pale but unafraid.

Alex drew to a halt at the entrance, sliding down the side window. His heart hammered wildly. The sentry moved towards him, bending to peer through the windshield, and Alex reached into his tunic, flashing Leading Seaman Hopkins' photograph and ID card.

As the sentry stooped to scrutinise it, Captain Matthews said on cue, 'Has Commander Wilcox arrived this morning?'

The sentry's eyes flickered. 'Commander Wilcox, sir?' he echoed, focusing his attention on Captain Matthews.

'HMS *Portree.*'

'I'm not sure. What time was he due?'

'He promised to meet me in the wardroom for breakfast.'

The sentry shrugged apologetically. 'I really couldn't say, sir. I only came on duty twenty minutes ago.'

The captain nodded, and with a cursory glance at Alex, the sentry stepped back, waving the limousine through. Alex felt relief flood through him as he pressed his foot on the accelerator. He let the breath escape from his body, exhaling softly with an almost imperceptible hissing sound. First hurdle successfully surmounted, he thought; at least they were on their way. He watched the base rising up in front, the brick-red buildings drably uniform. A movement caught the periphery of his vision and he felt a stab of alarm as an officer stepped through the guardroom door and signalled him brusquely to a halt. The officer gestured to the window, and without a word, Alex slid it down. The man leaned forward, staring at him intently.

'What's your name?' he demanded.

'My . . . my name?' Alex stammered, thinking desperately. 'Hopkins,' he whispered.

The officer frowned. 'Put a Sir on that,' he commanded with a warning glint.

Alex felt his stomach cringe. 'My name is Hopkins, sir,' he repeated frantically. 'Leading Seaman Hopkins.'

'Have you had an eye test recently, Hopkins?'

'Eye test, sir?' Alex blinked.

'For spectacles, you imbecile.'

Alex stared at him helplessly. Small and cadaverous-looking, the officer was eyeing Alex with an air of malicious smugness, clearly enjoying his moment of power. Up from the ranks, Alex suspected, good at his job probably, but with one fatal flaw – he thought respect could be won through fear.

The officer's adam's apple bobbed above the level of Alex's nose as he reached down and opened the door. 'Get out,' he ordered.

Alex hesitated.

'Out,' the officer bellowed sharply.

Gritting his teeth, Alex unclipped the seatbelt and climbed into the chill January air. The officer looked at him coldly for a moment, then walked to the front of the car.

'Come over here,' he snapped.

Alex joined him wonderingly. Suddenly, he saw what the officer was getting at. In the confusion of the last two hours, he had smashed the left-hand headlamp. Staring at it wildly, he remembered hearing a tinkling sound when he'd reversed into the roadway after tying up Hopkins. Damn fool that he was, he'd been too engrossed in the task ahead to check the car exterior. He sucked in his breath, trying hard to look calm and relaxed.

'Wouldn't you say a man would have to be virtually half-blind to miss a dent like that?' the officer demanded.

'I'm sorry, sir. I left rather early this morning.'

'Were you on the pop last night, Hopkins?'

'No, sir.'

The officer eyed him critically and something in his manner warned Alex he was in for trouble.

'Good God,' the man breathed. 'Have you taken a look at yourself?'

Seizing Alex's arm, the officer dragged him to the side of the car and pushed him in front of the left-hand mirror. Alex eyed his reflection unhappily. He had to admit he offered a poor image as a seaman. Hopkins' uniform was several sizes too small for him, and the tunic buttons were straining uncomfortably against his breastbone.

'What in God's name do you think this is?' the officer demanded in a harsh voice. 'A carnival show?'

'I'm sorry, sir,' Alex moaned.

'You're a bloody disgrace to the Royal Navy, that's what you are, a bloody disgrace. What's this?' The officer tore at his tunic front. 'You look like a scarecrow, man.'

'I couldn't help it, sir,' Alex protested. 'I sent the uniform to the cleaners and it shrank.'

He saw Captain Matthews lean forward in the passenger seat, sticking his face through the limousine window. 'Is this necessary, George?' Matthews asked gently.

'I'm sorry, sir,' the officer said, 'but have you seen how this man is dressed?'

'I agree he's a bit of a shambles. As a matter of fact, I had a word with him about it myself this morning. But I'd be grateful if you could save your comments till later, George. I'm really in a terrible hurry.'

'Very well, sir.'

Eyes narrowed, the officer placed his face barely an inch from Alex's own. 'Listen to me,' he said, lowering his voice. 'You will deposit Captain Matthews at his office and go immediately to your quarters. There, you will dress yourself in a proper manner and report back to this guardroom looking as a seaman of the greatest navy in the world should. If I find one button undone, one piece of material creased, one hair out of place, I will make you curse your mother for giving you birth, is that understood?'

'Yes, sir,' Alex croaked, his insides churning.

'Now get out of here,' the officer bellowed.

Trembling wildly, Alex scrambled into the waiting car.

Mike stopped the van on the riverbank and peered cautiously around. The road was empty in both directions. Beyond the hedgerows, flat fields reached towards the open sea, and directly below, he could see a line of motor yachts bobbing placidly at their moorings.

Mike took a deep breath. He didn't like this one little bit, he reflected. It had seemed a grand idea in the beginning, putting the frighteners up the bloody English, but Christ knew, those Argentines were crazy, hitting a fully-manned naval base. He didn't envy Alex and Collis. Inside those walls, they'd be trapped like squirrels, helpless and surrounded. Getting in was only the start of the problem. Finding the gear and spiriting it out, that was the hard bit. Luck wouldn't help them, he told himself. What they needed was a bloody miracle.

Mike eased cautiously along the wharf, checking each of the motor yachts in turn. They looked deserted in the January morning, their curtains drawn, their hatches battened. He chose one that appeared a little more salubrious than the others and eased himself on board, his feet making hollow clomping noises on the frosty deck.

To his surprise, the hatch was unlocked. He opened it easily and slipped down the metal ladder. The saloon looked comfortable and lived in, and a faint odour of cooking hung on the air as if someone had recently used the galley. Mike frowned. He'd expected the vessel to be abandoned for the winter. If it was still in use, the owners might reappear at any moment. He opened the door to the adjoining compartment and stood frozen, blinking in surprise. A half-naked girl sat on the narrow bunk, staring up at him owlishly. The sheets had fallen to her waist, exposing a pair of creamy breasts. Mike stared fascinated at the soft flesh and orange nipples. The girl's pupils were dilated, as if she'd been taking alcohol or drugs, and after eyeing him in silence for a moment, she said in a loud voice: 'Charlie?'

Mike heard a movement on the other side of the cabin and saw a figure emerging from the opposite bunk. Unshaven and dishevelled, the man peered at him blearily.

Mike gulped. 'Excuse me,' he stammered. 'I must've climbed on to the wrong boat.'

He slammed the door and scrambled back the way he had come, his limbs shaking impulsively. Bloody fool he'd been, blundering in like a bull in a china shop. He should have checked the boat was really unoccupied. Big mistake, taking things at face value.

He moved down the line of vessels and selected the one at the furthermost end. This time he tapped lightly on the hull with his fist. There was no response. He tapped again. Still no answer. Mike clambered warily on board and checked the hatch. It was secured with a heavy padlock. He glanced swiftly around, and taking out his knife, jimmied it open. Once he was satisfied the cabin was empty, he walked back to the van and began to unload the jerry-cans of petrol he had purchased that morning, dragging them across the icy dockside and stacking them into the yacht's interior. When the cans were all in position, he topped up the fuel tank and started the engine. A few light raindrops were falling as Mike released the rope, and pulling away from the shoreline, steered across the rivermouth towards the open estuary.

Outside the magazine, the sentry looked at Captain Matthews unhappily.

'I'm sorry, sir, no one's allowed inside today without special authorisation from Captain Chamberlain.'

'On whose orders?'

'Orders of the Admiralty, sir.'

Captain Matthews shifted impatiently on his feet, uncertain how to proceed.

Alex cleared his throat. 'Surely the orders don't refer to officers you actually recognise,' he said.

The magazine guard looked surprised. He glanced at Captain Matthews, clearly puzzled that an ordinary seaman would dare intervene in his officer's presence.

Glimpsing the danger, Captain Matthews quickly regained control. 'He's quite right,' he declared. 'The Admiralty regulations can't apply to officers serving on base.'

'I'm sorry, sir,' the guard replied firmly. 'The order came from Captain Chamberlain himself. No one, not even the admiral, is allowed to enter these premises without Captain Chamberlain's personal approval.'

'Why, for God's sake?'

'Something to do with that Argentine launch, sir. There's a big diplomatic barney blowing up in London, and they want the cargo kept intact till the politicians decide what's to be done with it.'

'Good God, man,' Captain Matthews exploded, standing on his dignity at last, 'do you seriously imagine I'm about to cause an international incident? I want to check on some stores, that's all. You're not going to waste my entire morning for the sake of some stupid security order?'

Alex looked at him approvingly. The captain was getting into the spirit of things, he thought. Matthews' eyes were blazing and a flush of colour tinted the skin above his cheekbones.

The guard, however, was resolute. 'No one is allowed to enter without written authorisation signed by Captain Chamberlain,' he repeated stubbornly.

Captain Matthews sighed and Alex gave him a nod towards the car.

As they slid back into the limousine, Collis, crouched behind the seat, said, 'What happened?'

'He wouldn't let us in. We need some kind of special permit. New rule.'

'How d'we get that?'

Alex peered questioningly at Matthews.

'We can try Captain Chamberlain's office,' Matthews suggested. 'It's in the large red building on the other side of the square.'

Not exactly a brilliant beginning, Alex thought, as he cruised slowly across the open compound. Still, they'd expected snags, obstacles, complications. Improvise as they went along, that was the secret. Roll with the punches. Compromise and adapt. The captain was playing his part to the letter, which was something to be thankful for. Alex watched uniformed seamen saluting Matthews as the limousine rolled by. Beyond the buildings, he could see a massive destroyer framed against the docks.

When they reached the admin building, they left Collis crouched behind the driving seat and made their way to Captain Chamberlain's office on the third floor. A young Wren in a starched white blouse smiled at Matthews apologetically.

'Captain Chamberlain's out this morning,' she said. 'He's not expected back before lunchtime.'

'Is he on base?' Matthews queried.

'No, sir, he's somewhere in town, I understand.'

Alex felt a stab of dismay. It seemed grotesque that having started out so promisingly, their progress was being dogged by insidious naval red-tape.

'Look here,' Matthews said reasonably, 'I have to get into the magazine to check some stores, and the damned sentry says I need some special bit of bumf or other. D'you know anything about that?'

The Wren looked sympathetic. 'That's perfectly true, Captain. There's some kind of flap on about that Argentine motor launch. The cargo's being held under top security regulations. No one's allowed into the magazine unless they can prove they have a genuine need to be there.'

'Well, dammit,' Matthews exclaimed, 'I have an inventory to complete. Can't you give me one of your authorisation forms?'

'I'm sorry, sir. Only Captain Chamberlain himself can do that.'

'But this is nonsense. Captain Chamberlain isn't even here.'

The Wren's face hardened. 'I'm sorry, sir,' she repeated. 'He'll be back at lunchtime. You'll just have to wait until then.'

Alex's brain was racing furiously as they strolled back down the staircase, heading for the door. Of course they'd got it under lock and key, he thought. The stuff was volatile, delicate, sensitive – destined, the British believed, for the Provisional IRA. No wonder they weren't taking chances. Nobody said it was going to be easy.

On the threshold, Captain Matthews looked at him. 'Look,' he grunted. 'You can't possibly remain undetected until Captain Chamberlain returns. You've given it your best shot, but it didn't pay off, that's all. Why not call it a day?'

'We're going back to the magazine,' Alex told him.

Matthews' cheeks blanched. 'If you're planning to use those guns, you can go to hell,' he snapped. 'I'll not help kill British seamen.'

'Nobody will be hurt,' Alex promised. 'Just do as we say, and I give you my word you'll soon be back with your family.'

They scrambled into the limousine and Collis hissed, 'Any luck?'

Alex shook his head. 'We'll have to use plan two,' he said. 'Are you game?'

'What the hell, I'm not going out empty-handed.'

'Then you'd better take off that stocking mask,' Alex warned. 'Somebody might spot you crossing the magazine lawn.'

His heart was beating wildly as they drove back the way they had come. Maybe Luke and Mike had been right all along, he thought. It was an insane stunt they were pulling. He didn't even know if he had the nerve to go through with it. But some strange, indefinable resolve was urging him on.

He kept his hands on the wheel, peering out at the uniforms drifting by; strange how familiar it all seemed – naval bases were the same the world over, he reflected absently – in a curious way, he felt completely at home. Then he saw the magazine, and with an intensity that startled him, his fear returned.

The guard snapped to attention as Captain Matthews approached. He was clearly worried by his earlier officiousness. Alex turned his back to the barrack blocks behind, and shielding his movements with his shoulder, drew the heavy replica revolver from inside his tunic, pressing it sharply into the sentry's stomach. The man's eyes bulged in disbelief. He stared at Captain Matthews as if he couldn't believe what was actually happening.

'I'm sorry, seaman,' Matthews told him sadly.

'Put your carbine against the wall,' Alex ordered.

The sentry obeyed, his eyes glazed with shock. Behind, Alex heard the limousine door slam as Collis emerged into the open air. Collis scuttled across the lawn and picked up the sentry's carbine, cocking it briskly.

'How many men inside?' Alex demanded.

'Two guards inside the door, and three clerks in the records office.'

The man spoke in a monotone, his tongue lightly touching his lips. He looked as if he was trying to build up enough courage to take on Alex by physical force, if necessary. Alex drove the pistol deeper into his stomach.

'It will be up to you to placate those men, to assure them that we have the necessary documentation. If you attempt to warn them in any way, or if they suspect, with or without your help, we are not what we seem to be, I will kill you without hesitation, is that understood?'

Stunned and defenceless, the man nodded, swallowing hard. He looked completely intimidated, all trace of resistance gone. Taking a plastic card from inside his tunic pocket, he slid it through a slot in the magazine door, and the door opened with a muffled click. They stepped inside, the guard leading, Alex, Matthews and Collis following close behind.

The interior was like a large communal cave, drab and windowless. Its green walls gave it an air of soulless austerity. On both sides of the narrow companionway, rows of rifles stood in line like regiments on parade. Two guards drinking coffee in the centre of the room reached for their carbines as the intruders entered, but recognising their companion, they allowed themselves to relax.

'What's up, Herbie?' one demanded. 'Too cold for you outside, is it? Come and have a brew. Warm the old cockles a bit.'

Suddenly, the men glimpsed Captain Matthews and snapped to attention. The pause gave Collis the opportunity he needed, and he moved swiftly towards them, wielding his rifle.

'Stay just as you are,' he commanded. 'Touch those carbines and I'll blow your bloody skulls off.'

At the far end of the hall, Alex could see the glass partition which separated the tiny records office. The three clerks were working inside, their heads bowed studiously. None of them had noticed the brief commotion in the outside room.

'Keep walking,' Alex told the sentry in front.

He picked up one of the guards' carbines, and slipped the replica pistol into his jacket pocket. His nerves almost at breaking point, he clutched the rifle to his hip and steered the sentry through the office door, following him swiftly. The men froze in their seats, staring up with uncomprehending faces. Their eyes looked glassy with shock.

'That's good,' Alex said. 'Nobody speak unless he's spoken to. Do as I say, and there's a good chance you'll come out of this unhurt. My colleague and I are prepared to kill ourselves if necessary, to get what we've come for, so don't imagine for one minute we'll hesitate to kill you if you attempt to resist or fail to co-operate.'

He nodded to the nearmost clerk. 'What's your name?' he asked.

The man moistened his lips with his tongue. 'Jenkins, sir.'

'I meant your first name, Jenkins.'

'Gregory,' the man said.

'Well, Gregory, I want you to show me where the cargo from the Argentine motor launch is being kept.'

'It's in the strongroom, sir, in a metal cage.'

'Can you open it?'

The clerk nodded silently.

'Good,' Alex said. He waved the gun. 'Everybody up. We're going in there together.'

The strongroom seemed cramped with everyone packed inside. Through the cage bars, Alex could see the diving-suits, machine-guns and limpet mines stacked on the metal floor. Each item had been carefully catalogued and tagged. The clerk's fingers trembled as he fumbled with the combination lock. Somewhere outside, a whistle shrieked piercingly. Alex heard a muffled click and the cage swung open.

'There's a staff-car parked on the forecourt outside,' he announced. 'We are going to load this cargo into the vehicle's boot. I want you each to take a piece of equipment and carry it through the front door, is that understood?'

The men nodded warily, and Alex glared back at them, hoping to God his expression looked menacing enough. He waved the carbine. 'All right, let's move,' he snapped.

CHAPTER EIGHT

Luke sat in the kitchen, the dummy Walther clasped against his thigh. Perched on breakfast stools in front of him, the family eyed his stocking mask in uneasy silence. The children had lost their initial fear and were now beginning to fidget, but something in their mother's manner kept them warily subdued. He hadn't bargained for this, Luke reasoned, terrorising women and children. A fine bloody hero he'd turned out to be. What would the girl, Deborah Robben, think if she could see him now? A fine sight he must look, smothered in this ridiculous pantyhose. Even the gun was only a toy – a collector's piece, the store proprietor had said, something to hang on the wall or stick in the china cabinet. And what was he supposed to do if the woman resisted? He wouldn't put it past her, she looked the gutsy type. Not one to scare easy – wasn't scared now, if the truth were known. Would rush him in a twinkling, he'd no doubts on that score, except that she was trying to be sensible and diplomatic; worried about her children probably.

'I suppose you think you're a brave man,' the woman said darkly.

Luke shifted uneasily in his chair. It was the first time she'd spoken all morning.

'Does it make you feel strong and important, threatening little children?'

'The children won't be hurt,' Luke told her soothingly.

'Me, then. Am I your target? That's just about your style, isn't it? You're the bloody Provos, aren't you? I knew it the

157

minute you stepped through the door. Is this your proud war of liberation, you Irish bastard?'

'Please,' Luke pleaded. 'I don't like this any more than you do, but everyone will be fine, I give you my word. I'll be gone soon, and you can go back to your lives as if nothing had happened.'

'And my husband?' she choked. 'What about my husband?'

'I told you, he'll be okay.'

'I know all about your Provo bloody justice. You don't like taking chances when you blow a man's brains out. You tie his hands, pull a hood over his head. I've seen some of your handiwork, you bastard. We spent eighteen months in Ulster, Raymond and I.'

'Mrs Matthews,' Luke said patiently, 'your husband will not be harmed. We're not doing this because we enjoy it. We have no other choice. If you'll just bear with me a short while longer, I promise your nightmare will be over.'

The little girl said something to her mother in a low voice, and the woman leaned over, listening intently. She peered up at Luke. 'She wants to wee-wee.'

Luke sighed again. He rose to his feet, thrusting the revolver into the waistband of his trousers. 'Where's the lavatory?'

'Upstairs.'

He jerked his head. 'We go together,' he said.

They trailed up the staircase, the woman and children leading, Luke following close behind. On the landing, Luke checked the interior. There was one tiny window immediately behind the cistern pipe, too small for anyone to crawl through. Satisfied, he waved the little girl inside.

In silence, he and the woman faced each other, the woman's gaze smouldering with hate, Luke's wary, miserable, embarrassed, shrouded by his ridiculous stocking mask. A minute passed, and they heard the lavatory flush. Luke smiled as the girl reappeared. Gently, he ruffled her hair.

'Leave her alone,' the woman snapped savagely, dragging the little girl away.

Luke shrugged. 'I didn't mean anything.'

'Don't you dare touch my children again,' she warned, her chest rising and falling rapidly. 'You can threaten us, you can kill us, but don't touch us. We're not your property to be fondled and patronised.'

Clutching the children on each side, the woman steered them across the landing and Luke shook his head as he followed them down the narrow staircase. Mrs Matthews made a formidable adversary, he thought. Little wonder the British empire had flourished so long.

In the kitchen, Luke fidgeted on his chair as the clock ticked remorselessly on. Nobody spoke. The brief burst of communication had been enough to emphasise their polarity. Now the woman remained silent, studying Luke in her dark vitriolic way.

If I closed my eyes, I could make her disappear, he thought; but he couldn't, he knew, so he tried turning his mind from the demeaning situation in which he found himself, focusing instead on things pleasant and diverting – like the girl, Deborah Robben – he could think about her all right. Was he fooling himself about Deborah Robben? What would she see in a slob like Luke Culpepper? And yet, he wasn't completely blind. She'd liked him, he'd bet money on it. He knew that as surely as he knew his own name. He wanted to see her again, wanted it more than anything in the world. There was no future for them, he realised, not in the face of what he had to do, but what the hell, there was no harm either. A man needed something to look forward to.

The clock chimes made Luke jump. He glanced at his watch, relief flooding through him. Thank God, time to go. He strode into the hall and deftly cut the telephone wire. When he returned to the kitchen, Mrs Matthews had picked up the children and was clutching them protectively to her bosom, clearly half-afraid he might decide at the last moment to eliminate the witnesses.

'It's all right,' he told her gently. 'Your husband will be back shortly. Please don't move until he arrives. He'll want to find you here.'

The woman didn't answer. She went on glaring at Luke with the same fiery mixture of hostility and hatred, and Luke sighed, making his way to the door. On the threshold, he paused to tear off the stocking mask before stepping out into the wintry morning. He felt his limbs stiffen and his wrists turn icy as, with disbelieving eyes, he glimpsed a police car pulling up the drive in front of him. Jesus Christ, he thought, I'm tumbled. He could see the occupants watching him through the gleaming windshield. For one wild moment he thought of ducking back into the house, but the car drew to a halt and the officer in the passenger seat climbed slowly into the daylight. He stared at Luke quizzically.

'Captain Matthews?' he queried.

Luke shook his head, scarcely able to speak.

'This *is* Captain Matthews' house, isn't it?'

Luke nodded, his stomach cringing.

'I wonder if we might have a word?' the policeman grunted.

He took out a handkerchief and briskly blew his nose. He did it with short, precise movements, folding the cloth between his fingers as if any unnecessary effort constituted a weakness of sorts. 'It's about our prize-giving ceremony on Saturday.'

Luke blinked at him. 'Prize-giving?'

'It's passing-out day for our new recruits. We were hoping ... that is, the Chief Constable was hoping that Captain Matthews, as one of our more distinguished local residents, would agree to present the winning certificates?'

Luke held on to his composure with an effort. I can't believe this, he thought. Now, they choose now, of all times, to call about a stupid prize-giving ceremony.

'Captain Matthews isn't here,' he said.

The policeman frowned. 'Any idea where we might find him?'

'He's gone to the naval base.'

'That's odd. We telephoned his office barely ten minutes ago. His secretary said he hadn't turned in this morning.'

The policeman studied Luke intently, his sharp eyes noting the unruly hair, the rumpled clothing, the suntanned features. 'Friend of Captain Matthews, are you?' he enquired.

'His brother,' Luke stated promptly.

'I see.' The policeman turned and glanced at his companion. Without a word, the second officer opened the door and eased into the sunlight. Luke felt his pulses racing. They were suspicious, he could tell. Damn the bastards. A few more minutes, and he'd have been clean away.

'Resident hereabouts?' the first policeman queried.

'No, no,' Luke said hastily. 'I live in Scotland. I'm just paying a social visit.'

'Couldn't we talk inside? It's a little chilly out here, don't you think?'

Luke swallowed hard. 'Well ... I'd like to, gentlemen, really, but the place is in a bit of a state. I know Mrs Matthews wouldn't be happy at the idea of strangers wandering about.'

'Mrs Matthews is out then, is she?' the policeman enquired casually.

'Shopping,' Luke told him. 'She'll be back around lunchtime.'

The policeman folded his arms. Again, he glanced at his companion.

'Then perhaps you can explain who the lady is at the up-stairs window?'

Luke felt his features blanch. He couldn't think, couldn't speak. Dumbly, he peered at the window above. Mrs Matthews stood framed against the curtains, her lips writhing as she fumbled with the catch, sliding it open.

'Look out,' she screamed hysterically. 'He's carrying a gun.'

Luke didn't wait for the officers' response. Leaping down the steps, he drove head-first into the leading man's stomach, feeling the hard resistance of the policeman's muscles tightening against the top of his skull. The impact jarred Luke's neck, an agonising spasm rippling through his body. Breath choked in the officer's throat, and he tumbled back against his startled companion, bringing them both to the ground. Turning, Luke sprinted wildly for the far end of the paddock. He could feel the blood pounding in his temples, and a wave of sickness rippled through his stomach. The fence reared up and he took it at a run, stumbling as he scrambled into the ploughed field beyond. His feet sank in the loose cloying earth. Behind him, he heard the policemen shouting as they started out in hot pursuit.

Luke switched direction, cutting diagonally across the neatly ploughed furrows towards a thicket which traced the fence on the opposite side. His breath rasped painfully as he fixed his gaze on the trees in front, trying to focus his strength in his lower limbs. Not far now. Twenty yards. Fifteen. Twelve. Coming up.

He didn't pause at the wire strands, but took them neatly, soaring into the air with the grace of a champion hurdler. The thicket gathered around him, and choking with terror, Luke plunged headlong into the underbush, fighting his way desperately through the clinging foliage.

Crouched in the motor yacht's cockpit, Mike spotted the naval base entrance ahead. Twin concrete gun-emplacements rose from the estuary, relics of World War Two. A large sign adorned the adjacent pier:

WARNING – BROWNFIELD NAVAL BASE.
This is a restricted area.
Do not proceed any further.
Military vessels only allowed to enter.

Mike could see camouflaged guard turrets framing both sides of the harbour. The sentries were watching his approach with casual unconcern. Grunting, he opened the hatch and eased himself below. Unscrewing the jerry can lids, he began to splash petrol all over the cabin interior. The rancid fumes pricked his nostrils as he moved round the main saloon, drenching the curtains and leather upholstery, spraying the doors and window frames, swilling the wooden floor. When he was satisfied the boat was suitably doused, he made his way back on deck and strapped the wheel firmly into place. The base looked much closer now, and the sentries in the guard turrets were no longer so indifferent; leaning on their parapets, they were eyeing him closely, puzzled by his continuing approach.

Crouching down, Mike took a handkerchief from his jacket pocket and lit it carefully, cupping the flames from the biting wind. When he saw the material was thoroughly alight, he tossed it through the open hatch. He hesitated a moment. This was the part he dreaded most, he thought. Without waiting for the petrol to ignite, he moved to the side and leapt deftly over the rail.

The icy water took his breath away. He could scarcely believe the coldness of it. His brain numbed, and for one awful moment, he thought he was going to pass out, but thankfully, his head broke the surface. Coughing and spluttering, he shook the moisture droplets from his tangled hair, treading water in the motor yacht's wake. He saw the hull buckle outwards in a monstrous eruption of smoke and flame. Sparks danced into the sky, casting a wave of breathless heat across the curling wave-crests. In the naval base entrance, men were shouting in astonishment and alarm.

For a moment, Mike remained stationary, watching the blazing vessel chug sedately towards the heavily guarded piers. Then he turned on his front, and clenching his teeth against the insidious chill, struck out gamely for the shoreline.

Alex heard the commotion as he slammed the limousine boot. Across the square, men were running towards the open quayside. Alex glimpsed flames rising, and saw the motor yacht swing into view, smoke churning in its wake as it drifted into the harbour.

He jerked his head at the little group of captives. 'Inside,' he ordered.

It had taken only a moment to transfer the equipment from the strong-room to the limousine, but already Alex's nerves were beginning to fray. It was only a myth, he thought, the idea that a man could go on playing the hero indefinitely; there was a limit to boldness, just as there was a limit to patience, and he had an awful feeling he was just about played out as far as bravery was concerned. Also, the first flush of shock had faded from the features of the captured seamen and he knew it would be only a question of time before they attempted to resist.

They shepherded their captives back to the strongroom and ordered them to sit on the floor.

'Not you,' Alex said, motioning at Captain Matthews. 'We need you in the staff-car.'

He slammed the door, locking it firmly, and for extra measure, slid shut the two metal bolts. 'That should hold them for a while,' he grunted with satisfaction.

When they reached the forecourt, the entire compound was deserted. Everyone had flocked to the harbour. Even the office blocks looked abandoned. Mike's diversion had worked a treat.

'Hop in,' Alex ordered, opening the limousine door.

There was no clear reason, no logical reason at any rate, why Captain Matthews should choose that particular moment to retaliate. He had behaved so submissively, Alex had almost begun to relax. Matthews might not have been over-eager, but the thought of his wife and children had prevented him doing anything rash. Now, unaccountably, he suddenly decided to fight back. Turning in a savage arc, he thrust his shoulder against Collis's carbine and swung his trunk to the right. Collis choked, doubling forward as Matthews' elbow sank deep into his stomach. Matthews leapt forward, and with a cry of triumph, whipped the dummy pistol from Alex's jacket pocket. He crouched forward, both arms extended, the barrel aimed unerringly at Alex's chest.

'Drop the rifle,' he bellowed. 'Drop it.'

Alex blinked, staring at the toy clutched in Captain Matthews' fingers. Oh, he was an admirable fellow all right, the good captain. Brave, stubborn, resourceful. Family or not, he'd decided to make a stand. With a strange contrariness, Alex almost wished he could have succeeded – God knew, he deserved to – but staring at the captain's eyes, Alex glimpsed a flicker of uncertainty as Matthews realised the weapon he was clutching was too light to be a fully-armed revolver. Then a strange sickness entered Matthews' features, and Alex knew he had guessed the awful truth. He stood peering at Alex with an air of stricken disbelief.

Choking with anger, Collis scooped up his carbine, and without hesitating, clubbed the captain across the back of the skull. Matthews dropped like a log, the pistol clattering from his grasp.

A shout echoed across the square, and Alex and Collis turned towards it, startled. A group of ratings were wandering up from the harbour. Frozen in their tracks, they blinked in disbelief at the rifle clutched in Alex's fingers, at Collis ruefully rubbing his stomach, at the prostrate figure of Captain Matthews sprawled motionless on the magazine lawn. Alex's lips moved wordlessly, as the seconds stretched.

The ratings spun round and began to sprint frantically back to the harbour, yelling at the tops of their voices.

'Into the car,' Alex bellowed.

Terror lanced through him as he quickly released the hand-brake and jammed his foot on the accelerator, screeching across the empty compound. He saw the parade ground, the flat lawns of the officers' married quarters, the white ensign fluttering gaily alongside the union jack. Foot hard down, he struggled for control as the limousine hurtled towards the exit gates. Men came running from the guard-room, shouting at him to stop, and Alex's stomach churned as he glimpsed the metal gates slowly closing. Cursing under his breath, he stabbed the accelerator, and with a thunderous roar, the limousine leapt forward.

The guards dropped to their knees, swinging their carbines into alignment. Spurts of flame pierced the morning sunlight and Alex heard bullets pinging through the vehicle's super-structure. His left fender caught the nearside gate and the windshield shattered with a deafening crack. Suddenly, they were skidding in a dizzy arc, tyres screeching as they spun across the open road. A milk truck coming from the opposite direction swerved frantically to avoid them; Alex saw it swinging to a halt, and clenched his teeth, waiting for the impact. A thunder of shattering glass jarred his skull as they hit the truck in a sidelong collision, denting its side like a battered tin can.

Alex slammed the gear into place, and with hooters squawking angrily around him, crashed a red light and tore off blindly through the morning traffic.

Luke crouched in the hedgerow, moistening his lips with his

tongue. His clothes were covered with dirt, and his dark features looked stippled where sweat had traced tiny rivulets through the dust caking his skin. It had taken him nearly an hour to throw off the two policemen, picking his way across country, hugging the fences and dry-stone walls. Time and time again, he'd been forced to dive for cover as vehicles cruised the adjacent roadways. Since leaving the house, his journey had been a nightmare, and now, when he'd finally reached the rendezvous point, Mike, damn him, was nowhere to be seen. For all Luke knew, he might already be in custody. Alex and Collis too, for that matter. He was lucky to be at large himself. It had been touch and go back there, with the bastards hot on his tail. He belonged in the saddle. Hadn't used his legs in years.

Luke felt his heart beating rapidly at the sound of an approaching vehicle. Craning his neck above the hedgerow's foliage, he felt relief flood him as he recognised Mike's battered grey van. The van slid to a halt, and Luke scrambled from his hiding place, scurrying across the grassy verge to tumble into the passenger seat.

'You're late,' he hissed. 'Where the hell have you been?'

'I had to change my clothes,' Mike told him.

Mike's garments were dry, but his hair hung damply over his forehead.

'Any sign of the others?' he asked.

Luke shook his head.

'For Christ's sake, they should've been here twenty minutes ago. What d'we do now?'

Luke folded his arms and leaned back in the passenger seat, watching the road in front. 'Damn all else we can do,' he said in a stubborn voice. 'We bloody wait, that's all.'

The limousine hiccupped and Alex glanced at Collis with alarm. 'We're slowing down,' he muttered.

'Try a different gear,' Collis suggested.

Alex shifted the lever. There was no response. 'The fuel gauge was practically full when we started. It must be the engine.'

Collis swore. 'One of those bullets probably hit something vital. Can you nurse her along a bit? We're almost at the pick-up point.'

'It's no use,' Alex cried. 'The bloody thing's crocked, I tell you.'

He pumped desperately at the accelerator as the vehicle's power faded. The engine spluttered, coughed, died, and the limousine slid to a halt.

'*Mierda*,' Alex exclaimed, hammering the wheel with his clenched fist.

The road was empty in both directions. There was nothing to see but broad fields and the rolling line of the distant hills.

'How much further?' he demanded.

'Can't be more than a quarter of a mile. We can do it on foot, if we have to.'

'There isn't time,' Alex said. 'They'll be on our tail by now. They have our licence number, remember.'

Collis grunted. Opening the door, he ran to the vehicle rear and tugged open the trunk. Alex watched in puzzlement as Collis took out one of the sub-machine-guns and slapped in a fresh ammunition clip. His cheeks were pale as he flicked off the safety catch and pointed it into the air. He glanced at Alex wryly, then gently squeezed the trigger.

Rat-tat-tat-tat-tat.

The shots echoed eerily in the morning stillness. Crouched in the van, Mike and Luke stiffened, staring at each other in astonishment.

'Hear that?' Luke hissed.

Mike blinked. 'Somewhere up ahead.'

'Alex and Collis. Got to be.'

Mike frowned at him. 'What in the hell are they shooting at?'

'Nothing, stupid. It's a signal.'

Mike's cheek twitched, as if his nerves were beginning to fail him, but without a word, he started the engine and pulling away from the roadside, sped furiously over the rise. The lane dipped, skirting between open pastures and heather-studded heathland. Mist hung above the ploughed fields and woodlands, blending into the wintry sky. Rounding a bend, they spotted the limousine parked in a ditch, Collis and Alex leaning against its bonnet. Mike screeched to a halt, and Luke felt his heart thumping rapidly as they climbed into the sunlight, staring at each other in silence. Alex and Collis looked tense and drawn, but physically unhurt.

The wind caught Alex's hair, scattering it wildly across his narrow features. Luke felt the breath stop in his throat. He stared at Alex, his eyes questioning, and suddenly Alex grinned. For a moment, Luke could scarcely believe his senses, then he whooped out loud as pandemonium broke loose. Howling and laughing, they began to leap about in the roadway, hammering each other's shoulders in jubilation and delight.

'We did it,' Luke yelled, tears streaming down his cheeks. 'It was impossible, bloody impossible, but we bloody well did it.'

They went on laughing and leaping and slapping, caught in a fit of helpless hysteria, letting the tension flood from their minds and bodies. Their madness lasted several minutes until Alex, sobering at last, brought them to a halt.

'We haven't time for this,' he stated. 'They'll shut the roads if we hang about much longer.'

Their laughter died as the gravity of their situation returned. Without a word, they scrambled to the limousine and began to transfer the guns, mines and diving equipment.

The only sound was the clanking of accoutrements and the laboured rasping of their own breathing.

When the loading was completed, Mike slammed shut the rear doors. 'Right,' he snapped. 'Jump in and let's get our backsides out of here.'

The sun faded and a light rain began to fall as they tore madly along the highway to the north.

The news reached Palmer's desk at eleven-thirty the same morning. He kept his face impassive as Ardrey, his deputy, outlined the events of the past few hours over the telephone. When he had finished, Palmer said in a quiet voice: 'Who knows about this?'

'Nobody yet. We've kept it under wraps, Charles.'

'Press?'

'So far, nothing. It's only a question of time though.'

Palmer drummed his fingers on the desktop. 'You realise they've made us look like a bunch of bloody fools?'

'You can't blame the navy people, sir. They were caught on the hop, that's all. I mean, only a lunatic would try a stunt like that.'

'What happened to the captain's driver?'

'The police found him tied up in a derelict barn. He's shaken, but unhurt.'

'Descriptions?'

'Plenty. The police artists are working on the pictures now.'

Outside, Palmer heard pigeons cooing on the empty window-sill. Traffic roared in the street below and somewhere a telephone rang, the sound muffled in the office stillness. Anticipate, prepare, Palmer thought. Cardinal rules for a man in his profession. After thirty-two years in the service, he'd learned to expect anything. But not this. He hadn't expected this. The sheer cheek of the raid almost took his breath away.

'Don't worry, Charles,' Ardrey told him reassuringly. 'Getting the equipment is one thing, smuggling it into Ulster is another. We're stepping up security at all the major exit points.'

Palmer was silent as he cradled the receiver against his chest and fumbled in his pocket for a cigarette. Something about the incident disturbed him, but it took a moment to identify what it was. He frowned as he leaned forward for his desk lighter. 'Did you say, Ardrey, that the raiders took only the Argentine material, nothing else?'

'That's right,' Ardrey confirmed.

Palmer drew hard on the cigarette, his gaze focusing on the filing cabinets at the opposite side of the room. Uncharacteristic, he thought. The IRA would hardly hit a Royal Naval armoury and pass up the chance of picking up a few extra carbines at least.

'Ardrey,' he said.

'Yes, sir.'

'What are the chances of getting a D-notice on this one?'

Ardrey sounded surprised. 'Is that wise, Charles? We can use all the coverage we can get, before the bastards scamper.'

'There's something wrong here,' Palmer told him. 'I don't know what it is yet, but I need a little time to play with. Couple of days should do the trick.'

'They'll never go for it, Charles. A story like this, they'll want to blaze it across the front pages.'

'Try, Ardrey. It's important.'

Ardrey sounded doubtful. 'We'd have to prove national security's involved.'

'Look, the Argentines already claim we're trying to discredit them at the United Nations over the gun-running incident. If this hits the headlines, the situation'll escalate out of all proportion. I want to prevent that happening.'

Ardrey sighed. 'What about the identikits?'

'Police stations and airports, but no media. I mean it, Ardrey.'

'Right, sir,' Ardrey promised. 'I'll see what I can do.'

Hanging up the receiver, Palmer sat for a long time, thinking deeply. The equipment had been sophisticated and specific. Diving-suits, limpet mines, even an underwater direction device. Everything pointed to a sabotage operation, but if it wasn't the IRA, who in God's name was it and where was their target?

Reaching a decision, Palmer stabbed the intercom button. The voice of his secretary, Miss Gavshon came on the line.

'Have Segunda brought here immediately,' Palmer ordered. 'Then phone Mosstrooper and ask her to meet me in G46. Tell her to wait in the anteroom. I'll signal if, and when, she's needed.'

'Yes, sir,' Miss Gavshon answered.

The set faded as Palmer flicked off the switch.

CHAPTER NINE

Mike's head was nodding as they approached the hotel entrance. Alex could tell he was practically asleep at the wheel. It had been a long hard journey, picking their way across open country, avoiding the main roads and motorways where police spot-checks would be in force. For a while, Alex had relieved Mike at the wheel, but his knowledge of the unfamiliar landscape had been too uncertain to navigate effectively, and in the end Mike had been forced to take over. Now it was early evening, and for the first time they were beginning to relax as they glimpsed the lights of the Barracula Hotel looming up ahead.

Alex sighed, leaning his head against the seat-rest. It had been a miracle, their escapade today. There was simply no other way to describe it. Somehow, against all logic and reason, they'd bungled their way through. The British hadn't imagined they'd have the bare-faced effrontery to snatch the equipment from under their bloody noses, that was the size of it. Audacity had helped them pull it off. That, and luck. A man couldn't get anywhere in this world, Alex thought, without a fair share of luck.

He felt his eyelids fluttering as Mike approached the hotel. He would sleep tonight, they all would. They were like zombies, shattered and stultified, still unable to believe the success of their operation.

Suddenly, Mike cursed under his breath. Frowning, Alex straightened, glancing sideways through the darkness.

'What's wrong?'

'We're being followed,' Mike said. 'Bastard's flashing his headlamps.'

Alex peered into the driving mirror. He could see the vehicle directly behind. In the rear of the van, Collis reached silently for one of the machine-guns and clipped in a fresh magazine.

'Pull over to the side,' Alex ordered, his pulse quickening.

The pursuing car cruised past them and drew to a halt directly in front. Alex saw two men emerge into the head-lamps' glare. They moved forward, their faces contourless in the dazzling beam. They were tousle-haired, ruddy-cheeked, and dressed, Alex saw, in denim trousers and donkey jackets. One walked with a marked limp.

Mike breathed a sigh of relief. 'It's okay,' he muttered. 'It's only Joe and Barry Robben from the neighbouring farm.'

He rolled down the window as the two men strolled up.

'Hey, Mike,' one of them said, 'we've been looking for ye all afternoon.'

'We've been climbing down at Aviemore,' Mike answered. 'Did Julie no' tell ye? We stayed in a guest house overnight.'

The man leaned forward, resting his arms on the window frame. 'Is Luke wi' ye?'

Alex frowned. How could this man know Luke? he wondered. Their orders had been explicit – keep to them-selves, avoid the local populace. He heard Luke shift un-comfortably in the van rear.

'Hello,' Luke said, glancing nervously at his three com-panions.

Alex blinked at him. Bloody fool. He'd been fraternising. That was Luke all over. Couldn't stay aloof. Couldn't keep his mouth shut. Had to communicate. Had to make friends.

The man grinned happily. 'We just wanted to tell ye the race is on for tomorrow.'

Luke flushed in the shadows. He could see Alex watching him, and his face was filled with guilt.

'We've been telling folks how good ye are,' the man went

on. 'They're fair looking forward to getting their own back on the Dunaven crowd for a change. Barry and me'll pick ye up at eleven o'clock. Race starts twelve noon prompt. Afterwards, we'll celebrate at the village dance.' He chuckled and winked. 'We'll gie 'em a Burns Night they'll never forget,' he promised.

Nodding to his companion, the man straightened and strolled back to the waiting car.

They watched it swing away from the roadside and disappear from sight, its exhaust fumes trailing lazily in the headlamps' glare. For a long moment, nobody spoke, then Alex said quietly: 'What the hell was he talking about?'

Luke seemed unable to meet his eyes. 'I . . . I ran into them the other day,' he explained. 'It was pure accident. I was out for a walk and I saw them standing in this paddock.'

'So you decided to stop for a chat?'

'I had to. If I'd walked on, it would've looked strange.'

'You're supposed to be keeping a low profile, you fool.'

'I forgot. I'm sorry, I forgot. I couldn't help myself.'

Alex shook his head resignedly. They should have anticipated Luke. He was too gregarious for his own good. No restraint, that was Luke's trouble. He liked to be with people. Any people. Sod orders. Sod the submarine. Luke cared only for the moment.

'What was that business about a race?' Alex demanded softly.

'Aye,' Mike put in, 'I heard about it at the village store, but in the excitement of the last few days, it must've gone clean out of my head.'

Luke wiped his moustache with the back of one hand. 'They had a mare,' he explained. 'They'd been saving her to run against the neighbouring village, but nobody could ride her. She was too wild, too wilful.'

'So you had to show them how good you were.'

'No,' Luke protested.

'God Almighty,' Alex growled. 'Do you realise what you've done? You've cost us another twenty-four hours, you clown.'

'How's that?' Luke cried.

'We can't hit the submarine tomorrow if everyone's expecting you to run in that race.'

'Why don't we launch the raid tonight?' Collis suggested gently.

Alex shook his head. 'We're too beat. We need rest.'

'*Compánero*, if we leave it much longer, the *Conqueror* could haul anchor and sail away.'

'I know,' Alex admitted wearily, massaging his forehead with his fingertips. 'But we've no choice. The place'll be crawling with people tomorrow. We'll have to leave it one more day.'

Collis eased back on his haunches. 'You're not seriously suggesting we let Luke ride?'

'If he tries to pull out, they'll want to know why.'

'But the police'll have our descriptions by now. Drawing attention to himself could start somebody wondering.'

'Not if he remembers to do one thing.'

'What's that?' Luke asked.

Alex turned to peer at him. His face looked hard and set. Only his eyes carried life; they glittered fiercely in the darkness of the early evening.

'Lose,' he said.

The room was bare and cheerless, its walls white, its floor uncarpeted. Foldable chairs stood around its rim and a glass panel opened into the chamber beyond, allowing spectators to view what was taking place in the adjoining cell without being observed in return.

Palmer sat on one of the chairs, watching Segunda interrogate the two captured Argentines. Though the conversation was conducted in Spanish, it was clear to Palmer that

Segunda was getting nowhere at all; the prisoners, unshaven and dishevelled, glared back at him defiantly, answering his questions with monosyllabic grunts.

As Palmer watched, the door behind him opened and Ardrey, his deputy, came into the room. Ardrey was a small man with a goatee beard and a slightly mincing manner. He peered over Palmer's shoulder at the scene in the cell beyond.

'Any luck?'

Palmer shook his head. 'They're sticking to their story.'

'After what happened at the naval base?'

'Segunda's not infallible, Ardrey.'

'Cheer up,' Ardrey smiled. 'Here's a bit of good news. Those identikit pictures we circulated – a taxi-driver at Glasgow airport claims he recognises the men.'

Palmer glanced up quickly. 'Police talked to him yet?'

'It was the police who contacted us.'

Palmer traced the side of his mouth with his tongue. He'd almost begun to think the raiders had vanished into thin air. Rarely had he known a case where the fugitives had been seen by so many people, and the sightings had been absolutely nil. Now, at last, a chink, a pinpoint of light.

'This is the first real lead we've had,' he whispered.

'You want me to send a man up?' Ardrey asked.

Palmer considered for a moment. He had learned a few things over the years. Politics could be dirty, and the secret was to stay cleaner than clean. If a sacrificial goat was called for, it might be wise to provide one and cover his back. He came to a decision. Leaning forward, he pressed the intercom linking him to the adjoining room.

'Ask Mr Segunda to step out here, will you?'

Segunda's face looked tired when he appeared in the doorway. The laughter lines had gone from his eyes, and there was a flush of anger on his craggy cheeks. Palmer could scarcely suppress a small glimmer of satisfaction as he peered up at him quizzically. Segunda had been so arrogant, so bloody sure of himself.

'Not as easy as you imagined, is it?' Palmer asked.

'Give me a knife and leave me with them for twenty minutes,' Segunda growled. 'I'll have them singing on the other side of their faces.'

'We do things differently in England, Mr Segunda.' Palmer examined his fingernails in the harsh fluorescent lighting. 'However, I do have some news for you. A driver at Glasgow airport has recognised the descriptions of the men who raided the naval base.'

Segunda frowned. 'Why are you telling me this?'

'I thought you might like to continue your investigation,' Palmer said with a shrug.

No reaction. Segunda was still eyeing him warily. He was nobody's fool, Palmer thought. Flippant on the outside, but sharp as ice underneath. Not one to be fobbed off easily. Good brain in his head.

'Our relations with Argentina are growing more sensitive by the minute,' Palmer explained. 'If things get out of hand, I want it perfectly clear that I bent over backwards to be reasonable and accommodating.'

Segunda chuckled dryly. 'And I'll make a perfect whipping-boy if anything goes wrong. I've got to hand it to you, Palmer, you're quite a hand at the survival game.'

'There's just one thing,' Palmer said. 'I can't allow you to go wandering around the British Isles unattended. It'd be more than my job's worth. You must operate under the direct control of one of my own officers.'

'You know I always work alone,' Segunda protested.

'This particular officer is something of an expert on your case, Mr Segunda. She knows you – academically speaking, of course – almost as well as you know yourself. You remember Mosstrooper?'

Segunda blanched as Palmer pressed a button on the panel

in front of him and a shadow fell across the open door. His eyes lifted slowly, reluctantly. The woman standing there was tall, slim and elegant, her hair dark and tumbling to her shoulders, her face bold and feminine. They could see the tension in her features.

Segunda knew the woman intimately. Years before, they had conducted a fiery love affair in the city of Paris when, on the instructions of her department, she had first seduced him, then left him to die in the Sahara Desert.* She was the only woman who had ever affected Segunda emotionally and he felt his muscles tighten.

Her eyes held his with a disconcerting brightness. Her spine was straight, the tilt of her chin defiant. He could see the challenge in her soft grey eyes.

'Hello, Mártin,' she said in a quiet voice.

The day of the race dawned bright and clear. A few storm clouds hung over the Charrach Dam, but in the east the sun lifted quickly and by nine, the clouds had vanished, leaving the sky a beautiful azure blue. At eleven o'clock, Joe and Barry picked up Luke at the Barracula Hotel and drove him to the improvised racetrack.

Luke was still stunned from the heady events of the day before, and like Alex and Collis, puzzled that no mention of them had appeared in the morning newspapers. It was as if the naval base raid had never happened. Luke found the silence weird, to say the least; in fact, in a funny sort of way, he'd almost begun to wonder if he hadn't dreamed the entire thing. It seemed almost dream-like – the long hours of waiting with Captain Matthews' family, the awful moment when he'd emerged through the door to glimpse the approaching police car, the desperate flight across the empty fields and hedge-rows – it was the stuff nightmares were made of, except for

* *Hour of the Gaucho*

Alex and Collis. They were just as baffled as he was. Did the media black-out represent some ominous warning? Were the security forces poised to pounce at that very moment?

The question seemed unsettling, and Luke found it difficult to focus his mind on the task in hand. After all, he hadn't asked for this race, despite what Alex and Collis claimed. He had done his best to wriggle out of it, if the truth were known. But they'd stuck his name on the list, and now, whether he liked it or not, he had to see it through.

The event was a strictly informal affair, the riders dressed in jeans and woollen pullovers. Under Joe and Barry's guidance, Luke went through the preparatory rigmarole, and at twelve noon, the bell rang for the jockeys to mount. Joe slapped Luke on the shoulder as he swung into the saddle and nudged the mare toward the starting line.

A row of flags marked the route. It ran in a direct line across the open beaches, ending where the promontory formed a natural barrier beyond the foreshore. The horses seemed skittish and excited, bobbing and whinnying as they took up their positions for the off, the riders fighting to keep them in line. Luke patted the mare's neck, feeling the tremors rippling through her hide. He peered at the spectators lining the cliffs above, filling his lungs with air as the jockeys fidgeted for position.

People had flooded in from all over the surrounding countryside, and Luke felt a tremor of unease as he studied them moodily. It didn't seem right somehow, throwing the race. Everyone was counting on him. Not just Barry and Joe. Not just Deborah Robben. All the residents of Sheilington. He sighed, filled with a sudden wave of despondency. Stop worrying, he told himself. He was still jumpy from yesterday's escape – a narrow squeak, it had been, romping across those empty fields. A man couldn't be blamed for feeling out of sorts after an experience like that. But Luke knew it wasn't yesterday he cared about – it was what was about to happen today. Money was changing hands, good money, hard-earned, frugally collected. He was letting them down. Everybody. He didn't feel proud of himself, and that was a fact.

He could feel the tension gathering as the crowd fell silent, watching, waiting. Stirrups clanked, horses snickered. Somewhere an aircraft droned lazily, its engine muted in the pregnant stillness. There was a scent of animal sweat mingled with the cold salt air.

Then Luke felt his senses leap as the tapes went up and with a thunder of hooves, the riders leapt away. He let himself merge with the others, picking up the rhythm with an easy fluid grace. The horses seemed to gather in a group, the jockeys tilted forward, their outlines blurring as the wind moistened his eyes. The group spread into an elongated column, a massive bay leading by three lengths. Luke could feel the chestnut straining to break loose. She was an animal in a million, he thought, experiencing a momentary surge of regret as he fought to restrain her. Sand and spray lashed into his face and the muscular body rippled against his thighs and knees. He lifted himself in the stirrups, forgetting style and deportment as he leaned forward along the horse's neck, excitement pulsing through him. *Qué caballo. Qué caballo mas hermoso.*

He bore to the left, the mare stampeding crazily as though nothing in the world could stop her, the cliffs whipping by in a breathless flurry. Dimly, Luke heard the roar of the crowd above the ocean breakers. He was starting to draw ahead. The mare was too fast, too strong. On his left, the bay was falling back, its rhythmic stride breaking. Length by length, the chestnut widened the gap. Luke was seized by panic. *Mierda*, he thought, I'll have to take a fall.

He was flat out now, every muscle and sinew straining, the mare working into her stride, eyes bulging, nostrils flaring, the pulsing flash of her hooves showering his cheeks with dust. The beach shimmered dazzlingly as he tugged back on the reins, forcing the chestnut to falter. He sensed the bay closing fast and gritting his teeth, rolled to the right, toppling from the saddle in an inelegant flurry of arms and legs. The ground tilted in his vision as he cartwheeled over, hitting the sand with a resounding thump. Before he could stop, he had tumbled into the shallow water. Cries of dismay rose from the watching crowd, and to Luke's surprise, the mare slithered to a halt and stood nudging at the incoming tide, the reins dangling loosely over her head. Stiffly, Luke clambered to his feet, the cold air causing the drenched clothing to cling icily to his naked skin. He stumbled towards the waiting horse, dusting himself morosely. Suddenly, he heard a voice rising above the clamour of the crowd.

'Come on, Luke.'

He felt his senses tingle. He recognised the voice's timbre. It was Deborah Robben. He could see her clearly framed against the sky as she cupped her hands to her mouth, bellowing down with a hoarse desperate entreaty. 'Come on, my bonny lad, ye can still win, I know ye can.'

Luke's features tightened. Something rose inside him, impossible to ignore. He was a simple man in many ways, artless and direct. He threw himself into life with a gusto that was totally lacking in restraint. He felt his spirits racing, the blood pounding in his temples. It wasn't simply himself he was disgracing. It was the girl too. It was all of them, all the people who had put their money and their faith on him. He didn't stop to consider the wisdom of what he was doing.

Spitting on the ground, he leapt into the saddle, gathering up the reins. The mare surged forward, responding rhythmically to the subtle pressure of his thighs, hide steaming as Luke bent over, rising up in the stirrups, squinting into the field ahead, seeing the rearmost riders kicking up dust as they pounded for the finishing line, seeing the gap steadily closing, knowing he was going to win, knowing it with a certainty that was utterly intuitive. Nothing could stop him now. They were part of each other, he and the mare together, a single unit, moulded and united, pounding across the open sands. Length by length, the chestnut drove past the stragglers, her muscular body reaching out to meet the challenge. Luke felt a surge of exultation as he gave the mare her head, the wind tearing at his hair, dimming his vision.

The bay was making the running, but the chestnut was eating up ground, thundering into second place with a ferocity that sent the crowd wild with delight. Luke's body undulated, hips taking the strain, sand spraying his throat and hair. The flags fluttered to his right as he closed with the bay, neck and neck now, fighting desperately for the lead. He could sense the bay weakening as the winning-post approached. Its tail swished, its head shook, and then, with a burst of elation, Luke saw its stride falter, and in a flash he had whipped ahead.

The sky tilted dizzily, the sea spreading into a contourless smudge; he balanced wildly in the stirrups, the wind screeching in his eardrums, the chestnut thundering, the air buffeting, and nothing up front but open sand. The post zipped by and he drew on the reins fighting to bring the mare under control. Steam rose in spirals from her glistening flanks as he wheeled back from the promontory.

The crowd went wild. Scattering, they came streaming down the slopes like people possessed. Yelling and cheering, they surged across the open beach, and Luke laughed as he felt himself being lifted from the saddle. Shoulder high, they carried him in triumph up the narrow pathway to the cliffs above. Eagerly, he peered around for Deborah Robben, but she was nowhere to be seen. Then he spotted Alex and Collis watching him accusingly, and with a chill of dismay, Luke realised what he had done.

*

In the village hall, bowls of mashed turnip and potato had been arranged on long trestle tables. Voices hummed above the clattering cutlery as plates of steaming haggis were passed along the exuberant rows. Ladies drifted up the aisles, filling the diners' cups from huge metal teapots. The room was filled with an air of muggy conviviality. Most of the men, Luke noticed, laced their tea from whisky flasks carried in their trouser pockets, and every once in a while, strangers would wander up to his table and despite Luke's protests, top up his drink with strong-smelling Scotch. Everywhere, people were smiling in his direction.

'Look at them,' Alex growled dryly. 'They think you're a bloody hero.'

'They'll have forgotten it by tomorrow,' Luke said.

'A small community like this, they'll be talking about it for weeks. A man who rides like you do is no ordinary tourist.'

'It was the horse,' Luke whispered hotly. 'I couldn't hold her back.'

'If the constable's got your description, it's only a matter of time before he twigs.'

'Why should he? It's not in any of the papers.'

Alex frowned. 'That's what worries me. We should have been front-page news this morning.'

'Maybe the Navy's trying to save face,' Luke suggested.

He paused as a figure leaned over the table, tipping whisky into his teacup.

'Hey, Jimmy, here's a wee tot tae keep oot the cold,' the man said with a wink.

Luke sighed. He couldn't imagine what had possessed him today. The sight of the girl had completely disarranged his senses. He forgot their raid on the naval base. He forgot their designs on the *Conqueror*. He forgot everything except Deborah Robben. All through supper, he looked for Deborah, but she was nowhere to be seen. Never had a girl affected him so. He wanted her, he realised, more than anything he could name, and that was the tragedy, for there could be no happiness for either of them in view of what he had to do.

When supper was over, the diners retired to the bar while members of the village committee folded up the tables, stacking them in the outside shed for the dancing to begin.

Luke, Alex and Collis stood at the counter, drinking morosely. Their gloom seemed in strange contrast to the merriment surrounding them. They were nice people, the Sheilington folk, Luke thought, simple and direct. They belonged to the land, to the mountains they lived in. Craggy, wind-reddened, they looked rough and ready, independent, but filled too with an innate friendliness and a ready warmth. He liked that.

Just before eight, Julie MacNally arrived, accompanied by her boyfriend, Jamie, a beefy young farmlad with a mop of thick hair. Julie looked lovely, Luke decided. It was the first time since their arrival they had seen her wearing a dress. She smiled at them, and wandered into the main hall as the dancing began, the young man's arm resting casually around her waist. Luke saw Collis staring after them, a strange look in his eyes.

A party of sailors filed through the door, eyeing the girls appraisingly, and Luke felt a tightening sensation in his chest as he realised they were part of the *Conqueror*'s crew.

'What're they doing here?' Collis growled.

'Same as us, I imagine,' Alex murmured.

Luke saw the sailors elbowing their way towards the bar and turned his back, staring into the mirror on the wall behind. He didn't want to meet any of his potential victims, he reflected; the job was going to be hard enough without complicating matters.

A man jostled him, and the glass fell from his hand, spilling across the counter.

'Sorry, sport,' the sailor said. 'My fault.'

'Forget it,' Luke grunted.

'No, no, I'll get you a fresh one. What's your shout?'

'It's nothing, I tell you.'

'Hey, Doris, fill up his glass,' the sailor bellowed.

He leaned against the counter, studying Luke with an expression of drunken cheerfulness.

'Hey, aren't you the geezer who won the race today?' the sailor asked with a friendly grin.

Luke nodded.

'My God, the way you rode that horse, it was like the charge of the bloody Light Brigade. You're not a professional jockey, by any chance?'

'No,' Luke told him.

'It was magic, pure magic.' The sailor chuckled happily. 'I've never seen anyone ride like that in my life. Where're you from, mate?'

'Winchester way,' Luke muttered vaguely.

'Winchester, is it? Do they all ride like that in Winchester?'

Striving to deflect the sailor's attention, Luke's heart suddenly jumped as he spotted Deborah coming through the door. Her red hair had been tied in a loose coil on top of her head, and she wore a simple dress that contrasted marvellously with the creaminess of her skin.

'Excuse me,' he muttered thickly, 'I've just seen somebody I know.'

He stumbled towards her, trying to appear sober, and she smiled as he approached.

'I thought you weren't coming,' he said.

'I live on a farm,' she grinned. 'I had chores to do.'

'You've missed supper.'

'That's all right. I've already eaten.'

She squeezed his wrist. 'I suppose ye know you're the local hero?'

He shrugged, his cheeks colouring.

'I saw ye fall. Were ye hurt?' Her eyes looked anxious.

'Jerked my shoulder a bit, that's all. Come on up to the bar and let me buy you a drink.'

She studied him impishly. 'Ye look like ye've had enough.'

'Well, I've been going at it sort of hard,' he admitted. 'I guess I'm just not used to all this attention.'

She laughed. 'If it's all right wi' you, I think I'd rather dance. You *can* dance, can't you?'

'I'm no Rudolf Nureyev,' Luke admitted, running his fingers through his thick dark hair, 'but I'll give it a try, if you will.'

Chuckling, she took his arm. 'Come on,' she said. 'Wi' Joe and Barry around, playing nursemaid is something I'm used to.'

On the dance floor, an accordionist and fiddler were hammering out a lively Scottish medley. Luke could feel the floor vibrating as the couples leapt and whirled, whooping in an impassioned kind of way.

'What kind of dancing is this?' he muttered.

'Scottish. Put your arm around me and give it a go.'

Dumbly, Luke did as she ordered, the music hammering at his eardrums. His entire body seemed to have lost co-ordination.

'Follow me,' Deborah commanded. 'One, two, three. Now back again, four, five, six. Turn and whirl me around. Come on, grab hold, I winna break. That's it.'

Desperately, Luke tried to follow the unfamiliar steps. Sober, he might have managed at least a fumbling attempt, but stewed as he was, he could not seem to control his legs. For several minutes, he stumbled around the dance floor until at last Deborah, laughing, took his arm and shepherded him back towards the bar.

'It's a good job ye ride better'n ye dance,' she told him.

Shaking his head dazedly, Luke headed for the counter,

but Deborah held on to his elbow, steering him towards the door. 'Ye've had a bellyful of that already,' she stated firmly. 'I'm taking ye outside for a breath of fresh air.'

And grabbing their coats from the cloakroom, she led him meekly into the night.

The music changed, became slow, dreamy, soothing. Julie closed her eyes as Jamie held her tight. Why did life have to be so complicated? she wondered. Until a few days ago, she'd been happy and contented. She had the hotel. She had Mike. Now everything had been turned topsy-turvy. He'd done that, the young man Alex. Strange, moody, truculent. He hadn't encouraged her, she told herself, not once. Not like Collis, who hung around her like some kind of shadow, making her skin crawl. Thought himself a ladies' man, did Collis. Proud of his appearance, proud of his charm – knew how to turn it on too. But no matter how hard Collis tried, it was Alex she wanted. Something about him had intrigued her from the beginning. It wasn't his looks, not that. She hadn't been strong on looks before. It was character she appreciated. Sensitivity. She glimpsed that in Alex. She could see the haunted look in his eyes.

She tried to imagine it was Alex holding her now, Alex's arms around her waist, Alex's body against her breast. Why was she thinking like this? she wondered. In a few days' time, she would never see him again.

She spotted Collis at the bar doorway, watching her across the sea of bobbing heads, and felt her stomach tighten. He was drunk, she knew, but it was more than drunkenness with Collis. There was something in his face which frightened her. Something deranged.

She felt Jamie's arm pulling her closer, and numbly, unfeelingly, pressed herself against him. Across the floor, silent and immobile, Collis's eyes followed her as the dance went on.

*

'Feeling all right, Jock?'

Alex blinked. A sailor was standing at his elbow, grinning at him amiably.

'You look a bit down in the mouth,' the sailor said.

Alex leaned back from the bar. He could see his face in the mirror on the opposite wall, his cheeks pale, his eyes slightly out of focus. 'I've had a bit too much to drink,' he admitted.

The sailor laughed. 'Don't knock it. It's the only way to be.' He glanced around at the swirling revellers. 'They know how to enjoy themselves all right, don't they? You'd think the end of the world was coming.'

Alex nodded.

'We're from the submarine down on the Sound,' the sailor told him conversationally. 'HMS *Conqueror*.'

'I guessed as much.'

The sailor chuckled. 'To tell you the truth, the boys weren't too happy when they knew we were coming here. We'd been promised a trip to South America, then at the last minute, they sent the *Dreadnought* instead. You can imagine how the lads felt. I mean, who wants to be in Scotland in the middle of January? However, the way the village folks have treated us, we can't really complain. It gets a bit boring at times, but nobody can say they haven't made us welcome.'

Alex blinked at the sailor, focusing his gaze with an effort. He saw a pale face, a friendly grin. 'How long are you staying?' he asked thickly.

'Just till the end of the month. Then it's Australia, if the rumours are correct.'

'Lucky man.'

The sailor grinned and held out his hand. 'Woolcott's my name,' he said. 'Harry Woolcott.'

Alex hesitated. I can't afford to talk to this man, he thought, I can't afford to know him. Blowing up a submarine

189

was one thing, but doing it with people on board, people he'd met, perhaps even liked, was unthinkable. However, there was no way he could avoid the exchange without appearing boorish.

He shook the sailor's hand. 'Alex Masters,' he said in a soft voice.

'You're not from around here?' the sailor muttered.

'What makes you say that?'

'The accent, of course. You're an Englishman, like the rest of us.'

'Oh.' Alex relaxed. 'That's right. We're up on holiday.'

'In winter?'

'We're climbers. We've come for the winter conditions.'

Woolcott laughed. 'Rather you than me. It's a mug's game, that climbing.' He leaned against the bar. 'Fancy another?'

Alex glanced down at his empty glass. 'Why not?' he grunted.

The sailor called the barmaid and ordered fresh drinks. He took out a packet of cigarettes and offered one to Alex. Alex shook his head.

'That bloke's a friend of yours, isn't he?' the sailor said. 'The one who won the race today.'

'That's right.'

'Hell of a rider. I'd have sworn he'd had it when he came off. But the way he remounted and went after them like the hounds of hell, that was absolutely bloody fantastic.'

'He had a good horse,' Alex muttered.

'Sure, he did. But the best horse in the world won't win unless he's got a rider to match. A bloke who can ride like that is wasting his time climbing mountains. He ought to be a jockey, a professional.'

'Yes,' Alex said. 'That's what we keep telling him.'

'Where are we going?' Luke asked as they walked along the road.

'Nowhere special.'

'I think I'm a little stiff from the ride today.'

'Aye, that and the Scotch,' she grinned. 'Never mind, ye deserve it. I was fair proud o' the way ye rode up that beach.'

'You mean it?'

'I wid'na say it if I didn't mean it.'

'Funny, nobody's ever spoken to me that way before.'

'Och, ye're all the same, you men. Ye'll say anything but yer prayers.'

'It's true. No girl anyway.'

Her eyes crinkled with amusement. 'Ye must've led an awful sheltered life, I'm thinking.'

'I've never been out with a girl before,' he admitted. 'Not in the real sense, the intimate sense.'

She laughed. 'Now I know you're teasing.'

'Look at me, for God's sake. I'm not exactly a maiden's dream.'

'I canna stand pretty men myself,' she said.

Luke spotted a group of children hanging around Cameron's fish-and-chip shop on the corner of Argyle Street. A solitary policeman strolled along the store windows, trying each of the doors in turn. In the dim light of the streetlamps, the buildings looked dour and chilling.

He shivered fiercely under his coat. 'Christ, I'm freezing half to death here.'

'Ye must have very thin blood,' she chuckled. 'This is nothing to the way it usually gets.'

She took his elbow and steered him into an alley. He saw dustbins and cardboard boxes littering the shadows.

'There's an abandoned shack behind Mulligan's laundry,' she said. 'It'll shelter us from the wind.'

'Is it warm?' he whispered.

'We'll make it warm,' she told him, her eyes twinkling, filled with humour and indecipherable promise.

The shack was small and scattered with straw. There was a smell of paraffin mingled with roof-tar. Someone had scrawled: 'Dunaven United are a bunch of pouffs' on the rear wall. An ancient oil lamp, its metalwork furred with rust, still hung, cluttered with cobwebs, from a nail beneath the roof.

Luke gasped as he ducked warily under the beams. 'What is this place?' he muttered.

'Just a shack. Lennie Fraser uses it to store some of his hay.'

'Sounds like you've been here before.'

'Meaning what?' she challenged.

'Meaning nothing.'

Smiling gently, she pushed him against the wall. 'Feeling better now?' she asked.

He nodded.

'Night air doing some good?'

'I guess so.'

'Och, you're a right bunch of softies south of the border.'

'It's my fingers,' he told her. 'They're like ice.'

'I'll show ye how to warm them.'

Calmly, she opened her coat, and taking his wrists, pressed his hands against her breasts. Luke's throat choked as he felt the softness of her flesh through the flimsy dance dress. She was smiling in the darkness, her eyes masked in shadow.

'That better?' she asked, pressing herself against him. Luke's blood rose thickly as she ran her fingers through his tangled hair. He tried to speak, but she seemed oblivious to his words, digging her nails into his skin. He kissed her hard on the mouth, and she opened her lips invitingly. He could feel the bulge of her pubic bone pressing against his groin. Something exploded inside his head and his senses swam as, with a muffled groan, he tore wildly at the front of her dress.

*

The music changed, losing its dreamy tempo, becoming harsh, forceful, tempestuous. Julie recognised the strains of the tango. Several couples left the floor, smiling embarrassedly and her muscles tightened as she spotted Collis moving towards her, his face hard and determined. She glanced up at Jamie who was dancing with his eyes closed under the music's hypnotic spell, but before she had time to warn him, Collis had seized her roughly by the arm. Jamie's eyes opened in a flash.

'I'm cutting in,' Collis told him brusquely.

With an air of savage insolence, he slipped his arm around Julie's waist and drew her backwards into the crowd. Blinking, Jamie recovered and lurched forward, his craggy cheeks reddening in anger. 'Hey Jimmy, what d'ye think ye're playing at?'

A dancer caught Jamie's shoulder, drawing him gently back. Julie saw him vanish into the sea of swirling faces. Collis was holding her so tightly, she was finding it difficult to breathe. She could see his face, cold, dispassionate, disdainful.

He swung into the dance's rhythm, the forcefulness of his movements taking her completely by surprise. There was no way she could resist, even if she'd wanted to. She felt her muscles tense as she struggled to follow his intricate dance patterns. Collis did not restrict himself to an individual area, but used the entire floor, swinging her wildly, sweeping from one end of the hall to the other with a brazenness that left the other dancers gasping. Desperately, Julie tried to accommodate his movements, dipping and swaying with each shift of limb and torso, conscious that Collis was no ordinary dancer, conscious that the other couples were shifting back, clearing a space in the centre of the dance floor. They gathered round appreciatively, clapping their hands to the music's beat as numbly, perplexedly, Julie let the dance absorb her.

*

'Hey,' a sailor said, popping his head through the bar-room door. 'You ought to see this friend of yours. He's a regular John bloody Travolta.'

Alex frowned. He closed his eyes and the room seemed to spin. He opened them, and it steadied again. Suddenly, he realised the bar had almost emptied. Everyone was filing into the dance hall conscious that something was happening there.

A feeling of uneasiness spread through Alex's body as he stumbled to the door, his stomach tightening. The crowd had parted, forming a circle around the edge of the floor. At its centre, Collis and Julie were going through the motions of the tango with a staggering bravado that took Alex's breath away. It was clear Collis was some kind of pro. He moved with the elasticity of a ballet dancer, his body poised, his head tilted arrogantly. He seemed to have lost all sense of time and place. Nothing mattered to him any more, only the dance, and the girl. Watching, Alex groaned softly under his breath. Collis was preening himself like a turkey cock, showing off to everyone in sight, and most of all, to Julie MacNally. Bloody fool, Alex thought miserably, what in God's name did he think he was playing at?

Julie heard the thunder of applause as the music drew to a close. Collis still held on to her hand, his chest rising and falling rapidly, a glint of excitement in his cold blue eyes.

She felt her senses chill as Jamie Blackmore came striding across the floor towards them. Blazing with fury, he grabbed at Collis's arm.

'Tek yer hands off her, ye crab-faced bastard, or I'll crack yer bloody skull.'

Collis stared at him imperiously. Around them, the audience, sensing a quarrel evolving, faded into silence. Collis's gaze focused on Jamie as if seeing him for the very first time, then he glanced down at the fist still gripping his jacket.

'Let go of my sleeve,' Collis commanded in a quiet voice.

'I'll leave go all right. I'll shove it doon yer bloody throat. Now get the hell out of here before I break yer bloody neck.'

Releasing Julie, Collis drew himself erect while the crowd watched with bated breath. This was even better than the dancing.

'Why don't we talk outside where there's more room?' Collis suggested.

'Aye,' Jamie exclaimed. 'Bet your bloody backside we'll talk.'

Her limbs caught in a state of semi-torpor, Julie watched the two antagonists stride angrily into the darkness. She hurried after them, pressing her fist against her lips.

The forecourt in front of the hall was packed with vehicles, and in a narrow clearing lit by a solitary streetlamp, she spotted Collis and Jamie confronting each other angrily. Collis was cold, drunk and determined; Jamie almost beyond the bounds of reason. A car sped by, heading south along the Carlton road. Julie saw the driver peering out, his face puzzled and bemused.

'Stop it,' she cried. 'Stop it this very minute.'

But the two men totally ignored her. They seemed intent on some elaborate and macabre ritual. Jamie lunged forward, swinging his arms in a series of wild uncoordinated blows which would surely have laid Collis flat if they'd landed, but Collis leapt back lightly, weaving his body from side to side. He was clearly no novice when it came to alley fighting. To Julie's horror, he lashed out suddenly with his foot, catching Jamie squarely in the stomach. As the Scotsman doubled forward, Collis clasped both hands together, bringing them down with stupefying force on the small knot of muscle and nerve tissue at the base of Jamie's neck.

As Jamie pitched to the ground, Julie felt fury engulf her. Screaming, she hurled herself at Collis, and taken by surprise, he staggered backwards, snatching at her flailing fists.

Someone came running from the hall doorway, footsteps ringing on the frosty cobbles. She saw Alex seize Collis, thrusting him roughly back. Alex glanced down at Jamie, then glared at Collis accusingly.

'You bloody fool,' he hissed. 'Are you out of your bloody mind?'

Collis's eyes faltered, and he stared guiltily at the ground. Julie had never seen Alex so angry before. He looked like a madman, his cheeks flushed, his eyes bulging.

He turned to face her, body quivering with fury. 'It was your fault,' he accused. 'You started all this.'

She could scarcely believe her ears. 'Me?'

'You lured him on. I watched you.'

She shook her head, unable to speak. It was some kind of nightmare from which she would quickly awaken.

'You've had your eye on Collis from the start.'

'That's a lie,' she protested wildly.

'D'you think I'm blind? I've seen the way he keeps hanging around you.'

'I can't help it,' she cried. 'He won't leave me alone.'

'You shouldn't encourage him. He'd never have started if you hadn't.'

'Encourage him?' she echoed. 'Why, why . . .'

Something inside her seemed to break. She felt fury hammering at her temples. 'Damn you,' she hissed. 'Damn you, damn you, damn you.'

And with tears streaming down her cheeks, she turned and ran swiftly into the night.

Julie lay in bed, staring at the ceiling. The pillow behind her head felt damp from her crying. She could scarcely believe the things she had heard tonight. She could scarcely believe the injustice of it all. That fool Alex, could he really be so blind? And poor Jamie, Collis hadn't given him a chance. The way he moved, deadly like a snake. Even drunk, he was as light on his feet as a feather. She knew Collis's type, unscrupulous, predatory. They all were, she told herself moodily. Alex too. Mike said they were old friends from his school days, but Mike was lying. Why? The suspicions stirred anew in Julie's mind, and gradually her anger faded. This had gone far enough, she decided. She was tired of wondering. She had to know. If any answers could be found, they would lie among their guests' belongings, a notebook perhaps, a diary, a letter from a friend.

Senses throbbing, she rose from the bed and pulled on her housecoat. They were still at the dance hall, the three Englishmen and Mike too. Julie padded across the darkened landing and entered the little dormitory where the visitors slept. Switching on the electric light, she glanced breathlessly around. The room was neat and tidy, the three beds carefully made. On the floor stood the suitcases containing their guests' belongings.

Heart thumping, Julie picked up the first one and propped it on the bedside locker. She rifled swiftly through the clothing inside. To her disappointment, she encountered nothing unusual. It contained exactly what she'd expected to find: toilet things, underwear, paperback novels, outdoor survival gear. The second suitcase was Collis's. Fumbling down the side, her fingers located a smooth oval-shaped bowl. It was made of polished wood and shaped like a coconut. Out of its solitary aperture, a slender bone straw protruded.

Julie studied the bowl in puzzlement. It was unlike anything she'd seen before. As she was puzzling over the strange phenomenon, a sudden creak on the landing made her catch her breath. Startled, she turned, her stomach tightening in alarm. She felt the blood throb in her throat and a surge of panic swept her body. Collis stood in the doorway, leering drunkenly at her, a crooked smile on his thin lips. His eyes took in Julie's frightened face, the open suitcase, the polished bowl.

'I saw the light on,' he drawled. 'Thought it might be burglars, so I sneaked around the back.'

'I . . . I . . .' Desperately, she tried to think. 'Someone was moving about in your room,' she whispered. 'I found the suitcase open on the locker.'

It was a futile excuse and she knew it, but she could think of nothing else. Collis considered the idea, scratching his temple.

'An intruder, eh? What happened to him, I wonder?'

'He must . . . he must have got out through the window,' she stammered, her body going hot and cold in turns.

Collis crossed the floor and peered outside. 'He'd have to be pretty agile. That's a thirty-foot drop out there.'

He turned to look at her, his eyes gleaming with a strange fire, and Julie felt her legs dissolving. She backed against the wall as he moved towards her, smiling thinly. Even from several feet away, she could smell the liquor fumes on his breath.

'Of course, he could've sneaked out the front when he heard you getting out of bed,' he said.

'That's right,' she choked in a hoarse voice. 'That's probably just what he did. Sneaked out the front.'

The wall brought her to a halt and panic rose in her chest as Collis moistened his lips with his tongue. His facial muscles looked curiously slack, his eyes slightly out of focus. He ran one finger down her cheek.

'Frightened you, did he?'

She nodded.

'You shouldn't have been frightened. Collis wouldn't have left you alone. Not a man to abandon a lady, is Collis.'

He tried to take her in his arms, but she pulled away,

placing her hands against his chest. He frowned. 'What's wrong? Feeling shy?'

'Please. Leave me alone.'

'I came back for you, didn't I?'

His hands found her breasts under the flimsy robe. She gasped as the hard fingers clutched her helpless flesh. His touch was rough, harsh, insinuating, shocking her senses into action. Shifting position, she brought her bare heel down on Collis's instep and saw his eyes flinch with pain. For a fraction of a second, his grip slackened and thrusting him back, she turned and darted through the bedroom doorway.

She felt almost weak with terror, her limbs moving of their own volition, carrying her dutifully, desperately, yet in some strange way, devoid of either strength or feeling. Down the darkened staircase she clattered, and out into the night, the housecoat flapping around her, the winter chill clutching her cheeks and throat. She saw the gloom of the empty paddock and the bare hillslopes beyond. Terror lanced her body, turning her flesh icy as she heard Collis coming after her, his shoes crunching in the stillness. Her bare feet scampered over the cindered forecourt and on to the road beyond, running in a daze, conscious that Collis was rapidly gaining.

'Help me,' she screamed. 'For God's sake, somebody help me.'

She felt something tear as Collis gripped her shoulder. His arms wrapped around her, his breath panting hot down the side of her neck as he dragged her, struggling, towards the nearby scrub.

Footsteps echoed in the night, and with a wave of thankfulness she spotted Alex sprinting out of the darkness. His eyes took in the scene in an instant.

'Let her go,' he snapped.

'Keep out of this,' Collis warned.

'I said, let her go, damn you.'

'This is a private matter, Alex. Keep out of it.'

'Let her go, you drunken bastard.'

Collis's face hardened. Roughly, he thrust Julie to one side.

'All right,' he breathed. 'All right, it's time we settled this once and for all.'

Panting with fright, Julie cowered at the roadside and watched the two men circle each other warily. The scene looked somehow grotesque, as if it belonged to some forgotten nightmare dredged from the unlit complexities of her mind. She struggled to control her trembling, sobbing noiselessly under her breath. Cat-like, the antagonists stalked each other, looking for an opening. Collis struck first. He leapt forward, his foot streaking out in a perfectly executed roundhouse kick, the toe aimed directly at Alex's jaw. Alex swayed, leaning back from the hips as Collis's shoe grazed the side of his cheekbone, then moving so swiftly his hands were a blur, he gripped Collis's ankle in his fingers, holding it firmly above his shoulder. For a full second, the two men stood frozen into a silent tableau as Collis struggled to maintain his balance on his one free leg, then calmly, and with precise deliberation, Alex kicked him hard in the crotch.

Collis's cheeks purpled as he sank writhing to the ground. For several moments he rolled in agony, his lips issuing harsh mewing sounds from deep inside his throat. Alex stood waiting, his face grim and determined as Julie shivered in the chill night air.

Somehow, Collis managed to stumble to his knees and drag himself to his feet. He swayed in the gloom as he attempted to straighten.

Alex moved in, pounding Collis mercilessly. There was little doubt Collis was the better fighter, but the kick had effectively disabled him, and Alex took full advantage to vent his fury, his blows hard, brutal, crippling. Collis's face was covered with blood when he rolled over and began to be sick in the gutter.

Without a word, Alex took Julie's arm and led her back to the hotel. She seemed to be in some kind of stupor.

'Are you all right?' he asked.

She nodded silently as he helped her upstairs. She sensed the change in him. The anger had gone now, the blind unreasoning rage he'd displayed at the car-park had faded completely. He was back to his normal self. She felt the gentleness as he paused at her bedroom door.

'D'you want me to come in?'

She nodded again.

He waited while she clambered into bed, shivering from tension and cold, drawing the blankets around her throat.

'I'll make you some tea,' he offered.

'No.'

There was a calmness in his eyes, an inherent strength she found strangely comforting. She felt her terror beginning to subside.

'I don't want you to leave me,' she said.

'You'll be all right. Collis won't harm you now.'

'Please.'

He hesitated, then glancing around, found a chair and settled down at her bedside. 'I'll wait until you're asleep,' he promised.

'I don't want to sleep,' she said. 'I want to talk.'

'About what?'

'Anything. Anything that'll take my mind off what happened.'

He looked at the floor and then at his hands. 'Those things I said tonight, I didn't really mean them. I was jealous.'

'Jealous?'

'Of Collis.'

'Why?'

He grinned wryly. 'I don't know. He's always so damned sure of himself. So damned confident.'

A smile lingered at the corners of his lips, and she thought how young he looked, how vulnerable. Dirt smeared his cheek where Collis had caught him a glancing blow. The horror of the evening began to disintegrate and she felt her shivering stop as the nightmare faded. He'd done that, just by sitting there. It was what she really wanted, she thought, having him near. Strong, quiet. Someone to rely on.

'Talk to me,' she whispered. 'Tell me about yourself. Tell me about Newcastle.'

'It's just another industrial town.'

'Please.'

'Dirty. Busy. You can't move for people.'

'I went to Newcastle once,' she told him.

'Really.'

'It wasn't Newcastle itself. It was close though. Carngill.'

'Carngill?' he echoed.

'Near the coast. You must know it.'

He nodded. 'My father used to take me there as a boy.'

'There was a paper shop on Grainger Market corner. Hogarth's. I had a schoolfriend whose family ran it for years. Just outside the station.'

'I remember,' Alex said.

'Is it still there?'

'Not any longer.'

'Pity. We had some marvellous times that holiday. Did you ever fish in the Braydon River?'

'All the time,' he smiled.

'They said it held the best salmon in the north of England.'

'Yes, we got some splendid catches.'

'Just think. I might even have served you. In the paper shop, I mean.'

'Isn't it funny to think so.'

They talked for a long time, exchanging platitudes in the dim glow of the bedside lamp. He seemed filled with an earnest need to comfort her, and gradually, Julie felt her nervousness subsiding. He was a nice man, Alex Masters, she thought. Patient, gentle. She liked him.

But later, after he had gone, she lay staring into the darkness, her brain in a quandary. As far as she knew, the Braydon River ran nowhere near Carngill, there had been no salmon in it since 1858 and she had never heard of a newsagent called Hogarth's on the corner of Grainger Market.

CHAPTER TEN

Julie paused, gasping heavily, and followed the ridge with her eyes. It bobbed and dipped, meandering in a series of zig-zag lines into the topmost peaks. Snowcapped summits towered around her, and to the east she could see the massive rampart of the Charrach Dam. The air felt keen against her skin. Snow coming, she thought. According to the BBC weather report, a severe frontal system was moving over Scotland from the Arctic. Julie shivered.

She had left immediately after breakfast, waiting until Mike and his guests had departed for the summits, then scurrying into the kitchen to pull on her boots and arctic clothing. For almost three hours she'd been trailing them at a distance of approximately half-a-mile. Now, however, Julie was puzzled. She could see the ridge ahead, twisting and undulating as it picked its craggy route up to the mountain's shoulder, but there was no sign of the English climbers. She frowned. They could hardly have eluded her. There was only one logical route and that lay along the ridge itself, unless – her brain reeled – unless the ridge walk had been nothing more than a diversion, a deliberate attempt to make observers think they were making for the summit when in fact they were heading for somewhere else entirely.

Heart thumping, Julie lowered herself flat on the ridge and gazed along the steep leeward flank. Her lips pursed as she spotted four figures picking their way down the bracken-covered hillslope, heading for Brachaigg Bay. Julie could see the bay quite clearly, a flat crescent of water protected on two sides by low rocky promontories. She considered her position quickly. Once she descended the hillslope, she would attract attention. She had to find a different route. Immediately below the ridge, a narrow scar in the mountain developed into a boulder-strewn gully which curved north, running parallel to the bay itself. It looked an ugly descent, but it offered a cover of sorts and would keep her concealed until she approached within spying distance of her quarry.

Heart thumping, Julie slid into the ragged scar and began to edge down the boulder-strewn streambed. It was hard going, following the narrow brook as it rolled and twisted down the mountainside, but she kept at it, taking her time, placing her feet judiciously with the sure knowledge that if she tumbled and came a cropper, she would probably lie for years before her body would be discovered.

At last the gully began to level out, and as it arced to the right, she realised she was approaching the foreshore. Panting, she clambered up the muddy bank and reaching the crest, peered through the spiky grass clumps. The bay lay directly in front of her, its grey sand lustreless in the gloomy winter morning. A beachcomber's shack stood derelict against an apron of rippling grey rock. She saw Mike and his three companions carrying bundles out of the hut's interior and packing them into their empty haversacks. Something in the delicate way they handled the cargo told her it was neither orthodox nor legal.

Watching the strange scene, Julie frowned darkly as she felt her bafflement deepen.

Mike and his guests were sitting in the kitchen when Julie got back to the hotel. Mike had brewed some coffee, and they were sprawled around the heavy oak table, talking in low furtive voices.

Julie tried to look unconcerned as she wandered in. She took off her anorak and hung it on the kitchen door.

'Been out?' Mike enquired casually.

'Just down to the village.'

He glanced at her boots. 'With those on?'

'It's muddy in the paddock. I didn't want to get my feet wet.'

She moved to the stove, blowing on her fingers and rubbing them energetically. 'Any coffee left?'

'Half the pot. I've just made it.'

'Heard the weather forecast?' Julie wondered. Mike nodded. 'Snow coming, according to the Met. office. I hope we've plenty of supplies in.'

'Dinna be daft. Think I'd leave the freezer empty this time of year?'

She poured herself a mugful of coffee, then flipped open the stove lid and peered inside. 'Running low,' she said. 'I'd better get some fresh logs.'

Alex rose to his feet. 'Let me do it,' he offered.

'What d'ye think I'm made of?' she smiled. 'Plasticine?'

The cold struck her as she scurried across the paddock. There'd been no sign of the mysterious cargo inside the house, so it had to be in the tool-shed. There was no other place.

The little shack was dark and musty. She spotted the four haversacks propped in a corner. Breath rasping, she knelt and unstrapped the first one, tugging loose the drawcord. Something hard and metallic pressed against her fingers. Wonderingly, she wrested it free, cradling it in the pale gleam from the open doorway. It was a heavy metallic M3-A1 sub-machine-gun. Julie's eyes widened with astonishment. Dear God, what was going on here? This was her home, hers and Mike's. Who were these strangers who brought with them implements of death?

She heard a movement in the doorway behind her and turned, startled, her cheeks flushing. Alex was standing on the threshold, watching her expressionlessly. Behind him, she could see Mike and Collis.

Slowly, Julie rose to her feet, her fear giving way to anger and indignation. 'Who are you?' she whispered. 'What are you doing here?'

No answer.

Julie fixed her eyes on her brother and Mike flinched under the intensity of her gaze. 'I want the truth, Mike. What, in God's name, is going on?'

Mike glanced at the others, stubbing at the ground with his toe.

'They're Argentines,' he said sullenly.

Somewhere outside, a plane droned lazily westward, creating a resonance on the chill wintry air.

She blinked. 'Argentines?'

'You know the submarine on Barracula Sound, the *Conqueror*? They've come to blow it up.'

Julie rubbed her forehead with her fingertips. She felt as if reality itself had somehow come askew. 'I can't believe what I'm hearing here. Are you in league with these men?'

'I'm doing it for the movement,' Mike stated fiercely. 'It's a dual operation. We're working together.'

'The SNLA? I thought you'd finished with those lunatics ages ago.'

'It's a chance to make our voice heard, Julie,' Mike explained in an earnest voice. 'It'll give us the kind of publicity we've always needed. After tonight, they'll have to take notice of us in Westminster.'

'You bloody fool, do you realise what you're involved in?'

Mike's face reddened. 'I'm doing this for you, Julie. For everyone in this valley. Those English bastards are grabbing Barracula Sound. How much more of this country do they intend to steal for their bloody military bases? We're trying to change things.'

'By committing treason? You'll change things all right.

You'll end up in a bloody mental hospital, which is where you probably bloody well belong.'

Alex interrupted impatiently. 'You can argue between yourselves later. Meanwhile, we've got a job to do. We can't move until it's dark, so someone'll have to stay with the girl. We'll stand guard on a rota basis.'

Collis grinned, winking at Alex knowingly. Though Collis's face was covered with bruises, he appeared, surprisingly, to bear Alex no ill will.

'I'll take first shift,' he offered.

Alex glared at him. 'You're excluded,' he said.

Julie lay on the bed, her arms folded defiantly across her thick-knit pullover. In front of the window, Alex stood staring out at the first snowflakes drifting across the empty paddock. She could sense his stubbornness, the almost palpable barrier between them.

'Storm's starting,' he said, trying to establish an air of normality.

'You'll be happy about that,' she told him dryly. 'It'll give you a cover to work under.'

He sighed. Something in his manner told her his detachment was deliberate, as if he was consciously steeling himself, shutting off nerve responses and emotions alike.

'I don't blame you for being angry,' he said.

'You used me,' she accused. 'You used Mike. You used all the people in Sheilington village.'

'If you want to know the truth, it was Mike's idea from the beginning.'

'I don't believe it.'

'Ask him.'

'I intend to,' she stated fiercely.

He turned to look at her, the light slanting across his hollow cheekbones. There was a faint coating of beard stubble on his chin and throat; it diminished in some way his air of sensitivity, emphasising the torment in his eyes. 'Anyhow, by tomorrow you won't have to put up with us any longer.'

'And a hundred men will be lying dead at the bottom of Barracula Sound.'

He snorted. 'Nobody will die.'

'How can you be sure?'

'Because we'll telephone a warning. As soon as the mines are fixed, we'll get the submarine evacuated.'

'Supposing something goes wrong? Supposing the mines go off prematurely? Supposing the telephone operator doesn't believe you?'

'For God's sake,' Alex snapped. 'We're doing everything possible. If our warning fails, it's the fortunes of war. They didn't give us a warning on the *Belgrano*.'

'The *Belgrano*?' she echoed disbelievingly. 'Is that what this asinine foolery is all about? The *Belgrano*?'

A sudden tension rippled through his body, stiffening the spine, bringing into sharp relief the jagged contours of his facial structure.

'I was on the *Belgrano*,' he said savagely.

Julie hesitated. 'So that's it. So that's what you're doing here. Revenge, is it?'

'You'll never understand. How could you? You're not Argentine.'

'Explain it to me,' Julie challenged.

He shrugged. 'With us, honour is a kind of disease. It's bred into our bones from the minute we are born.'

'Honour? Is that what you call it?'

'Yes, honour,' he snapped angrily. 'Sometimes we use a different name. We call it *machismo*.'

'*Machismo*?'

'It represents everything that's good and bad in our society.'

'And is that what's driving you now? *Machismo*?'

He caught the mockery in her voice. 'Don't laugh,' he

said. 'There's nothing amusing about *machismo*. It's easy for you, a Scotswoman. You know where you came from, you know what you belong to. As a race, we Argentines don't even have an identity. Over fifty per cent of our population came from abroad. Italians, Spanish, English, Welsh. They didn't mix, they kept to themselves. Even today, there are people who can't speak their national language. But the one thing we have got is *machismo*. It might be self-delusion, but at least it's Argentine.'

He paused as the door opened and Mike entered the room, carrying two mugs of coffee. He handed one to Julie who took it without a word, the other he gave to Alex.

'My shift,' he said. 'You'd better start getting your things together.'

Alex looked at him, frowning. Something in Mike's face bothered him. There were dark shadows under his eyes and he seemed to have lost his customary ebullience. 'Anything wrong?' Alex asked.

'Bit nervous, that's all.'

'Everyone's nervous,' Alex said.

'Aye, I ken that. Dinna fuss yersel', I'll be all right.'

Alex nodded, and clutching the coffee mug, quietly left the room. Mike pulled up a chair and settled into it, trying hard to avoid his sister's eyes. They fixed on him remorselessly, hard, bright, accusing.

'So you're the gaoler now?'

'Julie, be reasonable,' he groaned.

'Reasonable? Mike, you're in trouble, serious trouble. You're a traitor.'

'How can I be a traitor, when my country doesn't even have a government?' he cried.

'Don't give me that Scottish Nationalist guff. It's murder you're involved in, Mike, mass murder. What about the Scotsmen on that submarine? Are you going to sit here and let them die?'

'Nobody will die, nobody.'

'All it takes is a single misjudgement. A mistake on the timers, a crossed telephone line. More than a hundred men, Mike, young men like yourself. You saw some of them at the dance last night.'

'Shut up,' he snapped.

'Beginning to get a conscience, are you? Beginning to doubt if this is such a good idea? Beginning to wonder if you can go on living with yourself with a hundred men at the bottom of Barracula Sound?'

Mike's face twisted in torment. She could see the turmoil in him. His gaze fixed on hers with an almost desperate pleading.

'I don't want to hear about it,' he cried. 'I don't want to think about it, I don't want to talk about it. I just want you to bloody well shut up.'

'It may be nothing more than coincidence,' the airport official said, guiding Segunda and Louisa across the terminal floor, 'but when we pinned the identikit pictures on the restaurant noticeboard, one of our taxi-drivers felt sure he remembered the men. Have a chat with him, and see what you think.'

He stepped back to let them through the automatic doors. Segunda smiled at Louisa, alias Mosstrooper, but she studiously ignored him. She'd ignored him all morning, ever since his release from prison. Segunda felt unperturbed. He was not a man who was discouraged easily.

Something in the way Louisa moved told him she was holding herself together with an effort. He felt relieved at that. A man needed reassurance, positive proof that the things he'd cherished had not been illusory. He watched as she stepped in front of him, her high heels clicking on the pavement flags, her figure still trim, still vital beneath the deep folds of the gaberdine coat, her hair catching the subtle refractions of light glimmering beneath the outside canopy.

Segunda shivered as the cold wind blew into his face. He watched the airport official wave over a thickset individual with balding grey hair.

'This is George,' the official said. 'Tell them exactly what you told me, George.'

George shrugged disparagingly. He had the look of a man who hated being the centre of attraction.

'It's mebbe nothing,' George admitted, 'but I spotted these three characters coming through the doorway there. They looked awfu' like the pictures on the polis poster. I canna be certain, but the resemblance was uncanny. There were two reasons I noticed 'em. The first was, they looked so suntanned. I remember thinking: they did'na get yon tans in Bilbao, not at this time of the year.'

'Were they British?' Segunda asked.

'Aye, Englishmen, judging by their accents. One of them dropped something on the ground. It was a wee bowl thing wi' a straw poking through. His friend got awful hot under the collar. They were arguing right there on the pavement.'

'How was it shaped, this bowl?'

'Christ, I don't know. I did'na get a decent look. It was just a wee bowl, that's a'.'

'Round?'

'No, no, not quite round. More the shape of a rugby ball.'

'Or a coconut?'

'Aye, tha's right, a coconut.'

Segunda's eyes gleamed. 'A *maté* gourd,' he breathed.

'Does that have some significance?' Louisa asked.

'I believe so.'

He eyed George keenly. 'Any idea where the men went to?'

'Aye, as a matter of fact, that's the other reason I remember. A car came to pick them up, and I recognised the driver. It was Billy Hannah, a right tearaway. Used to be a bit of a hard man in the old days. When I saw him wi' yon new arrivals, I figured they must be hoodlums of one sort or another.'

'Where can we find this Billy Hannah?' Segunda demanded.

'If he's flushed, he'll be in Charlie Andrews' pub on Banavie Street. It's the only place he has'na been barred.'

Segunda took a deep breath, his senses tingling. 'Thank you,' he said softly. 'You've been a tremendous help.'

He was silent as they drove into town. Things hadn't gone too badly for a beginning, he reflected. At last, he was beginning to make some progress. Sitting in the passenger seat, he studied Louisa from the corner of his eye. He had almost forgotten her over the years. It seemed strange to be in such close proximity again. He'd learned slowly, painfully, that time was the great equaliser, the precious salve to old wounds. Even the scars healed sooner or later. He could still feel the terrible moment of loss, the first bewildering sense of amputation. Love had been a curious sensation for a man like Segunda. He'd thought himself beyond all that. Immune. Incapable, even. But he'd loved Louisa, loved her badly. Her betrayal had hurt him more than he cared to say.

Traffic began to build up as they approached Glasgow centre, and Segunda cleared his throat.

'Bit like the old days, us working together again.'

'We never worked together,' she stated. 'You only thought we were working together.'

'That's true,' he admitted. 'You were very convincing. Especially in bed.'

Her cheeks pinkened, but no expression crossed her face. Professional to her fingertips, she never allowed herself to be needled.

'Can I ask you a personal question?' he murmured.

'That depends.'

'I was just wondering. How could you do it, pretend like that? It *was* pretence, wasn't it?'

'Yes, it was pretence.'

'You've missed your vocation, Louisa. You're a talented lady.'

'Don't be gauche.'

'Gauche, is it? Well, I suppose gaucherie is an apt enough label for a man who's made a fool of himself. I really thought you cared for me.'

Louisa was silent as she switched gear. Something in her face, a touch of colour above the cheekbones, a tightening of her hands on the steering wheel told him her calmness was merely a façade.

'I had a job to do,' she said. 'I used the only weapon I had. If you think I gave a convincing performance, that's because it wasn't all play-acting. Part of the time, I really meant it.'

She glanced at him quickly. 'Don't get the wrong idea. We're not picking this up where we left off. That's in the past. This is business, nothing else.'

'Like leaving me to die in the desert?' he said. 'Was that business too?'

'You were dangerous. You had to be eliminated.'

'So you used the oldest bait in the book.'

'It worked, didn't it?'

He nodded. 'Close, damned close.'

'Then stop bleating. You've lots to be thankful for. You're alive, you're free. You're not even on our wanted list any longer. When this is over, you can go back to Argentina and forget it ever happened.'

He smiled at her, his eyes crinkling in the wintry light. 'That's what I like about you, Louisa,' he said. 'You have such a romantic way of looking at things.'

They found the pub after seeking directions from a local policeman. It was hardly an inspiring place. Its outer windows had been shielded by wire netting to protect them from vandals, and the building itself carried an air of squalor and decay.

Louisa remained in the car while Segunda stepped inside. Sawdust had been scattered over the bare boards and a sundry assortment of customers, young and old, sprawled at wooden tables gazing blearily at the open doorway.

Segunda made his way to the counter and ordered a large Scotch. 'Billy Hannah been in?' he asked the barman casually.

The man looked at him. 'Who wants to know?'

'An old friend.'

'Polis?'

'No,' Segunda said.

The man went on staring at him in a hard unflinching way, and with a shrug, Segunda took out his passport and laid it on the counter.

'How can I be a detective when I'm not even British?' he insisted. 'I've been looking for Billy all morning. They told me I'd find him here.'

'Well, they told ye wrong. I barred him six days ago. Up to his old tricks again, he was, brawling and fighting.'

'Where's he living now?'

The man sniffed. 'He's left the Sally Ann. Somebody must've given him a bob or two. He's found hisself a flat on Slawain Street.'

'Got the number?'

The barman yelled at a figure sprawled in the pub corner. 'Hey, Sharky, what's Billy Hannah's new address?'

'Ten, Corby Villas,' the man answered promptly.

'Satisfied?' the barman asked, fixing Segunda with a wary glare.

Segunda smiled at him, and dropped a crumpled banknote on the counter. 'Thank you,' he said. 'You've been very kind.'

*

215

The flat stood in a grey tenement building that had no elevator and no lock on the front door. To reach it, they had to climb several flights of stone steps worn smooth by the passage of a million feet. The walls were covered with slogans and graffiti.

Segunda stopped at number ten and tried the handle. He took out a penknife, jimmied it easily, and waved Louisa across the threshold.

For a moment, they stood in silence, listening hard. Somewhere, Segunda heard a baby crying. A dog barked twice, then its voice faded into the muffled roaring of the traffic.

Louisa's nostrils wrinkled as she glanced around the room. 'How can anyone live like this?' she whispered.

The apartment smelled badly of stale sweat and even staler whisky. The floor was uncarpeted, and the solitary sofa was torn and threadbare, its fabric covered with grease-stains. In the kitchen, they found the sink stacked with dirty dishes, and cockroaches littering the wooden bench. A half-eaten piece of bread lay on the floor alongside a glass of spilled milk, its texture yellow and congealed.

Hannah himself lay sprawled fully-clothed on the filthy bed, snoring unevenly. Empty bottles littered the floor and the air was filled with whisky fumes.

Segunda chuckled. 'Not exactly Cary Grant,' he muttered.

'Wake him up,' Louisa said.

'Unless I'm sadly mistaken, this man is in an alcoholic stupor.'

Segunda rolled Billy on to his back and slapped his face sharply. Billy snored on peacefully.

'It'll be hours before he comes to,' Segunda grunted, running his fingers through Billy's pockets.

He took out the contents, laying them along the top of the battered sideboard. He found a soiled handkerchief, a coil of fuse wire bound with white thread, an old bus ticket, a crumpled packet of cigarettes, an advertisement torn from a newspaper offering a new type of hair restorer, and three tattered envelopes.

'Anything interesting?' Louisa asked.

The first two envelopes contained final notices on unpaid bills. The third carried a rough pencil drawing. There was no letter, only the sketch itself, clumsy and amateurish. Segunda frowned as he studied it in the pale light from the dusty window.

'Looks like the map of a coastline,' he muttered.

Louisa peered over his shoulder, narrowing her eyes.

'Recognise it?' Segunda asked.

'Could be anywhere. There aren't any place-names.'

'There's one. Sheilington. Mean anything?'

Louisa sucked in her breath. 'It's a little village in the Highlands. I drove through it once on a touring holiday.'

'I have a feeling this could be the destination that Argentine motor launch was making for.'

Louisa's eyes glittered with excitement. 'I'll get the local boys to pick up Hannah and keep him on ice until he sobers up. Then we'll call the Sheilington police. Maybe they'll know something.'

It took them more than twenty minutes to find a booth which hadn't been vandalised, and Segunda waited outside while Louisa used the telephone. He stamped around in the icy chill, his hands thrust deep in his overcoat pockets. The streets looked grim and unfriendly, imbued with a kind of uniform drabness, as if the squalor had drained colour and perspective alike.

When Louisa came out, her face looked troubled.

'What's wrong?' Segunda asked.

'I can't get through. The entire north-west coast of Scotland has been hit by a blizzard. It's brought the cables down.'

'Did you call Palmer?'

'I tried both his office and his home address. Apparently, he's half-way between Oxford and Birmingham, returning from some damned meeting or other. They're not expecting him back until after eight-thirty. We'll have to use the car.'

'The car?' Segunda echoed. 'Where are we going?'

'Where do you think?' Louisa said. 'North, of course.'

CHAPTER ELEVEN

Alex stood in the doorway and watched the others loading the equipment into the rear of Mike's van. The snow had worsened with the first hours of darkness, and with the snow had come the wind, picking its way along the valley like a stampeding army. It seemed to swell as it thundered towards them, growing louder, stronger, every minute.

Alex shivered. Two more minutes and they would be on their way. It was all over, the waiting, the planning, the agonising. Time to show he still had it, he thought – some semblance of responsiveness, some modicum of perception. God knew, he'd responded all right the night Collis had attacked Julie. Damn near lost his head. He'd wanted to kill Collis, pound him into the ground in a fit of frenzied fury. He'd thought himself beyond that, beyond emotion of any kind, but the sight of Collis with the girl had brought alive his senses in the rudest way imaginable, and now the prospect of the ordeal ahead made his stomach tense, his wrists turn icy.

He watched Mike fixing snow-chains to the vehicle tyres to give them extra purchase, feeling a tremor of uneasiness as the young Scotsman tugged the metal links into place. Something had happened to Mike since their confrontation in the toolshed. He was a different man, almost unrecognisable. He looked furtive, riddled with guilt. It had to be the girl, Alex reflected, Julie. Somehow she'd got to him, pricked his conscience, shaken his resolution; the signs were inescapable – Mike MacNally had had a change of heart.

Alex frowned. He could be mistaken, he thought. It was

easy to misjudge people, easy to read things into the simplest, most innocent responses. Mike was nervous, and nervous people acted strangely. He'd been all right during their attack on the naval base. Had done his bit — reluctantly, it was true, but he'd followed his instructions to the letter. Still, there was too much at stake to risk jeopardising their lives on the strength of some dubious ill-begotten loyalty. If, as Alex suspected, Mike was beginning to regret his involvement, then clearly he had to be watched.

Collis came strolling across the yard, his face coated with snowflakes. Alex could see the livid bruises from their fight discolouring his cheeks and jaw, but there was no resentment in Collis's smile. It was as if their bizarre little encounter had never even happened. Alex felt glad about that. He liked Collis in some curious perverse sort of way. Collis was headstrong and rebellious, but a man couldn't ask for a finer ally when things got tricky.

'What about the girl?' Collis asked.

'We're taking her along.'

'She'll only get in the way,' Collis said.

'Well, we can't leave her here.'

'Why not? Mike can look after her.'

'I don't trust Mike any more. I think she's been getting at him.'

Collis frowned as he peered at Alex through the eddying snow flurries.

'Having second thoughts, is he?'

'Maybe I'm wrong, but I'm not risking it. Out there in the snow, there's damn all he can do. Here, who knows, he might get an irrepressible urge to pour out his heart to the local constabulary.'

Luke came up, ducking his head beneath his anorak hood. 'Everything's ready,' he announced.

Alex felt a strange reluctance to proceed, as if once they

left the sanctuary of the hotel, they would be inextricably committed.

'Alex?' Luke said, his eyes dark and serious.

'Yes?'

'When this is over, I'm not coming back.'

Alex frowned. 'What the hell're you talking about?'

'I want you and Collis to leave without me. I've made up my mind. I'm staying here.'

'Have you lost your bloody wits?' Alex snapped.

'It's my decision, Alex.'

'What kind of decision is that? When the mines go off, they'll grab every stranger in sight.'

'I'll take my chances,' Luke said quietly.

Alex looked at the sky, grinding his teeth in a spasm of helplessness.

'It's the girl, isn't it? Deborah Robben?'

Luke nodded. 'I want her, Alex.'

'You fool. How d'you think she'll feel about you after she finds out what you've done?'

Luke's face was hard and set. 'She's the one good thing in my life,' he said stubbornly. 'I'll set your mines, I'll help you sink that submarine, but after it's over, you go home without me.'

Nothing would shake him, Alex could tell. He sighed as they stumbled across the forecourt and clambered in the vehicle's rear. As if Mike wasn't enough, he now had Luke to worry about as well. Biology had a lot to answer for.

Mike started the engine, and turned towards Barracula Sound, driving at a snail's pace through the thickening blanket of snow. It was cold sitting on the metal floor, and the air steamed heavily with their breathing. Crouched in the rear, they listened to the storm's awesome clamour thundering around them.

Mike drove like a man demented. He could scarcely see through the blinding curtain of white. They had travelled only a mile before his windshield wipers folded under the strain and he was forced to lean through the open window and run his hand down the front of the glass. Despite the tyre chains, they were slithering all over the road, and Alex could feel the wind buffeting their tiny vehicle, threatening to turn it over altogether.

'How far to the Sound?' he demanded.

'Another quarter of a mile.'

'Stop the van. We'll walk the rest.'

Mike grunted, bringing the vehicle to a halt. Opening the doors, they began to drag out the equipment, wincing under the skin-stinging snow flurries tearing at them from all directions. Alex could see Julie crouched against the van rear, shoulders hunched, face hidden beneath the dark outline of her anorak hood. Already, she was coated with snow from head to foot. They looked comical, all of them, like mystic creatures from some mythical universe. Only the wind seemed real, driving against them in a constant mind-numbing spray.

Dazed, they shouldered the haversacks and set off into the storm, Alex leading, picking his way along the white-blanketed roadway. Hard to believe the snow could lie so fast, he thought. At this rate, there'd be several feet before morning. Worriedly, he considered their escape. If the roads were blocked, how in God's name would they get to Glasgow? That was Mike's department, supervising the retreat. He hoped to God he was wrong about Mike. Without him, they had no clear way of getting out of here.

The wind changed, gathering itself for another onslaught, the white veil lifting in all directions, whipping into a whirling living funnel. The entire world was blotted out; they couldn't breathe, couldn't feel, almost couldn't think. It was as if the storm had obliterated their last tentative link with normality.

Alex spotted a thickening in the mist, the wire fence

bordering the slopes above Barracula Sound. He waved to the others and turned towards it, clambering over the thickly-encrusted strands.

They picked their way down the slippery hillslope, negotiating heavy drifts and glistening ice-troughs. They didn't talk – it was too hard to talk in the deafening tumult – they didn't even bother to check the compass-bearing, using instead the slope's decline to guide them to the water's edge.

Something glimmered in the flurries ahead and Alex shielded his eyes with his hands. The Sound. He shuffled forward, finding a little amphitheatre of rocks which offered a blessed respite from the wind, and flopped inside, gasping. The others tumbled in, ludicrous creatures furred with white, their tortured faces caked with snow. Alex wiped his eyes with his gloved fingers and studied the little group speculatively.

'You stay here,' he said to Mike. 'The rocks'll give you a bit of shelter. Keep an eye on your sister.'

Mike nodded, sullen and scowling. Alex studied him worriedly, then he grunted at the others, and without a word they began to strip off their clothes and climb into their diving-suits.

Leading Seaman Harry Woolcott left his bunk in the junior ratings' quarters and climbed the metal companionway which led to the *Conqueror*'s Sonar Room. It was almost 1900 hours, time for his duty shift. He could feel the vessel rolling and pitching alarmingly, and knew it would only be a matter of time before the captain gave the order to head for the open sea. Here, they were forced to take the full fury of the Atlantic gales, but once out of shallow water, they could submerge and stay safely cocooned until the storms were over. That was the marvellous thing about subs, he told himself; when things got too unpleasant for comfort, you simply left the surface world behind.

Charlie Partridge was sitting in front of the sonar computer, his blunt head encased by heavy earphones. He grinned when he saw Woolcott approaching.

'What's up?' he asked. 'You're not due for another six minutes yet.'

'I couldn't sleep the way the old tub's bouncing around,' Woolcott told him. 'Anything happening?'

'Not a sausage.'

Woolcott picked up the spare headset and pulled it over his head. He could hear the refracted sound-rays which signified the distribution of the various wrecks littering the seabed.

'Notice anything different?' Partridge wondered.

Woolcott frowned, concentrating. Then he understood. 'The Pepperpot's gone.'

The Pepperpot was the nickname they'd given to an old paddleboat on the rocks directly beneath them. For days, it had been sending back signatures which were curiously distinctive.

'Right,' Partridge said. 'It must've broken up in the heavy swell.'

'We'll be breaking up ourselves if we hang around much longer,' Woolcott grumbled. 'It's like being inside a bloody washing-machine.'

Partridge chuckled. 'Well, if it happens, don't forget to wake me. I hate disagreeable wet dreams.'

Woolcott eased into the empty spring-seat as Partridge headed below.

The water seemed like a wall of sand. Swimming easily below the surface, Alex felt the current jostling him and tried hard to relax. The storm, which had been their ally on the long furtive approach, had now turned into their enemy, whipping up silt from the ocean bed and obscuring the route ahead. The heavy ear-protectors hugged his skull in a numbing grip.

Strange how silent everything seemed. The stillness was extraordinary. No wind, no thunder, no trees rustling, branches crackling. Hard to believe the deafening clamour taking place above.

Through the skin of his neoprene suit, he felt the coldness intruding. It was not debilitating. The chill helped to keep him alert. He reached up, pinching his nostrils, blowing hard to ease the pressure on his eardrums. He breathed shallowly, taking the oxygen in through his mouth, careful not to fill his lungs to capacity in case a sudden need to reach the surface led to pulmonary barotrauma.

Dangling from his weight-belt in a nylon webbing-harness were the two pillbox-shaped limpet mines. Once they had been fixed in position, the nitrogen bubbles in his neoprene suit would automatically carry him to the surface, but Alex was counting on the storm preventing any surveillance from the submarine's deck or bridge.

In his hands, he carried a sophisticated heat-seeking underwater direction device; without it, he knew their hopes of locating the *Conqueror* would be remote indeed. As it was, he was experiencing supreme difficulty in judging their actual depth. He glanced down at the luminous dials, and squinted into the gloom ahead. There was nothing real down here, no sense of perspective, distance, solidity. It was an alien world, strange and terrifying.

He moved rhythmically, letting the fins do the work, trying to counter the buffeting motion of the waves above. Odd, how dead the ocean seemed; no fish, no life, nothing — only that suffocating blanket of grey. If danger lurked, there would be no warning. No chance for flight. Easy to panic if you had the mind for it.

He felt a tremor of alarm as dimly, through the darkness, he glimpsed a monstrous shape rearing above their heads; for one crazy moment, he imagined they had stumbled into the lair of some grotesque sea creature, then he realised, with a wave of relief, it was the underbelly of the *Conqueror* floating innocently on the surface.

Rolling backward in a well-executed tight-puck technique, he gestured to the others, pointing upward. They nodded to show that they understood, then deftly, expertly, they flapped their fins and soared towards the motionless submarine.

Sitting in the *Conqueror*'s Sonar Room, Harry Woolcott felt bored. He didn't mind the long hours when something interesting was happening; picking up the transducer's readings, translating, identifying, could be a fascinating occupation, but tonight the sound-rays were depressingly neutral.

Woolcott reached for a battered paperback left by Charlie Partridge and skimmed through its ragged pages, whiling away the time. Another week and they would be out of here. He was pleased about that, in a way. He liked Sheilington, liked the people, but there was little to do except wander down to the local pub. Hardly a sophisticated place either. Not like the bars he was used to. Sawdust on the floor, smoke-stained ceiling. A drinking-house, that was all. And that storm out there. Harry Woolcott had never known anything like it. High seas, he'd seen before, but blizzards which blotted out the entire universe belonged to Scotland alone.

In six weeks, they'd be Australia-bound. Woolcott's spirits brightened at the thought. Something to look forward to. No blizzards in Australia. Only sunshine and surf, a pleasant pick-me-up after the last few dispiriting days.

A humming in his ears caught Woolcott's attention. He frowned, putting down the paperback. He could hear the noise generating through his skull, faint but distinctive, the waves changing in velocity as refraction began to occur. For a long moment he sat in silence, listening hard, then he called the duty officer.

Lieutenant Meggers was a slim man with heavily-greased hair.

'There's something funny on the transducer, sir,' Woolcott told him.

Meggers took the headset and pressed it against his ear. 'Sounds perfectly normal to me.'

'Those signatures, they shouldn't be happening.'

'Don't be silly, Woolcott, they're infinitesimal.'

'I know. But they're very close and moving closer.'

'It's just the old Pepperpot again.'

'The Pepperpot's broken up in the storm. We haven't picked up a sounding all night.'

'You're sure?'

'Ask Partridge,' Woolcott said.

Lieutenant Meggers frowned. He rubbed his nose thoughtfully with his thumb, then leaning forward, began to listen in earnest.

Cautiously, Alex felt his way along the metal hull. Though he had studied its replica for days on end, it was impossible to discern through the gloominess of the water which part of the submarine he was swimming under.

Protruding from the nearmost flank, he dimly spotted a flat oblong object vanishing into the dark. That would be the forward plane. He was too far in front.

Turning, he paddled back the way he had come, feeling along the *Conqueror*'s belly with his fingers. How different it seemed to the plexiglass model they had practised under. Even its texture felt different. There was simply no way of defining the correct target areas. He would have to take a chance and hope for the best.

The heavy ear-protectors seemed to constrict his buoyancy and vision. A waste of time, they'd been, from the start. Clearly the *Conqueror* was operating on 'passive' not 'active' sonar. The bulky headset was hampering him unnecessarily.

On an impulse, he tore it off and dropped it into the blackness below. Reaching down, he grunted softly as he eased the first of the limpet mines out of its nylon webbing. It was already primed, its electronic solid-state timer pre-set at four hours. He activated the magnet and pushed it towards the hull. The mine made a hollow clanging sound as it attached itself to the metal outer structure.

Alex moved to the other side of the vessel. He calculated the distance from his first emplacement, then taking out the second mine, carefully fixed it in position. Mission accomplished, he thought grimly, peering round for the others. A flurry of movement told him Collis was somewhere to his right, setting his charges alongside the diesel generators. Luke was further aft again, his target the emergency water tank and the torsion meter.

Alex flipped his fins, feeling the buoyancy take him now that the mines had gone. He trod water, struggling to hold his depth and position as silently, tensely, he waited for the others.

Commander Carnahan, the *Conqueror*'s captain, was sitting in the cubbyhole which served as his private cabin when Lieutenant Meggers entered.

'I'm sorry to trouble you, sir,' Meggers said, 'but we've picked up something on the sonar.'

'What is it, David?'

'Sounds like the old Pepperpot, sir. In fact, I thought it *was* the Pepperpot at first, but Seaman Woolcott seems to think it's something out of the ordinary. Could be a piece of wreckage caught in the swell, of course, but it bears investigating, I think.'

The captain sighed and rose to his feet. 'Better show me,' he said.

In the Sonar Room, the two officers joined Woolcott in front of the computer unit, and the captain listened to the headset in silence for a moment, his face dark and thoughtful. Then he said: 'Nothing irregular that I can see. What makes you think something's wrong, Woolcott?'

'The way the signature's moving, sir. It's carrying an integrated velocity vagary.'

'Could be bottom-bounce.'

'Too smooth and even,' Woolcott insisted.

'A piece of metal, possibly, caught in some seaweed?'

Woolcott shook his head. 'It's the first time anything's come through the transducer all evening, apart from the wrecks already charted. It's got to be alive, sir. And it's drifting along our hull.'

The captain grunted. He wasn't a fearful man, but he disliked taking unnecessary risks. A nuclear submarine was an awesome responsibility; there were too many people interested in its structure and design.

Swiftly, he made a decision. 'Let's switch to active mode,' he ordered.

The boom echoed through Alex's skull, vibrating wildly. He could scarcely believe the intensity of the sound. It was like a gong going off in an amplifying chamber, the reverberations rippling through his body in a series of violent shocks. His skin crawled. Oh God, he thought, they've turned on their active sonar gear.

In a daze, he pressed his palms against his ears, struggling to muffle the throbbing persistent clamour. Dogged and implacable, it echoed inside his head. He clenched his teeth, filled with a strange sense of helplessness. What an idiot he'd been, letting his headgear go. His brain was blurring, floating, drifting. I'm passing out, he thought.

He tilted backwards, bobbing against the metal hull. He felt as if his spirit had somehow come apart from his body and was drifting eerily among the wave currents. He saw Collis swimming towards him, eyes glittering behind his shiny face-mask. Collis hooked an arm around Alex's shoulder and began to drag him upwards. Helplessly, lifelessly, Alex let himself trail through the eddying water.

Commander Carnahan studied the sonar screens in silence. A configuration of signatures blinked up at him, their green lights winking eerily.

'Nothing extraordinary there,' he declared at last.

'Could be something too small to register,' Lieutenant Meggers suggested.

'Like what, exactly?'

Meggers shrugged. 'Visitors.'

Carnahan knew what Meggers meant. A nuclear submarine was a constant attraction for Soviet spy patrols. Though it seemed beyond credibility that an underwater reconnaissance unit would choose tonight of all nights, he couldn't ignore the fact that divers wouldn't register on the active sonar transducer.

'You're right, David,' he decided at last. 'It's probably perfectly innocent, but we ought to check it out. Sound the alarm bell and call the bosun, will you? I want some armed men on the deck immediately.'

Alex heard the alarm as Collis dragged him towards the shoreline. No longer weighed down by the limpet mines, they had broken surface and were swimming in unison against the swirling tide. Puzzled by the clamour, Alex shook his head to clear it, and rolling over, struggled to discern the submarine's outline through the flakes caking his face-mask. He felt better now that they'd left the sonar echoes behind. His brain was returning to normal, and his eardrums, though they still rang painfully with the refracted resonance, were beginning at last to settle down. He spotted men running along the metal deck, heard the clanging of their feet even above the screeching of the bell. Voices echoed on the storm-tossed air. A searchlight beam cut across the boiling water, eerily illuminating the feathery spray crests.

Alex gasped as the beam came streaking towards them, bobbing and dipping over the waves. He saw the figures bunching together on the metal hull, caught a flicker of movement, barely discernible, a muffled exlamation of protest, and then, to Alex's horror, the night erupted with the menacing stutter of machine-gun fire. Jesus God, he thought wildly, they're shooting back there.

He saw spurts of flame flashing rhythmically on the submarine's deck and breaking free of Collis, tried desperately to kick himself under, but the buoyancy of his wet-suit stubbornly kept him afloat. Bullets ripped into his oxygen cylinder, exploding it with a thunderous roar. Alex spun, fighting for balance. Righting himself, he tore the mouthpiece from his lips and sucked hard, filling his lungs with air. Then, battling to see through the mountainous foam, he kicked wildly for the shoreline.

Standing on the bridge, Commander Carnahan squinted down at the cluster of snow-caked figures struggling for balance on the deck below.

'Who fired those shots?' he bellowed.

'I did, sir,' a man admitted. 'I thought I saw something.'

'Who gave you permission to fire? Bosun, take that man's name.'

The man looked unhappy. 'It was something alive, sir. And moving.'

Commander Carnahan peered into the gloom. There was nothing to see but the frenzied ocean and the swirling spirals of snow.

'It looked like heads, sir,' the man maintained stubbornly. 'Three small heads, black and shiny.'

'Seals, you idiot.'

The man swallowed, shivering in the chill. He glanced

uncertainly at his companions, a look of rueful embarrassment settling over his features.

'Aye, sir,' he admitted. 'Now that you mention it, they did look a wee bit like seals.'

The captain glanced at Lieutenant Meggers, crinkling his eyes against the storm. Snow clung to Meggers' hair and cheeks, and his nose was a cherubic red.

'Get the men below,' the captain commanded. 'I'm taking her out to the open sea.'

'Submerged, sir?'

The captain nodded. 'We've had enough of this bloody hammering. Let's clear the Sound and sit it out till the storms subside.'

Marine Sergeant Kneeland heard the shots as he was opening his second can of soup. He had taken refuge in a little forestry hut, believing the slopes safe with the advent of the blizzards; it had seemed senseless to continue their patrol floundering about in the knee-deep snow, and the hut had offered a shelter of sorts, a primitive haven in which to while away the long hours of darkness. Now he paused, the cutter still in his hand, cocking his head to one side as he listened intently. His men stared at him, their faces tense and alert.

'A bloody machine-gun,' somebody whispered.

Sergeant Kneeland felt his stomach contract. 'The sub. It's got to be.'

'Provos?' a man suggested.

'Let's find out,' Kneeland snapped crisply. 'Forget the chow. Outside, the lot of you.'

Grabbing their weapons, the men surged through the doorway into the swirling snow.

Alex saw the beach looming out of the darkness. Rocky outcrops reared in the night, taking on shape, substance, definition. He spotted a movement in the shadow clusters ahead, and saw Julie slithering down to meet them, her face bright with panic and alarm.

'Mike's been hit,' she cried hysterically.

Alex cursed under his breath. Stumbling through the shallows, he scrambled up the slippery snowbank to where Julie was standing, trembling with emotion, tears streaming down her cheeks.

'Where is he?' Alex snapped.

'In the rocks.'

Mike was lying where they had left him, his eyes dim with pain. Blood drenched the front of his anorak, forming a crimson starburst against the drifting snow. Alex tore at the clothing, exposing the milky flesh. He could see the hole where the bullet had entered, the skin blue-rimmed and pulsing out blood.

'Get me a cloth,' Alex snapped.

Without a word, Julie took off her scarf and passed it across. Alex folded it into a makeshift pressure-pad and jammed it against the open wound. He nodded at Julie.

'Hold it in place and don't let it slip. We've got to stop that blood flowing. I'll get some adhesive tape from the first-aid kit and we'll strap it against his chest.'

'What about the bullet?' Julie whimpered.

'We'll worry about that later. Right now, we've got to get him under cover.'

Mike was shaking like a man demented. They could hear his teeth chattering even above the roaring of the storm. He looks bad, Alex thought. If it's clipped his lung, he'll be coughing up blood. They'd managed so splendidly, too, despite his momentary disablement. A good professional job, mines set, timers activated. And now this. It was lousy luck.

Deftly, Luke and Collis helped him with the dressing, moisture beads clinging to their cheeks and throats.

'His stomach's swelling,' Julie cried with alarm.

It was true. Mike's torso was ballooning upward as if, by

233

some grotesque circumstance, he had suddenly become pregnant.

'It's the shock wave,' Alex explained. 'The reaction from the bullet is pushing his intestines out. They'll settle back, if we can get him into shelter.'

Some hope, he thought gloomily. A man in this condition shouldn't be moved. A sudden jerk, an unexpected stumble, and who knew what damage might result? He felt sorry about Mike. He liked Mike, despite the Scotsman's changeability. He didn't want to see him die.

Hastily, Alex, Luke and Collis stripped off their wet-suits and pulled on heavy arctic gear. Alex felt a wave of relief as the clothing began to generate heat through his body. He took the diver's clasp-knive and strapped it to his webbing-belt. Then they re-packed the haversacks and picked up the sub-machine-guns.

'What about the diving gear?' Luke asked.

'Might as well junk it. We've enough to carry, as it is.'

'They'll find it in the morning.'

'Who cares? By then, with luck, we'll be far away.'

Easing the machine-gun across his shoulder, Alex knelt at Mike's side.

'Mike, can you hear me? We've got to get you back to the hotel. Think you can walk?'

'We shouldn't move him,' Julie protested.

'Leave him here and he'll die of exposure. The hotel's his only hope.'

Julie's face was white with anguish, and watching her, Alex felt his senses melt. There was no point in pretending. Her brother was in a bad way.

He nodded to Collis and together they hooked their hands under Mike's armpits, hauling him to his feet. For a moment, he stood balanced between them, his knees buckling, then with a monumental effort of will, he managed to find his balance.

'We're heading out into the wind now,' Alex said. 'Just keep moving your legs.'

They set off up the treacherous hillside, battling against the gale. Mike's weight seemed to wear Alex and Collis down. Tucking his chin against his chest, Alex tried not to think, tried to withdraw into the inner recesses of his brain as if he could, by a conscious effort of will, blot out the appalling world in which he found himself. Sliding, slithering, stumbling, they struggled doggedly upwards, Mike moaning in an incessant symphony of misery and pain.

Something moved in the darkness ahead, and Alex blinked. He saw figures filtering through the trees, taking on shape and definition. The marine patrol, he thought wildly. Damn fool that he was, he had forgotten their existence in the panic of the last few minutes.

Mike's weight seemed to intensify against his shoulder, then Alex realised to his horror that Collis was swinging his machine-gun in a rapid arc, bringing it into alignment. A paralysing chill froze Alex's spine.

'No,' he yelled.

But Collis was beyond listening. The night exploded in a deafening roar as the gun went off, reverberating backwards and forwards across the empty hillside. Crimson flashes turned the darkness into brilliant day. Tree trunks splintered. The din was deafening.

Collis threw himself into the snow, mouthing obscenties as he fired compulsively at the troops ahead. Alex saw them diving for cover, scattering into the dark curtain of woods.

Collis paused to rip out the magazine, jamming in a fresh one. 'Get him out of here,' he bellowed, nodding at Mike. 'I'll keep them busy until you're clear.'

Bloody idiot, Alex thought, but he didn't wait to argue. Seizing Mike's arm, he scrambled through the covering of trees, Luke supporting from the opposite side, Julie scurrying along at the rear. Branches brushed against his face, tearing loose his anorak hood. Breath rasping, he ploughed through the snow, sliding, slithering, fighting for balance.

Staccato flashes lit the sky as the gunfire started up again, rattling above the storm. Thank God for Collis. The horror of the moment had stunned Alex's brain. He'd been unable to think back there, unable to respond. Not Collis though. Collis always responded. Oh, he was a splendid man all right, wild as a March hare, but an invaluable asset when things went wrong. Collis was the ultimate survivor.

Panting, Alex followed the line of the hill where it offered the least resistance, scarcely conscious of where he was going any more.

'Stop,' Julie exclaimed hoarsely. 'For God's sake, stop. D'ye want to kill him?'

Alex floundered to a halt. Delicately, he eased Mike into the snow and flopped alongside his supine body.

Julie knelt at Mike's side, examining him anxiously, her eyes glistening in the freezing darkness.

'How's he doing?' Alex croaked.

'Still shivering. He seems to be in some kind of fever.'

Alex didn't answer. Exhaustion had taken away his capacity for speech. He lay quite still, chest rising and falling rapidly. Collis found them several minutes later. Alex spotted him stumbling through the trees, his light anorak almost indiscernible against the heavy blanket of snow. Collis was sweating, and there was a hint of excitement in his wild blue eyes.

Alex rose to meet him. 'I suppose you think you're a bloody hero?'

Drawing to a halt, Collis considered for a moment, panting hard. 'Yes,' he admitted modestly.

'Well, you're not. You damn near got us bloody killed back there.'

'We dodged them, didn't we?'

'For Christ's sake, all they've got to do is follow our tracks.'

'The way this snow is drifting, they'll be bloody lucky. Took me all my time to find your trail myself. Beside, they'll be careful now. They're not sure how many of us there are up here. That little broadside bought us precious time.'

Alex stared at him wryly. Collis was right again, as usual.

'Christ knows what we'd do without you, Collis,' he said, grinning through the darkness. 'Come and give us a hand with Mike. He's burning like a volcano, but if we can get him under cover, we might just save his life.'

CHAPTER TWELVE

The road led nowhere. It was impossible to see in front of the windshield, for the headlamps floundered against the blinding curtains of snow. Segunda tried the accelerator, pressing his foot down gently, delicately, feeling the engine roar, the wheels spin, the vehicle shudder. There was no surge forward. On both sides of the car, the drifts seemed almost level with the windows.

'We're stuck,' he announced.

Louisa swore softly under her breath. 'Sheilington's only five miles ahead.'

'Might as well be five hundred in this muck.'

'What are we going to do?'

'We'll have to abandon the car. There's a house about fifty yards back. I saw it as we passed.'

'We'll be hammered to death out there.'

'Better than freezing. Are you game for a try?'

She nodded.

'Then let's go.'

Segunda gasped as he felt the unbelievable power of the storm. He wrapped his arm around Louisa's shoulders, struggling through the knee-deep drifts. The wind came at them from all directions, there was simply no escape from it. It pounded their cheeks, drove into their necks, worked its way inside their clothing.

Segunda saw a shape looming out of the billowing shroud and shielding his eyes, dimly discerned a noticeboard which read:

SALACH TOWERS HOTEL
Open Easter to October
B & B, High Teas
FAMILY GROUPS WELCOME

'This way,' he croaked, and guiding Louisa through the drive, battled his way to the porch.

The front door was locked and barred. Stumbling about in the snow, Segunda found a rock and smashed one of the ground-floor windows. The catch jimmied easily, and he clambered inside, dragging Louisa behind him. They collapsed to the floor, their bodies grotesque bundles of feathery white. Segunda shook his head, wiping the snow from his lips and eyes. After the clamour of the storm, the silence of the empty hotel seemed strangely painful to listen to. What a night, he thought; it was like being in the middle of Antarctica. Segunda instinctively disliked cold and snow. He was a man of the sun, the warm pastures of the open *pampa*. Cold emasculated and demoralised him.

The room lay in darkness, its furniture concealed under heavy grey dust-covers. There was a musty smell to the air, an odour of mothballs and disinfectant. Segunda shivered as the draught from the window sliced through his drenched clothing.

'Come on,' he grunted. 'Let's find a warmer spot.'

They wandered through the darkened building, checking each of the downstairs rooms in turn. The electricity had been switched off, but Segunda found a box of candles and lit one carefully. He moved into the residents' lounge, gazing round with an appraising eye.

'This'll do,' he declared.

'For what?' Louisa demanded.

'A base.'

He grinned at her happily. She'd unbent a little, since their early hours in Glasgow, but there was still that maddening

239

defensive barrier. Segunda could sense it like a physical blockade. God knew, he hadn't expected to see Louisa again; he'd thought it over, that part of his life, forgotten for good. But now, finding himself thrust into her company, old feelings were being resurrected.

Delicately, he fixed the candle on the mantelpiece, and picking up a chair, began to smash it against the hearth. Louisa stared at him in amazement.

'What, in God's name, are you playing at?'

'Building a fire. We'll need heat if we're to survive the night.'

Louisa smiled wryly as she watched him shattering the furniture. There was a pleasing conciseness in the way Segunda moved, she thought. He'd always had grace and style. When he walked into a room, you noticed him immediately. He possessed a charisma that was impossible to ignore.

Louisa wandered into the reception hall and idly tried the switchboard. To her surprise, a dialling tone purred in her ear as she pressed one of the plastic buttons.

'The phone's working,' she called excitedly. 'The entire area can't be out of action.'

Squinting in the semi-darkness, she called Palmer's London home. The line rang several times before he answered. His voice sounded weary and resigned. 'Who is this?' he demanded.

'It's Louisa,' she said.

'Louisa, where on earth are you?'

'Stuck in a blizzard in the Scottish Highlands.'

'You're joking.'

'I never joke, Charles, you know that.'

'You were supposed to contact me this afternoon.'

'I tried. You're never home, Charles.'

'I had a meeting,' he sighed. 'Where are you now?'

'At a place called the Salach Towers Hotel, about five miles south of Sheilington. It's closed for the winter, but we

240

let ourselves in. It was either that or freeze to death in the car outside.'

'How's our gaucho friend shaping up?'

'Oh, he's a regular little boy scout. At the moment, he's smashing up furniture to build us a fire.'

She heard Palmer mutter under his breath, and smiled.

'Put it down to expenses, Charles. You're a master at that.'

'What happened at Glasgow airport?' Palmer asked.

Quickly, Louisa outlined the events of the past few hours. She told him about Billy Hannah, and about the envelope and sketch map they had found in his jacket pocket. She told him about the long drive north and the steadily deteriorating weather. 'We're almost at Sheilington now, but the roads are completely blocked. You've no idea what it's like up here.'

'I heard the Met. reports on the radio,' Palmer said. 'There's a freak blizzard sweeping down from the Arctic, hitting the entire Scottish coast.'

'The thing is, Charles, do you know of anything politically or militarily sensitive in this area, something which might offer a possible target for a sabotage attack?'

'Seems unlikely. Plenty of military installations in Scotland, of course, but around Sheilington there's nothing but heather and grouse. Give me a chance to scout around, and I'll call you back. What's the name of that hotel again?'

Louisa told him.

'And the phone number?'

Bending forward, she narrowed her eyes as she read the figures haltingly from the telephone dial.

'I'll make a few calls, and get back to you as soon as I can.'

Louisa said goodbye, hung up the phone, and lighting a fresh candle, wandered into the residents' lounge. Segunda was kneeling in front of the fireplace. At his side lay a pile of splintered wood. Flames crackled cheerfully in the grate, and he smiled as he leaned forward to warm his frozen hands, steam rising in spirals from his saturated clothing. She could see the dark hairs on his wrists, disappearing beneath the laundered shirt-cuffs, and something started inside her, an intense and impossible-to-ignore physical excitement. Be careful, her mind warned. He'd always had that capacity, that animal presence, that inherent earthiness. Once, the mere thought of his touch had been enough to send her senses reeling. Stop acting like a bitch on heat, she thought, as a flush spread through her body.

'Palmer sends his love,' she said in a jaunty tone.

'He's all heart, that Palmer.'

She sighed as she felt the fire's radiance penetrating her sodden dress. 'Thank God for some warmth,' she breathed.

'Better get that off,' he told her. 'You'll catch a chill.'

He rose to his feet, moving towards the door.

'Where are you going?' she asked.

'Find some food. If we're not going to freeze to death, I'd rather not starve either.'

The kitchen, Segunda discovered, was disappointingly bare. The massive fridge had been switched off at the mains, and the proprietors had clearly cleaned out the remains of their provisions, using them up during the last days of the summer season.

In a small pantry, Segunda found two tins of beef casserole and a tin of skinned tomatoes. Better than nothing, he thought, tucking them under his arm and heading back.

As he stepped through the door, he felt the breath catch suddenly in his throat. Stripped to her underwear, Louisa was drying her dress in front of the fire. He could see her body outlined from the waist down. There was no constraint in Segunda's character. Throughout his life, he had followed his emotions with an almost psychotic intensity. He'd loved this woman. He'd wanted her more than anything in the world. Now the years rolled away, and in one breathless moment he was back in Paris the first time they'd met. The longing, the yearning, the pain came back in a blinding rush.

She turned to face him, her eyes bright with alarm. He could see the nipples of her breasts through the silk net of her bra. Slowly she shook her head.

'No,' she whispered. 'I told you, it's over.'

But Segunda scarcely listened. Dropping the food cans, he walked towards her. She stood transfixed, her eyes locked on his. He seized her in his arms, kissing her wildly. For a moment, her body felt stiff, resistant, unyielding. Then her lips softened, her arms slid around his neck and she crushed herself against him.

'Damn you,' she hissed. 'Don't you listen to a word I say?'

They sank to the floor and Segunda peeled off the rest of her sodden clothing. He did it gently, delicately, like a man faced with something infinitely fragile and precious. Their bodies melted together and his control faltered as he entered her. He heard harsh mewing sounds issuing from her throat as, furiously impaled, she writhed beneath him. In a tangle of limbs and crumpled underclothing, they performed the timeless ritual of love.

Louisa lay in the dark, her head against Segunda's chest. The candle had burnt itself out, but the fire cast a flickering pool of light across the deserted hotel lounge.

Segunda's eyes were closed and she could feel his stomach rising and falling rhythmically. He was sleeping. A strange man, she thought, not like others in his business. Frank, open and direct, there were no hang-ups with Segunda. No complexes. Only that strange disposition to laughter. Never had she known a man laugh so much. He found humour in everything, even the most worrying situations. She supposed that was what had attracted her in the beginning, that unquenchable merriment, that implicit belief that life was meant to be enjoyed. He'd seemed handsome and charming, and always there had been that strong, indefinable animal quality she'd found impossible to ignore.

She could still recall the first time he'd touched her, gentle, anxious not to push the pace; he had made love attentively and she'd been surprised. After all, she'd been no dewy-eyed virgin ready to lose her mind and soul in the pursuit of some idiotic amatory entanglement, but he had given her so much she could never put a name to. Afterwards, she'd tried to forget. She'd gone back and thrown herself into her work, but it hadn't been easy. The memory of the sunbrowned skin and reckless smile had remained like an old scar which stubbornly refused to heal. Now, like a fool, she'd opened up the wound again.

Louisa felt angry with herself. She'd made so many promises, so many resolutions, and she'd broken them all without even thinking. She had no illusions about Mártin Segunda. Charming, he might be, but she'd read his file and knew his background. Segunda was an animal – a psychopath, the experts said – as mercurial as a snake and twice as deadly. Ruthless and self-motivated, the normal standards of human behaviour had no place in his consciousness. Emotion was a game he played. He murdered compulsively, with neither sentiment nor remorse.

The sound of the telephone made Louisa jump. She gathered up her dress, wrapping it loosely around her; the material was still damp but felt warm from the fire's glow. She wandered out to the switchboard and picked up the receiver.

Palmer's voice came on the line, shrill and discordant.

'We've found the Argentine target,' he told her breathlessly.

'Yes?' Louisa murmured.

His voice rose in an uneven crescendo. 'They're going to sink the *Conqueror*,' he said.

*

It was raining in Knightsbridge as the Home Secretary left his club and walked towards the limousine waiting at the kerbside. Jenkins, the detective assigned to protect him, was standing with his collar raised about his ears, holding open the rear door respectfully. Traffic rolled by, tyres hissing on the asphalt.

The Home Secretary grimaced. He hated London in the winter. When he retired, he was determined to travel between Christmas and spring. Somewhere hot, where the sun shone and the surf sparkled. As a man grew older, such luxuries became important.

He was about to climb into the car when he spotted a figure waving to him from the opposite side of the street. He recognised Charles Palmer of the intelligence service. Palmer was standing by the door of a blue Mercedes, his white hair hidden beneath a sombre homburg.

The Home Secretary frowned. It was unlike Palmer to approach him in such an unorthodox manner, and at such a late hour too. As a rule, Palmer was meticulously precise in matters of procedure and protocol.

'Wait, just a moment,' the Home Secretary said to his detective.

He watched as Palmer came trotting across the gleaming roadway.

'Thank God I caught you,' Palmer said. 'I was afraid you might have left.'

'Have you seen the time, Palmer?' the Home Secretary asked, peering at his watch.

'I know it's late,' Palmer admitted. 'But this is a matter of the gravest urgency.'

He glanced at the club doorway. 'Can we talk inside?'

The Home Secretary pursed his lips, then nodded. 'I'll be back in a few minutes,' he said to his detective.

The two men strolled under the canopy and entered the club through the revolving doors. Leading the way along the thickly-carpeted corridor, the Home Secretary ushered Palmer into a private office.

'It's the chairman's,' he explained, 'but he lets me use it in emergencies. Besides, he's never in on Thursday evenings.'

He waved Palmer to a chair. 'Please sit down, Palmer.'

Palmer shook his head. 'I'm afraid there isn't time, Home Secretary. We're running against the clock.'

'Good God, man, it's unlike you to be so dramatic. You'd better tell me what this is all about.'

Quickly, and as graphically as he could, Palmer outlined the events of the past few days. He described the capture of the motor launch, Segunda's arrest, the raid on the naval base, Louisa's phone call from Scotland, and the *Conqueror*'s torpedo trials on Barracula Sound. When he had finished, the Home Secretary stared at him, frowning.

'You're sure about all this?'

'As sure as we can be,' Palmer said. 'It's guesswork, of course, but there are too many links to be pure coincidence.'

'Dammit, Palmer, this shouldn't belong to your department at all. It comes under the jurisdiction of the Directorate General.'

Palmer sighed. 'There isn't time to go through the necessary channels, sir. We've set up a special operations room at the Admiralty and they're radioing a warning to the *Conqueror* now. In the meantime, there are two detachments of the Royal Marine Mountain and Arctic Warfare Cadre training in the Mulloch Valley. That's less than eight miles from Sheilington itself. They're the finest mountain troops in the world, Home Secretary. I need your permission to put them into the field.'

The Home Secretary looked pale and drawn as he stretched out his hand.

'Pass me the telephone,' he ordered curtly.

*

Numb with cold, Alex and Luke stumbled into the thundering storm, Mike supported between them. Snow lashed at them solidly, driving into their eyes and mouths. On both sides of the narrow road, trees merged into a swirling sky.

'He'll never make it,' Julie cried.

Alex paused, gasping, tilting his head as he studied Mike's features. Mike's eyes were closed and his face looked strangely contourless, as if pain and exhaustion had caused the muscles to consolidate. Snow coated the deep hollows beneath his cheekbones. It was clear he could not last much longer.

'How far's the hotel?' Alex demanded.

'Another mile, at least.'

'Then you're right. We can't keep dragging him along like this.'

'It's your fault,' Julie accused hotly. 'If you hadn't come here, he wouldn't be in this condition.'

Alex sighed. He would get no sense out of Julie, that was painfully clear. She was too emotionally concerned with Mike's welfare even to consider logic or reason.

He narrowed his eyes against the gale. He could see lights gleaming dimly ahead.

'What's that?'

'The Robben farm. Joe and Barry.'

'We'll take him there,' Alex decided.

'Is that wise?' Collis grunted. 'We're in a big enough mess, as it is.'

'We've got no choice. If we don't get him under cover, he'll be dead in an hour.'

With Luke leading the way, they wrestled Mike down the road and across the open farmyard. Snow clawed at their cheeks, caking their eyes and nostrils. It furred the outline of a battered old tractor parked at the paddock entrance.

Luke hammered on the farmhouse door, and they stood

waiting, the storm hitting them in successive waves. A footstep creaked inside, and Barry appeared on the threshold, peering out at them incredulously. Without waiting to be invited, Alex and Collis stumbled past him, manhandling Mike into the blessed warmth.

In the kitchen, Deborah, gathering the supper dishes from the table, glanced up in surprise as the snow-caked intruders burst into the room. Joe was reading the daily paper. He rose to his feet, reaching for his walking stick as Alex and Collis gently eased Mike into one of the vacant chairs.

'What the hell's going on?' Joe demanded.

'We have an injured man here,' Alex told him brusquely. 'He needs help.'

Joe frowned. 'For God's sake, that's Mike MacNally. What's happened?'

'He's been shot.'

'Shot?' Joe's eyes widened incredulously. 'Who shot him?'

Alex ignored the question, glancing at Deborah. 'Got any surgical dressings?'

She nodded. 'Upstairs.'

'Fetch them.'

Joe leaned over Mike, studying him intently. 'He looks bad,' he declared. 'Better get him into bed while we call the doctor.'

'He needs warmth more than rest,' Alex said. 'Let him sit in front of the stove.'

For the first time, Joe noticed the machine-guns slung across their shoulders, and his eyes narrowed as he stared first at Luke and then at Collis.

'Who the hell are you people?' he demanded in a quiet voice.

'Never mind,' Alex snapped. 'Just do as we say and nobody'll get hurt.'

Alex saw the recalcitrance creep into Joe's eyes. He was a plucky bastard, all right, not one to be intimidated easily, but they couldn't afford resistance at this delicate stage.

'Think of your sister,' Alex warned him quietly.

Joe's features hardened. His eyes looked murderous, but wisely he held his tongue. Watching, Alex thought: he'll kill me if he gets the chance. There was no clemency in Joe's face. No quarter. He looked savage and defiant.

The door burst open and Deborah bustled in, clutching the medical kit; she filled a bowl at the kitchen sink and tugged a clean towel out of a cabinet drawer. She did everything in a brisk, efficient manner, but Alex could tell her brain was working overtime, trying to decipher what on earth was going on. She glanced earnestly at Luke.

'Are you all right?' she whispered.

Luke nodded. There was an air of dismay on his face. He knew the pretence was over, the masquerade finished.

'What happened to Mike?' she demanded.

'Nothing.'

'Ye call this nothing?'

'It was an accident.'

'Accident, was it? Wi' guns?'

Deborah's eyes blazed accusingly, and Luke glanced at the floor, avoiding her gaze. She knelt at Mike's side, tearing open the sodden anorak, and Alex felt a surge of dismay as he watched the clothing drawn away. Mike's shirt and undervest were drenched with blood, and the makeshift pressure-pad he had applied at the water's edge had worked itself loose during the long hike back from the Sound.

Mike appeared to be in a stupor; his eyes hung open but were curiously out of focus. Despite the warmth, his body was still trembling, his lips trailing saliva down the front of his ravaged face.

'We've got to get him to a doctor,' Julie exclaimed.

'Not yet,' Alex told her.

She glared up at him, her eyes hot and angry. 'Ye want him to die?'

Alex sighed. 'Why should I want him to die? There are things we have to take care of first, that's all.'

'What things?'

'A hundred and three men on board the submarine, for a start.'

Joe's eyes flitted between them, shrewd and calculating. 'What submarine?' he demanded.

'HMS *Conqueror*,' Alex said dully. 'There are six limpet mines clamped to her hull, set to go off at eleven-fifteen. Unless we can get the vessel evacuated, her crew'll end up at the bottom of Barracula Sound.'

Something like understanding shone in Joe's eyes. 'Ye're the bloody Provos,' he hissed.

'Not Provos,' Julie told him in a flat voice. 'They're Argentines.'

Joe handled it well, Alex had to give him that, but there was no mistaking the incredulity on his face or the tremor of shock which rippled through his stocky frame. In an instinctive and purely unconscious gesture, he reached down and touched his missing leg. Alex guessed the conflict he was going through, the shock of realisation, the surge of personal resentment. Joe was tempering his emotions with an effort, but Alex wasn't fooled for a moment. Joe was a fighter. He would bide his time.

'Where's the phone?' Alex demanded tensely.

'In the corridor.'

'Show me.'

Joe hobbled from the room, Alex trailing in his wake. Behind them, Julie was working briskly to stem the flow of blood from Mike's shattered chest. They could hear her whimpering as Deborah took the bloody pads from her fingers, handing her fresh ones.

Joe stopped in the passageway, nodding to the telephone on a small table by the wall.

'Get me the Glasgow police,' Alex ordered.

'Glasgow?' Joe echoed, frowning.

'The local boys are too close for comfort. We've still got to get out of here.'

Joe lifted the receiver and held it to his ear, rattling the instrument rest up and down with his fingertips. Alex felt a tremor of uneasiness as Joe stared at him coldly.

'Line's dead,' he stated. 'Must be the storm.'

Alex snatched the receiver from his hand. No sound echoed in his ear. Panic rose inside him as he glanced at his watch. 'We'll have to get to the hotel,' he said. 'Will you take care of Mike?'

Joe nodded, his face expressionless. Alex knew perfectly well Joe would betray them the minute he got a chance, but without a telephone, there was little Joe could do. By the time he got word to the village, he, Luke and Collis would be on their way to freedom.

In the kitchen, Julie was putting the finishing touches to Mike's dressing. Mike looked weak and nauseous as his eyes struggled to focus.

'The phone's clapped,' Alex announced in a cold voice. 'We'll have to use the one back at the hotel. We'll leave Mike here. Joe and Deborah will look after him.'

He hesitated, glancing down at Julie. 'We'll have to take you along,' he whispered, his voice softening.

'I'm staying with my brother,' she snapped.

'I'm sorry. We have no choice. We need someone who knows the area.'

'I'm not leaving,' Julie stated fiercely.

Alex nodded to Collis who stepped forward, seizing Julie's arm, dragging her to her feet. Julie tore herself free, glaring at Alex, her eyes blazing with hate.

'You bastard,' she hissed, 'and to think I was actually beginning to like you.'

Alex sighed. 'We'll turn you loose the minute we feel safe. In the meantime, Mike'll be in very good hands.'

Deborah rose, fixing Luke with an accusing stare. 'Luke?' she said.

Luke looked back at her. In the pale light of the kitchen, Alex could see the misery in his eyes. Poor bastard, he thought. He'd imagined he could keep it from her, the truth; he'd imagined he could stay behind, ignore reality, pursue his private dreams of happiness. How sadly wrong he'd been. There was no future for Luke, or any of them for that matter, in this God-forsaken land. Deborah knew it. The answer showed clearly in her face.

'Goodbye, Luke,' Deborah said, staring at him intently.

Luke flushed. He nodded, moisture droplets gleaming on his moustache, then without a word, he shouldered his machine-gun and strode out into the darkness.

Grimly, Alex shepherded Julie through the door in front of him. He glanced back once, his eyes taking in the scene as if in some elusive way he wanted to imprint it indelibly upon his memory, then he slammed the door and followed the others across the farmyard. Heads bent, shoulders hunched, they set off into the clamour of the arctic night.

Joe stood at the window, watching them go, his eyes blazing with anger and excitement. 'Barry,' he hissed, 'get down to the village and tell Constable Whitgreave what's happening here.'

'What about you?' Barry asked uncertainly, his face curiously unformed beneath its thatch of unruly red hair.

Without a word, Joe opened the kitchen cabinet and took out a heavy 12-bore shot-gun. Opening a drawer, he tipped a box of ammunition on to the table and thrust the cartridges into his jacket pocket.

'No,' Deborah hissed.

'Hold yer tongue, woman. Ye think I'd let them get away wi' this?'

'They've got machine-guns,' she protested. 'What in God's name d'ye hope to do wi' that thing?'

'They took ma leg in 1982, but by Christ they did'na get the rest of me,' he declared grimly.

'Joe Robben,' she cried, 'don't ye dare go anywhere near that hotel.'

'What's wrong? Worried about your boyfriend?'

'I'm worried about you, idiot.'

'I'm coming wi' ye,' Barry said earnestly.

Joe glared at him. 'Do as I tell ye. Get Whitgreave. Ye want those men to die out there?'

Deborah felt the tears issuing from her eyes. 'They'll kill ye,' she sobbed. 'Ye'll no' stand a chance.'

'You're wrong. I've two strikes in my favour already. The first is, I know this country better than they do. And the second . . .'

He grinned at them wolfishly as he slipped in a pair of cartridges and took his anorak from the kitchen wall. 'I owe them something,' he said, 'and it's high time I paid the sodding bastards back.'

CHAPTER THIRTEEN

Standing at the window, Segunda spotted the flickering pinpoint of light gliding towards them down the distant hillslope. It looked unreal, like a firefly glimpsed at some impossible altitude. Pale and luminous, it wheeled and dipped as it made its slow inexorable approach.

'They're coming,' he said crisply.

Louisa joined him at the window. 'They didn't waste any time.'

They watched the light gradually growing larger until soon they were able to discern the outline of the vehicle behind, an armoured Daimler Lehmtrack personnel carrier with a snowplough front, a 375E chassis, and giant tractor-treads for traversing the steadily deepening drifts. Faces peered at them from the tiny porthole windows. The vehicle drew to a halt at the drive entrance, and they heard its engine revving loudly. After a moment, the hatch slid back and a man in a heavy parka came stumbling across the hotel forecourt, clambering over the window-sill. Tugging off his anorak hood, he grinned at them in the candlelight. He was ruddy-cheeked, and his features looked elongated, as if they had somehow slipped out of alignment.

'I'm looking for a lady with the codename Mosstrooper,' he said.

'I'm Mosstrooper,' Louisa told him.

The man held out his hand. 'Lieutenant Canby, Mountain and Arctic Warfare Cadre.'

'It's good to see you, Lieutenant. Did you bring us arctic clothing?'

The man chuckled, and taking off his haversack, tugged it open, drawing out padded overtrousers, fur-lined parkas and heavy climbing boots. 'I hope we got the sizes right. It was done in a bit of a rush.'

'Did Palmer tell you what we're looking for?' Segunda asked as he clambered into the mountaineering gear.

'Terrorists, the report said. An Argentine commando group, out to sink the *Conqueror*.'

'That's right. Three men.'

'Do we know what they look like?'

'Only a rough description. It's not much to go on.'

'Any idea where they'll be hiding, then?'

'Somewhere near Sheilington. It's the best we can do.'

The marine commander looked dubious. 'In this storm, it'll be like hunting a needle in a haystack. Without the Lehmtrack, we wouldn't have got here ourselves.'

'True. But there's one thing in our favour. The snow might stop the security forces getting in, but it'll also prevent the terrorists getting out.'

Segunda zipped up his anorak and studied Louisa critically in her bulky survival gear. 'You look like a pregnant polar bear,' he grinned.

She laughed. 'You're not exactly elegantly tailored yourself.'

Lieutenant Canby blew out the candle and stood at the window, extending his hand towards Louisa. 'Ladies first,' he said gallantly, helping her over the sill.

The hotel rose through the storm, dark and beckoning. Alex could see the low outline of the porch, its steps completely obscured by white.

He crashed through the door and stumbled into the passageway, stamping the snow from his boots. He found the telephone in the residents' lounge. His hand was shaking as he lifted the receiver. The others watched him, their faces taut and expectant. Alex's skin went cold when he realised the line was dead.

'It's crocked,' he announced, dropping the instrument on the table. 'The storm must've damaged the cables.'

For a long moment nobody spoke. Alex knew what they were thinking. There was no way now they could spread the alarm without becoming directly involved.

'What do we do?' Luke grunted.

'Let me think,' Alex said.

He walked across the floor, head bowed in concentration. He hadn't done much thinking since he'd come here, that was the truth of it. A fine mess they'd started, and no mistake. He'd wanted to feel again. Well, he felt something now all right. He felt dismay.

'We'll have to go back,' he decided at last.

'Back?' Collis echoed.

'To the sub. We'll have to defuse those mines.'

Collis's eyes widened in disbelief. 'You're crazy. It's not our fault we can't get a warning through.'

'It's not the fault of the *Conqueror*'s crew either.'

'So she sinks with all her men on board. It's sad and it's cruel, but it's no bloody worse than the bastards did to the *Belgrano*.'

'We were at war when they hit the *Belgrano*,' Alex told him.

'You think sticking mines on a nuclear sub isn't war?'

Alex frowned. He'd expected resistance from Collis. Collis always resisted, it was part of his nature. But something in Collis's face bothered him. This was more than just a gesture.

'There are a hundred and three men out there, Collis. You want them to die?'

'No, I don't want them to die,' Collis exploded. 'Dammit, I'd help them if I could. But not if it means saving the submarine.'

Suddenly Alex understood. 'I know what's eating you, Collis. It's the money, isn't it? If the *Conqueror* doesn't go down, we end up with nothing.'

'Yes, I want that money. I'm not ashamed of it.'

'Blood money, Collis.'

'It's not blood money,' Collis corrected. 'It's retribution.'

'Retribution? A hundred and three lives? This is just a game we're playing, Collis, a game, that's all.'

'It's a bloody serious game to me, Alex. Did you really believe we could pull off a stunt like this without spilling blood? For Christ's sake, man, you've more reason than any of us to hate that submarine out there.'

There was no mistaking Collis's seriousness. He meant what he said, every word. It was a revelation to Alex who had always believed, for some extraordinary reason, that their motives and intentions were roughly the same.

He turned to Luke. 'What about you? Are you going to let those men die, or are you coming back with me?'

'I'll come,' Luke told him softly.

Collis looked like a man cruelly and unexpectedly betrayed. He stared at them for a moment in fury and disbelief. Then, as they moved towards the door, he swung the machine-gun from his shoulder. The sound of its safety catch seemed strangely discordant against the muffled thunder of the storm.

'Hold it right there,' Collis snapped.

He stood facing them, the machine-gun clutched against his lower ribs. On the landing above, a clock began to chime, the sound echoing through the empty building.

'What do you plan to do with that thing?' Alex demanded.

'Kill you, if I have to. I need that money. I'm not going back to La Boca.'

'You'd put a price tag on human slaughter?'

'I'll do anything necessary to get the job done. Make

yourselves comfortable. We're going to wait. In three hours, it'll all be over.'

Alex didn't move. He stood perfectly still, and Collis's features tightened.

'Did you hear what I said?'

'Go to hell, Collis. Nobody's turning me into a murderer.'

For a long moment, they stood transfixed into a silent tableau, Alex and Collis confronting each other across the stained mahogany coffee-table, Luke and Julie watching the scene through tense fearful eyes.

The shot, when it came, was almost an anti-climax, its blast muffled by the falling snow. There was a dim, almost indiscernible retort like a branch snapping on some distant tree, and simultaneously the window behind Collis's head exploded into a million pieces, showering the room with glass. They dived for the floor, their differences forgotten.

Sprawled under the table, shaking window fragments from his hair, Alex struggled to think. His first impulse was that somehow the marine patrol had followed them here, but he dismissed the idea as absurd. The marines had been armed with Sterling sub-machine-guns. That had been a single shot.

Collis slithered to the window and peered warily outside. Faced with this new danger, his anger seemed to have vanished completely.

'See anything?' Alex hissed.

Collis shook his head. 'Too dark.'

'It was a shot-gun blast,' Luke declared from under the table.

Alex frowned. 'Can't be soldiers then.'

Collis eased slowly back, leaning against the wall. They could see his face gleaming in the semi-darkness. There was no hostility there, no rancour or resentment. He was part of the team again, weighing up problems, capable of switching allegiance with the necessities of the moment.

'Somebody's got to go out there,' he announced.

Alex hesitated. It was an unpalatable prospect. Outside, who knew what dangers waited? In the darkness, in the snow, terrors were somehow accentuated. And yet, Collis was right. They couldn't sit here, cornered and helpless.

'Volunteering, are you?' he asked dryly.

Collis shrugged. 'Why not?'

'You must want that money awfully bad.'

Collis glared at him. 'Just give me covering fire while I get through the rear door.'

Alex nodded to Luke and slithered to the window, unslinging his machine-gun. Together, they took up positions at either side of the shattered glass frame as Collis wriggled from the room, vanishing into the passageway.

Alex counted the seconds. One, two, three . . .

'Now,' he said.

Moving in unison, he and Luke thrust their machine-guns through the glass slivers and fired blindly into the night. The rattle of gunfire was like a thunderclap exploding inside the tiny lounge. Staccato flashes lit their faces, and the air reeked with the odour of smoke and cordite.

Julie crouched, flinching, as spent cartridge cases came clattering across the floor towards her. She felt grateful when the guns rattled empty and the two men crouched against the wall, switching magazines.

'What now?' Luke gasped, peering at Alex questioningly.

'We wait,' Alex said, squinting out into the swirling storm. 'There's damn all else we can do. We just wait, that's all.'

Joe crouched behind the toolshed, glaring fiercely into the gloom. Reaching down, he ejected the spent cartridges from his shot-gun and thumbed in fresh ones, snapping the barrels shut. The fumes from the blast still lingered in his nostrils. It had been a wild shot, reckless and foolhardy, but he hadn't been able to resist it. He'd seen the man Collis outlined

259

clearly in the window and it had seemed too good a chance to miss. Now he regretted his impulsive behaviour. He'd alerted them unnecessarily.

The snow drove into Joe's battered face as he reached up, tightening the strap on his anorak hood. What a night, he thought. It was like the end of the world.

There was no sign of movement from the hotel itself. Since the first frantic burst of machine-gun fire, the building had settled under a pall of silence. Through the storm clouds, Joe could see where the Argentines' bullets had stuttered impotently across the empty ground. They'd been miles off, he thought with satisfaction, but the momentary barrage had reminded him all too graphically that he was hopelessly outgunned.

Joe flexed his gloved hands, working the fingers to get the circulation going, then steadying the shot-gun across his arm, he leaned out from the toolshed and studied the hotel front warily. A sound reached him through the storm, strange, alien, distorted. The mist parted, and for a fleeting moment, he glimpsed the side of the house, its dour brickwork coated with panels of glistening ice. As he watched, a tiny, almost indiscernible cloud of steam drifted from the distant corner. Breath vapour. Joe felt his stomach muscles tense. Somebody was crouching there.

Quickly, he glanced around. No chance of a shot if he remained where he was. Even if his stalker moved into the open, the toolshed would obscure Joe's view.

A barbed-wire fence ran diagonally from the shed's opposite corner to the far side of the building. The wooden posts and wire strands had been furred with snow, offering cover of a sort. Joe decided to chance it.

Clutching the shot-gun across his chest, he wriggled through the knee-deep drifts, keeping the fence in front of him. Laboriously, inch by inch, foot by foot, he worked his way towards the furthermost corner of the building. He could see the man clearly now, pressed against the ice-glazed wall. Even in the darkness, Joe recognised Collis.

Gently, Joe brought the shot-gun to his shoulder. Cradling the weapon against his cheek, he took careful aim on Collis's mid-section. No sense trying for a head shot in this weather. Joe hooked his thumb across the hammers and began to ease them back. The lock held firm. He blinked, and pulled harder, feeling the metal tips digging into his flesh. With a chill of horror, he realised the firing mechanism had frozen solid.

He could see Collis's head turning. Collis had sensed something in the darkness and was shielding his eyes against the storm. Joe felt panic surging through him. Panting hoarsely, he clambered to his feet and began to stumble back the way he had come, following the fence through the whipping snow flurries. The night erupted as Collis opened fire.

Rat-tat-tat-tat-tat-tat-tat.

Joe could hear the bullets scything through the gloom, kicking up snow in small feathery spurts. He glanced back and terror made his stomach dissolve as he saw Collis running after him through the darkness, balancing the machine-gun against his hip.

Something caught at Joe's foot and he sprawled headlong into the snow. He tried to scramble forward, but his ankle held firm. He had stumbled unwittingly into a roll of discarded fence wire, and his artificial leg had become entangled. He could see Collis floundering towards him, his angular frame outlined against the drifting flakes. An inarticulate groan issued from Joe's throat as he reached down and began to tear frantically at his leg harness.

Crouching on the glass-strewn floor, Alex listened intently as Collis's machine-gun lapsed into silence. He peered at Luke above the carpet of shattered glass.

'Luke,' he said, 'we've got to defuse those limpet mines.'

Luke considered for a moment. 'Think there's still time?'

'At least we can try.'

'Supposing they go off prematurely?'

'Listen, you're no more an executioner than I am. Do you want those men's deaths on your conscience?'

'No,' Luke said.

'Then we've got to take the risk.'

Luke stroked his moustache with his fingertips. Snowflakes belched through the window, powdering his dark tangled hair. 'Okay,' he grunted. 'I'll go with you. But we'd better get out before Collis comes back.'

Alex grinned at him. 'Now you're talking sense,' he said.

Collis spotted something in the snow ahead. He paused, shielding his eyes against the wind. A line of tracks disturbed the surface at his feet, and there, tangled in a nest of barbed wire, he spotted the macabre outline of a man's leg. He blinked, and kneeling down, brushed away the powdery snow. The metal buckles of a hip harness gleamed in the darkness. An artificial limb. So the man he was trailing was Joe Robben from the neighbouring farm.

Collis straightened, his eyes narrowing. Robben couldn't go far, he reasoned, not with one leg gone. The toolshed would be about his limit. He was probably lying there now, waiting for Collis to approach.

Cautiously, Collis moved away from the fence, circling stealthily to come in from the rear. He had moved to within a radius of almost thirty yards when a movement on the hotel forecourt caught his eye. The mists parted, and for one fractional moment he glimpsed Alex, Luke and Julie scrambling towards the Barracula road. They were heading for the Sound, he realised. Anger rose in Collis's chest. Indignation. Betrayal. Blind with fury, he clambered over the fence and shuffled wildly in their wake.

Thirty yards away, quivering with fear in the tiny

toolshed, Joe felt a surge of blessed relief as he watched Collis change direction and set off in pursuit of his three companions.

When Barry Robben arrived, Sheilington looked like a village under siege. The single main street had been completely obliterated by drifting snow until it was impossible to tell where the pavements ended and the road began. The frosted windows gleamed like barriers of steel.

Barry gasped as he battled his way through the clinging drifts. He'd never seen anything like it. Even the church steeple was completely furred in white.

He made his way to the house of Constable Whitgreave and rang the bell. The door was opened by the constable's wife, a short compact lady in her early forties who had known Barry since childhood. She helped him over the threshold and stood fussing as he stamped snow from his boots on the plastic mat cover.

'Whatever brought ye out in such dreadful weather?' she demanded. 'Ye did'na walk in from the farm, did ye? Ye're lucky ye did'na freeze to death the way that blizzard's blowing.'

Barry shook the flakes from his hair, shivering violently.

'Come on into the kitchen,' she urged. 'Sit yerself in front of the stove while I get the kettle on. I'm sure whatever it is that's brought ye canna be important enough to catch pneumonia over.'

Stubbornly, Barry shook his head. 'I must speak to Mr Whitgreave,' he insisted. 'At once.'

Her eyes scoured his face, hard and searching. She could sense the panic in him, and deep inside, a kindred emotion responded instinctively. It was the kind of call she dreaded. It would take her husband out into the bleak arctic night.

'What's happened?' she whispered softly.

'Please, missus, I must speak to the constable right away.'

Upstairs, the lavatory flushed and they heard footsteps creaking on the landing.

'Who is it, Myra?' Constable Whitgreave called.

'It's Barry Robben, Stan,' she told him. 'He says it's important.'

Constable Whitgreave grunted. He came down to the porch, wearing his dark-blue service trousers, the braces dangling around his hips. His body looked pale and sinewy in the grey flannel undervest.

'What's up then, Barry?' he demanded in a gruff voice.

Breathlessly, Barry poured out the story of the past few hours. As he listened, Constable Whitgreave kept his face impassively grave, but behind him, his wife Myra twisted her hands dismayedly in her apron strings. It was worse than she'd thought, much worse. It wasn't merely the storm her husband would have to face.

When Barry had finished, Constable Whitgreave pursed his lips and opened the door to his private office. He sifted through a sheaf of papers and took out a photostated identikit picture, holding it to the light.

'I thought as much,' he murmured. 'Ever since that laddie won the Burns Day race, something about him seemed familiar.'

'Ye've got to hurry, Mr Whitgreave. Joe's gone after them wi' the shot-gun, and he has'nae a chance on that leg of his.'

'Och, the young fool's got more guts than sense. What about the submarine?'

'The mines are set to go off at eleven-fifteen. That's less than three hours' time, Mr Whitgreave. If we dinna get a warning through, she'll go to the bottom of the Sound and take the entire crew wi' her.'

Constable Whitgreave thought for a moment. 'Charlie Marriott got through from Drumartin and he reckons the phones are still operating there. If we can get word out, mebbe someone can relay a warning to the proper authorities.'

Barry looked at him hopelessly. 'The roads are blocked to a standstill, Mr Whitgreave. It took me damn near forty minutes to get here from the farm. By the time we make it to Drumartin on foot, the mines'll have blown.'

Constable Whitgreave considered the thought. 'We can try Bert Lamb. Bert's a radio ham, and that new set of his is the most sophisticated thing on the market. The storm'll be breaking up transmission, but if he can just get through to somebody, they can pass the message on. It's worth a try.'

He reached for his tunic and together, he and Barry battled their way through the snowdrifts and hammered loudly on Bert Lamb's door. It was opened by Lamb himself, his eyes widening when he saw them standing there.

'My God, ye must be oot of yer minds, venturing out on a night like this.'

'Let us in, Bert,' Constable Whitgreave ordered. 'We need your help.'

Blinking, Lamb stepped back and waved them over the threshold.

'That equipment of yours still working?'

'Not in this muck. Why man, it'd be like transmitting through a tubful of porridge.'

'Porridge or not,' Constable Whitgreave said, 'ye'd better give it a try. There are more than a hundred men facing death tonight, and you're the only bloody hope they've got.'

Inside the Admiralty, the special operations room was crowded. Typewriters clattered, telephones buzzed, and shirtsleeved officers strode earnestly between rows of print-out machines, computers and filing cabinets. Tension hung like an odour above the elaborate radio console where the headphoned operator struggled valiantly to arouse some life from the complex array of batteries and leads in front of him.

Palmer glanced at his watch and nervously lit a fresh

cigarette. His fingers were trembling as he pocketed the lighter. Three hours they'd sat here, trying to contact the *Conqueror*. It was unbelievable. During the Falklands conflict when she'd been operating eight thousand miles away, they'd maintained liaison via American satellite, yet here they couldn't even raise her a bare few hundred miles from home. The Scottish storms were breaking up frequencies, the operator said.

Palmer wrinkled his face in disgust as he tapped ash into an empty saucer. Crumpled paper littered the floor and the air was filled with a thin blue haze of cigarette smoke.

Commander Branscombe studied Palmer sympathetically. Commander Branscombe was a tall red-haired man with a fiery beard. He had a reputation for irascibility among his junior staff, but Palmer had found him unusually sensitive in crises which called for delicate handling.

'Don't worry, sir,' Commander Branscombe said soothingly. 'The storms can't last for ever. We're bound to make contact sooner or later. We'll just keep transmitting until we do.'

A young naval rating entered the operations room, saluted smartly and handed Commander Branscombe a typewritten message. The commander's cheeks blanched as he read it. There was no trace of emotion on his face, but Palmer was filled with an intuitive sense of calamity. He could feel the commander's dismay in the tilt of his chin, the unconscious bracing of his shoulders. Branscombe handed the message over.

'I'm sorry, Mr Palmer. Some radio ham got through to the RAF signals branch at Pitreavie Castle. It seems whoever your saboteurs are, their limpet mines are already in position. They're timed to go off at eleven-fifteen.' He glanced at his watch. 'That gives us less than two-and-a-half hours.'

'My God,' Palmer breathed.

A feeling of hopelessness overwhelmed him. They had

been so close, so unbelievably close. They didn't deserve to lose now.

Commander Branscombe stared at him for a moment, then he strode to the radio console. 'Any luck yet?'

The operator took off his headset, his eyes apologetic.

'Not a sausage, sir. It's like bedlam up there. Those storms are wiping out everything for damn near a hundred square miles.'

Branscombe's features settled into a weary mask. Lines of worry creased the corners of his mouth. He looked like a man to whom hope itself seemed an undreamed-of extravagance.

'Keep trying,' he breathed. 'Just keep trying. For the sake of *Conqueror*'s crew, you must make contact before eleven-fifteen.'

The rattle of the Lehmtrack lulled Segunda's senses. The cabin was dark and filled with heavy diesel fumes. Snow caked the tiny porthole windows, obscuring what filtered light there might have been. Only the driver, crouched at the front of the vehicle could see the road ahead. In the shadows, Segunda dimly discerned the twelve marines huddled on the hard wood seats, their bodies curiously unwieldly beneath their bulky duvet jackets. No one spoke, for the engine's roar made conversation uncomfortable. Lieutenant Canby was perched at the driver's side, watching their giant snowplough blades slice through the drifts in the glow of the single headlamp beam. The vehicle's hull shuddered alarmingly.

Segunda rubbed the porthole with his sleeve, and peered into the darkness. The night had no shape or texture. There was no substance out there, nothing to relate to.

He glanced at Louisa, perched at his side. She was sitting with her arms folded as if trying to generate heat into her frozen body.

'How far did you reckon Sheilington was?' he yelled above the engine's roar.

'Five miles,' she answered.

'We must have covered that by now. Can't be much further.'

'I hope not. My *derrière* feels like it's splitting in two.'

Segunda hesitated as the Lehmtrack shuddered to a halt. At the vehicle's front, Lieutenant Canby was rising to his feet, peering at the road ahead. Segunda watched him fling back the hatch, and steeling himself against the dancing snowflakes, plunge through the narrow opening. Segunda glanced at Louisa, and scrambling forward, followed the commander into the night. The wind came at him from all directions, hurling spindrift into his eyes. In the headlamp's glow, he spotted Lieutenant Canby crouching over a figure in the empty roadway. It was a one-legged man completely covered by snow, his eyes blazing with fury in the white furry mask of his face. An ice-glazed shot-gun lay clutched in his frozen fingers and his empty trouser leg flapped mournfully in the wind.

Glancing up, Lieutenant Canby nodded to Segunda, and together the two men dragged the grotesque figure to the Lehmtrack hatch, and hauled him, gasping, inside. The commander shone a flashlight into the newcomer's face.

'Who in the hell are you?' he demanded.

'Joe Robben,' the man grunted, brushing snow from his frozen features.

'What were you doing out there?'

'Heading for the farm. That's the entrance drive through the trees.'

'What happened to your leg?'

'I had to unbuckle it. It got caught in a coil of wire, and the bastards were coming after me.'

'Who, Mr Robben? Who was coming after you?'

'The Argentines, of course. The ones who've come to sink the bloody *Conqueror*.'

The lieutenant glanced at Segunda. 'We can't talk out here. I think we'd better get this man into shelter, and question him properly. Driver, turn in at the next opening.'

The farmhouse loomed out of the darkness, a squat grey building with roofs panelled by snow. Lights blazed in the downstairs windows.

The Lehmtrack slithered to a halt and the marines filed out, ducking their heads against the fury of the storm. Segunda and Lieutenant Canby clattered across the entrance porch, supporting the newcomer between them. Lieutenant Canby didn't bother to knock. He kicked open the door with his boot, and Segunda felt warmth bathing his frozen face. A woman screamed, startled.

In a room opposite the entrance hall, Segunda saw a lithe figure bending over a man sprawled by the stove. There was a surgical dressing strapped to the front of the man's chest, and beads of sweat clung to his throat and forehead. The woman was mopping him down with a cloth as they entered and, frozen with fright, she stood staring at them like a transfixed doe. Then a sob of relief burst from her lips as her eyes settled on the figure between them.

'Joe,' she cried, 'are ye all right?'

The man nodded breathlessly. 'That Collis damn near killed me,' he croaked.

Lieutenant Canby nodded to Segunda and they eased their burden into a convenient chair. He sat rubbing his stump with his hands, as if trying to get the circulation going.

'Now,' Lieutenant Canby said, 'tell us what this is all about.'

'There are three Argentine commandos out to sabotage the submarine on Barracula Sound,' Joe explained. 'They've set limpet mines scheduled to go off at eleven-fifteen.'

'They've also taken Julie MacNally as a hostage,' the girl put in.

'Where are they now?'

'Last I saw, they were heading back towards the *Conqueror*,' Joe said.

'For what reason?'

'Christ knows. Mebbe they want tae watch the fireworks when their mines go off.'

Segunda pursed his lips. 'Or maybe they're planning to detonate them by some form of remote control.' He looked at Lieutenant Canby. 'We've still got a chance to stop them.'

The lieutenant nodded. He looked capable and relaxed, ready to adapt. Changing situations were merely problems to be appraised and resolved. Moving across the room, he examined Mike critically.

'Get Phillips in here,' he commanded. He glanced at Segunda. 'Phillips is our medical orderly,' he explained.

Phillips' face was grave as he removed the bloodsoaked dressing and studied the wound carefully.

'How does it look?' Canby asked.

'Not good, sir. The bullet's still in there somewhere.'

'Can you get it out?'

'In these conditions, I'd be crazy to try. Besides, it isn't the bullet that does the damage. It's the pressure which precedes it and the vacuum which follows. Sucks in grass, dirt, bits of tattered clothing. See how his belly's swollen? That's the shockwave hitting everything in sight, heart, liver, lungs, spleen. His intestines are bunched up like a bag of rotten spuds.'

'Can't you do anything at all?'

'I can cauterise it, stop it from poisoning. Once the shock passes, his stomach should settle down a bit. If we can keep the wound clean, he should be fine till we get him to hospital.'

'Do what you can, Phillips,' Canby ordered briskly. 'We've got to move out. It's important. We'll pick you up on our way back.'

'I understand, sir,' Phillips said.

270

Straightening, the lieutenant nodded at his men. 'Back on the Lehmtrack,' he ordered brusquely. 'We haven't time to hang about.'

Grim-faced and determined, they filed into the night.

CHAPTER FOURTEEN

Alex grew wary as he approached the slope above Barracula Sound. If the marines who had attacked them were still in the vicinity, he didn't want to stumble on them unawares. He was grateful for the blizzard which obliterated not only their movements, but their tracks as well, filling their footprints in seconds.

He paused, as with breathtaking suddenness, the storm parted in front of them, lifting bodily like a theatre curtain on an empty stage and for one heartstopping moment, the entire Sound swung into focus. They blinked in astonishment as they stared down at the narrow sweep of water curving out to the far Atlantic. The respite lasted only a fraction of a second, vanishing almost instantly as the gale came swirling in again, but the brief glimpse had been enough

'It's gone,' Julie hissed

It was true. There was no sign of the submarine whatsoever. Only the water, lashed by the frenzied winds. The *Conqueror* had vanished.

Alex felt a chill settle on his stomach. 'They must have headed for the open sea. The Sound's too shallow to escape the storm. They're probably at the bottom of the Atlantic, waiting for the blizzard to stop.'

'So we're too late,' Julie exclaimed hoarsely.

Alex didn't answer. Well, what the hell had he expected? he thought. He'd known the game he was playing. No room for manoeuvre. No room for mistakes. Everything geared to clicking neatly into alignment. Life wasn't like that, clean and orderly. They should have expected it. They should have been prepared.

The stutter of a machine-gun echoed through the night. It came without warning, deadly and insistent. Alex turned, shielding his eyes against the storm. He saw spurts of flame lancing the darkness, bullets peppering the snow.

'Collis,' Alex exclaimed. 'The bastard must've followed us.'

Off to the left, the woods offered a sanctuary of sorts, forming a straggling line down the rim of a narrow gully.

'Into the trees,' he yelled, and taking Julie's arm, floundered through the knee-deep drifts towards the distant foliage.

There was a pause in the firing and Alex guessed Collis was switching magazines. Bloody maniac. God Almighty, they should have anticipated Collis. They should have watched him from the beginning. He was too mercurial, too unpredictable.

The night erupted into another deafening barrage, the trees tearing and splintering under the blistering hail of machine-gun fire. Foliage leapt into the darkness.

Tumbling into the scrub, they wriggled behind the safety of the narrow trunks, and gasping, Alex clawed the machine-gun from his shoulder. He didn't want to kill Collis, not unless he had to. He liked Collis, admired him even, and God knew, he didn't want another death on his conscience along with all the others. But they had the girl to think about, Julie MacNally. He would kill Collis to save the girl.

'See anything?' Luke panted.

Alex shook his head, watching for any movement, no matter how slight, which might signify Collis's approach.

Suddenly, they jumped in unison, as from an entirely new direction, gunshots erupted in the trees above. They were heavy and sustained, a steady line of fire concentrated on the spot where Collis had lain. The marine patrol, Alex guessed, attracted by Collis's shooting.

He laughed dryly. Collis was their friend, but Collis had acted like a fool. He'd endangered them all.

'Looks like he's got enough on his hands not to worry about us,' Alex exclaimed.

'Do we help him?' Luke asked.

'What the hell for? He brought it on himself. Let's think about our own necks for a change. Come on, we're getting out of here.'

Collis hit the slope with his shoulder, rolling dizzily as he heard the bullets ripping in around him. The thunder of gunfire almost obliterated his senses. He spun to a halt on the steeply banked snow, the M3-A1 clutched across his padded chest, and without pausing for an instant, rose to his feet and skidded into a nearby gully, zig-zagging towards the cover of the woodland. He could hear the marines shouting to each other as they galloped after him, their voices shrill and discordant above the howling of the storm.

He clambered up the gully's opposite rim, and tumbled into the outlying shrubbery. Pausing, he glanced back, glimpsing dark figures flitting across the open slope. Jamming the machine-gun against his hip, Collis squeezed off a burst and saw the figures diving wildly for cover. Grunting with satisfaction, he turned and began to crawl upwards, picking his way through the heavy timber.

It was hard going, the last few hundred yards where the hill steepened as it approached the wire fence. Collis kept slithering to a halt, sucking hoarsely at the frozen air. The precipitous gradient was wearing him to a standstill. Every once in a while, his pursuers would fire blindly into the darkness and Collis winced as he heard the bullets ricocheting through the trees above. He'd acted foolishly, he knew that now, alerted the troops, betrayed his position. And for what? Some crazy notion about finishing what they'd started. Damned idiot, he'd been. Turned against his friends and brought the enemy down on his neck. Was money more important than life itself?

Collis's breath was rasping hard in his throat when he saw the fence looming out of the darkness and, clambering over the wire strands, staggered on to the road beyond. It was impossible to see the road through the heavy curtain of snow, but he let the gradient guide him, picking his way by guesswork as he moved erratically through the storm. Even if he managed to elude the patrol, how long could he last in such ferocious conditions? The cold would get him eventually. He was shivering already, dammit. When the shivering stopped, the brain became befuddled, unstable. He had to shake off the troops and get under cover.

He was no saint, he realised, had never claimed to be, but they deserved better, Luke and Alex. He hadn't meant to let them down. He needed that money, that was the crux of the matter, had set his heart on it, his present, his future. If the submarine sank with her crew on board, it would be tragic and unjust. But if she didn't sink at all, it would be unthinkable. He couldn't go back to the life he'd led. Never. It was over, forgotten. He'd braced himself for a new beginning. Who could blame him for losing his perspective in the face of such disappointment?

Collis spotted something moving towards him through the buffeting darkness, and froze in his tracks, staring uncomprehendingly. The shadows blurred, merged, the snowflakes compacted. It was an eerie sight, a monster rearing up to meet him, an apparition, chilling and grotesque. At first he thought his sanity had come askew, then he spotted a headlamp beam and realised it was some kind of vehicle he was staring at. An engine roared in his eardrums. He saw a twin-bladed prow, parting the snow drifts, giant tractor-treads biting into the glistening ice.

The lights picked Collis out through the storm, and without pausing to think, he fired almost by reflex, the machine-gun purring against his hip. The tracer bullets arced gracefully into the night, and glass tinkled as the head-lamps shattered, plunging the roadway into darkness.

Collis ran. He cut across the adjacent snowfield, his feet sinking helplessly into the clinging drifts. The night erupted with gunfire, and for no reason he could determine, he was lying face down in the snow with his hand stretched in front of him. Something was seriously wrong with his side. He felt disjointed, out of alignment, as if his body had been inexplicably broken. There was no pain, that was the sur-prising thing, only a kind of creeping numbness. Sickness engulfed him, partly fear, partly something else – a sense of wretchedness, of dire emergency. He saw his fingers twit-ching in the snow. Get up, his brain screamed.

Gritting his teeth, he dragged himself to his feet. Pain lanced through his lower ribcage, his eyes bulging with the intensity of it. He groaned under his breath, and hugging his wound with his free hand, limped frenziedly into the darkness.

Segunda leapt from the Lehmtrack, the marines spreading out around him. His body was pulsing with excitement, filled with the urgency of action and danger. He scarcely noticed the biting wind.

Frantically, his eyes scoured the shadows in front, strug-gling to see through the great wall of wind-driven snow. Lieutenant Canby shone his flashlight on the ragged trail at their feet. Blood smeared its glistening surface.

'The man's hurt,' Canby said.

'He can't get far in this mess.'

'We'll have to follow him on foot. The Lehmtrack can't cross open country. Too many walls and fences.'

Segunda grunted. He was finding it difficult to restrain his impatience. His mad chase was nearing its end at last. Suddenly, nothing else in the world mattered.

'Somebody's coming,' a marine hissed.

The lieutenant switched off the flashlight, tucking it into the front of his duvet jacket. The marines fanned out, crouching in the snow. Ahead, the night danced and swirled as dark figures moved towards them. Segunda counted eight altogether.

A marine challenged them and the figures stopped, snow coating their anorak hoods. Lieutenant Canby rose to his feet, carbine at the ready.

'Step forward,' he ordered, and obediently, the newcomers shuffled towards him through the heavy snow-drifts. Segunda saw windproof parkas, Sterling sub-machine-guns, webbing-belts and respirators.

Lieutenant Canby looked puzzled. 'Who are you?' he demanded.

'Sergeant Kneeland, sir,' a man answered. '59 Independent Commando Squadron.'

'What are you doing here?'

'We've been protecting the submarine on Barracula Sound.'

Canby glanced at Segunda, his ruddy face dark with irony. He seemed embarrassed, as if the newcomers had let him down in some strange way.

'Bloody fine job you've made of it,' he commented dryly. 'In case you're unaware of the fact, there are six limpet mines attached to the *Conqueror*'s hull, timed to go off at eleven-fifteen.'

Even in the darkness, they saw the sergeant's eyes widen.

'Any chance of getting in touch with the vessel's control room?' Canby enquired.

'She's gone, sir,' Kneeland choked, his voice unnaturally strained.

'Gone where?'

'Christ knows. Out to sea probably, to escape the storm.'

'Then who were you chasing?'

'An intruder. He opened fire on us in the trees back there.'

'Was he alone?' Segunda asked.

'Hard to tell. We didn't spot anyone else.'

Segunda looked at Canby. 'There were three men in the sabotage team. The other two must still be at the Sound.'

'What about our wounded friend?'

'He's hurt. He can't get far. Let the sergeant and his men track him down.'

Lieutenant Canby hesitated. 'All right. You stay with the Lehmtrack.'

'To hell with that,' Segunda grunted. 'I'm coming with you.'

'Those men are armed and dangerous,' Canby protested.

'It's still my show, lieutenant.'

'What are you trying to prove? That you're some kind of superman?'

Segunda sighed. 'I'm just trying to finish the job,' he stated.

'You can leave that to us. It's what we get paid for.'

'I'm coming, lieutenant,' Segunda insisted, eyeing him coldly.

Canby sighed. 'What about Mosstrooper?'

'I'm coming too,' Louisa said gamely.

Gently, Segunda shook his head. 'You stick with the sergeant,' he told her. 'The man he's trailing has a machine-gun, but he's badly injured, and can't last long. It's senseless risking both our lives when one of us will do.'

For a long moment, she stared at him, flakes clinging to her cheeks and eyebrows.

'The lieutenant's right,' she whispered. 'What's wrong with you, Mártin? What insanity drives you on?'

'It's part of the game, that's all.'

'Is that what you call it, a game?'

'It's the only one I was ever good at, Louisa.'

'Are you proud of that? Does it satisfy your Argentine *machismo*, hunting, killing, never giving in? It's like a sickness with you. You'd rather die than let those men escape.'

'You're right. But dying won't come into it, because they're not going to escape.'

'We're wasting time,' Lieutenant Canby said impatiently.

Segunda kissed Louisa on the cheek. Even in the darkness, she could see the laughter lines crinkling the corners of his eyes. 'No heroics,' he warned. 'Let the sergeant and his men tackle the fugitive. We'll meet you at the farmhouse. Keep the coffee hot. We'll be back as soon as we can.'

She felt a prickling sensation in her throat as she watched the ragged band of commandos set off into the night.

In the smoky operations room, Palmer saw Commander Branscombe approaching. Branscombe's cheeks looked even more florid than usual, and there was a hint of excitement in his small green eyes. Shirtsleeved and sweating, Palmer rose to his feet, mopping his face with a handkerchief.

'Any news?' he murmured.

Branscombe looked sympathetic. 'About the *Conqueror*, no. I've just had word from the Foreign Office though. There's been another telegram from the Argentine government.'

'What are they saying now?'

'They're accusing Britain of deliberately causing an international incident to stir up tension in the South Atlantic.'

Palmer sighed. In the excitement of the past few hours, he'd forgotten the diplomatic row surrounding the affair. Things had moved so dramatically since then.

He glanced around, running the handkerchief over the back of his neck.

'Can I use one of the typewriters?' he enquired.

'Of course.'

Swivelling a sheet into the platen, Palmer began to hammer at the keyboard. Clinically and concisely, he outlined the chain of events in precise detail, beginning with Segunda's interrogation, incorporating the raid on the naval base, and ending with the anticipated assault on HMS *Conqueror*. When he had finished, he examined his report critically under the glare of the electric light. The sentences were full of typing errors and crossings-out, but their meaning was clear. Palmer called a junior officer and handed him the paper.

'I want this message transmitted to our embassy in Uruguay as quickly as possible,' he said.

The man nodded, accepting the sheet without a glance. For the umpteenth time that evening, Palmer fumbled in his pocket for a cigarette. That would set the cat among the pigeons, he thought. Give the Argentines something to think about. The evidence was irrefutable.

A voice called him from the radio console. 'We've made contact with the *Conqueror*, sir.'

Grunting with relief, Palmer dropped the unlit cigarette in an ashtray and scurried across the crowded control room.

Conqueror's captain, Commander Carnahan, heard the duty officer coming in to wake him. He blinked rapidly, staring up at the bulkhead. He could tell by the look on Lieutenant Hanson's face that something very serious was wrong.

'What is it, Donald?' he demanded.

'Trouble with one of the WT masts, sir. We had to surface to repair it. While we were up there, we picked up some signals traffic.'

Silently, Lieutenant Hanson handed Carnahan the radio message. As the captain read it, his cheeks whitened. 'Jesus God,' he whispered.

'They could be mistaken, sir. It's only guesswork.'

'It's no mistake,' the captain said grimly. 'In Barracula Sound, we noticed some signatures on the sonar gear. If this information is correct, that was probably the sabotage crew in action.'

He studied the message reflectively. 'Six limpet mines,' he muttered. 'It's almost unbelievable.'

'Scheduled to detonate at eleven-fifteen,' the lieutenant said, trying hard not to show his fright.

'What the hell were those bloody marines doing out there? They were supposed to be protecting us, for God's sake.'

'Shall I give the order to surface, sir?'

'Don't be a fool. We can't put the men on the life rafts in this weather.'

'We could take her up to periscope depth and see if our divers can locate those limpets,' the lieutenant said.

'Out of the question. The way the sea's rolling, they'd be chopped to bits.'

Commander Carnahan thought for a moment. 'Who else knows about this?'

'Just the wireless operator Thompson, sir.'

'Keep it under wraps, Donald, that's an order. I don't want the crew panicking. Until we sort this out, not a murmur to anyone, understand?'

'What are you going to do, sir?'

The captain sighed. In the semi-darkness, deep shadows etched the corners of his eyes. 'I'm going to turn her around and run for land,' he said.

Alex drifted uneasily between consciousness and sleep; exhaustion filled him, a dangerous lassitude which hung heavily in his limbs and brain. He was experiencing difficulty in determining the difference between reality and fancy.

Outside, the storm raged on. There seemed no end to it, Alex thought. He could scarcely believe anything existed beyond that suffocating shroud out there. He was grateful for their little refuge, which offered shelter of sorts, a sanctuary from the wind. They had stumbled upon it accidentally, a tiny shack hidden among the trees – a forestry hut, Julie said, housing brasher knives, wire-coils, and brooms for beating out flames during the early spring. Clearly, it had been occupied before. There were food wrappers on the ground, cigarette butts. The marine patrol had probably used it as a base. Sooner or later, they'd be bound to return. He couldn't afford to rest too long.

Alex thought about escape. He had no clear plan in mind. It had seemed simple, in the beginning – a safe-house in Glasgow, car ferry to the continent and a plane back home – but the bloody storm had fixed that. The storm, and Mike MacNally. Alex's features hardened when he thought about Mike. He felt sorry for the man, of course, sorry for anyone taking a bullet in the chest. But it was Mike who had got them into this. His idea, from the beginning. A man should stand by his own decisions. There was no room for second thoughts. They had planned everything to the minutest detail, and for what? Now he and Luke were running for their lives and a hundred and three British seamen were sailing blithely along, unaware they were facing certain death. Damn Mike MacNally. Damn Runcana. Damn Jaurez.

Alex's face softened as he looked at the girl. She was lying on her back, eyes closed, chest rising and falling rhythmically. She looked beautiful in repose, he thought. Sleeping, her defences fell. He couldn't blame Collis for wanting her so much. Who wouldn't, a girl with looks like that? But it was more than just looks, he reflected, much more. There was a giving quality in Julie. She wasn't like her brother, hot and cold in turns. With a girl like Julie MacNally, you knew where you were. He was sorry he'd dragged her into this. She had enough to contend with, one way and another. Lying there in the darkness, he made a pact with himself. Whatever happened, Julie would be all right. He would see to it personally.

A sound reached him through the blizzard. He started,

and lifting his head, listened intently. It came again, a soft sibilant hissing noise, alien to its surroundings.

Heart thumping, Alex woke his companions, pressing his fingertips against their lips. He reached for his machine-gun and scuttled to the door. There was nothing to see beyond the dancing curtain of snow, but someone was approaching, he felt it.

He turned to the others who were watching him in silence, their faces tense.

'We've got to move,' Alex stated. 'We can't go back to the hotel, they'd pick us up in a matter of hours. We've got to get out of the valley.'

'Why don't we follow the road to Drumartin?' Luke suggested.

'It's blocked solid,' Alex said. 'Besides, they'll expect that. They'll have it watched.' He looked at Julie. 'We can go over the tops, can't we?'

'You'd be killed. No one could survive the mountains in this weather.'

'How far is it to Drumartin?'

'Fifteen miles by road.'

'And if we traverse the summits?'

Julie hesitated. 'Following the ridge and skirting Charrach Dam, you can drop into the village from the west. That's about seven miles approximately, but in these conditions it might as well be seven hundred.'

'It's worth a try,' Alex stated.

'You're mad.'

'I know. I know, godammit. But I can't think of anything else. I'm not spending the rest of my life stuck in some stinking British prison. Get your things together. We're going over the ridge.'

'They've been here,' Lieutenant Canby said, indicating the trampled snow in the forestry hut doorway.

Segunda nodded. They were fresh tracks, he knew. Their quarry was on the move again.

The lieutenant pointed to a ragged trail leading up the hillside.

'They're heading for the mountains,' he said.

'In this weather?' Segunda's tone was incredulous.

'Desperate men will try anything. They know if they can get into the adjoining valley, they stand a bloody good chance of losing us.'

'Fools. They'll die up there.'

'Probably, but we can't count on it. Any experience in mountaineering, Mr Segunda?'

'A little. We covered climbing techniques at training school.'

'This is different. Snow-and-ice work calls for a special approach. You'd better go back and wait for us at the farmhouse.'

Segunda looked at him darkly. 'I told you before, I'm coming along.'

'You'll only slow us down.'

'I'm coming, I tell you.'

Lieutenant Canby sighed. 'If you think it's cold down here, wait till you get on the tops. I want nobody on those hills who isn't fully experienced, and that includes you.'

'You're not giving the orders, lieutenant. I'm a government agent. I make my own decisions.'

'Not when you endanger my men.'

'Nobody will be endangered, you have my personal word.'

'We're not dragging along a bundle of firewood,' Canby told him grimly.

Segunda's eyes narrowed, and he stared at Canby for a moment in silence. Then his face relaxed, and he grinned happily. 'Don't worry about me, lieutenant. I have a remarkable stubborn streak when it comes to matters regarding my own life.'

Canby could see there was no chance of changing Segunda's mind. Something about the man defied logic and reason, an air of fanaticism it was impossible to ignore. Bloody idiot, Canby thought. Let him find out the hard way, if he had a mind to. They had a job to do.

He nodded, signalling to his men, and moving in unison, the little group of Royal Marines shuffled into the night.

Inside the *Conqueror*'s control room, the atmosphere was electric. The captain was a quiet man as a rule, he showed little of his feelings. But now his tension was inescapable. The crew recognised the signs, sweat beads on the narrow brow, drumming of the fingertips, minute flickerings of the facial muscles. The captain was worried, and what worried the captain worried them all. The control room was uncustomarily silent as the vessel sped furiously eastward.

Commander Carnahan studied the charts for the umpteenth time, calculating currents, distances, checking them against his watch.

'Let's see if we can speed her up a bit,' he whispered to Lieutenant Hanson.

The lieutenant's face was pale with strain. 'We're approaching the continental shelf, sir. We're already going faster than we dare.'

'How much water have we got under our hull?' the captain shouted.

'Twenty fathoms,' came the answer.

Carnahan chewed his lip. Lieutenant Hanson was right. They were too close to shore to risk an all-out sprint. But the minutes were ticking by. The rate they were going, they would never make it.

He reached a decision. 'Revolutions sixty,' he ordered crisply.

General Guayabero was relaxing by his swimming pool when

the houseboy crossed the terrace and handed him a carefully sealed envelope. 'This came by special delivery from the British Embassy in Montevideo,' he said.

Sitting up straight, Guayabero took the cigar from his mouth and ripped open the envelope. His eyes narrowed as he scanned the typewritten pages inside. Suddenly, he began to laugh. Leaning back in the sunlight, he guffawed elatedly, his cheeks streaming with moisture. Picking up a glass from the table next to him, he waved towards the study doorway.

'Fetch me the telephone,' he ordered in a triumphant voice.

The polo game was already in full swing when Colonel Jaurez arrived. He could see the riders galloping frenziedly at the far corner of the field. The noise in the spectators' stand was deafening as he paused at the top of the stairs, preening himself deliberately. He liked to arrive late because it gave him a chance to make an entrance. He looked, he knew, resplendent in his uniform.

He saw heads turning in his direction, and a small smattering of applause rose from the spectators in the adjacent rows. Jaurez acknowledged the acclaim with a wave, and made his way to the bar at the stand rear. He didn't care for polo, if the truth were known. He enjoyed such functions for the exposure they offered, nothing more. In Argentina, a high-ranking military man carried a special aura, and Jaurez liked that.

The barman behind the counter saw him coming and poured the colonel's favourite drink, Bacardi rum with ice and lemon. He was smiling ingratiatingly as the colonel took his seat.

'Good evening, Georgio,' Jaurez said pleasantly. 'Big crowd tonight.'

'*Si*, it is an important one, señor. Manaya is always a major draw.'

'How much do I owe you, Georgio?'

The barman shrugged obsequiously. '*Mi coronel*, as always the first drink is on the house.'

Jaurez purred with satisfaction. He liked bartenders who got things right. It was, after all, no more than his due. In Argentina, a full colonel deserved recognition, respect.

The man sitting on Jaurez's left smiled at him anxiously, and the colonel recognised Señor Maquez, a local landowner and horsebreeder. He was neither rich enough nor important enough to warrant the colonel's full attention, but Jaurez was feeling magnanimous and he smiled back, rolling the rum glass between his fingers.

'How are you, colonel?' Señor Maquez enquired. 'We've seen little of you these last few weeks.'

'I have been busy,' Jaurez confided. 'Important military matters.'

'Not another coup, I hope.' Señor Maquez smiled disarmingly to defuse the joke. Political witticisms could be hazardous in Argentina when made to the wrong people. Colonel Jaurez declined to acknowledge the rancher's remark, and with a small gleam of worry in his eyes, Señor Maquez quickly changed the subject. 'I hear your son is doing well for himself in Mar Del Plata?'

The colonel nodded graciously. He enjoyed talking about his family. He was especially proud of his boy Ricardo who ran a boat-building business on the Argentine coast.

'His order books are full for the next two years,' Jaurez said. 'Who would have thought it? Our family have always been military men, yet it seems I have bred a financial genius.'

'Intelligence is hereditary, *mi coronel*. Your son is fortunate to have sprung from such talented stock.'

Jaurez acknowledged the gauche compliment with a fleeting smile. He was about to speak again when he became aware of a figure standing at his elbow. It was a young army major, breathless and embarrassed.

Jaurez frowned. 'What is it, major? Can't you see I'm relaxing?'

The major saluted smartly. 'I must ask you to accompany me, señor.'

'For what reason?'

'My men are waiting at the entrance gate. I will explain as we go.'

Colonel Jaurez's face darkened. 'Major, I am not in the habit of dashing off here, there and everywhere on the whim of a junior officer.'

'Please, *mi coronel*.'

Something in the officer's manner disturbed Jaurez. The man looked nervous but resolute.

The colonel sighed. 'Very well. Wait for me at the gate. I'll be down as soon as I finish my drink.'

The major picked up Jaurez's glass and emptied it into the sink behind the counter. The colonel's eyes widened in astonishment.

'You must come at once, *mi coronel*,' the major said in a quiet voice. 'You are under arrest.'

The phone rang as Señor Runcana was buttoning up his smoking-jacket. He heard Juan, the houseboy, pick up the receiver in the adjoining room.

'*Si?*' Juan said, his voice low, modulated, perfectly controlled. After a moment, he wandered into the study. 'Señor MacAngus is on the line,' he declared.

Runcana grunted as he picked up the telephone. Through the window, he could see his daughter Tania riding one of the stallions across the empty paddock. She looked superb in the sheepskin saddle, a splendid attribute to the Runcana family. If only his son Régis had been alive, then his satisfaction would have been complete.

'*Si?*' he said with the receiver to his ear.

'Roberto?' MacAngus whispered hoarsely, and something in his voice made Runcana's senses tighten.

'What is it?' he demanded.

'They've arrested Jaurez.'

For a moment, Runcana stood perfectly still, staring through the window. 'You are quite sure?'

'My friend Cesar saw it happen. They picked him up at the polo game.'

'On what charge?'

'Roberto, what else can it be? Something has gone wrong.'

Runcana considered for a moment. 'What are you going to do?' he asked.

'Get out, while I can. I'd advise you to do the same.'

'Impossible. This *estancia* has been in my family for six generations. I cannot abandon it now.'

'Be sensible, Roberto. Governments change, people change. Take a trip. An extended vacation. Travel to Europe, the United States. You can come back in a year or two perhaps. By then, our little enterprise will have been forgotten.'

Runcana felt his facial muscles tighten. This was no time to stand on dignity, he thought. He could hardly help the *estancia* if he was reclining in a Buenos Aires prison.

'You're right,' he breathed. 'I am grateful for the warning. Good luck to you, old friend.'

Runcana put down the receiver and summoned Juan, the houseboy.

'I want you to pack my things,' he said. 'I have decided to take a vacation. Call Torres and tell him to get the aircraft ready. I'll bring the flight plan with me.'

Forty minutes later, Runcana appeared on his verandah accompanied by Juan, carrying his suitcases. He was about to descend the steps to his limousine when a convoy of military vehicles came clattering up the drive. Runcana watched them impassively, no emotion on his face. Soldiers leapt from the trucks and ran towards him, carbines at the ready.

An officer saluted smartly. 'Señor Runcana?' he enquired.

Runcana nodded.

'I must ask you to accompany us, señor.'

Runcana sighed. 'I understand, gentlemen,' he whispered. 'I have been expecting you.'

Tall and dignified, he walked down the steps and climbed into the waiting car.

CHAPTER FIFTEEN

Collis reached down, touching his side. His fingers came away covered with blood. Blood was trickling down his leg, soaking ominously into the padded material of his duvet jacket. He felt no pain, only a disorientating numbness, as if his entire left side had somehow been encased in concrete.

The snow lashed stinging into his eyes, covering his face with a thin white film. He could hear the wind roaring in his ears as it thundered across the open fields. He was moving in a dream, unable to think straight, unable to make sense of the nightmare world in which he found himself.

The machine-gun dragged remorselessly at his shoulder. He longed to let it fall, to loose the leather strap and drop it thankfully into the snow, but he knew the weapon would probably be needed. They were still following, the men who had shot him. His only chance was to stay ahead.

Clutching his side, he shuffled laboriously through the knee-deep snow, unable even to walk upright any more, lurching and wallowing like Quasimodo. The cloud grew thicker. It was hard to believe another world existed out there – in warmth, comfort, security; how pleasant to rest, how pleasant to let oblivion take him. I am not yet defeated, he told himself grimly. It was a sustaining thought, though God knew, it took all his willpower to keep it in focus. Amazing the things a man clung to with death staring him in the face. Collis was scarcely even conscious of his deteriorating strength – that part of him belonged to the outer shell, the painful bloody shapelessness of his body; inside, was where the stubbornness still glowed. He concentrated on that, on keeping the flickering spark alive.

Something drifted into his line of vision. He paused, hugging his side, wiping the snow from his eyes. A wire fence loomed through the eddying flurries. He saw a sign which read:

Dangerous Mine – Keep Out

Roof ready to collapse

YOU HAVE BEEN WARNED

Panting, Collis wormed his way to the wire barrier. A mine meant a tunnel, and a tunnel meant shelter. Anything was better than this interminable buffeting. He had to get out of the snow.

Collis took out his diver's clasp-knife and prised furiously at the wire, tearing it away from the post. When he had loosened enough strands to wriggle through, he shrugged off the machine-gun, and pushing it in front of him, slithered into the enclosure. He saw the mine entrance etched beneath a gaping fold of rock. Gasping, he stumbled inside, the storm's fury subsiding as he felt his way along the jagged walls. The roof was low. In places, it hung down so far he was forced to duck his head, in others it arced upwards, allowing him to move freely. Water streamed from the rock, making eerie dripping sounds which echoed backwards and forwards along the empty corridor. The air smelled stale, chilling his throat and cheeks.

Holding on to his bleeding wound, Collis stumbled grimly into the tunnel as the darkness closed around him.

Louisa and the eight marines picked up the mine's fence in the glow of their flashlights. They could see scarlet splashes trailing a distinctive spoor among the deeply-etched footprints, vanishing discreetly through a gaping hole in the fluttering wire.

'He's heading for cover,' Sergeant Kneeland declared, tilting his head against the wind.

'The mine?'

'Looks like.'

'He'll be trapped in there,' Louisa hissed fiercely. 'Only a fool would go to ground in an empty tunnel, with one way in and one way out.'

'The man is hurt,' Sergeant Kneeland said. 'He needs shelter more than he needs escape.'

'Are we going in after him?' Louisa asked.

Sergeant Kneeland hesitated. He looked unhappy, Louisa thought, and she couldn't blame him. She didn't relish the idea of an eye-to-eye confrontation in that miserable little pest-hole herself.

'I can't think of any other way,' Kneeland admitted. 'Somebody's got to winkle him out. You can wait here.'

Louisa took a deep breath. 'If we go at all, we go together,' she insisted.

'The man is armed, miss. There's no sense all of us getting our heads blown off.'

'Don't patronise me, sergeant. I'm not some shrinking violet. It's my job.'

The sergeant sighed. 'Okay,' he said. 'Come along, if you have to. But remember, I'm not responsible for what happens in there.'

Louisa felt her heart beating wildly as they clambered through the wire, and spreading into a straggling line, followed Collis's tracks to the tunnel mouth. Moving quickly to avoid being framed against the night, the marines darted across the gloomy threshold. Louisa gasped as the rough-hewn walls closed around her. It was a blessed relief to escape from the wind, but ahead, the tunnel looked eerie and menacing.

'Hug the walls,' Sergeant Kneeland ordered. 'And be ready to turn off those flashlights if the bugger starts firing.'

Cautiously, fearfully, they picked their way along the echoing corridor, their movements delicate and controlled as they inched deeper into the steadily narrowing mineshaft. Water dripped incessantly in Louisa's ears. Their flashlight beams bathed the bulging ceiling in a macabre blanket of orange light, picking out fissures, cracks and crannies, chillingly reminding them, if they had needed reminding, that the roof was ready to collapse at any moment. What madness was she engaged on? Louisa wondered. What stupid, stubborn pride had forced her into this? Segunda had sent her back with the sergeant because he'd thought it the safer alternative. A wounded man lost in the snow, his strength deteriorating, helpless and frightened. A doddle. Some hope, Louisa thought. She couldn't have asked for a nastier situation. A wounded man was like an injured animal. When he went to bay, there was no telling what he might do.

Breath steaming on the damp air, they furtively moved deeper and deeper. The marines seemed amazingly calm, machine-guns balanced against their speckled combat jackets, flashlights gripped in their mittened fingers. Something echoed in the recesses ahead. It was nothing Louisa could put a name to, but she knew instinctively the sound had been alien. Too metallic, she thought, for dripping water or creaking roof beams.

'*Down*,' she shouted, hurling herself against the rocky floor. The marines dropped where they stood, switching off their flashlamps, plunging the mine into abrupt darkness.

Almost instantaneously, a thunderous roar reverberated along the narrow tunnel. It was like the opening salvo of an artillery barrage, stunning in its intensity, echoing backwards and forwards between the solid rock walls. Spurts of flame lanced the shadows ahead, and Louisa heard bullets pinging across the hanging ceiling.

The marines opened up, and she shuddered violently as the world disintegrated into a maelstrom of intensified sound. *Crack, crack, crack, rat-tat-tat-tat*. The strafing went on, the marines' hands in constant motion, manipulating their weapons with a skill and familiarity made instinctive by countless hours on the firing-range, the air choking with smoke, ejected shell-cases clattering across the floor. Louisa lay still, holding her ears, narrowing her eyes against the gunfire's blur.

After a moment, the clamour faded away. Louisa shivered convulsively. The air seemed heavy with the smell of cordite. She heard a marine cursing in a dull impassioned kind of way. He had landed on a rock.

'You all right, miss?' Sergeant Kneeland asked.

Louisa grunted. She couldn't see him in the darkness. It was like being wrapped in a suffocating shroud.

'What are we going to do?' she whispered. 'If we move forward, he'll pick us off easily. If we retreat to the tunnel mouth, we'll be outlined against the night.'

'Don't worry. He's in a far worse position than we are. I'll try a stun-grenade and see if we can rattle him into doing something stupid.'

The sergeant spoke crisply in the gloom. 'Rawlings, Laughton, when I say the word, give me covering fire, understand? Keep shooting until I hit the floor.'

'Right, sarge,' a man grunted.

There was a moment's pause. Louisa heard Sergeant Kneeland shuffling about on the ground beside her. Something clicked metallically against the rock and she felt her tension mounting.

'*Now*,' Sergeant Kneeland snapped hoarsely.

The cave lit up as the machine-guns roared. *Rat-tat-tat-tat-tat*. The mine erupted in pandemonium, the staccato flashes dazzling and blinding. Louisa could see the sergeant illuminated clearly in the rapid bursts of flame. He drew back his arm, swinging it forward in classic fast-bowler fashion, hurling the stun-grenade into the murky darkness ahead. The explosion was almost simultaneous, a blinding ball of phosphorous light, turning the cave into brilliant day. The roar of the detonation buffeted their bodies, rolling over them like a tidal wave. And then, before the reverberations had died, Louisa heard something that froze her senses. Rising dimly on the periphery of her consciousness, a deep, stomach-freezing, cracking noise seemed to echo in the depths of her very soul, making her skin crawl, her blood freeze, filling her body with terror and dismay.

'The roof's caving in,' she screamed.

'Out,' Sergeant Kneeland bellowed. 'Everybody out, for Christ's sake.'

Somehow, Louisa dragged herself to her feet, sprinting desperately back the way they had come. There was no rhythm to her movements, no conscious co-ordination, only a desperate urge to put the cave behind her, to leave the suffocating tomb that even now was closing in like a vice, the walls shuddering, vibrating, taking on life, force, energy. She could hear the marines panting beside her in the damp cold air. She gasped, sucking in her stomach muscles, her ragged strides becoming erratic, hysterical, not caring any more about being framed against the tunnel opening, thinking only of escape, stumbling into rocks, knees buckling, vision tilting. Somewhere behind, a frenzied roaring noise rose ominously, gathering momentum, hammering her eardrums with stupefying force. Dust particles peppered her spine and neck. She saw the mine entrance looming up, and sobbing deep in her throat, lunged towards it in a last desperate spurt, staggering, almost tripping, pulling herself erect and bursting into the open with a whimper of triumph and relief.

A thunderous eruption echoed inside the tunnel as the ceiling collapsed, bringing down thousands of tons of rock and shale. Dust belched from the cave mouth, covering their faces. Panting and choking, they stared at the scene of devastation behind them.

'Poor sod,' Sergeant Kneeland muttered grimly.

'Think it killed him?' Louisa asked, pressing her fist against her heaving chest.

'Let's hope so. It'd take six months to dig through that little lot.'

Louisa shivered in the chill. The wind picked up again, driving spindrift against their cheeks. Sergeant Kneeland pulled at his anorak hood, his eyes glowing like dark coals.

'Let's get down to the farmhouse,' he said. 'No point in the rest of us dying of exposure.'

Collis sat down. Weakness swept through him, draining his body of life. He'd thought for a moment he would choke back there, in the aftermath of the roof-fall, for the air had seemed solid with dust. Now, though he was breathing easier, his side had begun to pain him again, lancing through his lower trunk in waves, intensifying with each beat of his pulse.

The darkness gathered around him, black and stupefying. There was nothing to see, not even the dimmest glimmer of a reflection. It was like being completely blind.

The tunnel was blocked, he thought dully. Soon the air would go. He would suffer asphyxiation, eventual death. He felt sad it had ended so ignobly. And yet, he was lucky, in a way, to have these moments to reflect on. A man deserved that, the right to appraise himself in the light of inescapable truth. His had been a sorry existence, to be sure. He wasn't proud of the things he'd done. Regrets, he'd had plenty, but if he were honest with himself, absolutely and brutally honest, would he have done them any differently? He doubted it. Except perhaps for Luke and Alex. He'd have changed that, if he could. It seemed wrong for a man to leave the world with the taste of betrayal on his lips. But it was too late now for change. Too late for anything. Only rest, sleep, emptiness.

Clutching his side, Collis closed his eyes in the heavy darkness and waited patiently for death.

The ridge vanished into the darkness ahead, its jagged shark-tooth rocks shrouded in feathery blankets of snow. The mist made it difficult to discern the level of the ground. Alex was panting hard as he beat a path up the steadily ascending crest. The wind flayed them, stampeding wildly across the distant summits. Sometimes, its power almost bowled them over in their tracks.

The others were moving well, Alex noticed approvingly. Julie, despite the appalling conditions, clearly knew how to handle herself in the mountains. Luke, too, showed no sign of slowing down.

Alex had no idea what they would do when they reached the adjoining valley, but at least there was still the possibility of escape. Here at Barracula, their liberty would end with the dawn. A major security operation seemed inevitable. They had to put the mountains between them. It was their only hope.

Groggily, they picked their way higher, Alex leading, Luke bringing up the rear. There was nothing to see but the few square feet on which they moved, a nightmare world, drained of density, drained of colour and perspective. Alex was conscious of the discomfort racking his tortured body; his hips ached, his calves trembled, his skin stung under the stupefying gale. He thought of Buenos Aires, of Patagonia and the high mountains. It all seemed so long ago. Time lost its meaning in such surroundings. A man could live his entire life in the space of a few fleeting seconds. Pain and misery absorbed him into the texture of the earth itself.

Ice coating the snow made their passage hazardous, and Alex slowed, kicking shallow steps into its crusty surface. One slip would take them into oblivion, for on both sides of the ridge, dark cliffs hung menacingly.

Then with a suddenness that started them all, the wind dropped leaving them gasping in the stillness. It had not vanished altogether, but protected by the hump of the adjoining mountain, they were cushioned from the main force of its blast. They found the transition dramatic and breathtaking. Alex blinked, peering ahead. The route seemed to level out, going nowhere.

'What happens now?' he asked Julie.

She wiped snow from her face. 'There's a narrow col joining the ridge's flank to the central massif,' she said. 'We've got to cross it.'

'Where?'

She shook her head. 'I don't know. It's somewhere down there in the darkness. There's a cairn marking the point of descent, but we'll never find it in this snow.'

'Is there no other way?'

'None. The col lies directly under the ridge's summit, a narrow saddle of rock connecting the two mountains together. Miss it and you can wander around for hours.'

Alex's lips tightened. Covered with snow, the rocks looked like marshmallows rearing out of the night.

'We must have reached the highest point by now,' he decided. 'The gradient's levelling. We'll drop down the slope and see if we can locate that col.'

Luke eyed the route dubiously. 'Pretty steep,' he declared. 'Almost perpendicular. The snow could give way at any minute.'

'We'll take it easy,' Alex promised.

'Those are sheer cliffs down there, amigo. One slip, and we'll be dancing on thin air.'

'I know, but we haven't any choice.'

Alex set off, picking his way down the precipitous slope, kicking out steps with his boots. The others followed, placing their feet in the holes he had left them, testing the surface cagily as they worked their way gingerly down the mountainside. Mist swirled below, a veritable blanket of mist, for which Alex felt grateful since it shut off the gully, shrouding the cliffs, cloaking their awesome exposure. There was nothing to see but that swirling platform of white. The snow lashed into his eyes, blanketing the slope, turning notches, crannies, protuberances into a smooth featureless slab.

Cautiously, he lowered a leg, dug his toe into the crispy surface, carefully transferring his weight as he hugged the mountainside with his free arm, his eyes anxiously scouring the darkness for any thickening in the mist which might signify the presence of the narrow saddle. He saw the top of the cliffs emerging and paused, frowning worriedly. If they missed it, he realised, they would have to retrace their steps, not an easy manoeuvre in such a delicate position. He heard Julie scream, and turning sharply, saw her fall, her body out of control as she went streaking past him, skidding helplessly into the dark. Her face peered up, white and pleading, her fingers clutching the snow as she gathered speed, slithering towards the jagged precipice which would plunge her into the void below.

'Julie,' Alex yelled, his muscles convulsed.

There was nothing he could do but stare, knees driven hard against the slope, pulse-beat accelerating, eyes rigid with horror, watching impotently as she turned in a dizzy spin, clawing at the ground, and then – he felt his muscles contract – she slithered to a halt, her body wedged between two craggy outcrops, the precipice yawning directly below. Trapped and helpless, she lay staring up at them, her features frozen with terror.

'Don't move,' Alex shouted. 'For Christ's sake, don't move. I'll try and reach you.'

Muscles trembling, he leaned out from the slope and began to kick his way down, moving less cautiously now, conscious of the need for speed. His chest ached as he filled his lungs, digging his boot tips into the loose cloying snow.

In the darkness, he dimly glimpsed the outline of the col above and cursed inwardly. They had come down too soon. Another hundred yards would have taken them to safety.

Inching lower, Alex felt terror rising from his stomach as everything suddenly dissolved around him, sending him slithering helplessly into space. Uttering an inarticulate cry of protest, he went skidding earthwards through a blinding curtain of snow.

Coming up the ridge below, Segunda and the small party of Royal Marines heard Alex's stricken cry and stopped in their tracks, squinting fiercely into the darkness.

'Hear that?' Segunda hissed.

Lieutenant Canby nodded. 'Somewhere to the left, I think.'

'What in God's name are they doing down there?'

'Looking for a way out, I imagine.'

The lieutenant turned to his men, shielding his face against the storm. 'Use the ice-axes, lads,' he shouted. 'And move carefully. The snow's too fresh, too ready to give.'

Someone thrust an ice-axe into Segunda's hand.

'Used one of these before?' the lieutenant asked.

'Not for a good many years.'

'Lean on the shaft to give you support. Keep it on the mountain side of the slope. If you feel your feet giving way, dig the blade into the ice and press down on the adze with the lower part of the chest. Think you can remember that?'

Segunda nodded, and strung out in a ragged line, the marines pressed on into the night.

Alex gasped, holding hard to his senses. He lay where he had fallen, wedged against Julie in the apex of the craggy buttresses. His ribcage ached with the impact of his inelegant descent. He could see his route in the snow above, and his stomach dissolved as he thought of the emptiness beneath.

Julie's breath fanned his cheek, and he could feel her heart thumping through the confines of her padded overclothing. He dared not move for fear of dislodging her. The slightest slip, he realised, would send them plummeting through empty air.

He could see Luke warily working his way towards them. Sweat streamed from Luke's cheeks as he slithered downwards, snowflakes dancing around his narrow spine. Alex felt a dryness in his throat as he watched Luke's perilous descent. Luke was no mountaineer, he knew. He hated the mountains. He belonged to the *pampa*, the Argentine flatlands. Alex knew the terror nestling in his friend's chest, knew the monumental effort of will it took for Luke to continue his delicate approach. Dry-mouthed, slack-jawed, he watched Luke reach a point directly above, balancing gingerly as he leaned out from the slope.

'Can you move?' Luke croaked.

Alex looked at Julie. He could see tension riven in her features.

'Take the girl first,' he shouted.

Gritting his teeth, he slipped an arm around Julie's waist, heaving upwards, adding his own strength to hers as she wriggled desperately out of the rocky aperture. Luke stretched towards her. Julie balanced, shifting her weight in small, delicately judged manoeuvres. She seized Luke's proffered hand and began to kick her way towards him. Panting and gasping, with Alex pushing below and Luke hauling from above, Julie worked her way up the perilous snowslope until she had reached a point of comparative safety directly above Luke's head and diagonally to his right.

'Kick out a stance and stay there,' Alex called. 'We'll join you in a minute.'

He watched approvingly as, ashen-cheeked, she flattened the snow into a flimsy platform beneath her boots.

Holding on to the slope with one hand, Luke reached

down with the other, and grunting, Alex began to ease himself out of the narrow apex. He picked his way cagily, studying the route ahead, testing the snow with his fingers before pressing on. Not too fast, he thought. Too much haste made a man reckless. He reached out, digging in his nails, following with his foot, worming his way upwards like a gymnast. His hand gripped Luke's and their fingers locked together. He could feel the strength in Luke's wrist as he rose steadily, ignoring the emptiness below, focusing his mind on one solitary direction. Up.

He was parallel with Luke now, their arms stretched across the snowslope, uniting them in a fervent clasp. Alex nodded to show he was okay, and releasing himself, picked a wary route towards Julie's stance on the narrow platform. When he reached her, she was trembling uncontrollably. He took her in his arms, feeling the tension steady inside her.

'All right?' he whispered.

She nodded.

He glanced back to Luke, seeing Luke's facial muscles tense as he began his difficult ascent. Poor bastard, Alex thought, it's been a nightmare for him.

Luke's tongue darted out, moistening his thin lips as he inched nervously upwards, making each move as deliberate as possible. Alex watched approvingly. He was doing all right. Scared, but coolheaded. Not a man to panic easily, never had been, buoyant, resilient, optimistic to a fault. Lost his head a bit over that girl, Deborah Robben, and who could blame him? Probably wishing he was with her now, instead of perched like a beetle on the side of this stinking mountain. Probably wishing he was anywhere. It was no picnic clinging to such a perilous rampart. Come on, Alex thought, a few more feet should do it.

As Luke drew closer, Alex leaned down, extending his right hand. He saw Luke's eyes focus feverishly upon it. Luke stretched towards Alex's beckoning fingers.

'Not yet,' Alex cried. 'You'll over-reach.'

But Luke seemed oblivious to the warning. The sight of the proffered hand was too tantalising to resist. With a desperate grunt, he lunged forward, disregarding holds, disregarding gravity. Sweet Jesus, Alex thought. For a full moment, they stared at each other, eyes locked in a gaze of hopelessness and dismay. Alex saw Luke's anorak hood scattered by the wind, saw the moustache coated with snow and the fear in the pallid cheeks. He clawed frenziedly at the air as Luke's body receded before him, face stricken, eyes frozen – not with panic, Alex thought, not terror even, just an inborn awareness of imminent death.

He heard Julie cry out, felt horror clutching his throat. There was something incongruous about that downward flight, for Luke's outline remained in exactly the same position, right arm flung forward, his gaze fixed unerringly on Alex.

Luke passed the outcrops where Alex and Julie had jammed, hit the lower slopes in a blinding flurry of spray, his speed quickening as he hurtled towards the precipice. So elegant did Luke's descent appear that for one moment Alex almost believed he might, by some incredible miracle, fly from the mountain like a mystic bird. Then Luke hit the rocky overhang and his body catapulted outward in a dizzy curve. Alex glimpsed him framed against the mist, cartwheeling in a spiral of churned-up snow, his body strangely diminished as he dropped sickeningly earthward. He hit a rocky projection, bouncing with a vicious thud, his grace shattered at last, vanishing wildly into the eddying storm.

Transfixed with horror, Alex and Julie clung together, the snow buffeting around them. Alex felt nausea sweeping up from his stomach as he stared mesmerised into the chasm where his friend had gone. Beside him Julie was sobbing hysterically.

A shout from the ridge brought Alex to his senses. He shook Julie savagely, making her teeth chatter.

'Don't look down,' he ordered. 'Do you hear me, don't look down. He's gone. There's nothing we can do about it. Turn around and climb to the ridge top. Climb, damn you. We've got to make that col.'

Pushing from below, he manhandled her slowly, painfully back up the slope.

Collis frowned as he detected something scuffling in the darkness. For a long time now, he had heard no sound at all. He had tried to imagine in his fevered, disorientated way that he was dead already, but the pain in his side reminded him, with irritating stubbornness, that the flame of life still flickered. He listened hard. The sound came again. Something was moving in the mine tunnel.

Collis shook himself. Clutching his side, he wormed his way up the rocky wall until he was standing unsteadily on outspread feet, then fumbling in his jacket, he took out his cigarette lighter and flicked it with his thumb. A tiny glow of light flickered in front of his face. He saw the craggy walls, the swirling spirals of dust still drifting lazily on the rancid air. His stomach lurched in a chill of revulsion as he glimpsed red eyes watching him through the gloom. Rats. There were dozens of them, creeping stealthily about the fissured floor. Their humped backs and slender tails merged in a seething carpet of living fur, and Collis recoiled, gripping his wound as he backed towards the roof-fall. He felt sickness rising from his stomach, and the hair prickled on his neck in nausea and disgust. Then his gaze narrowed as a startling realisation dawned on him. The lighter flame was dancing in front of his chin. He held it up, examining it intently. He hadn't been mistaken. Somewhere, there was a draught of air.

A spasm of hope lodged in Collis's chest as, with a hoarse

croak, he stumbled forward, ignoring the rats which scampered furtively from his path, following the tunnel as it probed deeper into the mountain. The air-flow was stronger now. He could feel it, like an almost imperceptible wave fanning his fevered cheeks. The breath rasped in his throat as he quickened his pace, shuffling in a grotesque semi-crouch, blood oozing into his already drenched clothing.

Collis paused, peering upwards. He could see a narrow chimney in the ceiling above. It must be the ventilation shaft, he thought. There could be no other explanation.

Senses tingling, he unslung the machine-gun and tossed it on the ground, then gritting his teeth, he worked his way up a narrow flake until he had reached the chimney opening. He switched off the lighter, slipping it into his jacket pocket, and blinking furiously, reached out in the darkness, groping with his fingertips as he wormed his head and shoulders into the chimney entrance. The pain in his side was excruciating. It passed through his body in waves, darting into his lower ribs. He turned his mind from it, concentrating on the simple task of picking his way upwards. He jammed himself against the chimney wall, leaning back with his arms, drawing up his thighs and thrusting his feet against the rock in front, then using the pressure to keep his body poised, he began slowly, nervously, to inch increasingly higher. It was an agonising process. The hard slab bulged against his spine, bruising his skin through the heavy duvet jacket. He could feel its coldness against his palms. He moved by instinct, picking his way by touch and guesswork, desperately fatigued.

The minutes ran into each other as if he had reached a point in time and space where only infinity existed. Wedged inside the narrow air-shaft, he wrestled doggedly towards its mouth. For an immeasurable period, he went on climbing, ascending into the stifling darkness, his mind drifting, caught in a strange never-never land of dreamless images and fevered consciousness. He had little strength or awareness left. Perhaps I am dead already, he thought. Perhaps this infernal funnel up which I move is the gateway to heaven itself, a Jacob's Ladder to oblivion. When reality dimmed, he would plummet earthwards like a graceless stone.

He had no idea how long he had been climbing when the chimney suddenly began to open out. He felt cold air bathing his cheeks and throat. Blinking, he saw clouds swirling over the basin above. A wave of elation swept through his body as he realised he had reached the chimney mouth. Sobbing deep in his throat, Collis jammed his feet against the rock, and wriggling and scrabbling, wormed breathlessly into the storm-laden night.

For the umpteenth time that evening, Palmer glanced at his wristwatch. His stomach tightened, and a coldness settled remorselessly inside him. Eleven-fourteen. Only one minute to detonation. The *Conqueror* was still at sea. There could be no hope now for the men inside its metal hull. It would be their tomb, icy and eternal.

He looked at Commander Branscombe, hating the sympathy he glimpsed there. Dammit, he didn't want the man's pity. He'd done his best, they all had, but luck had been against them.

'Any word?' he asked the operator at the radio console.

The man shook his head. 'Nothing for the past twenty minutes now, sir.'

Palmer rubbed his forehead, hopelessness creeping through his body. Thirty seconds to go. 'God help the poor bastards,' he whispered.

Inside the *Conqueror*'s control room, Commander Carnahan stared fixedly at the clock on the metal bulkhead. He could see the second hand ticking inexorably round. Sweat trickled between his shoulderblades and the muscles tightened along his jawline.

'We're approaching the Sound now, sir.'

Carnahan ignored the shout. He was staring at the clock, transfixed. They were only seconds from oblivion.

The captain was not a cowardly man, but he wondered about the moment of extinction. Would it be swift – one blinding dissolving flash – or would it be slow and agonising? He pictured the hull crumpling inward like a battered tin can, the sea streaming through the shattered bulkheads, flooding the oiltanks, the diesel generators, shutting off the escape towers. He envied the men. They had the blessed solace of ignorance. They would die without knowing, blindly, uncomprehendingly.

Commander Carnahan's muscles clenched as the pointer sped remorselessly round. Five seconds to go. Four, three, two, one ... He gritted his teeth, cheeks whitening as he waited breathlessly for the moment of eruption.

The pointer moved on. Eleven-fifteen and ten seconds. Eleven-fifteen and twenty seconds. Eleven-fifteen and forty seconds.

'We're in the Sound now, sir.'

Carnahan glanced at Lieutenant Hanson. Hanson's cheeks were grey and sweaty. He stared back at the captain with a sickly look in his eyes.

Commander Carnahan stepped to the periscope, seizing the clipped-up handles and pressing his face against the eyepiece. He could see a swinging vista of white water and sky. The dark outline of the coast reared above. He snapped open the voice-pipe.

'Slow ahead,' he bellowed. 'How much water underneath?'

'Twelve fathoms, sir.'

'Stop both,' Commander Carnahan shouted, and stepped back from the periscope, his features trembling.

'Take her up,' he yelled. 'And break out the life rafts. I want this vessel evacuated as quickly as possible.'

*

The col was narrow and difficult, but Julie felt a wave of relief as they stumbled across it and glimpsed the mountain rising in front of them, its glistening icefields blurred by the drifting snow.

She moved in a daze, her senses dulled with shock. That last dreadful glimpse of Luke cartwheeling headlong over the precipice seemed imprinted indelibly into her memory. She would never forget it, she knew. The stricken look in his eyes, the sickening thud as he'd hit the rocky outcrop. It would live with her always.

She stumbled on the icy surface and Alex seized her elbow, hauling her erect. The warmth of his body seemed strangely comforting. Ahead, the massif loomed above them and Julie studied it with dismay. The narrow path which wound precipitously between the slabs of fractured rock had been covered completely. There was nothing but a contourless wall of glistening white.

She swallowed hard. 'We're trapped.'

Alex chewed at his lip, staring into the darkness. He tested the surface with his boot toe. 'We can do it,' he told her gently. 'Trust me, and we can do it.'

'It's too soft. It'll be like climbing through porridge. Besides, we've no ice-axes.'

'We've got this,' Alex said, drawing the clasp-knife from his webbing belt.

He hacked at the snow, carving out a great bucket-hole for his boot to nestle in. Moving rhythmically, earnestly, he worked on another, chopping a diagonal ladder up the precipitous snowfield. She watched him go, marvelling at his balance, feeling a tremor of admiration at the tireless way he sent the snow flying.

Within minutes, he had carved out a series of hand and footholds to a spot almost fifty feet above the col. They were not the usual one-chop jobs of high-altitude mountaineers, but mini-platforms designed to hold her feet steady and her body stable. He knew the dangers they were facing. The snow, with its soft underbelly, was ready to give way at any second, and without ice-axes, ropes or crampons, their ascent would be hazardous in the extreme. But Alex, taking his time, was making the way easy for her and she felt grateful for that.

He paused, peering down through the snow flurries. 'What are you waiting for?' he bellowed.

Julie took a deep breath and raising one foot, jammed it into the first toe-hold, slipping her fingers into the holes above. Moving rapidly, confidently, she followed hard on Alex's tracks. Within minutes, she was close behind him, twisting her head as he sent snow and ice granules cascading into her cheeks. Now that she was literally suspended on the mountainside, her sense of exposure returned. She could dimly see the col below, its narrow saddle half-obscured by the drifting mist. She felt thankful that the wind had dropped, for clinging as they were, they would have run a serious risk of being ripped bodily from their flimsy perch.

Chunk, chunk, chunk. Alex ripped and tore with the clasp-knife blade, moving expertly, inexorably upwards.

Shutting her mind to the dangers, Julie dutifully followed.

Segunda saw the col taking shape through the darkness. There was ice on its narrow crest. He negotiated it cagily, placing his boots in the footprints of the man in front.

Somewhere up front, the mists were hardening. He felt his spirits sink as he watched the ice-wall looming out of the night. It looked immense. Had their quarry really come this way? He could scarcely believe it. But through the dancing snow-flurries, he spotted a series of toe-holds meandering diagonally into the mists above.

Lieutenant Canby studied them soberly. 'They look firm enough,' he announced.

He turned to Segunda. 'This is where it starts to get tricky. I can't spare the men to take you back.'

'I'm not going back,' Segunda told him.

'Ever snow-and-ice climbed before?'

'Not for a good many years.'

Canby sighed. 'I wish you'd left this to the experts. We're only a matter of yards behind them.'

'I haven't slowed you yet, have I?'

'All right,' Canby nodded grimly. 'We'll put you in the middle of the rope. Stick to the footholds and use your ice-axe for balance. We'll move in stages, one man at a time. It'll hold us up a bit, I know, but this snow's ready to crumble at any second and I don't want to lose anyone through unnecessary impatience.'

The marines strapped crampons to their boots, and Segunda watched in silence as a man tied him to the centre of the rope. He felt the nylon knot pressing against his belly.

Lieutenant Canby led off, picking his way up the makeshift ice-ladder, testing the holds before climbing on, his men paying out the rope beneath. When he had reached a point some fifty feet above, he hacked out a platform in the snow, belayed himself to his ice-axe shaft and brought up the second man on the line. Moving in sections, each climber bringing up the figure at his rear, the little party of Royal Marines slowly, warily scaled the snowfield, following the trail of footholds in Alex and Julie's wake.

Commander Carnahan sat in the life raft, staring dumbly at the submarine bobbing in the centre of the Sound. High waves crashed over its metallic grey hull, hurling spray across the oval-shaped conning tower. Its snort masts and periscope looked curiously unreal, etched against the swirling sky. As Carnahan watched, the vessel tilted against the swell, and he glimpsed the dim projection of its forward plane pointing inelegantly towards the shoreline. The wind whipped in, whirling around in a moving funnel, and Carnahan struggled for breath as snow clogged his nostrils and eyes. Around him, the other life rafts danced perilously on the writhing ocean. He glanced at Lieutenant Hanson who was watching him in bewilderment. Carnahan knew what Hanson was thinking. Why hadn't the submarine blown? Had the Admiralty signal been a hoax? Were they evacuating the vessel for no reason?

Commander Carnahan shook himself. He would worry about that when the storm subsided, he thought. Tonight, he had his crew to think about.

The wind leapt in again, hammering his spine, pounding his cheeks with stupefying ferocity. He wiped his face with his sleeve, fighting to see through the buffeting blizzard. 'Head for shore,' he shouted hoarsely. 'We can't sit around here much longer. We've got to get the men into shelter before they die of hypothermia.'

The operator called Palmer from the radio console. 'We're picking up a new transmission, sir. It's pretty faint, but just discernible.'

Palmer blinked. He was sitting in the communications room, his feet propped on the desk in front of him. He scarcely knew what he was doing here. If the *Conqueror* was sunk, the job of arresting the saboteurs belonged to Special Branch, not his department. But the thought of returning to his empty flat depressed Palmer. He couldn't face it alone, the weariness of defeat.

'It's from a lady called Mosstrooper,' the operator yelled.

Palmer stubbed out his cigarette and scurried across the room. He took the microphone from the operator's hand and spoke into it hoarsely.

'Louisa? Where are you?'

There was a sizzling sound on the receiver, then a voice

broke through the static, cracked and discordant. 'Charles?'

'Are you all right?'

'I'm fine. I'm in a farmhouse near Barracula Sound.'

'Where did you get the radio?'

'From the *Conqueror*'s wireless man.'

Palmer's eyes widened. 'The submarine's still intact?'

'She was an hour ago, Charles. The crew are all here, sheltering from the storm.'

Palmer filled his lungs with air, breathing deeply, holding it in, letting it out slowly, willing his arms and legs to relax with each individual breath. His head began to spin, and for a moment he held on to the radio console as relief swept through his body. Reaching up, he nipped the bridge of his nose, the mucus in his mouth dry and sticky. Then he said: 'What happened?'

'The mines didn't go off. Not on schedule at any rate. The captain had time to evacuate his men.'

'Thank God,' Palmer said. 'Thank God.'

'We're sitting tight until the snow stops. It's like a nuclear war-zone up here. We've got an injured man who badly needs hospital attention.'

'Segunda with you?'

'No, Charles.'

Palmer frowned, a faint uneasiness stirring inside him. 'Where the hell is he?'

'Chasing the saboteurs.'

'Alone?'

'He's got some Royal Marines with him.'

'Louisa,' Palmer said hoarsely, 'I warned you not to let him out of your sight.'

'I know, Charles, but I had no choice. The men were getting away.'

Palmer felt his anxiety rising again. His stomach squirmed as his relief gave way to apprehension and dread. 'Don't you realise Segunda's a psychopath?' he croaked.

'I trust him, Charles. Really. And the marine commander will keep him in line.'

'I hope to God you're right, Louisa. There'll be hell to pay if he starts his Gaucho tricks over here.'

'He won't, Charles. I give you my word.'

Palmer sighed. 'Keep me posted on any new developments. I'll radio RAF Kinloss and see if they can get a chopper out to you as soon as the wind drops.'

'Thank you, Charles,' Louisa murmured.

Palmer put down the receiver as the transmission went dead.

Alex felt the gradient slackening and knew they were coming up to the final pitch. Already the strain had moved from his knees. Another twenty feet, thirty maybe, and they would be back on level ground again.

His arms ached from the interminable chopping. A clasp-knife was no substitute for an ice-axe, he thought. His palms stung and he was panting hard from the strain of exertion. He couldn't have kept it up much longer.

Behind him, Julie moved slowly, easily, placing her hands and feet in the holds he'd vacated, trusting him without question. He was grateful for that trust. He had no right to expect it, he knew, but he couldn't have made it without her.

His brain still reeled when he thought about Luke, about the awful moment of realisation when, their eyes locked, they had each known intuitively he was going to fall. Alex shuddered as he recalled Luke's body cartwheeling through the snow-flurries. It didn't hurt, they said, falling from a mountain. The mind separated from the body, became a different entity. But Luke had caught the overhang. There had been no separation there, no release, no immunity from pain.

Alex tried to put Luke from his mind as he concentrated on the gruelling task of carving out the last few snowholds.

Soon the ground began to slope gently forward, and filled with blessed relief, Alex thrust the clasp-knife back into its sheath, stumbling upward with a cry of triumph. They had reached the shoulder of the main massif.

But Alex's exuberance was short-lived. As he gazed at the solid wall of ice-glazed cliffs in front, he felt his spirits sink.

'Which way does the path go?' he hissed.

Julie studied the wall balefully, her chest rising and falling as she filled her lungs with air. 'It zig-zags up the face of the rocks,' she said. 'When you can see it.'

Alex swore. 'We'll never cut our way through that lot. There must be another way.'

She shook her head. 'You've got to get to the top of the massif if you want to drop into Drumartin.'

Alex felt anger stirring inside him. Bloody storm. It had bamboozled them at every turn. He'd come so far too. Climbing that snowfield without ice-axes had been a miracle, nothing less. He couldn't quit now. He couldn't face the thought of imprisonment. He couldn't bear confined spaces, they tortured him.

Eyes hot, he peered into the night. On the one side, the ground slipped into a narrow gully. He could see a river dancing at its bottom, darting pearl-grey over boulders coated with ice. 'Where does that lead?' he demanded.

'Up to the dam.'

'What lies above?'

'Nothing. Just high cliffs on every side. It's a natural rock basin.'

'There'll be shelter on the dam. A place to rest.'

'I imagine so. But you'll be trapped if they come for you. There's only one way in and one way out.'

Alex grunted grimly. 'I'll think about that tomorrow,' he said. 'Since we can't go up and we can't go down, we might as well spend the night in comfort. Come on.'

Without waiting, he stumbled into the gully and began to pick his way up its twisting belly. Sighing deep in her throat, Julie trailed along in his wake.

Segunda stood on the narrow snow ledge, sliding the rope across his waist and shoulder as he brought up the man behind him. He was belayed firmly to his axe-shaft, but despite the comforting grip of the nylon sling, he felt perilously exposed on the sheer mountainside. He was no climber, God knew, and there was nothing to give him solace or hope, no rocky projection, no comforting jughold – only the ice, flat and implacable, to which they clung like a swarm of insects.

His briefing had been swift and precise. Use the axe to belay, clip the karabiner to the rope at your waist, hold the line taut when bringing up your fellow, control its progress with the fingers of the right hand. Easy enough, Segunda admitted, if you had the nerve and stomach for it, but crouched on such a godforsaken perch, he felt dreadfully alone and dangerously insecure.

He scarcely knew what he was doing here. Why can't you quit? Louisa had asked with that shrewd and penetrating stare. Good question, Segunda thought. Why couldn't he? What solitary madness drove him on so remorselessly? Those people in front meant nothing at all. If they escaped, his life would not be one single jot poorer. Yet here he was risking everything on this indefensible pursuit. Did Louisa despise such ruthlessness? he wondered. You never knew with Louisa. She could be ruthless herself, as she'd proved so graphically when she'd left him to die in the Sahara. But perhaps, in some curiously perverse manner, that was the very thing which attracted him so. Women had never troubled Segunda before. He'd used them to satisfy his needs as he might have sampled a pleasant wine or a good cigar. But emotional involvement lay beyond his understanding.

Why then did he feel so perplexed when he thought about Louisa Carleton? What devilish magic had she wrought, that after all these years, after the pain and anguish of her previous betrayal, he still wanted her, wanted her badly? That was madness of a sort. He had always prided himself on his capacity for coldness. Laughter, he understood. Caring, never. Caring was a weakness for a man in his profession. It led to compassion, guilt, remorse. It led to this, he thought sourly, a reckless manhunt over a storm-tossed mountainside, with no prize at the end of it except a dubious salve to his own manic pride.

He watched the climber beneath making his cautious ascent, checking the line of footholds methodically before proceeding. The man's breath steamed on the frosty air. Beyond him, Segunda could see only the chasm, awesome and inspiring; even the narrow col had receded into the swirling blanket of mist.

Dry-mouthed, Segunda followed the marine's progress, admiring the confidence with which the man moved; there was a curious symmetry to his actions, like that of a dancer going through a well-rehearsed routine. He showed no fear, only a cool professional absorption as he edged steadily upwards, Segunda gathering in the slack as quickly as he could.

He shivered as the wind switched direction, hurling spindrift into his cheeks. He could see the man's face clearly now, the eyes steady, cool, appraising, the legs and shoulders moving in unison, slow, rhythmic, filled with the ballet dancer's grace. There was no questioning the man's expertise. It was not his fault the snow chose that particular moment to give way. Its suddenness took Segunda completely by surprise. Avalanches, he'd imagined, were dramatic, awe-inspiring things. They roared and thundered and took their time. This one was instantaneous. One second, the surface texture was there, the next it was gone, as simple as that.

Segunda saw the white blanket peeling out from the rock like the skin of a rotten orange. He saw the man drop, his body strangely controlled as it plunged backwards into the night, the rope wriggling from his waist like a grotesque umbilical chord.

With a chill of horror, Segunda hurled himself against the ice and waited for the impact. The rope scoured his palm, zipping taut across his shoulders. He felt the thud as the climber jerked to a halt. The line gave like a string of elastic, and suddenly the man was swinging crazily in a pendulum motion, streaking across the cliff in a breathless arc. Eyes bulging, Segunda saw a second man torn from his perch, then a third. In a fountain of churned-up snow, the three marines spun crazily into the night, kicking and twisting in a flurry of panic and alarm.

Strapped to his ice-axe shaft, Segunda clawed at the rope and prayed to God he could take the strain.

CHAPTER SIXTEEN

It was hard going in the narrow gully, but Alex and Julie climbed steadily, following the bed towards its source. Julie's hips ached remorselessly, sending slivers of pain lancing into her chest. From the knees down, she was conscious of only a skin-tingling numbness. She fixed her gaze on Alex shuffling ahead, placing her boots in his footprints with an air of glassy incomprehension. Her body had lost its capacity to think. It operated by instinct, driven on by the demands of the moment.

She felt her stomach lurch as she glanced ahead and saw, towering above them like a vision of God, the outspread veil of the massive dam. Viewed from beneath, it looked immense, a breathtaking rampart of incredible size. Beyond it, the mountains reared into the darkness. Julie swallowed, numbed by the sheer scale of the thing. She had seen it many times before, but never from this angle, and never in such grotesque circumstances.

Alex headed towards the dam's right-hand rim, and Julie saw a steel ladder embedded into the concrete cliff, tracing a spidery route to its upper parapet. Alex picked his way up the slippery snowbank to the bottom of the ladder. She heard his boots clanging on the lower stanchions as he began the precipitous ascent.

Without pausing for breath, she reached out, gripping the handrail, and followed blindly.

The sinews rose on Segunda's neck. His muscles trembled as he held hard to the rope. Behind him, driven deep into the crusted snow, his ice-axe secured him to the mountain by a nylon sling. The line bit into his shoulders, straining across his spine. The three men dangled helplessly below, clawing at the wall in front of them.

Segunda heard a scraping sound as Lieutenant Canby approached. He didn't dare turn his head – he knew if he did, he would be totally engulfed by fright.

'Hold on,' the lieutenant grunted, almost at his elbow. There was something unnaturally calm in the timbre of Canby's voice. He seemed utterly unshaken, as if such events were commonplace. The snow rustled as he hammered in an ice-piton and clipped himself to it with a nylon sling, his movements swift, yet unflurried. He slipped the spare rope from his shoulder, belayed it to the cliff-side and tied it swiftly around Segunda's waist. Then he leaned forward, seizing the rope in Segunda's hand, adding his own strength as a secondary anchor. Segunda felt a wave of relief as the strain slackened. The three marines dangled directly beneath them.

'What the hell are you playing at?' Canby shouted. 'Get yourselves back on that snowfield! D'you want to drag us all off?'

Painfully, the two lower marines managed to reach the cliff and kick themselves steps in the sheer white wall. Segunda let himself relax, sweating heavily as Lieutenant Canby hammered in more pitons to make the belay secure.

'Will they hold?' Segunda croaked.

'They'll have to,' Canby said. 'There's no other way.'

He cupped his hands to his mouth and shouted down the mountainside.

'Anybody hurt?'

One of the marines called up: 'Bradbury's moaning, sir. Looks like he's broken his leg.'

Canby cursed. 'Just like the sodding thing. We'll have to lower him down to the col.'

'Think we've got the strength for it?' Segunda asked dubiously.

'We'll spread the weight out a bit, rig up a pulley system with the pegs and slings. It'll work, you'll see.'

Briskly, efficiently, the lieutenant hammered in parallel rows of pitons, clipped on karabiners and threaded the rope through zig-zag style to form a crude leverage device. When he had finished, he tied a sliding friction knot to serve as a brake.

'It's primitive, I know,' he admitted, 'but it'll have to do.'

He bellowed to the men beneath. 'Get Bradbury into a harness. We're dropping him down to the col.'

It took only seconds for the marines to fashion a makeshift seat and strap their injured companion into it. When he was secure, they waved at the lieutenant above.

Canby looked at Segunda. 'Right,' he said.

And with Segunda operating the safety knot, they began slowly, tentatively, to ease their delicate burden through the network of karabiners.

Collis's body seemed filled with a strange buoyant feeling, as if he was floating above the storm. The world rippled and blurred, ice granules peppering his fevered skin. He was shivering from head to foot, his breath coming in short rapid bursts. He had no idea where he was going. He had lost all sense of direction. He moved with a strange shuffling motion, his mind drifting between reality and illusion. Sometimes he saw green fields and summer sun. He could feel its warmth radiating through his tortured limbs like a blessed salve. Sometimes the world vanished, and he felt he was drifting through a vacuum like a man caught in some immeasurable bubble. In his head there were wondrous images, ephemeral fragments conjured from the inner recesses of his soul. He saw swallows diving above jungles flecked with dew, craggy islands and blossom-studded pastures. Creepy-crawlies plagued the night, waiting to haunt him in the awesome bloody clamour. No escape from this stomach-sickening, spine-crawling hullabaloo. No noble principles to provide sustenance or hope. Only conflict and suffering, that was the ghastly reality.

Am I afraid? he wondered. Hardly. Fear is relative, like hunger. I shall not sell my soul at the moment of extinction. I shall not call for dubious solace in the face of this final indignity. Let it be slow or fast, however it chooses, I shall remain intact. But I wish I had someone to tell it to, he thought. It would be so satisfying at the moment of my sad inglorious exit to make a final declaration, one last farewell utterance. A single paragraph would phrase it all.

An hour passed, then another. Still, he floundered onward, fired by a strange vibrating power. The storm leapt in, driving against him in a great whorl of white. Blinking, he glimpsed a thickening in the mist ahead. Have I lost my senses, is reality wavering in the face of this pounding pandemonium? Something is out there, truly. Tangible. Beckoning.

Fighting for breath, tottering on his exhausted legs, he leaned into the wind and staggered blindly towards it.

Julie felt the coldness of the metal rungs chilling her fingers. They were half-way up the ladder, the dam wall reaching out around them. It looked unreal in the drifting mist, a blank featureless cliff, no cracks, no buttresses or fissures, only the wall, silent and implacable.

She felt terribly exposed as she picked her way gingerly upwards. Alex was somewhere far ahead, an unimaginable distance above. He looked minute, perched against the dam, his body moving evenly as he scaled the spidery ladder. She could hear his boots clanging on the metal rungs.

The wind caught her as she moved higher, coming in blasts from the valley below. They were losing the protection of the central massif. She flinched as the gusts sent needle-sharp ice-granules into her cheeks, hitting her in successive bursts. She held on grimly, the ladder shuddering beneath her, shutting her eyes to the gaping veil of the dam wall as she focused her attention on the simple act of working one foot above the other.

When she reached the parapet, Alex helped her over the concrete rim. She saw the dark sheen of the mountain lake and the amphitheatre of precipices surrounding them. Alex unslung his machine-gun. He picked his way across the narrow rampart, stepping delicately where the wind had cut intricate patterns in the surface snow, moulding it into an icy crust almost as hard as the wall itself. Julie followed, her feet sliding dangerously. She saw the dark hump of the engineer's office. Alex tried the door but it was locked. He stepped back, kicking it open with his foot, and thankfully they tumbled inside, shaking the snow from their sodden clothing.

Alex switched on the light. The office was small, but comfortably furnished. There was a low settee, a row of filing cabinets, charts pinned to a wooden noticeboard. An electric kettle stood on a bench beside a tiny washbasin. Julie saw a teapot and a cluster of dirty mugs.

Two doors faced them on the opposite wall. Alex tried the first, disclosing a small broom cupboard. Brushes and cleaning materials lined the shelves and an odour of floorwax and disinfectant drifted into their nostrils. The second was locked. Alex prised it open with his clasp-knife and Julie glimpsed a narrow staircase leading down into the dam itself. Alex flicked on the light and explored as far as the lower landing, then satisfied, he returned, closing the door behind him.

She watched him sigh with relief as he pulled back his anorak hood, ice glazing his hair, melting in trickles which ran down his wind-battered skin.

'Fancy some tea?' he asked.

He plugged in the kettle and switched on the electric fire.

She watched as he dumped the mugs in the sink, rinsing them under the tap.

She moved to the reddening bars, holding her hands above the blessed circle of heat. 'I thought I'd never be warm again,' she said.

Steam rose in spirals from his saturated clothing. 'I want you to stay here,' he told her.

'For how long?'

'Till somebody comes. You've risked enough.'

'What about you?'

'I'm moving on as soon as it's daylight.'

She was silent for a moment. How strange, she thought, her aggression had gone. A few hours ago, he'd been her enemy, someone to outwit, oppose. She'd hated him then, or imagined she had. Now, everything had changed. Despite what he'd done, they had gone through too much together even to consider anything so petty as hostility. She wasn't part of his private war, she thought. She felt no loathing, no fury or indignation. He was human, he was vulnerable, he was real. She'd liked him in the beginning. She liked him now.

'You can't escape, you know,' she said in a reasonable voice.

'I can try.'

'There's no way out of that rocky basin.'

'I'll find a way.'

'Give yourself up,' she pleaded. 'Do you want to finish like Luke? Is anything really worth dying for?'

'Look at your watch,' he said.

She glanced down. It was nearly midnight.

'Now do you understand?' he whispered. 'The *Conqueror* sank at eleven-fifteen.'

His guilt was manifest, tangible. He understood the enormity of his crime, he hadn't forgotten, not for a moment. Not even on the mountain.

'A hundred and three men,' he murmured. 'They'll put me away for twenty years. I couldn't stand it. Enclosed places drive me crazy. It's escape or die.'

The truth hung between them, chastening and indisputable. A shrill whistle filled the room as the kettle began to boil.

Segunda stood on the narrow col and watched Lieutenant Canby examine his injured man. As the lieutenant ran his fingertips expertly along the length of the swollen leg, the patient winced but made no sound. There were dirt streaks on the marine's cheeks, and his breath had frozen to his beard stubble in a milky film.

'No fracture,' Canby declared. 'Sprained, I'd say. Pretty badly too, but the bone seems intact.'

'Thank Christ for that, sir,' the casualty moaned painfully.

'Can you move your toes?'

'I think so.'

'We'll leave the boot in place for the moment. No sense getting frostbite.'

Canby straightened, turning to Segunda. 'I can't leave him here,' he stated. 'He'd freeze to death in this muck. I'm sending him back with a four-man escort.'

'It's a long way down.'

'He'll make it. They can take turns giving him support. It might be a good idea if you went too.'

'No,' Segunda said.

'Be sensible, man. You don't know what you'll be running into up there.'

'I have to go. It's my job.'

The officer studied him critically in the darkness. 'Are you trying to impress me, or something?' he demanded.

'Why would I do that?'

'Because you're an Argentine, that's why.'

325

'You're talking like a fool, Canby.'

'What do they mean to you, these men? What makes them so important you're prepared to die, if necessary, rather than let them get away?'

'It's the only way I know,' Segunda told him.

'Well, you're doing no bloody good up here at all. That accident cost us several hours, at least. We'll have to double our speed.'

'Don't worry, I'll not slow you down.'

'Go back, for God's sake. This is your last chance.'

'I'm coming,' Segunda insisted grimly.

Canby stared at him for a long moment, his eyes cold behind the plastic snow goggles. Then he spat on the ground and reached for his ice-axe as, for the second time that evening, they prepared to scale the treacherous snow wall.

It was strange sitting in the engineer's office. Like being cocooned, Julie thought. Outside, she could hear the storm raging, the wind cannoning towards them up the narrow valley, but inside their concrete shelter, the air was warm, the room muggy. She felt drowsy as she sprawled back on the ancient settee. Something had revived within her, the essential spark that kept her alive. Now at last, her brain was beginning to work again. It was necessary to think, she told herself. She had to define her duty, she had to define the role she must play. She had to settle her mind realistically and unemotionally. Tonight, Alex Masters had killed a hundred and three British sailors. She had no right to help him escape. And yet, was he a murderer? Not in the real sense, the true 'meaning to' sense. He was a strange man, full of complexes, inhibitions she could scarcely begin to guess at. But his humanity was inescapable. He had brought her here against her will, it was true, but she could scarcely blame him for that. Mike, it was, who'd dragged her into it. Poor dumb Mike.

Julie's features fell as she remembered her brother. So hectic had been their last few hours, she'd scarcely had a chance to think about him. Now the worry came back with stultifying force. What if he died down there? God knew, he'd looked bad enough. It was an ugly wound, ragged and uneven, and he'd been bleeding hard.

Sitting beside her on the sofa, Alex glimpsed the concern in her eyes.

'What's wrong?'

'I was thinking about Mike.'

'He'll be all right,' Alex told her.

'They'll never get him to a hospital in this weather.'

'There's a doctor in Sheilington, isn't there?'

She nodded.

'They'll get the doctor,' Alex said.

He was silent for a moment, studying her curiously. He was no Robert Redford, she thought, quite plain-looking really. Face too narrow, chin too long. But something in his eyes was irresistible. Kindness, warmth. Pain too – she could sense the pain like a physical force.

'You're very close, the two of you,' he said. 'You and your brother.'

She smiled. 'In some ways, I still think of him as a little boy.'

'Some boy.'

'Oh, he's a husky specimen all right, a great protector in the old days, growing up in Glasgow. Nobody took liberties when Mike was around. Then he grew older and got into the wrong company.'

'Criminals?'

'Revolutionaries. They filled his head with daft ideas.'

'And that's how we came along.'

She nodded, smiling.

'Plan to go on living here, when all this is over?'

'Running the hotel, you mean? Why not?'

'Bit lonely, I'd have thought. Especially for a girl like you.'

'I don't find it lonely at all. I love the hills.'

'Good place to hide in.'

She looked at him sharply. 'What would I be hiding from?'

'Commitment,' he suggested.

'To what?'

'Life.'

She took a deep breath, her fist clenching involuntarily in her lap. He was too damned perceptive for his own good. He smiled, as if trying to defuse his remark. 'Fancy a refill?' he asked. 'It's not exactly *maté*, but it's the next best thing.'

She watched as he rose to his feet, filling the kettle at the sink. He lacked Collis's supple grace, but he carried something more, an air of ideality that was difficult to define.

'What's *maté*?' she asked curiously.

'A drink. We brew it on the *pampa*. We make it out of holly leaves.'

'Sounds awful.'

'You're wrong. It's very refreshing.'

He flopped back beside her on the sofa, and she could see the marks of the storm on his cheeks and nostrils. There was a strange fragility in the way he held himself intact. Confused, tired and bewildered, he was hanging on in the face of dire adversity. She warmed to that. It told her something about his character. She knew so little, she thought, about the dark forces which had fashioned him, the influences which had created his psyche.

'Tell me about Argentina,' she whispered. 'What's it like?'

'What do you think it's like?'

'I don't know. Lots of dust. Sleepy towns. Peasants sitting in the sun. That's how I imagine Argentina.'

He chuckled dryly. 'You'd be disappointed. It's not much

different to here. The grass, the trees, the texture of things, even the feel of the air. It's exactly the same.'

'And the people?'

He grinned. 'Not quite. We're a hotch-potch in Argentina.'

'You're British really, aren't you?'

'Way back. All of us were one thing or another. Argentina was one of the big melting-pots of the nineteenth century. Just like the USA.'

'Immigrants?'

He nodded. 'Millions. They came from all over, refugees fleeing the political purges of Eastern Europe, Irish families escaping the potato famine, hungry people fed up with poverty and disillusionment. They wanted a second chance, a new life.'

He grinned at her. 'Did you know at the turn of the century economists prophesied that the two major powers of the future would be the United States and Argentina?'

'What happened?' Julie asked.

'Politics happened. One damned general after another. In South America, it's always the military who rule. It opens the door to corruption. As a population, we're too diverse. In Patagonia, you'll find people who only converse in Welsh. Italians who only speak Italian.'

'That's incredible.'

'Yes, we're a mixed-up nation all right, but don't imagine we're not proud of our country. To us, *machismo* is very real. *Machismo* is something you can't define. You have to feel it. In here.' He tapped his chest, chuckling. 'It's a sort of exaggerated masculinity. We have to keep proving ourselves, it's in our blood.'

'Was it *machismo* that brought you here?' Julie asked.

He was silent for a moment. The electric fire threw ribbons of scarlet across his narrow cheekbones.

'No,' he said. 'That was something else.'

'The *Belgrano*? After all these years?'

'Some things you never forget.'

No, she thought, I can see it in your face. To certain men, war was a game. Others, it destroyed completely. 'You must hate us a great deal,' she whispered.

'Hate?' He looked surprised. 'You've got to be alive to hate. I lost that a long time ago.'

'What made you do it then?'

'I wanted to see if I could still function as a human being.'

'And has it worked?' she asked bitterly. 'Has it brought you back from the dead? Has it turned you into living flesh-and-blood, the knowledge that you've sent a hundred and three men to the bottom of Barracula Sound?'

His body seemed to flinch, his shoulders stooping in a posture of despair. Still and lonely he crouched, his eyes filled with misery.

'Patriotism can bring out the worst in men as well as the best,' he breathed.

She felt her spirits melt. There was no mistaking his torment. It emanated from every contour of his body. He was caught in the nightmare of his own private hell. What have I done? she thought.

'Alex?' she whispered.

He looked at her.

'Put your arm around me.'

Martha Higham turned up the hurricane lamp, and putting on her spectacles, settled down to read in front of the blazing log fire. Outside, she could hear the storm hammering at the window panes. She liked the sound, she liked the cosy feeling which surrounded the cottage's hearth. Though they had been without electricity since early evening, the inconvenience seemed an exciting novelty to Martha and her sister Cecilia who found something fascinating in being snug and warm

330

while the blizzards thundered impotently around them.

Martha Higham was forty-six years old. She was plain and horsey-looking, with an angular body which bore little resemblance to the soft curves and gentle valleys of the classic female form. She had never married. Apart from one brief courtship during her early twenties, she had never associated in an amatory sense with a man. Martha Higham, as she was all too depressingly aware, was progressing into spinsterhood with an inexorability which it seemed impossible to escape.

She lived with her sister Cecilia in the cottage left by their aged father, running a home-based crochet business which helped to pay their meagre bills. Several years older than Martha, Cecilia had embraced the aridity of their empty life with the stoicism lack of choice engendered. The two sisters, homely and dour, continued the tenure fate had mapped out for them with a loneliness and dissatisfaction few of their associates suspected or recognised.

As Martha turned the pages of her magazine, pictures of glamorous fashion models stared up at her, and she allowed her mind to drift, imagining herself vibrant, alluring, filled with verve, dash, elegance. It seemed a different world out there, one she scarcely believed in, and yet she clung to its resonance with an impassioned stubbornness as if, in some elusive way, she needed it to moderate the incalculable unfairness of life.

The door opened and her sister Cecilia came in, clutching her topcoat tightly around her. Flecks of snow beaded Cecilia's hair and shoulders, and her cheeks were pale, her eyes bright with alarm. Martha blinked as she put down the magazine.

'What's wrong, Cecilia? Ye look as if ye've just seen a ghost.'

'There's a man in the woodshed,' Cecilia gasped, shuddering.

Martha frowned. 'A man? Are ye sure?'

'He's lying on top of the logs. I think he's ill. He's shivering something awful.'

Still frowning, Martha rose to her feet. She strode into the workroom and opening the cupboard, took down the double-barrelled shot-gun their father had used for hunting rabbits. Of the two, she was the stronger. Her illusions vanished in the face of stark reality. She could kill a fox, could – and had – delivered a baby. Emergencies were fuel to her flame.

She loaded the gun carefully, and with her face grim, made her way to the front door. Cecilia followed, biting her lip with fear and apprehension.

The woodshed lay at the other side of the paddock, its low roof smothered under a heavy blanket of snow. The door creaked as Martha gently entered, gripping the shot-gun protectively in front of her. A smell of tar and linseed oil hung heavily on the cold night air. In the darkness, she discerned a figure huddled on the pile of severed logs. It was shuddering violently, its spine arching as spasms racked its narrow frame.

Martha lowered the shot-gun. It was clear the man was in no condition to present any danger. She moved forward, squinting into the shadows. A great patch of scarlet drenched the left side of his jacket.

'He's hurt,' she whispered hoarsely. 'We'll have to get him into the house.'

'Is that wise, Martha?' Cecilia asked. 'We dinna ken who he is or where he's come from. What happens when he wakes up?'

Martha propped the shot-gun determinedly against the shed wall.

'If we dinna get him into the warm, he'll no' be waking up at all,' she declared.

Somehow, working together, they wrestled the supine

figure off the pile of logs and hooking his arms around their shoulders, manoeuvred him, staggering feebly, across the snowbound paddock to the cottage front door.

'We'll put him in father's room,' Martha said. 'The bed's made, an' we can light a fire in the grate.'

They dropped their fevered burden on to the heavy spring mattress, and Martha examined him critically in the pale light of the hurricane lamp. The man's cheeks were flushed, his eyes bulging. Stubble coated his throat and chin, and his skin carried the texture of melted wax. He was, she noticed instantly, a remarkably good-looking young man, and as she studied him, his lips drew back in a crooked smile.

'*Perdone me, señora,*' he murmured in a husky voice. 'I ask your forgiveness for intruding so rudely, but I was very cold.'

Martha felt a tremor in her chest. It was a curious sensation, as if some dark barrier, some secret stronghold had been unexpectedly pierced. The young man's smile filled her with a fierce and inexplicable physical awareness, and Martha flushed hotly. She was not experienced enough or perceptive enough to recognise the emotion, but she was conscious of a tension within her, a scarcely recognisable longing.

'Dinna talk,' she whispered. 'Ye must save your strength. We have to get ye warm again.'

'*Mil gracias, señora,*' the young man breathed.

His body shuddered convulsively, and Cecilia clucked deep in her throat as she tugged open his jacket and shirt.

'This man has been shot,' she exclaimed.

Martha frowned, peering at the open wound.

'The bullet's gone straight through the fleshy part of his side,' Cecilia added excitedly. 'In one end, out the other.'

'He's lost an awful lot of blood,' Martha said.

Cecilia stared at her, eyes widening. 'He must be a criminal of some kind.'

'Aye. Seems likely.'

333

'We'll hae to call the polis.'

'How?' Martha demanded. 'The phone lines are down.'

'Then we'll hae to fetch him on foot.'

'In this storm? Only a maniac would venture out in such weather.'

'Martha, what are we going to do?'

'Do?' Martha echoed grimly. 'I'll tell ye what we're going to do. We're going to keep him here. Fetch me some hot water and the first-aid kit from the medical chest. I'll clean his wound and dress it properly, and we'll get some food into him. Tomorrow, when he's strong enough to talk, we'll listen to what he has to say. Then we'll decide about the polis.'

It was still dark when Alex awoke. He sat for a moment, breathing deeply, Julie's head resting in the crook of his arm. Something was different, he knew. His eyes flitted around the office interior. Through the window a strange pervading greenness seemed to ripple in a gentle see-saw motion. The mountains had vanished. He frowned, and gently easing Julie's head from his arm, padded across the concrete floor. Close to, the greenness seemed more pronounced than ever. He could see spidery tendrils eddying beyond the window panes, and something drifted into his line of vision. He felt his wrists turn icy. There was a man up there, floating eerily in the current, his arms dangling in a silent embrace. His face was grey, the muscles limp in the flat impassivity of death. Alex recognised his features. It was Harry Woolcott, the sailor from the *Conqueror*, the man he had met on the night of the Sheilington dance. He spotted similar figures drifting past the window. The night seemed to be full of them, bodies swaying, eyes flat and accusing.

Numb with horror, Alex stepped backwards. He wanted to scream. He wanted to protest. He covered his face with his hands, shaking his head in anguish, and then, in a strange inexplicable transition, the scene suddenly faded. Warm sunlight bathed his head and shoulders. He saw open grasslands reaching away to the far horizon. Tree stumps studded the empty *pampa* and water meadows nestled on the open pastures. Bewildered, he stared about him in confusion.

Hoofbeats echoed in his eardrums. Turning, he glimpsed a horseman galloping towards him, the wind curling the rider's sombrero brim, plucking at the baggy *bombachos* covering his knees and thighs. It was Luke, Alex realised, and he was laughing wildly. Beneath the moustache, his teeth flashed in the sun. A leather *rebenque*, or lariat, dangled from his wrist, and he leaned forward in the sheepskin saddle as he dug his heels into the belly of his foam-streaked *criollo* pony.

He drew no closer, that was the strangest thing. No matter how hard he galloped, his body remained in exactly the same position. His laughter rose on the sundrenched air, loud, mocking, brittle. Then, as Alex watched wonderingly, Luke's body crumpled like an old tin can, face, neck, ribcage, everything collapsing inwards in a grotesque welter of flesh, bone and bloody viscera.

Alex turned. Stricken with panic, he began to run. It was a strange world he fled through, a world glimpsed in a fairground mirror. He recognised the dam, its grey wall rippling eerily. Julie was sitting on the parapet, washing her hair in the waters of the loch. He called her name and she smiled, beckoning. As he moved towards her, the smile altered. Her eyes grew venal, malevolent. Blood trickled from her dark damp hair. Suddenly, he realised the entire loch was a monstrous pool of blood.

He began to scream. Soft hands gripped his chest. Someone shook him. His eyes opened and he saw daylight streaming through the office windows.

'Wake up,' Julie whispered urgently. 'Wake up, for heaven's sake.'

He blinked at her. It had been a dream, nothing more, a nightmare, vivid and demoralising. He glimpsed the pale grey of the early dawn. The storm had stopped. There was a hint of sunlight amid the heavy grey cloud.

'You've got to get out of here,' she snapped.

He struggled to refocus his vision. Had it been purely imaginary then? No blood. No Luke. No Harry Woolcott.

'What's happened?'

'They're coming up the gully.'

'The gully?'

He shook his head vigorously to clear it, and trembling, rose to his feet, peering through the office window. He could see the mountains clearly defined in the early morning. Deep snow coated the hillslopes. Some immeasurable distance below, a tiny party of men threaded their way up the narrow depression, heading towards the base of the dam.

Alex's nightmare was forgotten as he glanced furiously around.

'What are you going to do?' Julie hissed.

'Stop them. There must be a way of opening the dam.'

'You're crazy.'

'I've got to, Julie. I couldn't stand it if they sent me to prison.'

'But the water output's controlled by the hydro-electric scheme below.'

'They'll have an emergency valve. If the loch gets too deep, they'll need a way of releasing the pressure to keep the dam from cracking.'

He tore open the door and stumbled down the steps leading to the dam's interior. Lightbulbs threaded the grey stone walls. A smell of concrete, dust and cleaning fluid filled the air.

On a landing below, they discovered a complex array of

insulated pipes, dials, gauges and barometers. Alex stared at them helplessly. 'It must be here somewhere. There's got to be a way of opening the sluice gates.'

Three metal wheels protruded from the adjacent wall, firmly secured with heavy padlocks. Alex reversed his machine-gun and swung the butt hard, smashing each of the padlocks in turn.

'Alex,' Julie cried.

He looked at her.

'Open those gates, and you could kill those men down there.'

'That's precisely what they're planning to do to me,' he said.

Slinging the machine-gun across his shoulder, he began to haul furiously at the metal wheels.

Coming up the gully, Segunda heard the distant roaring noise. He paused in his tracks, frowning, his body stiff from the long night's climb. Above, framed against the morning sky, they could see the majestic expanse of the Charrach Dam. The roaring sound grew more insistent, like a roll of thunder heard on the periphery of a deep sleep. Segunda felt his senses tighten. The others, he realised, had heard it too. Swaying with exhaustion, they stood blinking up at the distant dam.

Segunda felt his genitals twitch in an involuntary spasm. Something was bearing down on them from an immeasurable distance above. An avalanche. He thought at first the cornice had given way near the top. But this avalanche was not of churned-up snow, it was a wall of boiling foam surging towards them down the narrow gully.

'Somebody's opened the dam,' Lieutenant Canby gasped. 'Get up the side, lads, quick.'

Segunda clawed at the icy slope, the strength draining from his body. The long night's haul had worn him to a standstill. Somehow, his feet refused to stay in one place. Every step he took seemed to slide him further backwards. The gully, which had looked so unimposing, suddenly appeared immense.

Segunda saw the barrage of water heaving towards them, filling the craggy defile almost to its rim. The foam curled beneath his feet, lashing his body with icy spray. He could scarcely believe the coldness of it. It surged around them, sweeping towards the dip. Segunda's arms were aching in their sockets as he clung to the one protuberance he could still get a grip of, a ragged nobble of slippery rock. The water rose to his knees, drenching his clothes, sucking him downwards. He felt it pummelling his thighs and waist. He slipped, sliding back, falling into the swirling torrent. The water carried him, coughing helplessly as moisture flooded his nasal passages and streamed into his throat. Something caught him a stunning blow and his head went under. Gasping, spluttering, he broke the surface, lungs screaming for air, glimpsing the banks flashing by in a dark vivid blur. He fought wildly, thrashing in a numbed disjointed fashion, but like a living force intent on his destruction, the current carried him remorselessly on.

Julie watched Alex rummaging through the cupboards in the engineer's office. He discovered a coiled nylon rope and tested it firmly with his fingers.

'How far d'ye think you'll get with that?' she asked.

'It's better than nothing.'

'You're trapped. I warned you what would happen when you got here.'

'I'm going up the crater,' he told her bluntly. 'I've been studying the cliffs. There's a possible route up the rocky escarpment adjoining the waterfall. With luck, it might go.'

She glanced through the window at the basin beyond. She could see the escarpment at the far side of the loch. It was flanked by a bubbling cascade which fell sheer from the mountain rim, seven hundred feet or more. Its roar seemed curiously muffled by the heavy curtain of ice. More ice glazed the escarpment itself, and to Julie, studying it from below, it looked virtually unclimbable. There might have been a route, she considered, on a warm summer's day with the rock free of verglas and the falls less swollen by the winter floods, but in present circumstances only a madman would attempt it.

'You'll be killed,' she said simply.

'I'd rather die on the mountain than rot in a British gaol.'

He found a small metal axe and hefted it in his hand. 'Might come in useful as an ice-hammer.'

'You think I'll stand here and let you throw your life away? Nobody could climb that cliff in these conditions.'

'They might, if they're desperate enough.'

'Give yourself up, Alex,' she pleaded. 'I'll tell them you tried to warn the submarine's crew.'

'Think they'd believe you? Your brother started this mess, remember.'

'Joe Robben saw you make that call.'

'Joe's got a damned good reason for hating all Argentines.'

Her eyes moistened as she felt the tears starting. She couldn't help herself. Why should she care, she wondered, if the damn fool lived or died? But somehow she did care, there was no escaping that fact. He had touched some part of her she couldn't explain, even to herself. A few days ago, she hadn't known he even existed. Now, she couldn't bear to think of life without him. Watching him, feeling the vulnerability which nestled in his narrow frame, feeling the defiance and determination, she loved him suddenly, blindly, passionately. She felt no need of affection in return. It was just a simple moment of singular love. She loved him for being human like herself. Was this what love meant? she wondered. She'd always thought love would be an exhilarating thing, happy and uplifting. This love was tearing her up inside.

He frowned, glimpsing her tears. 'Why are you crying?'

'I'm coming with you,' she whispered.

'You're crazy.'

'If you're prepared to try it, so am I.'

'I'm leaving you here, Julie.'

'When you reach the top of that cliff, you'll need someone who knows the country. There are a dozen ridges you can follow. Choose the wrong one, and you'll end up back where you started.'

'I'll take my chances,' he said.

'No,' she choked, her throat seizing inexplicably. 'No, you won't, because I couldn't live with myself if anything happened to you now.'

His face tensed, not hardening exactly, but taking on new definition like a man faced with some precious and undreamed-of truth. He reached out, pulling her close. She felt his heart through the heavy jacket, his beard stubble tickling her cheek. She kissed him softly on the lips.

'It's a strange world,' he said, smiling. 'Last night, I actually wanted to die. I wanted it more than anything in the world. Now suddenly, without even realising, I've found something worth staying alive for.'

She was still crying as she kissed him again.

Segunda shivered as the wind bit through his sodden clothing. He had never felt so cold in his life. It had taken every ounce of strength he possessed to fight his way out of that thundering torrent, dragging himself like a drowned rat into the calmer water and up to the gully rim beyond. Now his body felt weak and trembling.

He spotted the bedraggled marines sprawled in a narrow hollow. They were drenched to the skin, their berets gone, their hair wet and gleaming. Two had bloodstains on their combat jackets, and Lieutenant Canby's cheek had been scraped raw.

Segunda picked his way down the snowslope towards them. Canby was wringing out his gloves as he approached.

'That bastard damn near killed us,' Canby growled.

'Anyone hurt?' Segunda asked.

'Matlin's taken a nasty bump on the head. Coming up like a football. No sign of concussion though.'

'What about the climbing equipment?'

'Most of it's intact. Raymer lost his haversack in the first rush, but we're still in business if we can get out of this saturated clothing.'

Segunda peered at the dam above. 'There must be shelter up there. Some place we can hide from the wind.'

'We may have to fight for it,' Canby declared grimly.

Segunda grunted as his shivering intensified. 'In this cold, we've very little choice, lieutenant,' he said. 'We either fight, or we die.'

CHAPTER SEVENTEEN

The sun rose swiftly as Alex and Julie traced the rim of the mountain lake. It was not warm, Julie reflected, but after the fury of the night, it offered a compensation of sorts, an assurance that the world was about to renew itself. There was less snow inside the basin, as if the amphitheatre of precipices had somehow protected it from the blizzard's main onslaught.

Alex picked his way across the narrow curtains of scree. He could see the waterfall ahead, dropping out of the gorge in a silvery ribbon. The escarpment glistened in the morning sun.

Alex carried the coiled rope slung across his shoulder. In his hand, he clutched the metal axe. He looked strong and purposeful in the early morning. Julie enjoyed watching his limbs take the slope in rhythmic eager strides. He'd changed with the night, that was apparent. The change was evident in every subtle movement of his body. She'd done that, brought him out of his melancholy, given him something she didn't even understand herself. The haunted look had gone from his eyes and in its place she glimpsed hope, optimism, things she'd never expected to see there.

She was glad. There'd been no sense to it, living on forgotten guilts and torments. They couldn't change the past, but at least they could change the future. More than anything in the world, she wanted him to escape. He'd aroused within her emotions she'd scarcely even imagined. Not for years had her senses felt so keen, so elated, so alive. God knew, she couldn't bear to lose him now.

Alex paused at the foot of the jagged cliff, peering up at the way they would go. Julie followed his eyeline, and her spirits sank. It looked treacherous beyond belief. In places, the rock was completely glazed with ice. In others, the great tumult of the falls had turned its surface into a slippery bastion devoid of holds. Spray from the water fanned her cheeks.

'Ye really think it'll go?' she whispered.

'I didn't say it'd be easy, but if we keep our nerve, I'm sure we can do it.'

'The walls are streaming with moisture.'

'They'll be tricky, all right. But not impossible.'

They roped up and Alex set off, chipping away ice with the metal axe, picking his way delicately up the first precipitous pitch. A thin crack rose from the ground, overhanging for the first twenty feet or so then branching slightly to the left. Here, it joined a narrow chimney which opened on to a wide buttress of seemingly contourless rock. Moving gracefully, expertly, Alex forced a route across it until he had reached a narrow ledge some forty feet above, and belaying to the wall, prepared to bring her up on the rope.

'Come on,' he shouted. 'Just concentrate on taking it step by step.'

Swallowing hard, Julie started up the cliff. The first few feet were relatively straightforward, for he had chipped away the verglas, leaving her solid rocky projections to get her toes and fingers into, but soon the gradient steepened, and she found herself straddling the open chimney, jamming her boot rims against imperceptible niches in the rock. Her hands danced across the icy surface, scrabbling for fingerholds, crannies, fissures. She could see Alex nodding encouragement from above.

She came to a jutting roof and paused, ducking her head beneath the ugly overhang. The route lay to the left, cutting diagonally across the sloping contourless buttress. Gritting her teeth, Julie swung on to the open slab. Her boots clawed at the rock as she shifted her weight, edging cagily upwards. An ice-glazed knob gave her a foot-stance, and then she was wrestling up an open groove, jamming her arms against the smooth parallel walls. It was a slow, strenuous, stomach-wrenching ascent, but bit by bit she made it, dragging herself breathlessly to the narrow slab on which Alex had made his belay.

'You weren't lying about your climbing,' he said. 'You did that pitch like a veteran.'

She flushed, absurdly pleased at the compliment, then her heart sank as she studied the route ahead. The cliff grew steeper after the first sixty feet or so, and in places meandered into the path of the waterfall itself.

'Don't worry,' Alex grunted. 'We'll be at the top before lunchtime.'

Julie didn't answer. She hadn't the heart to tell him she thought they would never make it.

The engineer's office was deserted when Segunda and the four marines burst in. There were signs of recent occupation, tea-cups on the table, a rumpled cushion on the battered settee, but the room itself looked strangely abandoned.

Segunda and his companions gathered around the electric fire, shivering uncontrollably in their drenched clothing.

'We haven't time for this,' Segunda hissed, fighting to control his chattering teeth. 'We've got to get after them.'

'What are you talking about?' Lieutenant Canby growled. 'They're getting away, for Christ's sake.'

'If we try to follow them in this state, we'll die of exposure.'

Segunda felt panic starting deep in his chest. Canby had had enough, he could tell. They all had. Weak and trembling, they were struggling desperately to rekindle some blessed spark of warmth inside their frozen bodies. They couldn't quit now, he thought. Not when their quarry was so close.

'You're letting them escape?'

'I've got my men to think about. I'm not sacrificing their lives on some lunatic bloody steeplechase.'

'Damn you,' Segunda cried. 'You think I came eight thousand miles to sit here like a fool while those *hijos de puta* climb their way to freedom?'

'Look at the state we're in,' Canby declared. 'We're dripping wet, for Christ's sake. We'd freeze within an hour in those conditions outside. Who cares if the fugitives get away? The police'll pick them up anyhow, when they reach the other side of the mountain.'

'Those people belong to me,' Segunda growled. 'I've chased them half-way around the world. I'm not letting go now.'

In a frenzy, he began to tear open the office cupboards, hurling equipment over the open floor. The marines watched him, blinking in astonishment. Segunda was like a man in the grip of some terrible fever as, almost demented, he hurled papers and implements wildly across the room.

On a narrow shelf, he found a cluster of denim overalls, and picking them up, hugged them tightly against his chest.

'We can put these next to our skin,' he announced. 'They're dry and warm. If we pull our wet duvets over the top, they'll insulate our body heat.'

Canby stared at him. 'You're crazy, d'you know that?'

'The overalls will keep the chill out,' Segunda cried, his voice approaching hysteria. 'At least we'll still be in the game.'

Canby sighed. His eyes looked weary in the craters of his scratched and bloody cheeks. Turning, he picked up the kettle and filled it at the tiny sink.

'They can't get far in that rocky basin,' he said. 'We might as well have a brew before we go.'

*

For nearly two hours, Alex picked his way up the towering cliff-face, bringing up Julie on the rope below. She marvelled at the way his body swung into every curve and defile, appraising problems, testing, surmounting, pressing on. He was a natural climber, his balance uncanny, his energy limitless, his long limbs ideal for the strain and stretch of buttress, groove and chimney. There seemed to be no stopping him. Never had she seen a man so full of purpose. The loneliness, the sense of isolation that had hung about him like a cloud had gone completely. Now, he was sharp, alert, eager. She could scarcely believe the change. Her own uncertainty began to recede. For the first time, she felt a ray of hope. How could a man so determined possibly fail? They were a team, united and resolute. Nothing could stop them. Nothing.

At one point, they reached a glassy slab which looked to Julie, studying it from below, almost unscalable, but without pausing, Alex began to chip away ice with his hand-axe and balancing precariously on boot tips and fingernails, picked his way fly-like along a series of barely discernible grooves to bring her up on the rope, smiling exuberantly. She had never seen him smile before. Always, his face had been dark and sombre. Now, he looked transformed.

The route traversed to the right, then vanished into a narrow crack down which the waterfall tumbled in noisy confusion. Ice glazed the rock, and water streamed beneath its frozen outer layer.

'Looks like we'll have to get our feet wet,' Alex said cheerfully.

It was a nightmarish pitch. The icy water poured into their sleeves, and Julie gasped as she felt it chilling her naked skin.

At the top, soaked and breathless, they paused on a narrow chockstone. Far below, Julie glimpsed a ragged line of men clambering towards the escarpment's base. Even from that height, she could see the matchstick muzzles of their shouldered carbines.

'Here they come,' she whispered, her lips trembling with cold.

Alex nodded. He looked sanguine and undismayed. 'They're too far back,' he stated. 'We'll be at the top in another hour. They haven't a hope of catching us now.'

Lieutenant Canby took out his field glasses and trained them on the minuscule figures climbing above. The great wall looked dark and ominous, its hanging buttresses gleaming wetly in the pale glow of the wintry morning. Snow flaked the narrow ledges. He saw the man climbing freely, the girl paying out the rope behind.

Matlin fingered his carbine, looking at the lieutenant for approval. 'I reckon I could pick him off from here, sir, using the telescopic sight.'

Canby lowered the glasses, shaking his head. 'Kill the man and you'll drag the girl off too. We'll have to go after them on foot.'

He looked at Segunda. 'You'd better go back to the dam and wait for us there.'

'You're not leaving me now,' Segunda said flatly.

'You bloody fool. You'll never scale that wall.'

'Put me on the rope. I can do anything your boys can.'

Canby glimpsed the stubbornness in Segunda's eyes and sighed. 'Very well,' he said. 'But if you get stuck, I'm warning you now – we'll tie you to the rock and you'll just have to sit there until we bloody get back.'

'We're trapped,' Julie said. She gazed at the route ahead, blocked by a massive overhang. 'We'll never get past that roof.'

'Of course we will. It'll be a doddle.'

Alex scrambled towards it, crouching awkwardly beneath

347

its rim. She watched breathless as he reached out, feeling along the glistening surface. Nothing stopped him, that was the crazy thing. He was like a man on fire, restless, earnest, unable to rest, even for an instant. Retreat had no meaning for him. Defeat was an irrelevancy.

'There's a crack here,' he yelled. 'It'll give us a pressure hold.'

'It's too narrow,' she protested.

'Nonsense.'

He worked his hand inside, clenching his fist to form a makeshift chockstone. Julie couldn't believe what he was about to attempt. He's insane, she thought. She watched him balancing on his flimsy stance, then, as Julie gasped involuntarily, he swung himself outwards, letting his fist take the weight of his entire body, hooking his free arm over the roof's lip and wriggling up to the shelf above.

Julie felt her muscles trembling. God Almighty, did he imagine she was some kind of Olympic gymnast? It had been a miracle, finding a hold above that overhang. If he'd failed, what then? There'd have been no way on earth he could have worked his way back to the rockface.

The rope zipped taut and she heard him calling. She struggled to quell the panic rising inside her. She mustn't disgrace herself, whatever happened. She took a deep breath.

'Climbing,' she shouted.

Nervously, she lifted her foot, snaked it sideways across the open slab, found a narrow projection of rock and delicately transferred her weight to it, then reaching up, scoured the glistening surface with her fingers as her other boot slid tentatively upwards. She felt the pressure of the rope tugging at her waist, her damp clothes clinging unpleasantly to her skin. She was panting hard as she inched slowly, fearfully to the craggy underbelly of the jutting overhang. For a moment she crouched there, steeling her nerve, then reaching out, she thrust her fingers into the crack and clenching her fist, jammed it tight inside the rocky fissure. Now, she thought. Don't hesitate. Don't look. Just do it.

Fighting to control her fear, she let her body swing backwards on her slender wrist. Sweat streamed into her eyes as she hooked her free arm over the fractured lip, gasping with relief as her fingers located the jagged jughold. Panting and choking, she squirmed her way up to where Alex stood waiting, perched on a narrow platform.

'Okay?' he asked.

She nodded breathlessly, not trusting herself to speak.

'Gets even trickier ahead,' he said. 'But we've reached the crux of the climb. Beat the next bit, and we're home and dry. It's plain sailing all the way to the top.'

Following his gaze, she felt her throat turn icy. Directly above, the cliff bulged outward, and wet snow which had not yet cohered with the surface beneath, clung to the glistening sandstone slabs. There were no holds Julie could see.

'We'll never make it,' she whispered.

'We've got to. There's no other way.'

'Alex, it's madness to attempt that pitch.'

He kissed her lightly on the forehead. 'You think I'd let those bastards catch us now?' he said. 'We're almost at the summit. A few more minutes, and we'll be on our way out of here.'

He moved up, tracing a spidery fissure, leaning expertly to one side as he applied a series of delicate pressure holds. Julie payed out the rope behind. Take your time, Alex. Don't push it. Don't hug the rock. Relax. He reached a point some twenty feet above and paused, his body frozen into the shape of a narrow question mark, his hand clutching some indefinable fingerhold above.

'What's it like?' she called.

'Nothing much to hold on to.'

A pause, then . . . 'I think I'm stuck.'

'Can't you traverse to the right?'

'Not without losing balance.'

'Alex, come down. Come down, for God's sake.'

'Hold on. Just give me a minute to catch my breath.'

Something in the way he clung there, tense, rigid, told her he was in serious trouble. Oh God, she thought, what had they got themselves into? She gathered in the slack, pressing herself hard against the rocky cliff. A shambles, that's what it was. A fiasco. No way up, and no way down, except the hardest one of all. She must have been mad to let him attempt it. Out of her tiny mind.

He leaned to the right and began to move up again, climbing more quickly now, his confidence growing as he delicately negotiated the treacherous bulge. My God, he's doing it, she thought.

He reached a narrow flake and paused for breath, glancing downwards. She could see his cheeks, flushed with exertion.

'There's a stance here,' he yelled. 'It's not much, but if I can get you up to this point, the next bit's a piece of cake.'

'There's no place to belay,' she protested. 'What if I come off?'

'Don't worry.'

She saw him thrust the rope into a narrow crack, and taking a loose pebble from the rocky flake, jam it in behind, forcing the line around it.

'That'll never hold,' she called.

'Better than nothing. Just take your time.'

Julie swallowed hard. She closed her eyes for a moment, willing her fear to subside. Then sucking in her breath, she clenched her teeth fiercely, and without peering down, started to climb.

A hundred feet down the cliff, Lieutenant Canby eyed Julie's progress through his field glasses.

'She's almost up,' he shouted.

'Not yet,' Segunda bellowed. 'There's still another fifty feet to the top.'

'Easy stuff. Little more than a scramble. We'll never catch them now.'

Belayed to the rock, Segunda glared up at him, squinting against the harshness of the sun. He could see Canby's moulded rubber soles, clogged with dirt, splayed out against the incline above. Below, roped and belayed, the marines clung to their individual perches.

'We're not done yet,' Segunda protested.

Canby let the glasses flop against his chest, his breath steaming on the chill morning air. 'It'll take us an hour to scale that pitch,' he yelled. 'By then, they'll be halfway to Drumartin.'

'Move faster,' Segunda told him angrily.

'I'm doing the best I can. I told you before I'm not risking the lives of my men. If they escape, they escape. It's not our fault they're better climbers than we are.'

Fury pounded in Segunda's skull. Damn the man, they couldn't quit now, not with their quarry almost in reach. His body was trembling all over, like someone in the throes of an emotion too powerful to control. In desperation, he crouched back on his narrow ledge, peering about him wildly. Three feet away, one of the marines stood belayed to the rock, paying out the line to his companions above. Segunda reached inside his clothing and drew out his knife. Moving swiftly, he leaned across the rockface and cut the harness from the marine's carbine, dragging it from his shoulder. The man glanced around, startled, his lips opening in an involuntary cry of protest.

Segunda jammed himself against the cliff and thrust the carbine against his cheek, flicking the safety-catch with his thumb. Above, he heard Canby's voice, hoarse and desperate, bellowing into the wind.

'Don't shoot, you bloody fool. You'll kill the girl.'

351

Segunda ignored him. Focusing rapidly, he trained the sights on the figures above, and gently squeezed the trigger.

Peeeerrrrchewwww.

The bullet ricocheted crazily from the cliff-face, causing Julie to jump. She felt her fingers lose their grip, and terror filled her as she realised she was falling. Oh God, she thought, clawing desperately at the rock, her body slithering downwards, gathering speed, rocketing over the glassy slab, kicking up dust in a feathery spray. Above, she could see Alex straining to hold her, teeth clenched, eyes bulging with exertion and alarm. Her feet touched a narrow projection and she dug her toes into it, bringing her momentum to a shuddering halt. She heard the ping of Alex's belaying pebble shooting out of its crack. Then her stomach cringed and her brain froze as Alex, like some incredible bird, came soaring over her head, his body arcing gracefully as he plummeted into the void below.

Clutching the carbine against his chest, Segunda leaned into the cliff, watching Alex fall. There was something almost eerie in the way he somersaulted like an athlete executing an intricate dive. The rope snaked crazily from his waist as, still turning, he hurtled past the girl and plunged headlong over the jutting overhang.

Segunda saw the nylon line expand and contract, spinning its living burden across the cliff, swinging him wildly like a macabre human pendulum.

Frozen to the rock, Segunda and the marines watched dry-mouthed as the desperate drama unfolded above them.

Julie felt the rope zip taut across her shoulders. She reached out, sliding her free hand frenziedly across the cliff-face. Her fingers located a narrow flake and she swallowed wildly as she clung to it. She could see her knuckles gleaming through the skin.

The strain of the rope was tearing her body in two. In another minute, it would drag her from the cliff completely. She could feel her strength diminishing. Alex, she thought. Oh God, Alex. With a chill of horror, she realised she was facing the last desperate moments of her life.

Above the dam, the sun's glare struck at her unprotected eyes.

Forty feet below, swinging wildly on his slender thread, Alex felt dizzy from the shock of the sudden drop. His shoulder ached, and there was a tight constricting pain around his middle as he careered from side to side like a man trapped on some macabre flying trapeze. Because of the overhang, he was unable to reach the cliff nearby.

He peered upwards, narrowing his eyes against the sun. He could see Julie clinging desperately to the fractured rock. His weight was too strong, he was pulling her off. The rope creaked weirdly as he spun across the cliff. Below, the loch dipped and blurred.

A feeling of bitterness engulfed him. They were caught, helplessly and inextricably. There was no way out. It was cruel, cruel when they had been so close, salvation merely a breath away.

He tried to move, but his body whirled inelegantly like a button on a thread. He saw the splintered wall of rock rippling in and out, its snow catching the sun's rays, piercing his eyes with shafts of refracted light. The injustice of the moment seemed almost more than he could bear. He'd thought himself beyond the reach of human comfort, and she had given it to him, brought him back from the dead. It was the final irony, he realised, deliverance and death in the same breath. No escape. Nowhere to run to. Collis had seen it with his shrewd and capable eye, but he himself had been too blind, too self-absorbed, too conscious of his own pain. Well, it was too late now. Too late for anything. He was finished. Down and out. Kaput.

And then, in one of those strange incongruities which bedevil human existence, he was filled with an inexplicable feeling of happiness. Loving her for a moment had been a victory of sorts. She'd given him life, hope, completeness. For that alone, he should be grateful. Dying was illusory. It was merely a point of culmination and release. Love was real. Love, like time itself, was tractable and expanding. Love, not death, was the final truth, the ultimate reality.

He coughed, scarcely able to breathe, a dreadful lassitude drifting through him. The rock swayed mockingly in front of his eyes.

What he felt now, he thought, was the sum total of his experience as a human being, and nothing could detract from that, nothing could diminish it in any way.

He was smiling gently as he drew his clasp-knife, and with a neat, infinitely precise motion, cut the nylon rope.

Crouched against the cliff, Segunda watched Alex rocket past him, his dark body turning as he streaked down the thundering falls, plummeting out of alignment into the boiling cauldron of the rocky basin below. Even at that height, Segunda heard the sickening thud of flesh striking rock.

Gritting his teeth, he pressed himself fiercely against the fractured cliff.

Julie felt she had been absorbed into the sandstone wall. Her mind lingered in a dreamworld between consciousness and fantasy. Nothing seemed real any more.

She did not think about Alex. She had seen Alex plunging earthwards, had closed her eyes before the moment of impact. They were still closed, the lids locked as if she could somehow withdraw into the unlit complexities of her mind, shutting out the world beyond.

She heard the scrape of boots against rock, the rattle of pitons, the clatter of karabiners. A hand touched her shoulder, a rope looped her waist.

She shuddered uncontrollably as a voice murmured into her ear: 'Relax, miss, we've come to take you home.'

The farmhouse was crowded when Julie and her little team of rescuers arrived. She blinked dazedly as they stumbled through the door. She recognised Barry, and the village policeman, but the other occupants were strangers to her. They were dressed in woollen sweaters, denim fatigues, naval uniforms.

She spotted Joe Robben, and he shuffled towards her, balancing on a shoulder crutch. His empty trouser leg had been fastened to his thigh with a safety pin.

'Ye're all right then, Julie. They got ye safely back?'

'Who are these men?' she asked.

'They're sailors from the submarine. We put them up during the storm. They're getting ready to leave now. The danger's over.'

'Where's Mike?'

'Upstairs in bed. Dinna worry, lass, he's fine. The surgeon from the *Conqueror* managed to get that bullet out, and he's been sleeping like a baby ever since.'

'Is he under arrest?'

Joe looked puzzled. 'Why, in God's name, would he be under arrest? He's a bloody hero, that's what he is. They'll be pinning a medal on him when all this is over. They're sending a helicopter now to lift him out to hospital.'

'Can I see him?'

'Aye, lass, of course ye can. He's in Barry's room, second door on the left upstairs.'

Julie paused when she reached the landing, and stood for

a moment, closing her eyes. Her skin looked pale, almost transparent, plunging into the deep hollows of her cheekbones. She was filled with a sense of her own mortality, as if her body, driven beyond endurance, had somehow started to disintegrate. She could still see Alex soaring from the flake like some graceless inelegant vulture. She felt naked, stricken, full of sadness and desolation. She'd scarcely known him, when you came right down to it. A few casual encounters, a few intimacies exchanged in the seclusion of the night. You didn't get to know a man like Alex Masters that way – he was too complex, too deep. And yet, sometimes she felt she'd known him even better than she knew herself. Oh, Alex, she thought.

Mike's eyes were closed when Julie entered the room. His cheeks looked ashen, but the fever had subsided. His chest was rising rhythmically.

'Mike?' she said.

He looked at her, his lips twisting into a painful grin. His hair hung tangled across his eyes, causing him to blink.

'How do you feel?' she asked.

'Like I just lost an argument with a battering-ram.'

She found a chair and pulled it up to the bedside. At least she still had Mike, she thought. Thank God for Mike. He was staring at her sheepishly, his face filled with guilt.

'What did Joe mean, calling you a hero?'

Mike's cheeks coloured. 'Is that what he said?'

She nodded. His eyes held hers, not flinching any more, not pleading, just anxious, earnest, sober.

'They think I was a hostage. They think the Argentines were holding me prisoner. Are ye planning to tell them the truth, Julie? What really happened.'

'I don't know what really happened, Mike. I don't know why those men are even down there. They should be at the bottom of Barracula Sound by now. The mines were set to detonate at eleven-fifteen.'

Studiously, he studied the bulge of his toes under the bedclothes.

'Mike, why didn't the mines go off?'

His face looked hard, his lips tight. There was no arrogance there, no smugness, only an air of resignation, as if he had let himself down in some indeterminate way.

'I took the charges out,' he whispered.

Julie frowned. 'You did what?'

'I sneaked in while they were lying in the toolshed.' He stared at her hopelessly. 'I could'na go through with it, Julie. I thought I could, but when the moment came, I could'na do it.'

'You disarmed the limpets?'

'Aye.'

'But how?'

'Easy. We learned about the *Fouillis* with the SNLA. Textbook stuff, but I knew enough to put them out of action.'

Julie leaned back in the chair as the implication of Mike's words sank into her numbed brain.

'So the whole time we were out there, the whole time Collis, Luke and Alex were swimming under the Sound, the mines were useless?'

'That's about the size of it, aye,' Mike admitted.

A feeling of relief swept Julie. Tears sprang to her eyes, streaming down her cheeks.

Mike stared at her with alarm. 'You're crying,' he said.

She nodded, weeping helplessly.

'But I thought ye'd be glad.'

'I *am* glad,' she choked. 'I'm really very glad.'

The clock ticked in the corner, echoing through the silent room as Julie, shoulders shuddering, pushed her face into her handkerchief and sobbed remorselessly on.

The voice on the loudspeaker sounded hollow and discordant: 'British Airways announce the departure of their flight BA

310 to Madrid. Will all passengers please proceed at once to Gate 21.'

Segunda and Louisa rose to their feet. Across the airport terminal, people were beginning to move towards the departure lounge.

Segunda glanced at his watch. 'Right on time,' he said.

'They're always on time when you don't want them to be.'

He smiled down at her. 'You could always come with me as far as Madrid. I've got a six-hour wait before I make the connecting flight.'

She shook her head. 'That would only make it more painful.'

'On the other hand, you could come all the way, if you felt like it.'

'Don't be silly.'

'It's not such a bad town, Buenos Aires. Very like Paris. You'd like it there.'

'I could never leave England. This is my home. Besides . . .' She hesitated. 'I have someone else to consider.'

'Your daughter?'

She nodded. 'She's coming up to her finals shortly. I couldn't uproot her now.'

He studied her in silence for a moment, his face dark and thoughtful. In the pale glow of the overhead lights, he looked disarmingly attractive.

'You're not telling the truth, Louisa. That isn't the reason at all.'

She flinched, trying to avoid his gaze. Then she shook her head. 'I couldn't live with you,' she whispered. 'Not in the real sense, the permanent sense. Not in the sense that matters.'

'Why not?'

'Because of what you are.'

'A man?'

'A special kind of man. You're forgetting something. I've read your file.'

'Files are full of facts, but they don't always tell the truth.'

'I know everything about you, Mártin. The torturing, the killing. *La guerra sucia*.'

He shrugged. 'Someone had to do it. Our nation was disintegrating.'

'And the victims?'

'They were expendable. Don't tell me it's any different in your country, Louisa.'

'I think it's different,' she said, staring into his eyes.

He sighed. '*La guerra sucia* was a long time ago. People change.'

She shook her head. 'No, Mártin, I saw the way you went after those men. You couldn't quit, you couldn't give in. It was like a sacred crusade. Nothing stops you when you put your mind to it. You might have mellowed with age, but underneath, you're still the Gaucho.'

'Is that what it comes down to then, my dissolute past?'

'Not just your past, Mártin. Your present and future. I couldn't live with that.'

'You've never tried.'

'Every time you came home, I'd be wondering what you'd been up to during the day.'

'You forgot it quickly enough in Paris.'

'Paris was an illusion. They sent me to do a job. The job's finished. This is finished.'

He saw the resolution in her face, and a feeling of desolation filled him.

'Kiss me,' she said. 'Kiss me and go. I don't want you to stay any longer, because if you do, I might just forget myself, and that would be a disaster for both of us.'

He felt tears from her eyes running into his mouth as they embraced. She was breathless when he let her go.

Still crying, she turned and walked swiftly across the airport lounge, her heels clicking on the hard linoleum floor.

Segunda watched her till she had vanished from sight, then sighing gently, he joined the crowd flocking through the exit gate, and wandering down, boarded his plane.

Palmer watched the pallbearers hoist the coffins to their shoulders and set off up the narrow path behind the cemetery chapel. It was raining heavily, and the little party of mourners, locals from the nearby village, huddled together instinctively beneath their dripping umbrellas.

Palmer followed the cortège, walking slowly, his nostrils filled with the odour of damp earth and burning rubbish. Tombstones glistened in the driving downpour. There was an air of desolation and decay.

Palmer stood at the grave-opening as the two corpses were laid side by side.

'Almighty Father,' the clergyman intoned, 'everlasting God, in whose hands we are, in life as in death . . .'

Palmer barely listened. He had travelled up on the morning train, hiring a cab at Aviemore station. A tiresome journey. He scarcely knew why he had come. After all, there was nothing he could do here. The incident was over, tucked in the filing cabinets and computer banks, wrapped-up and forgotten. But he was a tidy man by nature. He liked to see things squared away. No loose ends, that was his motto. Everything trim and shipshape.

He was glad the locals had decided to attend. It would have been unthinkable somehow, if he'd had to face the service alone. One of the women was crying, a young girl, pretty, with a smattering of freckles across her delicate cheeks. Palmer watched wonderingly as the girl's shoulders shook and trembled. She was, he realised, the young woman who had been the Argentine hostage. The newspapers had made a big thing of her mountain-top ordeal. She'd turned down lucrative offers, Palmer knew, for the serial rights to her story. He recognised the young man holding her as the one who'd defused the limpet mines. Apparently he'd been allowed out of hospital especially for the funeral.

As the minister's address drew to a close, a figure moved from the adjoining crowd and took his place at the clergyman's side. He was ruddy-cheeked, tousle-haired, and walked with a distinctive limp. Clutching his cap in front of him, he looked at the mourners huddled in the rain.

'I just want tae say one thing,' he announced in a quiet voice. 'I had more reason than anyone to dislike these men. It was their country that took ma leg in 1982. I thought it was over, the fighting, the dying. But they came here to open up old wounds. They came as our enemies, on a mission of destruction, and God knows, we canna overlook that. But we canna overlook what they did either. One gave his life tae save Julie MacNally.'

The young man hesitated, then smiled. 'The other gave us a Burns Day we'll never forget. He was a bonny lad wi' the horses right enough.'

Stooping awkwardly on his bad leg, the young man plucked a couple of flowers from the wreaths and placed one on each of the coffins. 'From the people of Sheilington,' he whispered. '*Orananaoig* – when victory shines on life's last ebbing sands, oh who would no' die wi' the brave!'

He stared down at the open graves as the coffins were slowly lowered, and Palmer watched him curiously. There was no mistaking his regret. Palmer could feel it like an aura in all the people surrounding him. There was an air of sadness here. Of human warmth and human comfort. It seemed a strange valediction for enemy saboteurs.

The rain pattered on Palmer's umbrella as he turned back towards the waiting car.

Martha Higham laid the food on the silver tray, placing a cover over the poached eggs, and a tea-cosy over the steaming metal pot. As an afterthought, she took a rose from the flower display in the window bay and laid it on the empty side plate. It was only a plastic bloom, but it looked real enough in the pale light of the wintry morning, and in any case, she reflected, it was the thought which counted.

Martha paused to preen herself in front of the kitchen mirror. She had changed in the few weeks since the young man's arrival. Not so people would actually notice, but she felt the change like a palpable force. He had done that, Leo Collis. He had altered her entire outlook. She'd thought herself washed-up and derelict. Now, for the first time in years, she'd begun to realise she was still a woman.

Cecilia, her sister, just couldn't understand. Cecilia had wanted to inform the police, but Martha had forbidden it. The police indeed. Cecilia had no sense of propriety. Martha had warned her to utter not a word about Collis's existence to a living soul. Collis was their little secret. He'd been frank and informative. No subterfuge, no excuses. He'd confessed everything, how he'd been shot by a jealous husband, how he'd been lucky to escape with his life. Martha smiled thinly. That was Collis all over. Honest to a fault. He'd made no attempt to shield them from the truth. His candour made him so easy to forgive.

And he was such a handsome young man too, she thought, as she carried the tray upstairs, elegant, sophisticated, unrelentingly charming. He'd awoken responses within her she'd thought dead and forgotten.

She was humming softly as she tapped on the bedroom door and entered. Then a cry burst from her lips and she froze on the threshold, dismay settling like a wedge inside her stomach. The bed was empty, the sheets thrown back. The wardrobe door hung open, and she saw at a glance the clothes she had washed and mended were gone. Sometime during the night, Collis had left.

Martha put down the tray, her anguish giving way to a feeling of bitter resignation. She'd always known it would come to this. She'd always known that one day Collis would depart. For a few weeks, he had given her something she scarcely understood, but ultimately, she'd realised her happiness had been an illusion.

She sat on the bed, running her palm down the indentation where his body had lain. She was still sitting there when Cecilia found her more than an hour later.

Collis stood at the rail as the Norwegian ferry pulled out of harbour. The sky hung low over the snowcapped peaks, and north, gulls wheeled lazily, squawking as they followed in the steamer's wake, hoping for garbage scraps from the galley window. Sirens hooted on the chill morning air and a cold wind swept the deck, hurling spray into Collis's cheeks. He could see traffic drifting along the coastal road, and the great sprawl of the city creeping up the incline behind. A fishing coble bobbed on the wave-crests, its nets slung across the prow to dry. Behind him, a group of red-faced young men were cheering lustily at strangers on the shoreline. A football team, somebody had said, heading for the European quarter finals.

He stood for a long time watching the land recede into the distance, then he gathered his coat around him and made his way below. It was, after all, just an ordinary coastline, and it was very cold.